This had to be one of her brother's jokes...

Jessie glanced down at his companion. "A troll. Nice costume, kid. Aren't you a little young to be one of my nerdy brother's friends?"

The man who called himself Captain Viator raised a finely sculpted black eyebrow. "Ensign Drakus is not a child. He is a Trucanian."

She snorted. "From the planet Trucania, I suppose."

"The planet Trucan," the troll corrected with glee.

"Right. And I've been kidnapped by aliens." She rolled her eyes. "Give me a break. I'm not going to fall for that gag. I recognize Tim's handiwork here."

"Captain, she does not believe—"

The tall man held up his hand. "She will."

At his flat tone, the hairs on the back of Jessie's neck rose. An uneasy feeling settled in the pit of her stomach. She shook it off. "I like your outfit, big guy. Pretty authentic looking." Hobbling on one shoe, she circled the Captain, examining him. "You're quite an improvement over the geeks Tim usually hangs with." She stopped behind him. "Great buns."

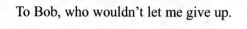
To Bob, who wouldn't let me give up.

Switched

***

Diane Burton

ImaJinn
Books

SWITCHED

Published by ImaJinn Books, a division of ImaJinn

Copyright ©2001 byDiane Burton
Printed and bound in the United States of America. All rights reserved. No part of this book may be reproduced in any form or by any means (electronic, mechanical, photocopying, recording, or otherwise) without prior written permission of both the copyright holder and the above publisher of this book, except by a reviewer, who may quote brief passages in a review. For information, address: ImaJinn Books, a division of ImaJinn, P.O. Box 162, Hickory Corners, MI 49060-0162; or call toll free 1-877-625-3592.

ISBN: 1-893896-51-X

10 9 8 7 6 5 4 3 2 1

Books are available at quantity discounts when used to promote products or services. For information please write to: Marketing Division, ImaJinn Books, P.O. Box 162, Hickory Corners, MI 49060-0162, or call toll free 1-877-625-3592.

Cover design by Patricia Lazarus

ImaJinn Books, a division of ImaJinn
P.O. Box 162, Hickory Corners, MI 49060-0162
Toll Free: 1-877-625-3592
http://www.imajinnbooks.com

ONE

"Damn. I slept through the ending." Jessie Wyndom yawned as the credits for *Star Trek IV: The Voyage Home* scrolled up the screen. Never mind, she'd seen the movie at least thirty-seven times—okay, slight exaggeration, but it was still her favorite.

She flipped off the TV then rolled her shoulders to remove the crick in her neck as she walked to the kitchen to let the dog out. With chagrin, she did a U-turn and headed down the hall to her bedroom. Old Whiskey had gone to that Great Fire Hydrant in the sky. Man, she must really be tired.

If she was to make *The Ms. Fix-It Shop* a going concern, she needed to put in long hours. Her hard work had paid off right from the beginning. Much to her parents' dismay. They'd be only too happy to see her fail.

Grateful that tomorrow was Sunday—the only day she closed the repair shop—she sat on the edge of her bed and toed off one athletic shoe. Maybe she could sleep in past six. Before she could remove the other shoe, a blinding light pulsated through the room.

She shielded her eyes with her hand. For weeks, something fishy had been going on in the farmhouse across the road. She knew the cops would catch that guy.

Intending to race to the window, she was halfway off the bed when the light swelled in intensity. She squeezed her eyes shut. Instantly, her stomach plummeted the same way it did on the Millennium Force at Cedar Point. But the monster roller coaster didn't make her ears ring. Or buzz...or...

Thunk.

"Ensign Drakus, that is *not* Cindy Crawford."

Jessie's eyes flew open. Where did that deep male voice come from? Where was her bedroom? Where was she?

"Xykr skizbat—"

She twisted around at the sound of another, higher-pitched voice. Who was speaking? She was alone, sprawled on an elevated platform in a gray, windowless room filled with what looked like computer equipment. A low hum, like that of a finely tuned machine, surrounded her.

"Please use twenty-first century English, Ensign. To speak in our own language is impolite to our guest."

This was one of her brother's pranks, Jessie decided. Tim and his buddies must have 'kidnapped' her again.

"I'm sorry, Captain. Shall I send her back?"

Jessie searched the room for the men who were speaking. *Nobody.* Computers along one wall hummed. A pedestal console stood in the middle of the room. Her cozy bedroom had been replaced by this sterile high-tech center. Just the sort of place Tim and his geeky friends would love.

"It is too late, Ensign. We are already beyond Earth's orbit." Pause. "Where is Lieutenant Qilana?"

Beyond Earth's orbit? *Yeah, right.* Jessie stood and planted her hands on her hips. "Okay, you guys. You've had your fun. Quit hiding and come out where I can see you."

"She sounds annoyed, sir."

"Interesting. Usually, they are afraid."

"Is this some kind of joke?" She stumbled off the platform. She wore one shoe and the same T-shirt and jeans she'd had on in her bedroom. She must have been so exhausted, she'd dropped off to sleep the minute she sat down on her bed.

"What do we do now, Captain?"

Jessie looked at the ceiling. No camera. *How could they see her?* "Did Tim put you guys up to this? You tell my brother I've had it with his gags."

This had to be her brother's doing. Despite her nap on the couch, she'd fallen back to sleep. Since she slept like the dead, Tim and his buddies must have kidnapped her, just like last year when they left her—in her nightgown, no less—near the old bell tower on the University of Michigan campus. Tim would pay for this.

At the whisper of a whoosh, she spun around again. A portion of the wall parted to reveal a doorway. A tall man in a burgundy and silver jumpsuit strode into the room.

Oo-whee. What a hunk. Raven black hair and brows. A blade-straight nose and a strong jaw. No five o'clock shadow for this guy. He had soot-black lashes to die for and silver eyes. Silver eyes? She shivered at their intensity. Not in fear but in a purely feminine reaction. *Yowza. Get me a fan.*

"My name is Captain Marcus Aurelius Viator of the Alliance starship *Freedom*. This is Ensign Drakus, a member of our Security team." The tall man pointed to his considerably shorter companion.

Intent on the hunk, Jessie hadn't even noticed the little guy. She stretched out her hand to the hunk. "Hi, I'm Jes—"

"We know who you are." The 'Captain' consulted the pedestal monitor. "Jessica Marie Wyndom. Age: twenty-nine. Home: Ann Arbor, Michigan, USA, Earth. Occupation: repairman."

She dropped her hand. "Repair *person*. Is there a secret salute I should know? Okay, I'll play along." She glanced down at his companion. "A troll. Nice costume, kid. Aren't you a little young to be one of my nerdy brother's friends?"

The man who called himself Captain Viator raised a finely sculpted black eyebrow. "Ensign Drakus is not a child. He is a Trucanian."

She snorted. "From the planet Trucania, I suppose."

"The planet Trucan," the troll corrected with glee.

"Right. And I've been kidnapped by aliens." She rolled her eyes. "Give me a break. I'm not going to fall for that gag. I recognize Tim's handiwork here."

"Captain, she does not believe—"

The tall man held up his hand. "She will."

At his flat tone, the hairs on the back of Jessie's neck rose. An uneasy feeling settled in the pit of her stomach. She shook it off. "I like your outfit, big guy. Pretty authentic looking." Hobbling on one shoe, she circled the Captain, examining him. "You're quite an improvement over the geeks Tim usually hangs with." She stopped behind him. "Great buns."

A spot of red appeared on the man's neck above the silver Mandarin collar of his burgundy one-piece suit. She noticed a small black mole just behind his right ear.

The troll, whose uniform was forest green, looked up. "She appears a bit slow, Captain Viator. Perhaps she doesn't understand. I've heard Terrans have minimal intelligence but—"

"Slow? Minimal intelligence? You techno-weenies think nobody is as smart as you are. This is one of your conventions, isn't it?" She walked over to a computer against the wall. Lights blinked, foreign symbols raced across the screen.

"Please, do not touch." Captain Viator stood beside her.

She jumped. Intent on the monitor, she hadn't seen or heard him move. "I have to hand it to you guys. This stuff looks pretty authentic. Tim told me about your games."

"Cap-tain," the little guy muttered. "She thinks this is a game. Terrans like to play simulations of space adventure. I understand they even have gatherings for fans."

"Terrans? Wait a minute. Aren't you guys supposed to say 'Earthlings'?"

"*Terra* means earth in one of your ancient languages," Drakus explained as if speaking to a child. He peered at her. "Sir? Doesn't she look familiar?"

"Yes." The Captain gave her an odd look. "Where is the officer who was in this room when you arrived?"

"No one was here." She glanced from the Captain to the troll. "Why are you looking at me like that?"

"It is of no importance." The Captain silenced the troll with a sharp glance.

"You guys and your secret games." She sighed. "All right. As long as I'm here, give me the Grand Tour, and then I want to go home. I've had a long day and an even longer week. I'm tired and I want to go to bed." Then, she groaned as she realized what she'd just said.

Neither of the men reacted to her slip of the tongue. No wink, no lewd comment, no elbow jostling. These guys really took their roles in this fantasy game seriously. They seemed awfully interested in one of the monitors.

"Ensign, locate Lieutenant Qilana. I am displeased she abandoned her post. Have Engineering check on the transport signal while I escort our visitor to the bridge. I need to discover why we left Earth's orbit. I do not want another malfunction when we return."

"Aye, sir." The troll disappeared through the doorway.

Captain Viator opened a drawer beneath the pedestal console in the middle of the room. He held out a flat black disk about a quarter inch in diameter. "Please allow me to attach this behind your ear. It will help you understand the crew."

So, that wasn't a mole behind his ear. This must be part of the ritual. She'd play along until Tim decided to show up. Nobody would accuse her of being a poor sport. "Whatever turns you on, big guy." She grinned.

His fingers grazed the tender skin behind her ear. She shivered at the tingle. That's odd. She didn't usually react to a man so instantaneously.

This close, she could see fine lines radiating from the corners of his eyes. She guessed he was a few years older than she was. Early-thirties, maybe.

Another ripple skitted from her ear down to her belly, and lower. She felt his heat, and a corresponding heat came over her. Strange. What was this guy doing to her?

Her nose twitched. No heavy cologne, just a clean male scent and something she couldn't identify. Faintly exotic. Woodsy? Spice? Whatever it was, he smelled damn good. Her breathing quickened at his nearness. She tried to concentrate on his watch. It was one of those high-tech gizmos that probably told everything from the weather in New Zealand to the stocks on the NASDEQ besides the time in all fifty states. It had a mini-monitor and even a tiny keypad.

He fumbled with the tiny disk. *Was he affected, too?* Nah. Guys weren't overcome with passion around Jessie Wyndom, all-around good sport, confidante, one-of-the-boys.

Quickly, he pressed the object behind her ear and stepped back. "Follow me." He strode toward the opening.

Her gait awkward due to only one shoe, she half-ran to catch up with him. The low hum seemed a little louder as they walked down a long, gray-carpeted hall that curved to the right. People dressed in a variety of costumes passed them. All nodded with respect to her companion.

"So, big guy, what is this? A Trekkie convention or something? Whoa." She swiveled around to gawk at a green-skinned, eight-foot tall character passing by. "Who did that guy's make-up? I can't get over the costumes here. No wonder the ceilings are so high. They'd have to be to—"

Still gawking over her shoulder, she ran right smack into the Captain who must have stopped and turned around. His strong arms encircled her, steadying her against a hard, muscular chest.

"Sorry." Her face flamed at being held by this superb specimen of manhood.

Those spectacular silver eyes seemed to sear her soul. A tremor rippled through her. Her breath caught in her throat. *Geez, I need to get out more.*

The Captain abruptly released her. He looked almost as discombobulated by their 'close encounter' as she felt.

He tapped the keypad on his wrist and a portion of the wall parted. She was about to ask how they managed to conceal the doors when she was stunned by the large room. Eyes wide, she followed him in.

"This is marvelous. Your set designer did a fabulous job." She looked around. "Is that a rear-projection screen? Wow. Looks like we're traveling through space. Just like in the movies."

Slowly, she turned toward a crew of four seated at different stations. One looked human. The others were outfitted to look like alien species. "Your costumer and make-up artist must be professionals. I can't get over this. It's like I'm on the bridge of a spaceship."

"You *are* on the bridge of a spaceship, as you call it. More accurately, this is the research starship *Freedom.*"

His pompous tone was back. She couldn't resist. "Whatever you say, big guy." Then she gave him a wink to let him know she was willing to play along with his fantasy.

He stiffened his already straight shoulders.

"Don't get all huffy on me now, Captain. Are they supposed to be your officers?" She waved at those seated at computer consoles around the room. "Hi, guys."

He shot her another look before pointing to each person. "Navigation Officer Glaxpher, Science Officer Xaropa, Communications Officer Cabbeferron, and First Officer Klegznef."

The last person eyed her as if he was a vulture and she was roadkill. He made her shiver in a totally different way from Captain Viator. She looked away. "Like I'm going to remember all their names," she muttered. She lifted her chin. "Okay, Captain. Where are we really? This place is big enough to be Cobo Hall."

He looked puzzled before he tapped the keypad on his watch. "Cobo Hall: a large place of assembly in Detroit, Michigan, USA. Detroit, a city known for the manufacture of despoilers of your atmosphere. Primitive vehicles you call cars."

Great. An environmental nut. "Yep, that's the Motor City all right." She pointed to the Captain's wrist. "What is that?"

"It is called a link. It is a communicator, plus it connects us to the ship's main computer," he replied.

"C'mon, now, Captain. What's really going on?"

"You are no longer on Earth. You are traveling through space, as you so quaintly observed."

God, he lectures just like Dad. This guy needs an attitude adjustment. "Get off your high horse, buster. I'm no dumb broad."

He snapped his head back. Out of the corner of her eye, Jessie saw the reaction of the crew. *Looks like nobody talked to the big guy like that. Oops.*

He cleared his throat. "No offense was intended. Your planet has made serious errors in its quest for progress. It is not prudent to poison the atmosphere that gives you life."

Your planet, too, big guy. She gave him an indulgent, if exasperated, smile. "C'mon, Captain, loosen up." She held up her hands. "O-kay. Enough is enough. This has been a rough week. I've worked over seventy hours, and I'm too tired to play your games. Get my brother to take me home. I'm going to wring Tim's neck for pulling this prank."

Captain Viator's silver eyes dulled to the color of pewter. "Terrans are such a violent race. Even the female of the species. How sad."

A chill ran through her at the grief flickering across his face. As if he'd witnessed a terrible tragedy.

She shook off the involuntary shudder. "This is a little too deep for me, Captain. C'mon, just beam me back to my farm." She pasted her brightest smile on her face. "You go your way and I'll go mine."

He gave a slight shake of his head. "Something is wrong with our transport signal. As soon as—"

"Captain." The deep, masculine voice carried a sense of urgency. It belonged to the only other human-like character. He was seated at a console to the back of the room. The Science Officer, she thought. "A Tegrorian frigate is cruising toward us."

"No Tegror ship is supposed to be in this sector," proclaimed the Navigation Officer. This guy's make-up was fantastic. Blue scaly skin, yellow eyes, and tightly curled indigo hair. "It could have been stolen by the Praetorium."

Viator stiffened. "We can take no chances. Have they sighted us, Mr. Xaropa?"

"No, sir. The range of that ship is much shorter than ours."

"If it is the Praetorium, they cannot be allowed to capture this ship. Mr. Glaxpher, prepare to engage the hyperdrive."

"Aye, Captain, preparing the hyperdrive," Blue Boy announced.

Jessie pursed her lips. "Hyperdrive? Aren't you supposed to go to warp eight, or something?"

"Engage the hyperdrive, Mr. Glaxpher." Captain Viator then stared down at Jessie with a look she remembered from her eighth-grade teacher.

"Hey, you aren't related to Mr. Nutt, are you? He—"

The room lurched. She would have fallen except for the Captain's grip on her upper arms. His wide stance, steady like a sailor on a ship in high seas, supported them.

A frisson of fear shot to her fingertips. This was a little too authentic. A whole room couldn't lurch, could it? Some sort of machinery in the floor must simulate that kind of movement. He released her.

"Sir, they are still following," the Science Officer announced.

"Evasive action, Mr. Glaxpher."

"Still following, sir."

"By the Intrepid Ones, we are traveling too far from Earth." Viator strode to a console against the far wall. "Lieutenant Cabbeferron, is there any communication from that vessel?" He spoke to a female.

At least, Jessie assumed she was female. Right now, anything was possible. The Communications Officer had bumps in all the right places and soft features, even though the markings on her face resembled hexagon chicken wire.

"No, Captain, but they are still following." If the soft, feminine voice was any indication, Chicken Wire Face—aka Lieutenant Cabbeferron—was, indeed, female.

Captain Viator stepped back, widened his stance, and clasped his hands behind his back. His broad shoulders seemed even broader. Here was a man obviously used to command. A leader. *Where did Tim find this guy?*

"They must have improved their tracking system," Viator speculated.

"Maintain speed, sir?" the blue-skinned Navigation Officer asked.

"Red Alert, Mr. Xaropa, and cloak. Then dead stop, Mr. Glaxpher."

"Aye, Captain," they both replied.

Red light filled the room, which lurched so strongly Jessie fell to the floor. In the huge screen, a dot zoomed closer until she could make out a long, sleek spaceship that looked like something out of a sci-fi movie.

"Ninety degrees port." The Captain's words were calm, as if he didn't see the ship racing toward them at tremendous speed. "Then, dead stop again."

She braced herself, and it still took her stomach three seconds to catch up after the sudden stop. A cheer rang out from Blue Boy and Chicken Wire Face. The human-like character and the Captain merely smiled. The gray-skinned 'Vulture' eyed Viator in stony silence.

"Thank the Intrepid Ones, they shot past us," the Science Officer reported.

"Excellent, Mr. Xaropa. Thank the Intrepid Ones, indeed. Deactivate Red Alert. Maintain cloaking device. Take us out of here, Mr. Glaxpher." The Captain folded his arms across his broad chest and looked down at Jessie. He expelled a deep breath. "What shall we do with you?" He reached down to assist her.

Despite the shakiness of her knees, she ignored his outstretched hand and scrambled to her feet. "What—"

"Security, have you located Lieutenant Qilana?" He spoke into the keypad-monitor on his wrist.

"Yes, sir." A froggy voice came from his wrist thingy, the *link*. "Lieutenant Qilana is on the bridge."

Jessie looked around. The Captain just looked startled. Whoever this Qilana person was, she wasn't on the bridge.

"Security," the Captain spoke slowly, "please repeat Lieutenant Qilana's position?"

"According to our genetic identification sensors, Lieutenant Veronese Qilana is standing next to you, sir."

"Hah. Your scanners have a glitch. Ain't nobody here 'cept us chickens," Jessie quipped. Then, she realized everyone on the bridge was looking at her. "What?"

"Security, run a diagnostic on the identification sensors. Contact me in my quarters." The Captain turned to Jessie. "Come with me."

Since he appeared to be in charge, she figured he was her best hope for getting answers. She gallumphed after him, wishing she'd taken off that shoe. If she took time now, she'd probably lose him.

His long legs, hard muscles evident beneath the form-fitting uniform, stretched out as he strode down the wide hallway. *Yes, indeed, very tight buns.*

"Would you slow down?" She panted as she tried to keep up. She definitely needed to make time for exercise. "What do you mean what should you do with me? I told you what you can do. Take me home. This isn't funny. I never liked pretending. I prefer my fantasy on television or in the movies. I don't want to play your silly games."

They continued along the corridor. Again, she noticed how it curved, as if they were traversing the perimeter of a large central room. He stopped, tapped his *link,* and a door appeared on the right. They entered a room, smaller than the two she'd been in. Though spartan in decor, books on shelves and objects in a display case made the room seem personal.

"Books? Gotcha." She smirked in triumph. "If this is some advanced culture, why do you still have paper books? Don't you have electronic readers? Even in our *primitive* culture we have electronic readers."

He gave her that 'Mr. Nutt' look. Made her feel downright stupid. Most of her teachers had made her feel that way. Her parents still did.

"I prefer using the tactile senses while reading for enjoyment," he said. "Those volumes are very old. Rare."

As soon as they entered the room, the door had whooshed behind them then disappeared into the wall. Ice snaked down her spine. She was alone with this stranger. A stranger who indulged in make-believe. *Could he have gone around the bend?* She'd heard about fantasy players who became so involved in their games that they lost touch with reality.

"I want to go home." She hated the tremor in her voice. She was no wimp, but this situation was beginning to frighten her. Where was her brother? Surely Tim should have appeared by now, if only to gloat over how he'd pulled off another gag. But what if Tim wasn't involved? What if—

"I would like nothing better than to return you to your home." The Captain rubbed the bridge of his nose. "We never meant to transport *you.*"

"What?"

"The directional signal for our transport must have developed a minor 'glitch' as you call it. Actually—" a red tinge crept up his neck "—we wanted Cindy Crawford."

Well, if that doesn't take the cake. Figures they'd want some model instead of me. "Glitch! I'll say you had a glitch. I don't look the least bit like Cindy Crawford."

His unnerving silver gaze traveled down her body and up again. "Yes, I know."

She yanked her baggy T-shirt over her jeans in a futile attempt to conceal the extra weight she carried on her hips. She was going to lose those fifteen pounds one of these days. As soon as grocery stores stopped carrying mint chocolate chip ice cream. Or butter pecan. Or Mackinac Island Fudge. Or...

She pursed her lips. "Fat chance Cindy Crawford would come to one of your conventions."

"I did not mean to insult you."

"Well, you did." She folded her arms across her chest then dropped them when she realized he was staring at her breasts. *Damn it.* He was not going to do this to her. She would not let this...this fantasy player make her feel self-conscious about her well-endowed attributes.

"This is not a convention," he said. "I told you before, you are on the Alliance research starship *Freedom.*"

"Right." She prowled the room. The unusual furniture invited relaxing. *They even designed futuristic furniture for their games?* "From another galaxy, I suppose."

"That is correct. Our homeport is in what you call the Andromeda Galaxy."

The finality in his voice shook her conviction that this was all an elaborate ruse dreamed up by her brother.

"Okay, big guy, you really had me going there for a few minutes. That sequence with the other ship? I almost believed you. But you blew it with the Cindy Crawford bit. Geez. You really know how to tromp on a girl's ego."

"I apologize. Again." He stood quietly in the middle of

the room, watching her.

She never knew anyone who could stand still that long without fidgeting. He unnerved her. She wandered over to the display case. Several carved animals lay in various poses on the shelves.

"So, why did you want Cindy Crawford? Besides the obvious." She rolled her eyes as she picked up one of the miniatures. The beast had a prehistoric quality, yet looked like nothing she'd seen before. *Fur and wings?*

He walked over to a small alcove. A short shelf jutted from the wall about waist-high. "Would you care for refreshments? Perhaps a cup of xephod tea. You may find it quite soothing."

"What, no Earl Grey?" She smirked. "Captain Picard would offer Earl Grey."

He rubbed the bridge of his nose then looked at her. Was that pity in his eyes? "If it eases your mind to believe this is a *Star Trek* convention, so be it. I understand that is a popular pastime for aficionados of what you Terrans consider science fiction." He held out a steaming container.

She accepted the handleless cup and stared briefly into the depths of the deep red liquid. "This isn't some sort of drug, is it?" She sniffed. The fragrance reminded her of cinnamon and citrus. "Like you'd tell me if it was," she muttered in self-derision.

"I will drink first to ease your mind." He raised his own cup, inhaled the aroma, and took a swallow.

"How long before you keel over?"

He stared at her.

"Okay, okay. Just joking." She sipped the aromatic liquid. Pure, unadulterated pleasure flowed over her tongue. As she swallowed the tea, warmth coursed down her throat and radiated outward. The tension in her neck and arms disappeared, leaving behind tranquility. "Whoa. I could really use this after a long day. Is this stuff legal? I'd give my eyeteeth for some to take home."

The tight muscles in his face relaxed and he smiled. His silver eyes lit up and the corners of his eyes crinkled in amusement. Those tingly feelings started skitting over her skin again.

Good God, what a smile.

"Alliance Space Fleet regulations prohibit illegal substances aboard starships," he pontificated. He had to spoil things by sounding like her dad again.

As he perched on the arm of a chair, his uniform stretched tightly over the hard muscles of his thigh.

She nearly choked on her tea. *Geez, Jess, get your mind above his waist.*

He took a swallow and then rested his cup on his knee. "My crew has become quite lax about exercise."

That certainly wasn't his problem. He probably worked out every day.

"Most of the crew are scientists," he continued. "More concerned with gathering research than keeping fit. Our medical officer thought Ms. Crawford would give them an incentive to exercise."

"Gotcha, again," Jessie gloated. "She doesn't even live in Michigan—especially not out in the sticks like me. How the heck did you mix us up? Another glitch in your identification sensors? Like your transporter? Like mixing me up with that Qilana person? You've got big problems with your equipment, buddy." Her face burned. *His* equipment looked pretty good.

"I believe you are correct." He didn't even notice her gaffe. Thank goodness.

She set her cup on a table and held out a carving. "What's this? Looks like a cross between a vulture and a kangaroo."

"A korvapid, which is indigenous to Trucan."

She gave him a droll look. "The home planet of your little troll friend. I remember."

"You still do not believe, do you?" He shook his head.

"What?" Distracted, she picked up another carving. This one had antlers, a duckbill, and webbed feet.

"That is a rumiduck. It is native to my planet, Serenia." He paused, thoughtfully. "Perhaps it is better you do not believe. That will cause you less anxiety. And if you ever do return to your home, you can convince yourself this was all a dream."

"Whoever carved these had a wonderful imagina—" She whipped her head up. "What do you mean *if* I ever return home? Look, mister, I have a business to run, a loan that rivals the national debt, car payments on a truck older than me, and the IRS wants their thirteen hundred dollars in estimated taxes by next Thursday, so you'd damn well better figure out how to get me home." She inhaled sharply, trying to catch her breath. The calming effects of the tea had completely disappeared.

When he began to stroke his whiskerless chin, she forgot everything. Her anger, her fear. She stared at his face. Having received a few whisker burns, she wondered what it would be like to kiss a man with a face so smooth.

A jolt ran through her. *What am I thinking?*

"I like your spirit, Jessica Marie Wyndom." His killer smile, coupled with his deep voice, struck a resonant chord deep within her.

Whew. That tea must be an aphrodisiac.

"You are not fearful like the others."

She bobbled the carving of a unicorn, the only beast she recognized. Again, cold trickled down her spine. "Others?"

"Periodically, we orbit your planet. The younger members of my crew like to listen to your rock-and-roll music." He grimaced. "I admit, the music is better than the raucous sounds from Zorf. Of course, none can compare to the soothing quality of the music from my home, Serenia. On occasion, I have indulged my crew by allowing them to transport a rock star aboard. Like you, they thought this is a science-fiction convention. However, we did not disabuse them of that concept."

Zorf? Serenia? He's into play-acting a little too deep.

He smiled—that killer smile again—which made her heart do a little tap dance. "Our purpose is research. We are observers of civilization. Yours is a primitive culture, much like we were once. We find Earth quite...interesting."

She'd humor him. Maybe he had to deliver his whole spiel before admitting this was all make-believe. "Okay, if you're really an alien from a 'galaxy far, far away,' how come I can understand you and your crew?" She gave him a triumphant look.

"The universal translator I attached behind your ear provides two-way translations. It converts our terms into comparable concepts in your language. The Intergalactic Alliance is comprised of many planets whose inhabitants are of various races and species. Our translators enable us to communicate with one another."

When he tapped the black spot behind his ear, she noticed his long, slender fingers which, like his hands, were devoid of hair.

"Without our universal translators," he continued, "it would be impossible to communicate with the members of the Alliance or to understand the inhabitants of the primitive planets we research, like Earth."

She ignored the reference to primitive. "So, you're like—voyeurs?"

He frowned. "Observers."

"This is too much. Next, you're going to say you want to impregnate me to carry on your species because your planet is dying." She quirked up the corner of her mouth. "Right?"

He arched that eyebrow again. "Why would I wish to mate with an inhabitant from such a primitive culture?"

"Talk about adding insult to injury," she huffed with exaggerated affront. "I'm outta here. First, I'm kidnapped by aliens—by mistake, no less. And now you're telling me no sex?" She gave him a droll look before stalking across the room. "Bummer."

She touched the wall. *Was this the way out?* She should've paid more attention when she entered. She'd been too busy watching those tight buns. "Before I leave—and I really must—tell me how you make the doors appear."

She felt the blank wall for a crack in the plaster. Only it didn't feel like plaster or wallboard or any other substance used for walls. She looked at the ceiling for a device that would sense her presence. Nothing.

Beneath her fingertips, the gray wall vibrated in sync with

the hum. Now used to the constant sound, she'd nearly forgotten about it. Her mechanic's ear picked up a slight hesitation in the hum. "Somebody needs to check—"

A doorway opened, catching her by surprise. She stumbled across the threshold.

"How did you open— Whoa. This is some bedroom."

***

Marcus Viator rubbed the bridge of his nose. Of all the Terrans he could have transported aboard, why this brash female? Like all Serenians, he abhorred emotional outbursts. He stopped rubbing the bridge of his nose and took a calming breath. The inhabitants of Earth were such volatile creatures.

He eyed her rounded figure. His crew would not resume a regular exercise program because of her. This Terran enjoyed her food a little too well. He doubted she even knew what aerobic exercise meant.

While baggy clothing hid her form, he remembered the feel of her lush body when she had run into him in the hall. Not altogether unpleasant, he thought with surprise.

On the rare occasion when he coupled with a female from his home planet, he enjoyed the hardness of her body. A firmness developed through rigorous exercise and strict adherence to a diet of healthful food.

Jessica Wyndom, on the other hand, was not firm. He should have been repulsed. Yet, for a brief moment, he wanted to touch her softness again.

Other commanders with less scruples than he coupled with their Terran 'visitors.' He would never take advantage of a guest on board his ship.

But this Terran, with her lush curves and tousled hair the deep red-brown color of the xephod tree, tempted him to put aside his unwritten rule. He dismissed the wayward thought and followed her into his inner chamber.

"Wow. You actually sleep in here?" As she slowly looked around, her blue eyes—the shade of Lake Domare on a cool morning—opened wide. "It's like being in a planetarium."

He glanced at the transparent bubble protruding from the room into the hull of the ship. He had grown accustomed to that amenity reserved for commanders of star vessels. It unnerved a few who preferred more secluded sleeping quarters. Not Marcus. Lying awake, staring at the blackness of space with its pinpricks of light soothed him, reminding him of sleeping outdoors under the stars on his uncle's farm—the one place where he yearned to live. Yet, instead of striding across the fertile soil of his own land, he raced across galaxies.

He dismissed the more and more frequent regret that the Elders had dictated his life. "Would it please you to rest here?"

Her mouth curved up in a wry smile—a smile that did not reach her eyes. "Cleverly done. That's quite a line." She lifted her chin and walked over to the bubble. "Didn't my brother tell you not to bother propositioning me? I'm just one of the guys, a grease-monkey who'd rather take apart an engine than romp between the sheets." She looked out into space, her arms crossed in front of her.

He recalled treatises on Terran body posture. Her rigid back, the toss of her head, the trembling of her fingers as they cupped her elbows revealed her inner turmoil. He did not understand why his reference to sleeping upset her.

"I do not know your brother. Therefore, it would be impossible for him to have warned me about you." He stayed in the portal where he would not be tempted to reach out and touch the vulnerable length of her neck revealed by the gathering up of her hair high on her head.

She whirled around. "I don't like this game." Her lower lip quivered. "Please have someone take me home." She straightened her shoulders, lifted her chin, and bit her bottom lip. At last, she restrained her emotions.

He admired her control despite her dawning fear. "If you care to rest, I will leave you in peace. No one will disturb you." He stepped back, indicating his good faith.

She seemed less sure of herself, now. Perhaps she was beginning to realize what had actually happened to her.

"I apologize for the distress our equipment malfunction is causing you. We will return to your planet as soon as possible. We must avoid detection by the Praetorium. They are renegades who prey on our ships. Also, we must discover why our transport signal erred. If it does not operate properly, you may not be returned to your home."

Her blue eyes widened.

"In fact," he continued, "an errant signal could send you to a different continent. Or even another planet."

TWO

"This is not hap—"

A signal sounded, interrupting his guest from Earth. Marcus touched the link on his wrist. "Yes."

"Drakus here, sir. Chief Hrvibm instructed me to run a diagnostic on our genetic identification sensors. Everything checks out A-OK."

Marcus winced at the Terran expression. "Have you located Lieutenant Qilana?"

"Lieutenant Qilana is with you in your quarters, sir."

"If the equipment is running properly, why does it insist that Jessica Wyndom is Veronese Qilana? Run another diagnostic."

"Y-Yes, sir."

"Captain?" This time it was Communications Officer Cabbeferron. "I have a time-delayed communiqué from Lieutenant Qilana. I am transferring it to your vid unit."

"On screen." He turned to the vid unit built into the wall above his desk. After a moment, a face appeared on the screen. A face remarkably similar to his Terran guest's. He and Drakus had been correct about their unexpected visitor.

Marcus glanced at Jessica, now standing in the portal to his inner chamber. Her eyes widened as she stared at the replication of her image on the vid screen.

Jessica approached the unit. "She looks exactly like me."

Like all Serenian females, Lieutenant Veronese Qilana had black hair and was slender with a firmness of body attained by vigorous exercise. Marcus raised his left eyebrow. "I daresay she does not look exactly like you."

The Terran blushed. He found that...charming. Perhaps,

though, she was embarrassed he compared her to Qilana. He did not intend to cause her discomfort.

"Captain, I have left this message to explain," Qilana spoke in typical Serenian tone, devoid of emotion. "The transport signal did not malfunction. I realigned it to bring Jessica Wyndom on board. She and I are victims of the Gemini Experiment." Qilana visibly swallowed, as if distressed.

Marcus controlled his surprise. Few knew about that aberration within the scientific community. The Elders had wrapped the project in so much secrecy the information was supposed to be unattainable. Apparently, Lieutenant Qilana had accomplished the near impossible.

"I will explain. Thirty years ago, a scientist from Serenia transported fetuses from Earth to volunteer host mothers from our home planet. Dr. Cenamola, being compassionate—" she spit out the word "—only removed one of a set of twins, leaving one child for the Earth mother."

Veronese Qilana and Jessica Wyndom are identical twins, thought Marcus. *That explains the error in the identification scanners. Their genetic make-up would be identical.*

Qilana pursed her lips. "Dr. Cenamola desired an answer to the eons-old question of nature versus nurture. To what extent does heredity determine an individual's make up, or does the environment in which one is raised have greater influence? Would the Earth twin grow up to act identically to the Serenian twin?" She appeared upset as she twisted her short-cropped black hair above her right ear. Her Serenian discipline seemed to have vanished.

"The experiment was halted as soon as the Elders discovered what Cenamola was doing. The Elders ordered him to return the unborn children to their rightful mothers. He did, with a few exceptions. He could not return me since I was born prematurely while Jessica was not. Our 'honorable' scientist buried the research. At least he did not bury me," Qilana said with scorn.

Intent on the screen, Jessica pulled from a stretchy fabric band a strand of hair above her left ear. Absently, she began to twist the hair around her left index finger. A mirror image of

Qilana. "This is unbelievable," Jessica muttered.

It was not unbelievable. Marcus knew the experiment was true.

"I grew up thinking I was different," Qilana's message continued, "even though my host mother never showed by word or action that I was anything other than Serenian. When she lay dying, she finally broke her oath of silence. I have been searching for my true genetic parents ever since. Fortuitously, Dr. Cenamola added a control to his experiment that aided me. He chose twins from the same area on Earth—Ann Arbor, Michigan, USA. At last, I have found my parents. And my twin."

Jessie shook her head. She couldn't believe this story. "No, this is not happening. This is a dream. All because I fell asleep during a *Star Trek* movie."

"My plan is to transport to Earth and transport my twin to the ship. Soon, you will receive a message that I am ready to talk to you directly." Even as this woman finished her recorded message, the Captain's link beeped.

"Sir, Lieutenant Qilana is hailing you. Since we are beyond the range of her *link*, her message is being relayed by a Trucanian vessel, the *Adventure*."

"On screen."

"Greetings, Captain. And to you, my sister, Jessica."

Jessie gaped. *What the hell?* The woman on the video monitor no longer looked like the slender, hard-edged officer from the previous message. It was like looking in a mirror. The woman appeared rounded, softer. Gone was the military-style cut of her black hair. Instead, her now-long, now-auburn hair was caught up in a ponytail with a bright yellow scrunchie. Just like Jessie's. Instead of a uniform, she wore jeans and a T-shirt like Jessie. But, the room behind the woman was the biggest surprise.

"She's in my bedroom," Jessie gasped. That was *her* antique sleigh bed, the stranger sat on. *Her* grandmother's double wedding ring quilt folded neatly over the footboard. Those were the lilac dotted-Swiss curtains *she*—Jessie—had sewn. Now, a stranger—a stranger who was a dead ringer for her—was in *her* house, in *her* bedroom.

The Captain shoved up the sleeves of his uniform. His forearms were hairless, she noted. Odd, given how dark the hair on his head was. "You have an explanation, Lieutenant." The quiet tone of his voice contained an edge that Jessie was glad wasn't directed at her. Made her forget all about his hairless arms.

"Yes, sir," the woman's voice faltered. She twisted a strand of hair above her right ear. Twice, she'd used that gesture—one Jessie often caught herself doing in times of stress. Jessie dropped her left hand. Unconsciously, she'd been doing the same thing.

"I have switched places with my twin."

"I don't know about you, *Captain*," Jessie interjected, "but I'm sitting down for the rest of this." She edged past him and sank into a chair that immediately conformed to her shape, giving her comfort as well as support.

"You are new to my crew, are you not, Lieutenant?" he asked.

"Yes, sir. When I discovered your destination was Earth, I specifically requested transfer onto your vessel. I came aboard during the last refit."

He clasped his hands behind his back. "You have a reason for your unorthodox behavior?"

"Would you two get on with this? How did that Stepford Wife get in my bedroom, and how did I get here?"

"Lieutenant," he continued as if Jessie hadn't spoken, "we are observers of primitive cultures. Our mandate forbids interference."

The woman stood up straight. "How is what I have done different from transporting rock stars or a fashion model aboard the *Freedom*?"

Jessie saw his adam's apple bob as he swallowed. Red tinged his ears. He was embarrassed, she mused.

"You left your post without permission, Lieutenant."

"Yes, sir." The woman on screen visibly swallowed. "But, I have to find out if this is where I belong."

"I'd like to know how she changed her appearance," Jessie

interrupted. "She sure didn't look like that before."

A flicker of guilt crossed the woman's face. "Genetic nucleotide duplication."

"Oh, right." Jessie rolled her eyes. "That explains everything."

"Lieutenant, use of GND is forbidden by Alliance law."

"Yes, sir." The woman gulped. "But—"

"Listen, lady, as long as you were going to all that trouble, the least you could have done was given me your old body. Great mask, sweetie. My brother has a lot to answer for. I'm royally ticked that he let a stranger into my house." Jessie jumped up. "Okay. I've been a good sport. But, I've had about enough of this game." She looked upward. "Beam me home, Scotty, there's no intelligent life here. You guys have fun at someone else's expense."

"Jessica, please listen to me," the woman on the screen said. "I want you to learn about my world just as I will learn about yours. I must meet the family I never knew. And, then, my sister, I will meet you face to face. Please understand. I only—"

The screen went blank.

The Captain touched his link. "Communications? What happened?"

"We lost the connection, sir. The *Adventure* does not answer our hail. We are attempting to contact other vessels in the quadrant in an effort to discover what went wrong."

"Keep me informed. Viator, out."

"Just what rabbit hole have I fallen into?" Jessie mused. "I think I'd like more of that tea about now."

"I believe this calls for something a little stronger." He strode over to a cabinet and removed a dark bottle and two narrow, fluted glasses. He poured a measure of aquamarine liquid in each and handed one to her.

She held the glass up to the light then quirked the corner of her mouth. "Don't tell me. Romulan ale."

"Romulan?" He gave her a quizzical look. Then his silver eyes brightened. "You are referring to a beverage on the television and cinema fantasy called *Star Trek*, are you not?"

"I don't know how you people did it, but that was a very good mask on that woman. It's so life-like I can almost believe she's my twin." She twisted the glass, glancing from the swirling liquid up to the man. Her heart gave a little lurch as she looked into his silver eyes. They seemed to bore into her, quickening her heart, sending tiny shivers through her bloodstream. What did he see?

"You still have doubts." His voice was flat, no question, as if he understood her confusion. That frightened her almost more than if he'd denied her fears.

"Wouldn't you?" she snapped. Then, she took a shaky breath. "This is not funny anymore. I need to get home. I don't believe for one minute this is real. Tim put you up to this. I know he did. Otherwise..." The horror of what she was contemplating hit her. *What if this is true? What if—*

Marcus observed her confusion. He pried the glass from her icy fingers. "I agree, it must seem unbelievable, but what Veronese Qilana said is true. Although it is highly classified information, I am aware of the Gemini Experiment. What she said did happen." *And more than once. Qilana, apparently, only knew about the last time, when Cenamola's treacherous work was discovered.* Not even Space Fleet Command was aware of the other times.

Jessica stumbled to her feet. She had the look of one stunned by horror. He had seen that same look in the eyes of young soldiers after seeing firsthand war's devastation. Thank the Intrepid Ones, since the Intergalactic Alliance was formed, war was no longer an acceptable method of settling differences. Since the war ended, the planets in the Alliance had enjoyed peace.

But, with the Praetorium—that band of cutthroats and hoodlums—striking out at isolated ships, the Alliance might have to take other measures. However, that was another issue. Now, he needed to reassure his guest.

"Apparently, our equipment does not have the 'glitches' we had assumed. Our transporter did not malfunction and our genetic scanners would be correct in identifying you as Lieutenant Qilana."

She shook her head. "I don't understand."

"Identical twins have the same genetic signature."

She gave him a wry smile. "Nature's clones?"

"Yes."

She still looked dazed.

"Perhaps you would care to rest and think about what you have learned." He motioned for her to precede him into his sleeping chamber. She quickly looked away from the clear enclosure as if realizing for the first time the blackness outside was actually space.

"Would a concealing screen make you more comfortable?" he asked.

She stared, as if seeing him for the first time. The fear in her eyes caused a curious sensation in him. He resisted the impulse to gather her in his arms and offer comfort. In all likelihood, she would misinterpret his concern for sexual aggression. *That would never do.*

"I will leave you. You have had a shock. More than one, in fact. You need time to adjust to what has happened. I will do everything within my power to return you to your home." He opened the drawer of the table next to the bed and withdrew a spare *link*. "Press this button to lower the concealing screen. After your rest, one of my crew will assist you. You have full access to this vessel, and you may talk to anyone. You are not a prisoner here. Again, I apologize for inconveniencing you."

Jessica—he liked how her name slid through his mind—twisted a curl of hair. Odd. Veronese Qilana used that same gesture.

Her movement pulled loose the stretchy yellow material in her hair. Without conscious thought, he caught the hairband as it fell. Now, her hair looked even more tousled, as if she had just awakened from a restless sleep. He rather liked it that way instead of caught up high like an animal's tail. He reached toward her to touch the deep fire of her tresses. She flinched.

"Pardon me." He dropped the yellow band into her hand. Then, he spun on his heel and left his quarters.

By the Intrepid Ones, what was I thinking? Touching a Terran? Very nearly lusting after her?

He had not lusted after Veronese Qilana. In fact, he had given her no more than a cursory glance on his visits to Engineering. Jessica was softer than her twin, her jaw more rounded and her mouth lusher, more enticing than the normal hard line of Qilana's. *More enticing? What am I thinking?* He caught himself scrubbing a hand down his face. He stifled the impatient gesture and maintained proper Serenian control as he strode purposefully toward the bridge. Perhaps communication had been restored between the ship and his missing officer.

Lieutenant Veronese Qilana had much to answer for.

***

Jessie prowled the Captain's quarters. She was still convinced her brother was at the bottom of this hoax. And hoax it had to be. How else could she explain what happened?

Tim delighted in playing tricks on his older sister. Usually, she just went along with his gags. Despite the disparity with which they were treated by their parents, she loved her brother dearly. She never held her academic parents' preferential treatment against him. It wasn't his fault he was brilliant. And she wasn't.

She had given up long ago trying to garner their approval. She threw all of her energies into her business. *The Ms. Fix-It Shop,* named after her favorite Girl Scout badge, was her pride and joy. She enjoyed her work and, by golly, she'd better get back home before Monday, so her hard work didn't go down the tubes.

Staring through the bubble into space, she rubbed her arms. This seemed so real. How could it be? She might be a sci-fi fan, but she didn't really believe in this stuff. Oh, she loved *Star Wars* and *Star Trek*. During a TV show or movie, people could live on other planets. Aliens from other worlds? Alternate universes? Yeah, for a couple of hours, she believed. But when the TV went off, reality kicked in. This just wasn't possible. Was it?

The bed beckoned. Exhaustion won.

She staggered over to the bed and kicked off her lone shoe. Maybe if she closed her eyes, she'd wake up back in her own bed.

That was a futile hope. This wasn't a dream. It wasn't a hoax played by Tim and his band of Trekkie wannabes. She really was cruising among the stars in a spaceship. Chills shot through her body. She curled up, pulling the soft covers nearly over her head. Maybe this would all go away.

She peeked out at the transparent bubble. She was in space. With a hunk right off a Chippendales' calendar. She started to grin.

Captain Marcus Viator, super stud. What a body. Muscles without bulges. Eyes that sent zings through her blood. Her nerve endings tingled just thinking about those silver eyes.

Eat your heart out, Cindy. This could've been you.

Just before sleep captured her, her ears picked up that odd sound again. She should get up and check it out. She would. In just a minute.

***

"Captain? What are you going to do about the Terran visitor?"

Standing in his usual spot on the bridge, behind the Captain's elevated chair, Marcus looked down at Ensign Drakus. "She has to go back to Earth, of course. As a member of the Security team, I am sure you are aware of Lieutenant Qilana's message."

Before Drakus could respond, a booming voice resounded. "Captain. We have a problem."

Stifling an impatient sound, Marcus turned to his Chief Engineering Officer who had just burst through the portal onto the bridge. As usual, Luqett ignored procedure. Instead of using the *link*, he used his burly presence in personal confrontation.

"Yes, Chief. What is it now?"

"Ye must stop these herky-jerky maneuvers."

"*Herky-jerky?*" Marcus raised an eyebrow.

"He's been watching Terran television," Drakus muttered.

"I canna keep the engines from tearin' apart."

Marcus never heeded Luqett's hysteria. Like the fable of the youngster who cried 'pterix' too often, Luqett lacked credibility. "What is happening to your speech?"

"Terran television," Drakus repeated. "He's trying to sound like Scotty on *Star Trek*, the original series."

Luqett shot the Trucanian a searing look. "We must return to Serenia, Captain. I canna fix the transport signal while we're cloaked. And now the hyperdrive—"

That caught Marcus's attention. "What is wrong with the hyperdrive?"

Luqett rolled his eyes dramatically. Eschewing the Serenian custom of restraint, the Chief frequently indulged in melodramatic behavior. It must be, as Ensign Drakus pointed out, too much Terran television.

"If ye would only listen, sir. The hyperdrive is na respondin'. After that last burst, she croaked."

She? Croaked? Marcus made a mental note to restrict the signals his crew beamed aboard. Terran colloquialisms were inappropriate on a Serenian vessel.

"Explain, Chief. What is wrong with the hyperdrive?"

"I dinna know, sir. We checked ev'rathin'. She just doesn't have any more to give. We're shuttin' down all systems until we find the problem. That fancy analyzer those know-nothing bureaucrats back home insisted we install is na worth the space it's sittin' on."

"What do you need?" Marcus knew Luqett had not come up to the bridge just to rant. He always had a plan. The Chief made problems look bleak in order to appear the hero when they were fixed. Since Luqett was a master at repairing anything, Marcus tolerated his idiosyncrasies.

Luqett straightened his shoulders. "If we maintain normal speed only, we might be able to diagnose the problem. Uncloaking, of course."

"Captain," wailed Drakus, "that would make us a sitting duck for the Praetorium."

Sitting duck? Yes, entirely too much Terran television. However quaint Drakus's expression, he was correct. The renegades needed Serenian technology. They especially could not be allowed to capture the *Freedom*.

Marcus strode in front of the viewscreen. *Sitting duck.* An apt description. Perhaps, he was too hasty in his decision to curtail television viewing. There might be value in learning the language of early twenty-first century America. The Serenian language did not have such a colorful vocabulary. Words were utilitarian. They meant what they said. No strange metaphors like 'sitting ducks.'

"Chief, how soon can we return our guest to Earth?"

"Sir," Luqett said with exasperation, "the last burst from the hyperdrive shot us through a quantum flux—out of the Milky Way Galaxy and into ours. We are too far from Earth to go back."

"Do what you can, Chief. Extensive repairs can be made when we reach Serenia." He stopped when he realized he was pacing. Serenians did not pace. Restraint was primary. He clasped his hands behind his back before turning to Luqett. "We *can* return to homeport, can we not?"

"It'll take a miracle, sir, but I'll give it my best shot."

Marcus shook his head, barely concealing his grin. "Miracles are your department. That is why I depend on you."

"I willna fail ye, Captain." Luqett spun on his heel and disappeared through the portal with the same energy with which he had entered.

"Mr. Glaxpher," Marcus spoke to the navigation officer, "steady course to Serenia."

Confident his order would be carried out, Marcus left the bridge and walked toward his quarters. Jessica should have had time to contemplate her situation. He did not relish another confrontation, which he abhorred as much as he did outward displays of emotions.

As he strode down the hall, he thought derisively that he had chosen a fine occupation if he wanted to avoid confrontation. He was a starship commander. During the Great Intergalactic War, fresh out of the Academy, he had even commanded a warship.

However, *chosen* was hardly the appropriate term for his career. If he had been able to choose, he would be striding to the top of a knoll where he could oversee his farm. A rolling expanse of freshly-tilled loam. Rich, fecund, waiting for the seeds of new life. The scent of fertile soil would fill his nostrils.

The buildings would be off in the distance. Barns, animal pens, storage facilities. A two-story farmhouse, encircled by a wide porch. The house would be white with dark green shutters. A rocking chair—no, a swing—would grace the front porch. There he and his soulmate would sit at the end of day to enjoy the sunset.

He stopped. Farmhouse? White with green shutters? The images in his fantasy were from Earth.

Engrossed in his daydream, he walked past his quarters. He turned around, flustering the young researcher who apparently had been trying to get his attention.

"C-Captain, Mr. Klegznef requests your presence in the C-Conference Room." Lieutenant Melora, a distant relative from his homeport, stumbled over her words.

"Why did he not contact me on the *link*?"

She scurried alongside him. "S-Sir, I do not know. He sent me to find you, but he said I must be very discreet."

Marcus stopped at his quarters. "Thank you for the message, Lieutenant."

"B-But, sir, Mr. Kleg—"

"That is all, Lieutenant."

Dismissed, Lieutenant Melora reluctantly walked away.

Klegznef had not been Marcus's choice for second in command. However, the Alliance wanted to show the Zorfans they were accepted as equal members. So, Marcus was saddled with this particular Zorfan, Klegznef.

Marcus would deal with his First Officer in a moment. He wanted to check on Jessica. All was quiet when he entered his quarters, the lighting low. He stood in the portal to his sleeping chamber. A lump in the middle of his bed left no question as to the whereabouts of Jessica Marie Wyndom.

She had burrowed under the thick michen feather coverlet. Only the top of her head was showing, her dark red hair a contrast to the white bedlinens.

For a moment, he watched her sleep. When he turned to leave, she rolled over. An anxious sound escaped her lips. She threw her right arm out wide, pushing the coverlet aside.

He was surprised at the muscularity of her forearm and

how strong her fingers and hand appeared. Earlier, he had been distracted by her hair and generous breasts. He rarely allowed primitive urges to distract him.

Her hand showed evidence of manual labor—fresh nicks and scratches, old scabs, calluses on the pads of her fingers and palm. Marcus reached out to touch her hand, to soothe the damage that marred her tender skin.

He drew back. Touching an unwilling visitor was totally inappropriate.

Her hair, a glorious mane of hidden fire, lay in disarray across the pristine white pillow. Her lush breasts moved up and down slowly beneath the white garment emblazoned with the words 'LET Ms. FIX-IT DO IT.'

What did Ms. Fix-It do? An image flashed through his mind of Jessica and him thrashing around together on his bed.

Startled, he realized he was aroused. He exerted control over his body. What was it about her that called to him in such an elemental manner? He was not attracted to full-blown females. He never indulged in fantasy. He never thrashed around on his bed, with or without a female. Furthermore, he did not couple with an alien species.

With a jolt, he realized how thoroughly he accepted Serenian culture as his own. Jessica was not an alien.

***

When Marcus entered the Conference Room, Klegznef did not rise from his seat at the large oval table. Although strict military procedure was not adhered to on a research vessel, the simple courtesy of rising upon the entrance of a superior officer was usually accorded.

Ignoring the breach of protocol, Marcus pulled out a chair and sat down. He forced himself to appear relaxed, his hands loosely folded on the table.

Hawkish in appearance and personality, Klegznef was better suited to a battle cruiser. If the Praetorium escalated their random outbursts, Klegznef would get his desire, the command of just such a ship.

At the end of the Great Intergalactic War, vessels of destruction had been converted into peacetime use. A beating of swords into ploughshares, if he remembered the Terran symbolism. Despite the peace that had reigned for nearly half Jessica's age, unrest stirred throughout the Alliance. On Serenia, as well as other planets, dissidents used the recent raids by the renegades to inflame the already worried inhabitants. The media called for the recommission of starships to prepare for a war that Marcus hoped could be avoided.

Officers like Klegznef would rejoice at the opportunity to engage in battle.

Klegznef was a native of Zorf, a planet whose barren plains and rugged mountains bred a warrior people. The Zorfan rulers had recently entered into the Alliance only because of the necessity of free trade which raised them above a spartan level of existence. The strictures of peace rankled them.

Klegznef stared. "The renegades have become bolder."

Marcus nodded, knowing his First Officer would make his point quickly.

"You did not fire on that vessel."

"No." Marcus would not rise to the temptation to explain. Klegznef knew why they did not fire upon a hostile ship. The *Freedom* was a research vessel, even though it carried appropriate armament. Attacking a renegade ship could very well plunge the Alliance into war.

Klegznef's gray complexion darkened. "Their actions were hostile."

"Yes."

"You should not have run."

"We did not run. We evaded."

"That was cowardly."

Marcus compressed his lips. "I am commander of this ship. And *you* are out of order." He pushed back his chair but did not rise. "Was there more you wished to discuss?"

"I have spoken to General Porcazier."

Marcus raised his eyebrow at the mention of his superior officer, the Commander of Alliance Space Fleet.

"I apprised the General of the situation with the Praetorian vessel," Klegznef said, and Marcus knew his first officer was looking for a reaction. Marcus did not give him one. "She was not pleased that you transported a Terran aboard."

The word 'tattle-tale' came to mind. Marcus allowed a small grin to curve his lips. American slang had its uses. He stifled the smile. "You are dismissed, Mr. Klegznef."

"Sir—"

"I said dismissed." *And don't let the door hit you on your way out.*

Yes, American colloquialisms definitely had their uses. He eyed Klegznef who stood but did not leave. *Would he challenge Marcus's authority?*

Fortunately for the Zorfan, he did not. He slammed his fists on the table before storming out of the room. Klegznef might have his own agenda, but he was still a product of a military environment. He would no more defy authority than Marcus would.

THREE

Jessie awoke with a start. There was that sound again. It had niggled its way into her dream. Damn. It had been such a good dream. An erotic thriller with Captain Marcus Viator in a starring role.

She looked around and her heart sank. She was not in her bedroom. She was not at home. She was in the Captain's quarters on board a spaceship.

Maybe she was dreaming she was dreaming. If so, this was one weird dream. The only good part was the Captain. Damn, that man was hot.

Hold it right there, Jess. Is he a man? Or one of those creatures who takes on the shape of a human? A shape-shifter.

He had felt pretty solid when she literally fell into his arms earlier in the hall and, later, on the bridge as the ship lurched into hyperspace. Those brief moments while he'd held her conjured up all kinds of interesting scenarios. Like the one in her dream.

She sat up straight. She believed his claim that she'd been beamed aboard a spaceship? That he and the rest of his crew were no fantasy players but real, live aliens? The realization made her take a quick breath. She brought her hand to her mouth. Oh, dear God.

What was wrong with her? Was she so enamored of science fiction she accepted the idea of beings from other worlds? Beings who could invade the space above Earth without detection by the country's defense systems? If this spaceship was sighted on radar, you could bet your boots all sorts of defensive and offensive measures would've gone into action by the military.

So, Jess, what makes you think it hasn't? How would you know if World War III hadn't already started? Or even War of the Worlds? Nah. Now, she was getting paranoid.

Why would she believe a total stranger? Albeit, a good-looking one. Was she so infatuated with Captain Tight Buns she believed everything he said? Was he really from another world?

What if he was one of those reptile creatures who lived inside humans? Like on that show—what was its name?—where the alien came out of the guy's mouth?

She shuddered. She hated creepy shows like that. *Remind me never to let the Captain kiss me.* As if he would. He'd made it perfectly clear he considered her beneath him.

His condescending attitude was exactly like her dad's. And hurt just as much. She climbed out of bed. Why did she care? Was she still looking for approval? Ridiculous.

She looked around. This place better have some sort of facilities. Maybe aliens didn't have to go to the bathroom.

She saw the *link* he left on the nightstand. She slipped the device onto her wrist and touched the symbol of an open door. An opening appeared in the wall. So that's how they did it. She entered a small room. Yep. Even those from superior cultures had to relieve themselves.

When she finished, she padded in her sock-clad feet around the rest of the Captain's quarters. Drawn once again to the carved miniatures, she marveled at the intricacies. Now that she realized these were actual animals—and not someone's wild imagination—she studied them more closely.

She cocked her head. That sound again. She had to tell somebody to check out whatever was making that noise. Although it was intermittent and barely perceptible, she always had her ear tuned to the sound of machinery. It was both a gift and a curse.

Once, she told a date his engine needed a tune-up. Even

offered to do it. The owner of the high-performance car had looked down his nose at her. How could *she* diagnose what his mechanic had missed? Last time she went out with that sucker.

She couldn't ignore the sound. What if it signified something crucial? Stalled on the side of the road was one thing, but broken down in space? Not while she was on board.

Where was the door to the hall? She'd been so busy following the Captain she hadn't paid attention to where they'd come in. She aimed the *link* toward each wall of the sitting room and pushed the button. Finally, a doorway appeared.

Out in the hall, she had no idea where to go. Follow the sound. *Yeah, sure.* When the sound was everywhere?

"Do you need assistance?"

Jessie whirled around. The man of her dreams, Captain Tight Buns himself. Heat filled her face as she remembered her erotic dream. Conscious thought flew out the window. *Sure, Jess, like they have windows up here in space.*

"When do I get to go home?"

"We are working on that," Captain Viator replied. "Were you able to rest?"

Heat flared in her face again. He gave her a questioning look. Dear God, she hoped he wasn't telepathic. All she'd need was another caustic comment about mating with a primitive species. *Do superior cultures do it better?* She blushed even deeper, if that was possible.

"You look...unwell," he observed. "Perhaps you need nourishment."

Unwell? Strangling over her hyperactive imagination was more like it.

"Come," he said.

As they walked down the hall, a door opened, startling her. A crewmember passed through, and the door disappeared.

"I gotta ask," she said. "I figured out how to make a door open, but how do you even know where a door is supposed to be?"

"The *link* will indicate the position of a portal." He clasped her wrist and aimed it at the wall. A symbol of a door appeared on the monitor.

His touch was firm yet gentle. Just as she had imagined it in her dream. An image of his hairless hand in a particularly intimate position flashed through her mind. Then, she wondered if he had *any* body hair. Oh, dear God, she was getting hot again.

To cover her fluster, she asked, "Do you just guess where a door should be?"

"You will look here." He pointed to the corridor wall. "Do you see this wavy outline?"

She peered at the gray wall, a lighter shade than the carpeted corridor. Everything in this place was a variation on the color gray. Looking head on, she couldn't see an outline. When she turned to ask him, she saw out of the corner of her eye a minor change in the wall. An outline of a door.

"Why so mysterious? Why not just put doors that look like doors in the first place?"

"The *Freedom* was originally the flagship of the fleet." At her perplexed look, he said, "It was the Commander-in-Chief's ship during the Great Intergalactic War. Disguising portals was intended to confuse the enemy if they boarded the vessel. After the war ended fifteen years ago, military vessels—like this— were converted for other use. The ship's computer controls access to the portals as well as the *links*."

"Things should look like what they are intended to be."

He wrinkled his forehead. "This irritates you. I do not understand."

"Look, sweetie, I want to go home." She gulped as she realized what she had called him. She was more disconcerted by his presence than she realized. "Sorry. When I don't understand things, I get irritated."

"I understand your concern." He paused thoughtfully. "You are probably hungry, also. You have been on board for ten hours."

"Ten hours! That can't be." She began waving her hands. "I have to get home. My business. People will be coming to get the stuff I've repaired and bringing—"

"Be calm." He clasped her hands and stared into her eyes.

"Do not become excited over what you cannot prevent."

His silver eyes mesmerized her. Tension flowed from her body as his hands telegraphed tranquility. She looked down at their entwined hands. Again, she found them gentle yet firm as they engulfed hers. She felt strength in those hands. A reassuring strength.

Disconcerted, she pulled away. He gave her a searching look and then began walking again. "This way."

He ushered Jessie into a large, softly-lit room. "The lounge is an area of relaxation. You missed lunch, what we call Midday Repast. I will demonstrate how to obtain something to eat." He explained how to order a snack from a food replicator.

He led her to a plush booth—in deep red. *Ah, hah.* A color other than gray. *Geez, I'm losing it. He holds my hand, and my brain self-destructs.*

She looked around. Other occupants of the room indulged in quiet conversation in secluded areas. Soft music played in the background. She didn't recognize the tune or the instruments. After four years of high school band, she could usually distinguish the sounds of various instruments.

"Tell me, Captain, what—"

"You may call me Marcus." A smile belied his stilted manner. That smile turned her insides all gooey.

Ridiculous. She needed a good kick in the behind.

"Marcus." She liked the sound of his name. Not bad. Now, if she could just stop the idiotic way she reacted to him. She cleared her throat. "What kind of music is that?"

He smiled again. She felt the warmth of his smile all the way to her toes. *Down, girl.*

"It is traditional music from Serenia."

"Your home, right?"

"That is correct. You would call it 'folk' music, I believe. Our ancestors played primitive string instruments to accompany the recitation of legends. What you are hearing now is a replication of the ancient instruments."

"It's very soothing." She popped into her mouth a piece of the snack he had selected and munched. The small dried chip exploded with a strikingly vivid taste. "Wow." She brought her hand up to her jaw.

He chuckled. "Your vegetables do not taste like that?"

"Of course they don't."

She placed another chip on her tongue. *Yowza.* Better than ice cream. Forget mint chocolate chip. Forget Moose Tracks. She'd eat nothing but veggies if they tasted like this.

"Captain?" A voice came from his *link.* Sounded like Chicken-Wire Face, the Communications Officer. "You are needed on the bridge."

He rose. "Excuse me."

She started to follow.

"Please finish your snack. Our Evening Repast—you would call it dinner—will occur shortly. I will send someone to escort you to the dining area."

He left the lounge, shoulders back, spine arrow straight, stride determined. A man with a purpose. Her gaze lingered on his backside. She gave her head a little shake. She had to quit fixating on his rear.

As she finished the last of the chips, the music stopped. Once again, she heard the engine sound—and the slight hesitation. That just showed how flustered she was in the Captain's presence. She had forgotten to tell him about the sound. She got up and looked for a receptacle in which to dispose of the container.

"May I help you?"

Jessie whirled around at the musical voice. A young woman waited patiently for a response. She wore the one-piece suit that seemed to be the uniform around here. The only difference was some uniforms had silver collars—indicating rank? Maybe the color indicated the department where they worked. This female's uniform was pale blue with a silver collar. Unlike the Captain's, her collar had no stars.

"A waste basket? Oh, there." Jessie followed the actions of an officer and deposited her trash. Then, she turned to the small female in blue. "I need to find— Oh, what do they call it on *Star Trek?*" She snapped her fingers. "Engineering. Yeah. Where's Engineering?"

The woman gave her a worried look. "Mr. Klegznef

assigned me to assist you. I am Lieutenant Aurelia Melora.
You may call me Aurelia. May I escort you to Provisions for
appropriate attire?"

"I'm fine. Just point me in the direction of the ship's
engines. I can take it from there."

Aurelia looked even more worried. "Engineering is a
restricted area. I am allowed to show you other places on the
ship, though."

So much for the Captain's assurance I can go anywhere.
Jessie thought for a moment. "Sure. A tour is just the thing."
She followed as the young woman glided down the hall.
"Aurelia. That's a pretty name. The Captain's name is similar,
isn't it? Marcus Aurelius Viator, right?"

"Yes. We are—" She concentrated for a moment. "You
would call us 'cousins.' Aurelia—Aurelius, for a male—is a
family name."

"You're from the same planet, then? Serenia? Like
Lieutenant Qilana?"

Aurelia's eyes widened. "*That* is who you look like."

Jessie grimaced. "I know."

"You could be dupes."

"I beg your pardon."

Aurelia looked startled at Jessie's offended tone. "Dupes.
Duplicates. Is that not what you call them?" She scrunched
her eyes. "No. Twins is your word. My translator must not be
working properly." She touched behind her ear. "I am sorry. I
meant no insult."

"No problem. I put my foot in my mouth all the time."

Again, the guide looked startled. She glanced down at
Jessie's sock-clad feet. "Was that a colloquialism?" Aurelia
smiled. "Foot in mouth. That is amusing."

"Think we can get this show on the road?" Jessie grimaced.
"Sorry. The tour can begin any time."

"I believe you will be more comfortable with footwear
and proper attire."

"If you insist." She really needed to get to Engineering,
but if changing her clothes would get her little guide to hurry
up, she would do it.

Aurelia led her down the hall. She stopped and touched her *link*. A doorway opened to a very small room.

"What is this?" Jessie waited before entering.

"We call it a *conveyance*, but I believe it is similar to your elevator. Come." Aurelia beckoned. Once Jessie was inside, Aurelia called out, "Provisions."

The conveyance moved smoothly downward. When the door opened, Jessie followed her guide. Provisions gave her a pale blue jumpsuit and soft, leather-like shoes. In a private dressing area, she stripped down to her underwear and stepped into the uniform. The front closure appeared to be similar to Velcro without the bulkiness or teeth that snagged on everything. Yet, she had no doubt the long opening would stay closed. Good thing she'd already gone to the bathroom. This thing would be a bear to get out of.

The material of the uniform felt like silk against her skin. A very sensual feeling. A very feminine feeling. One she was not used to. Her normal attire was just what she'd had on, well-worn jeans and baggy T-shirts.

She looked at herself in the mirror and grimaced. Her breasts looked too large. She turned around and craned her neck to see behind. Well, she never claimed to have tight buns. It was all the fault of those ice cream guys in Vermont.

She found Aurelia waiting patiently outside the dressing room. "I'm ready for that tour now."

Aurelia first showed her where to deposit her jeans and shirt for laundering. Then, she showed off the labs where she worked, and the transport room. Jessie had intimate knowledge of *that* place.

Just outside a gathering area much larger than the lounge where Marcus had taken her, Aurelia excused herself for a moment. Jessie walked to the doorway. Small tables were scattered around the lounge, with three or four chairs at each. In the middle, several tables had been shoved together to accommodate a larger group.

Crewmembers in jumpsuits of various colors lounged and chatted, many with glasses containing colorful liquids in front of them. Some of the crew looked human, though a few were quite exotic. Considering the uniforms—and if she was correct in her previous guess—this lounge was for non-officers. No silver collars here.

The soothing sounds of quiet music—much like what she'd heard before—floated through the air. An alien—okay, they were all aliens but this one *really* looked alien—stood behind a bar. Bright colored feathers formed a halo around his head. Round black eyes on either side of a tan face scanned the room. The bartender nodded to Jessie. Including the halo, he had to be at least seven feet tall. Maybe he doubled as a bouncer.

All talk ceased as the crew noticed her at the entrance. Even the music stopped. For the second time since she'd landed in this strange place, she felt afraid. It was one thing for Marcus to reassure her. He wasn't here right now. And the natives looked restless.

Suddenly, the sound of Bob Seeger's "Old Time Rock and Roll" erupted in the silence. She burst out laughing. These aliens couldn't be all bad if they liked rock-and-roll music.

Grins creased the faces of the younger members at the pushed-together tables. Some even got up and danced in the open space where the tables had been. They beckoned to Jessie. She couldn't resist. She danced her way over to the group, her body swaying, her arms over her head, clapping. *God, this feels good.*

Just as suddenly as it began, the music stopped. In the center of a circle surrounded by the others, Jessie lowered her arms. The man nearest her mumbled what sounded like a curse.

"What's wrong?" she quietly asked her companion.

"What is this nonsense?"

She turned in the direction of the deep, commanding voice. "Oh, no, the Vulture?"

The crewmembers came to attention, deliberately blocking her from the Vulture, who seemed to be searching.

"This unseemly behavior will cease."

"That guy sounds like Darth Vader with a cold," she said out of the corner of her mouth.

The curse-mumbler choked back a laugh. "That is First

Officer Klegznef. Do not make him angry."

"Why? He'll throw me in the brig?"

"Do not joke."

Darth— Oops. Kleg-whatzit was still scanning the room. Finally, he turned to the exotic bartender. "There will be no more playing of that alien noise. Is that clear?"

The bartender nodded, bright feathers bobbing.

"Such frivolity is unseemly on an Alliance vessel." With that parting shot, Klegznef did an abrupt one-eighty and marched out.

Once he was gone, the crew began muttering and milling about, their high spirits dampened.

"Mr. Popularity, huh?" she said.

Just then, Aurelia came running up. "We must leave."

The curse-mumbler stood in front of Jessie. "Welcome aboard. We heard you are unable to return to your home, and we did not want you to...feel bad."

She grinned. "You made me feel very good. Thank you."

A pale and obviously shaken Aurelia tried to hasten her away. "Come. We must leave."

"Thanks for the dance, guys." Jessie waved good-by.

Agitated, Aurelia led her out to the hall. "I should not have left you. They should not have danced with you."

"Hey, lighten up, Aurelia. They meant no harm."

"You do not understand. Come. There is much to see."

Yeah, like the way to Engineering. But Jessie kept quiet. She understood Aurelia's reluctance. Engineering was the perfect place for a saboteur. No way would she be able to convince her guide she just wanted to help.

"That Kleg-whatzit guy is a real pain in the—rear." *Totally different from Captain Tight Buns.*

Her guide stopped and gave her a frightened look. "Mr. Klegznef is not a person to annoy."

"Was he looking for me?"

Aurelia glanced quickly around. "I understand," she said softly, "that he is not pleased you are aboard. In fact, he reported to Space Fleet Command that Captain Viator did not return you to Earth immediately."

Jessie laughed. "I see gossip is alive and well in your *superior* culture."

Aurelia clapped her hands over her mouth. Her eyes widened. "I should not have said that."

"Sure you should have. Hey, what's in there?" Jessie pointed to a wall with warning signs. Even if she didn't know the language, she could figure out the symbols.

"That is the conveyance to Engineering. A force field protects that area. No one can engage the conveyance without authorization. Chief Luqett is very protective of his area." She urged Jessie away. "Down this hall..."

After a tour that seemed to go on forever, Aurelia's *link* beeped. They had just returned to the first lounge where Marcus had taken her for a snack.

"Please excuse me again," Aurelia said. "I must leave you for a few minutes to return to the lab. Statistics for my current research project are ready. You may wait in there. I will return shortly."

"Sure," Jessie lied. "Take your time. I'll be fine."

She waited until Aurelia was out of sight before walking out of the quiet lounge. Blessed with a good sense of direction—when she wasn't distracted by the Captain—Jessie backtracked toward the forbidden area of Engineering.

When she saw the warning signs, she scanned the *link* on her wrist for the symbol of a door. Maybe she should call the head of this department first. What was his name? Aurelia had mentioned it.

"What are you doing here?"

She knew that voice without turning around. Darth Vader with a cold.

"I asked you a question, Terran."

With reluctance, she turned around. "Don't get your knickers in a twist, mister. I heard you the first time."

First Officer Klegznef glared. *Oops. Wrong thing to say.* When would she learned to watch her mouth? The gray bristles on his head quivered, and his mouth hardened into a straight line. He looked steamed.

She was five-seven, but he towered over her by more than

a foot. "Anyone ever tell you you'd make a great basketball player? They have basketball on your planet?"

His sharp, obsidian eyes bored into her. She shivered at their cold intensity.

"Guess not, huh?" She glanced down the hall to her left. Empty. Same on her right. *Oh, sugar jets.* This was worse than facing a mugger with a switchblade. *Brazen it out, kiddo.*

"Mar— The Captain said I could go anywhere on the ship." *Geez, Jess, what a wuss.*

Klegznef's sharp features tightened in disapproval. From his short, quill-like gray hair to his corpse-gray chin, his face became even more rigid. He'd fit right in on Mt. Rushmore. If he didn't have a stroke first. He spoke with controlled fury. "You will leave this area immediately."

Sweat dampened her hands. Her mouth turned to cotton, and she couldn't have spoken if she'd wanted to. She clenched her hands so he wouldn't see them shaking.

Her feet, clad in her new shoes, became iron blocks stuck to a magnetized floor. She swallowed a nervous giggle as she imagined Klegznef using her for a rock'em-sock'em punching bag.

"Is there a problem, Mr. Klegznef?"

Jessie breathed a sigh of relief. Captain Marcus Viator to the rescue. A charging cavalry wouldn't have been more welcome.

Her mouth unstuck. "Hi, guy, er, Captain."

Marcus glanced from his First Officer, bristling with fury, to an over-bright Jessica. Before he interrupted, he had seen absolute terror written across her face.

"I see Mr. Klegznef has been entertaining you, Jessica." Not for a moment did he believe that. He needed to get her away from his First Officer.

"The Terran should not be here."

Despite Klegznef's hostility, Marcus remained calm. "She will be returned to her home as soon as possible."

"You—" Klegznef pointed to Marcus "—should confine her to quarters."

Marcus lifted his chin. "She is not a prisoner. She is free

to come and go as she wishes."

"It is possible for her to sabotage the ship. You will forbid her to roam freely."

Klegznef was giving *him* an order? Marcus looked closely at the Zorfan's implacable expression. "You need not concern yourself with our visitor, Mr. Klegznef."

"But I—"

"She—"

"Thank you, Mr. Klegznef," Marcus interrupted their simultaneous protests. "Our visitor may roam the ship at will. Now, I will resume her tour."

For several seconds, Klegznef stared at him. Would his First Officer defy him?

The Zorfan visibly struggled to contain his anger. Marcus wondered if Klegznef's warrior persona would overpower his military training. Insubordination could end his career with the Alliance.

The First Officer grimly nodded once. He continued to stand with his arms crossed in front of him. Marcus decided it prudent to remove the Terran from the area.

"Come." He nodded to Jessica. "You will, perhaps, be interested in seeing how we grow that snack you enjoyed."

"Listen, I need to tell you about—"

"Not now," he cut her off.

When the hall curved enough for them to lose sight of Klegznef, she said softly, "Why does he hate me?"

Marcus waited until a small group of crewmembers passed before answering. "I do not believe he hates you."

"Oh, yes, he does. You didn't see how he looked at me. God, he about froze me to death." She shivered.

"Let us continue this conversation in my quarters." He led the way. "I understand Lieutenant Melora has already given you a tour of the ship."

She looked puzzled for a moment. "I'm getting so confused with the names. You mean Aurelia?" She smiled. Color had returned to her cheeks, and the sparkle was back in her eyes. "She took me to Provisions and gave me this uniform."

He had already noticed the way the uniform molded her lush body. Entirely inappropriate thoughts tantalized him. He must have revealed his interest because she looked away.

"Aurelia showed me the labs," she spoke hastily. "And I'm sure you already heard about the scene in the lounge."

He smiled. "Klegznef does not approve of Terran music."

"He doesn't approve of fun, either."

Marcus had to agree, though he did not say so. He opened the portal to his quarters and motioned her ahead of him. The door quietly closed and disappeared. "Please sit down."

"Can't. I'm too wired." She paced the sitting room, stopping to examine a book here, a carved miniature there. "That guy scared the sh— Oops. He really scared me."

Marcus rubbed the bridge of his nose. How to proceed? He sat, then crossed his ankle over his knee. "Mr. Klegznef was recently assigned to the *Freedom*. His adjustment to the atmosphere of the ship under my command has been...difficult."

"Maybe he wants your job."

He raised an eyebrow in acknowledgment. "Mr. Klegznef is from a culture that values confrontation. Zorfans believe peacekeeping is a waste of time. Cowardly, even. For economic reasons, however, they joined the Intergalactic Alliance and reluctantly obey Alliance regulations."

"This Alliance. Is it some kind of government?" She finally sat down and looked at him with avid interest.

Though her overly emotional reactions were directly opposite to what he valued, her eagerness to learn, her boldness, even when frightened, appealed to him. Yet she disconcerted him with her unusual way of phrasing things.

"The Alliance was formed after the Great Intergalactic War fifteen Earth years ago. The leaders of the member planets realized they never again wanted to endure destruction of that magnitude. Whole civilizations were decimated. Planets totally destroyed. With peace has come prosperity."

"That ship you avoided didn't have peace on its mind."

Her quick grasp of situations surprised him. His understanding of American culture indicated that the higher the intelligence, the less manual labor was involved. She worked with her hands. Therefore, he surmised, she would not be qualified for work requiring higher intelligence and, consequently, not looked upon with regard. That would not be true on Serenia, of course. All talent was valued. He did not believe that was so on Earth.

Yet, she appeared quite intelligent. Her command of the language—though colorful—indicated enhanced mental capacity. She adapted easily to captivity. He wondered how he would fare if he landed on Earth and discovered he could not return to his ship or his home.

"Not all inhabitants of the Intergalactic Alliance are content with what they have," he observed. "Greed is a powerful motivator."

"Even in superior cultures?" She settled back in the chair and gave him a smug grin.

He raised an eyebrow. "Touché."

"Go on. So you've got a faction that wants power."

"The Praetorium is a band of renegades and hoodlums. Dissidents from several planets have joined together to upset the natural order. To date, their activities have been minor skirmishes. Irritating but of no real consequence. However, they appear to be getting bolder and better organized. Their stolen technology more advanced."

"A threat?"

"To peace? Perhaps."

"To your ship?"

"Definitely."

"Could Mr. Klegznef be a member of this Praetorium?"

He controlled the urge to bolt from his seat at her preposterous suggestion. "Absolutely not. Zorfans may be a warrior race, but they are the product of rigid adherence to military order."

She shrugged. "Just a thought."

Could Klegznef's actions be a warning? He strode to the vid unit above his desk. "Computer, access crew profiles."

"Access denied."

The ship's computer denied him access?

"Computer, this is Captain Viator. Access crew profiles."

"Access denied."

Jessica walked up behind him. "Another glitch?"

He shot her a speaking glance. "Computer, this is Captain Marcus Aurelius Viator, identification number Alpha two seven five, Delta six. Access."

"Access denied."

"Maybe you should just give the computer a good whack. Let it know who's boss." Her eyes twinkled.

He had no time for twinkling eyes or smart-aleck remarks. "Bridge," he ordered the computer.

"Access denied."

He tapped the *link* on his wrist. "Security."

"Access denied."

He strode to the exit portal and tapped his *link*. Nothing happened. "This cannot be."

"What's wrong?"

He took a deep breath. He must not allow Jessica to worry. Unable to return to her home was threat enough. After the fright with Klegznef, witnessing Marcus's alarm would upset her further. As Captain, he was responsible for protecting her. He would say nothing until he confirmed his suspicions.

Not seeing the outline of the portal disturbed him. "May I have your *link*? Mine appears to be malfunctioning."

She handed it over. He pointed her *link* toward the wall where the portal should be. No image of a door appeared on the monitor. He tapped the correct button. Nothing.

"Bridge, respond," he spoke into the *link*.

"Access denied."

He tapped again. "Security, respond."

"Access denied."

She put her hands on her hips. "Houston, we have a problem."

FOUR

"Hiya, sweetcakes!"

Startled by the overly-friendly male voice, Veronese Qilana looked up from the workbench in Jessica's garage. Because of the stifling heat, she had raised the large door.

Veronese set down the narrow screwdriver, a primitive tool but all she had to work with as she tried to repair her *link*. "May I help you, sir?"

"Oo-o, aren't we all la-de-da." The man tipped up the brim of his cap, emblazoned with an Old English 'D'.

That was the symbol of the Detroit Tigers. She thanked the Intrepid Ones she had researched the social and entertainment customs of the area in which her twin lived. Was her visitor a member of that baseball team? Beneath the man's cap, clumps of dark blond hair stuck out in several directions.

In an effort to decipher his strange speech, she examined his tone and facial expression. "La de da?"

"You got anything to drink, sweetcakes? I'm all out over there." He jerked his thumb toward the dilapidated farmhouse across the road. So, that was how he came upon her without her hearing. He simply walked across the dirt road. She was relieved that her surprise at his arrival was not due to her intense concentration on her work.

"I am able to give you coffee." At his scowl, she realized that was not what he expected. She should have included subtle speech context in her preparation for switching places with her twin. There was so much she had not been prepared for. This trip was not going as planned.

"Got any beer?" he asked in an exasperated tone.

His greeting indicated he was on friendly terms with Jessica. But, something about him did not seem right. His eyes darted from one side of the work area to the other. From the time he had greeted her, he never looked directly at her. The longer she stared at him, the edgier he became. Perhaps he was not a friend.

"Water would refresh you. A dispenser is over there." She pointed to her left.

"Hey, you got a water cooler out here. Not exactly what I was looking for, though." He sauntered over to the dispenser. He filled and drained a paper cup several times before crumpling it up and dropping it on the floor.

Smacking his lips, he returned to the front of the workbench. "My, my, that sure was good. Nothing I like better'n a cool drink of water."

His tone sounded sarcastic, but she was uncertain.

"'Course a good brewski would've tasted better." He *had* been sarcastic. If she could not return to the ship, she would have to learn the nuances of speech. "'Specially on a hot day like this," he added.

The day *was* very warm. Late September in Michigan was supposed to be temperate weather, like Serenia. Not this heat that left her—rather, Jessica's—T-shirt sticking to her skin. Unused to such long hair, she had gathered it high off her neck.

The man's vocabulary confused her. "'Brewski'?"

"A beer, sweetcakes. A beer."

She should have studied twenty-first century American linguistics in more depth. She was in way over her head, as they say here. She picked up the screwdriver and continued taking apart the *link* she had brought from the *Freedom*. She had lost contact with the ship twelve hours ago and had not been able to contact any Alliance vessel.

This did not make sense. At least two other research vessels were assigned to this sector. The *Adventure*, the farthest from Earth, had relayed her transmission to the *Freedom*. Why was the *Freedom* out of range? It should still be in orbit around Earth. Normal research time was at least two Earth weeks.

Once communication was severed, she had not been able to contact anyone. Perhaps her *link* had become inoperable.

"Say, what was that bright light last night?"

"Light?" She looked up from her work.

"Yeah, around midnight. Two big flashes of light." Thankful for the strict discipline she had been taught on Serenia, Veronese controlled visible emotion. Inside, she quaked that others might have seen the flashes from the transporter, once for Jessica and once for her. She thought making the switch at night would be less noticeable. Why had she not thought about the light?

"Midnight?" She arched her eyebrow.

"Thereabouts. Your whole house lit up."

Her stomach clenched. *Was this man watching Jessica's house?* "I was asleep."

"Really?" He stared. "Your bedroom light was on."

A strange sensation lifted the hairs on the back of her neck. Was that fear? She bent to work on her *link*. Perhaps the man would go away if she did not talk.

"What's that you got there, sweetcakes? A mini-TV?"

His interest disconcerted her. Serenian technology was quite advanced from that of Earth's. If the man wanted to think the *link* was a small television, she would let him. Better that he not look too closely.

Silently, she bent over her work, hoping he would leave.

"You sure aren't very sociable." He stuck his hands in the back pockets of his jeans and rocked on his heels.

"I am working."

He held up his hands. "Hey, I can take a hint. See ya later, sweetcakes." He gave her a mock salute and then swaggered down the driveway.

With a sigh of relief, she blew upward, ruffling her bangs. Even if it meant losing the cooling breeze, she closed the overhead garage door. That should deter visitors. Before switching places, Veronese had secretly monitored Jessica and then practiced imitating her twin in the privacy of her quarters. Startled by the visitor from across the road, she had forgotten to mimic Jessica's speech. She would have to be more careful in the future.

She set the *link* aside. She would attempt to contact an Alliance ship later. Now, it was time to do what she had come here for. With her heart thumping in anticipation, she went into the old farmhouse, Jessica's legacy from their grandmother, and prepared herself to meet her biological parents.

***

"Okay, big guy." Jessie propped her hands on her hips. "Tell me what's going on. Are we locked in?"

The Captain looked like he was debating what to say.

"Give it to me straight," she persisted. "Can we get out of here?" That darn computer kept repeating 'access denied.' Sure sounded like somebody had shut him out.

"There is a malfunction in the ship's main computer."

She snorted. "Somebody changed your access code. My money's on the Vulture. He's got it in for you."

"Vulture?" He was still trying to get the computer to open the door. Without success.

She wished he'd stop. Though the female voice of the computer was pleasant, Jessie was getting darn tired of hearing her say 'access denied.' "Yeah, your First Officer. Kleg-whatzit. He looked ready to spit nails when you said I could have the run of the ship. By locking us in here, he certainly fixed that."

"Spit nails? How quaint." He shook his head. "Mr. Klegznef would not program the computer to block my access or confine me to my quarters. That is tantamount to mutiny."

"If you say so." She shrugged. He certainly had some pre-set notions about the loyalty of his crew. "So what do we do now? Scream for help?"

"With its regular complement of over a hundred crewmembers, the rooms were soundproofed to ensure privacy. I am afraid screaming—" he gave her a distasteful look "—will not help."

Well, wasn't I put in my place? "So, there're a hundred people on board?"

"No, a research vessel carries only half as many as a

warship—as this once was."

He walked back to his desk, sat down and pulled out a drawer. He rifled several squares of black plastic, similar to computer disks yet larger. Maybe six inches square.

"You going to tell me when I can start panicking?"

He gave her his *look*. "There is no need for alarm."

"That's rich. We're locked in your quarters, you can't even raise Security—let alone the janitor to let us out—and you say there's no need for alarm. What would constitute need for alarm? Being attacked by aliens?" She snapped her fingers. "Oh, I forgot. That's already happened."

He glanced over his shoulder and raised his eyebrow before inserting a black square into the bottom of the video unit above the desk.

"God, I hate it when you do that." His look made her feel stupid. Growing up, she'd had enough of that from her dad as well as her teachers. She paced the sitting room, which was getting smaller by the minute.

"I beg your pardon?" He sounded distracted. Figuring out how to open the door, she hoped.

She sighed. "Never mind."

After watching the video monitor over his shoulder, she started examining his neck. Precision-cut hair. Must have been recent, as there was no new growth down his neck. Either that or his hairline had a perfect edge. His jaw was still as smooth as when she had first seen him.

"Did you just shave?"

He looked over his shoulder. "I beg your pardon?"

Heat burned her cheeks at the inappropriately personal question. She gave him a sheepish look. "Uh, never mind." She really needed to think before opening her big mouth.

He wasn't having success. Tension vibrated from his body as he tried one black square after another. Well, she wasn't standing around any longer waiting for him to rescue them. She scooped up her *link* before opening cupboards. She wasn't sure what she would find—an override switch, maybe?

Nothing.

She must've left the bedroom door open when she was

here before. Or, whoever locked them in Marcus's quarters made sure the interior doors were open. She went into the bedroom and opened a closet. Burgundy uniforms hung in precise order. "Hey, don't you have any casual clothes?"

She stooped and poked around under the clothing, feeling along the walls and tapping, hoping to find an opening.

"What are you doing?"

She came up under one of his uniforms and brushed the silky pantleg from her face. "Looking for the service hatch to the bathroom. There's gotta be a way to get at the plumbing."

He pulled her up. "Come." Despite their current situation, his clasp was warm, reassuring. Her hands, in contrast, felt like ice.

She followed him into the bathroom. He pressed a button near the top of a tall cabinet that spanned a short wall from floor to ceiling. Though it looked like a linen closet, the cabinet had no doors. Earlier, she couldn't figure out how to open it and hadn't spent the time exploring.

With a whirring noise, the cabinet swung out from the wall. Pipes, plastic-like tubing, and thick wires ran vertically between wall studs, branching out under the floor.

She stepped closer and looked down. "Hmm. A little snug, but it might work."

He came up behind her. His heat, his scent surrounded her. Butterflies in her stomach started doing the macarena. *Oh, my.*

She heard his sharp intake of breath.

"You are not thinking..." He stepped back. "You cannot consider..."

In the limited time she'd known him, Captain Viator was never at a loss for words. He had a weird look on his face.

"What?" she asked.

"Are you considering going down through that...that maintenance conduit?" His Adam's apple bobbed as he swallowed.

"Sure. We could shimmy down the pipes."

"That is impossible." He walked out of the room.

"Got a better idea?" She followed him back to his desk

where he began fiddling with the black disks. "Hey, Captain. What's the problem? I think the hole is big enough."

"No," he said calmly, as if they weren't in a real bind.

"But I think we could—"

"No," he snapped.

Surprised at his vehemence, she went back to the bathroom to look again. Maybe the hole wasn't big enough. He had pretty broad shoulders. She studied the opening. The maintenance conduit appeared to go down about three levels. At each level, the pipes branched off.

She had a good eye for measurement. They could do it. They could make it through, shimmying down one at a time.

She looked up. Some of the pipes and wires continued above the ceiling, making a ninety-degree angle. This must be the top level of the ship. Maybe they could go up and wiggle across the ceiling and then come down in the room next door.

Could they make the ninety? Looked awfully tight. She stood on the lid of the commode and hoisted herself up, then whacked her head on the ceiling.

"Damn." She pushed her shoulders forward, leveling out. The edge of the opening cut into her belly.

"What are you doing?"

Startled by Marcus's voice, she whacked her head on a support beam above. "Damn it."

She wiggled forward into the space above the ceiling. Suddenly, she couldn't go any farther. "Oh, sugar jets." Was she ever off on her guess-timate of the space.

She was stuck. She tried wiggling forward. Nope. Then she tried backward. Nope. Didn't that just frost her cookies. Her butt was stuck. All because she was on a first name basis with the purveyors of gourmet ice cream. Bet Cindy Crawford wouldn't have gotten stuck.

"Do you need assistance?"

Oh, God. There she was hanging out of a hole in the ceiling, and Captain Tight Buns was staring up at hers. "Nah. I think I'll stay up here for a while." *Yeah, like for the next hundred years.*

"That would not be wise. You do not look comfortable."

"I was being sarcastic. Don't you people use sarcasm?"

"I believe you are stuck."

"Now, there's a news flash. I think I'll just stay up here." *Until I lose those fifteen pounds off my butt.* She felt like Pooh stuck in Rabbit's Hole. Only it wasn't a friendly Piglet looking at her backside.

"Would that not be uncomfortable?"

He had no idea how uncomfortable she was. The ceiling digging into her stomach couldn't match her embarrassment.

"They forget to program a sense of humor in you, Captain? Why don't you just go back and straighten out the Computer Babe and let me figure out how to get out of here?"

She felt a small tug on her feet. *Great.* He was trying to pull her down. "You don't need to do that, Captain."

"Did I not ask you to call me Marcus?" He gave another tug, this time with more force.

Like a cork released from a champagne bottle, she shot out of the opening, first whacking her head again, then tumbling into his arms. He tried to catch her, but she fell on top of him, knocking him to the floor.

Of all the humiliating scenes she could have dreamed up, this one took the cake. Klutzy Jessie Wyndom had just flattened the sexiest man she'd ever met. And now she lay sprawled on top of him. Her breasts were flattened against his chest, and he was cradling her against him. From breasts to knees, she was molded to his body.

She closed her eyes. She wanted to die. First from humiliation. Then from sheer pleasure. Delicious sensations coursed through her body. Tiny flames of desire flickered through her veins, arrowing down to the feminine spot between her legs. How sweet it was. She could die now.

She felt every hard line of his body, the muscled planes of his chest, his firm, flat stomach, the ridges of his hips and— Oh, boy. He was aroused!

Her eyes flew open. He stared at her, his silver eyes glittering with desire. For her?

Couldn't be. Any female squashing him would probably have the same effect. She tried to get up. His arms tightened around her. He wanted her to stay? She couldn't. She couldn't face the disappointment in his eyes when he realized it was only klutzy Jessie Wyndom in his arms, not some babe like Cindy Crawford.

She scrambled to her feet and gave him a cocky smile. "Another fine mess you've gotten us into."

She glanced down at him still lying on his back on the floor of the bathroom. He had the stunned look of a guy run over by a truck. Yeah, a truck named Jessie.

Mortified at how intimately they'd been entwined, she offered him a hand up. He accepted her help. The clasp of his hand sent more tingles up her arm. She jerked away.

What is wrong with me? She never got this way around a guy. Maybe it was the Captain. He must be the kind of alien who can enchant a woman, making her lose her inhibitions.

Wait a minute. She couldn't lust after him. Right from the beginning he'd made her feel inferior. She'd never be attracted to a guy who looked at her like she was dog doo-doo. Damn it, nobody was going to do that to her.

She dusted the backside of her uniform. "Guess going through the ceiling wasn't such a hot idea. Looks like we'll have to try the floor."

He straightened his uniform, even though he didn't look mussed. Not like her. Her hair had fallen into her eyes. She raised her arms to reposition the scrunchie that still clung to a few clumps of hair like a burr on a dog.

He avoided her eyes, for which she was eternally grateful until she realized he was staring at her breasts. The pale blue uniform stretched smoothly, outlining in every detail the lace of her bra along with the points of her nipples. She fixed her hair quickly then dropped her arms.

He cleared his throat. "I do not believe descending into the conduit is a good idea. I will continue trying to access the computer." He turned to walk away.

She grabbed his arm and spun him around. "It'll work. The hole in the floor is bigger than the one in the ceiling. They probably didn't need to make that one very big because that's the end of the line. We won't get stuck going down."

He stared at her. She dropped her hand.

"Okay, okay. *I* won't get stuck again. I'm sure of it. You won't either if you turn your shoulders to get through. It's wider under the floor. We can make it."

He glanced at the hole in the floor. The creases next to his mouth whitened. "No."

"What is wrong with you? We have to get out of here. I need to get home, and I sure can't do it stuck in here."

Without answering, he returned to the sitting room.

"Okay," she called after him. "You play with the Computer Babe. I'll go roust the cavalry." She sat down on the floor and inched closer to the pipes.

Shimmying down the pipes? Was she crazy? *You can do this, Jess. You have to.* How else was she going to get out of here? How else would she get home?

What if she slid so fast she crashed at the bottom? Splattered like a pumpkin on the sidewalk. Her body a broken mess. A broken, *lifeless* mess.

No. She couldn't die. Not up here in space. Nobody back home would know. And where would that leave the Serenian twit who had switched places with her? Hah. It would serve that Veronese Qilana right for pulling this trick. She'd be stuck on Earth.

Jessie stared down into the conduit. What did they do with dead bodies up here? In the *Star Trek* movie where Spock died, they put him in a photon tube and shot him into space. Would they do that to her poor, battered body? Stuff her into a black casket? Would Scotty play 'Amazing Grace' on the bagpipes in memory of her? And then would they shoot her out and let her drift through space like garbage?

The hand dropping on her shoulder nearly sent her over the edge. She shrieked.

"You are going down there, are you not?"

She slowly released the death grip she'd had on the pipe. "Geez Louise, Captain, you nearly scared the sh—bejeebers out of me. Don't ever do that."

He stooped next to her, his eyes averting the hole. "I apologize. You were concentrating on the best way to descend, and I interrupted you."

That wasn't all he'd interrupted. She wasn't going to mention her death scene and subsequent space funeral.

"I, uh, I was looking for handholds and where to put my feet. Are you coming, or do I have to send a rescue team when I get down to the next floor?"

He blew out a long breath. "I will come with you. If you become stuck again, you will need assistance."

"Gee, thanks, guy. Another tromp on the old ego."

He cocked his head to peer at her. "Are all Terrans overly sensitive?"

She pursed her lips. "I can't speak for the rest of my species. But *you*, buster, have all the finesse of a bull elephant in rut." She squeezed her eyes shut. *Damn. Damn. Damn.* She would have to remind him of their earlier 'moment of togetherness.' "One of these days, I'm going to think before I shoot off my mouth."

She opened her eyes. A small smile curved his mouth. What a cute smile. For a moment, he looked like such a nice guy. Just a regular guy. Not an alien.

"I find your speech...entertaining."

"Yeah, that's me. A laugh a minute. Okay, here goes." Just as she swung over to a pipe, she caught sight of a vertical ladder. "Why the heck didn't they put the ladder in plain sight? This will be a piece of cake."

She lowered herself until she could grab a rung. "Come on, Captain. We can do this."

She scrambled down several rungs of the ladder before looking back up. He still sat on the edge, his long legs dangling over. He wasn't moving.

"Contemplating your death scene?" she asked.

When he leaned forward, she could see a muscle ticking along his jaw. *Is he clenching his teeth?*

"Hey, Captain, tell them to forget 'Amazing Grace' at my funeral. I want the 'Hallelujah Chorus'."

"Jessica, now is a good time to think before you speak. I would appreciate your silence." Slowly, he wrapped his hand around one of the pipes. "Where is the ladder?"

"Is it all right for me to tell you where it is, or would you rather I shut up?"

He looked down to give her, she was sure, that nasty 'Mr. Nutt' look when he closed his eyes and went stock-still.

What the heck is going on?

"Please, instruct me where to put my foot."

"Okay, you do want my help. Slide a little to your left. Now, look down and to the right. Captain, you really need to open your eyes to do this. The ladder is under the floor. Looks like somebody miscalculated where the hole in the floor should be. Maybe your planet awards the building of spaceship contracts to the lowest bidder, just like the good old U.S. of A. So much for superior cultures."

"Jessica, instruct me where to put my foot," he said with a touch of impatience.

"Okay, okay. Swing your leg over a little more to the right. Oops. Your other right." She grabbed his ankle to guide it to the rung of the ladder just above her head. His nerves vibrated beneath her fingers. Something wasn't right.

"Do not pull. I am capable of descending on my own."

"Sure. Whatever you say, big guy."

As she climbed down the rungs, she wondered what was going on with the Captain. Had she hurt him when she flopped on top of him in the bathroom? Maybe he injured his head when he hit the floor.

"You okay up there, Captain?"

"I have asked you to call me Marcus." He sounded like he was talking through clenched teeth.

Light from the bathroom shone only partway into the conduit. Worklights were located at each level. "Hold up a minute. I'm at the next level." She wrapped her arm around the rung to better secure herself. "I'll try to push the cabinet aside." The cabinet wouldn't budge. "Is there a magic button out here that'll move this sucker?"

"Try your *link*. I am certain the Engineering crew must use a *link* to access the room when necessary."

"That would be great." She let the sarcasm drip. "I could be taking a shower and in walks one of your janitors? Sure would spoil my day."

"I believe they would announce themselves first."

While she tried the *link*, he nearly stepped on her fingers. He was looking straight ahead at the wall and not down where he was putting his feet.

"Hold up, guy. My *link* doesn't work." She used the flat of her hand and slammed as hard as she could against the wooden cabinet. "Hey," she yelled. "Anybody home?"

He winced. "Please warn me the next time you plan to make so much noise. I will attempt to cover my ears."

"Good one, Marcus. You made a joke."

"I was not joking," he muttered.

"I heard that. What's under your room?"

"A storage facility. Are we continuing our descent?"

"A storage facility? Nobody would be in there. Why the heck didn't you say so in the first place?"

"I was under the impression that you had taken charge of our expedition."

"You're a real comedian, Captain."

She backed down the ladder, her arms aching from the need to hold onto the rungs. She tugged his pantleg. "You can come down a little faster. I'm not that slow."

"Do *not* touch me." His shout startled her.

"Geez, have a cow. Sorry."

"I apologize for raising my voice."

"Raising your voice? That's a euphemism if I ever heard one. Get the lead out, Captain, we're nearly to the bottom."

He mumbled something that sounded suspiciously like a prayer of thanksgiving.

"Uh, oh."

"What did that mean? 'Uh, oh.'" He sounded nervous. "Is there a problem?"

"Yeah. We can't get out. There's a door down here, but it's locked from the other side. Shoot. It's a full-size door, too. Nobody would get stuck."

"Maybe you need to push harder on the door."

"You want to come down here and try?"

"I do not believe there is room for both of us."

"We can switch places." She flattened against the wall, waiting for him to climb down. The moment she glanced up to see what was taking him so long, she wished she hadn't. She stared straight at his crotch. A mere two inches away.

FIVE

Marcus knew using the maintenance conduit to escape from his quarters was not a good idea.

He flattened himself as far away from Jessica as possible. Clinging to the vertical ladder with one hand and bracing himself against the wall with the other, he turned himself at a right angle to the ladder. She tried to do the same. Their bodies brushed in passing, bringing back the memory of their earlier encounter on the floor of the sanitary room.

As before, sensations raged through his body. Sensations caused by runaway hormones. So...Terran, he thought with disgust. Again, he tried to exert control over his body's reaction to Jessica. Again, the combination of Serenian discipline and his own strong will had little effect.

Her breathing quickened. As did his. She was level with him now. Her breasts pressed against his chest. Her heart thudded, or was it his? She stared at him, her lush mouth parted. The blue of her eyes was nearly obscured by the dilated pupils. In those brilliant eyes, he saw naked desire. The same look he thought he had seen earlier. When they had lain on the floor after she tumbled out of the ceiling in the sanitary room.

At first, he had put his arms around her to keep her from being injured as she fell. Then, he found that he liked the feel of her pressed against him. The lushness of her full breasts against his chest invoked disturbing images. Images of Jessica and him, together in the most elemental way.

With their bodies so close now on the ladder, hunger flashed through him. Its strength caught him by surprise. A hunger unfamiliar in its intensity. Hunger for this female from Earth.

Serenians experienced a mild pull toward each other, a pleasant feeling of attraction. Nothing like the force of this allurement—this magnetism—between him and the Terran woman now pressed against him.

Her pink tongue crept out to lick her lips. He wanted to capture her tongue, draw it into his own mouth, let her feel the hunger she induced by— He shook his head.

By doing nothing. By being in this deplorable situation, by scrambling around in the bowels of the ship. He was mistaken. She could not be as aroused as he. That was not desire he saw in her widened eyes. She was afraid. Her quick breathing, the thudding of her heart, the flush on her cheeks, her dilated eyes had to be the result of fear.

Fear induced by falling from the ceiling, climbing down this wretched ladder, being incarcerated on a starship with little hope of returning to her home planet. Fear of the alien she thought he was.

He released his grip and dropped to the floor. He ignored her gasp of surprise as, unintentionally, his hands trailed down her body from shoulder to breast, from hip to ankle. Of course, it had been unintentional. Holding his hands behind him would have brought him even closer to her. Raising them over his head had been the only solution.

Was lying to oneself a Terran trait? On Serenia, truth— especially to oneself—was paramount. Trailing his hands down her body had been...delightful.

She scrambled up several rungs of the ladder. "I-I'll get out of your way." She sounded breathless. Fear, he reminded himself. She was afraid of him.

While he tried to open the hatch at the bottom of the ladder, she climbed to the next level. He glanced up. With each movement, her uniform stretched and twisted across her hips.

Serenian females did not have generous hips. Yet, the roundness of hers enticed him. He wanted to touch, to run his palm over her curves. At the sudden warmth, he loosened the neck clasp of his uniform.

He shook off his wayward thoughts. Thoughts he never had about a Serenian female's trim hips. Fantasizing would not help Jessica and him escape from confinement.

He did not understand how his *link* and his computer could have been reprogrammed to deny him access to the main computer. Only executive officers had the authority to change the main computer: the Captain, the First Officer, Navigation and Science Officers as well as the Chiefs of Engineering and Security. Normally, the Communications Officer belonged to the executive staff. Just prior to leaving Serenia, the *Freedom's* Communications Officer had taken ill. A replacement was unavailable at such short notice. Cabbeferron, even though only a lieutenant, had to assume the responsibility. But without the incumbent authority.

First Officer Klegznef made no secret of his desire to command. He chafed at the strictures of the Alliance and the peace it ensured. But, Zorfans were warriors who prided themselves on their ability to do battle. His First Officer would not attempt to wrest control in such a devious manner. He dismissed Klegznef as a suspect.

Security Chief Hrvibm had served with Marcus for the past three tours. Claiming it was better to have a superior officer she knew than what she might get, she had even turned down a planet-side job to stay aboard the *Freedom*.

Chief Engineer Luqett had served with Marcus since the Great Intergalactic War. Despite his disregard for abstaining from excess food and volatile emotions, Luqett was loyal to the Alliance and a faithful friend, as was Science Officer Xaropa. Navigation Officer Glaxpher had been Marcus's friend since the Academy.

With no degree of false modesty, Marcus knew the reason his executive officers stayed aboard the *Freedom* was their loyalty to him. He valued their friendship, just as they valued his. He dismissed each of them as the perpetrator of his imprisonment. Yet, whom did that leave? Someone at Space Fleet Command? Remote access to a ship's computer was possible by authorized personnel. But, the *Freedom* was no ordinary ship and had special safeguards to prevent remote access, even by authorized personnel.

He gave one more thrust of his shoulder against the door.

To no avail. He found no manual override to release the locking mechanism. His bruised shoulder ached from slamming it against the door to break the latch. Brute force rarely worked. Yet, he had to try.

"Marcus, I think I've found a way."

Glancing up, he saw her feet disappear through a side opening. He had seen the narrow access tunnel on his descent. A descent he would have preferred to avoid.

"Come on. We can do this." Her muffled voice came from inside the tunnel.

He climbed the ladder. At least it was not down. Descending a vertical ladder was not one of his favorite exercises.

Not one of his favorites? To whom was he lying?

He reached the opening to the tunnel. Ahead, he saw her feet and then the sway of her all-too-enticing hips as she crawled ahead. The passage was just wide enough for his shoulders but not even a meter high. Emergency lights, spaced every ten meters, gave minimal illumination.

As he stretched to pull himself into the opening, he made the mistake of looking down. He froze.

The all-too-familiar tingling began in his fingertips and traveled up his arms. His stomach lurched. He broke out in a cold sweat. Blackness edged in from the corners of his eyes. Heights always unnerved him. He opened the top portion of the front placket of his uniform. The environmental controls must not be functioning in this area.

He cursed the weakness which had plagued him all his life. It made little sense how he could fly far above the surface of planets and not feel the disturbance in his equilibrium that always came from looking straight down.

He could don a jetpack to perform extra-vehicular activities in space and was never affected. Yet looking straight down, even one story, gave him the willies.

What an appropriate colloquialism. His Terran visitor made him think in her language. How odd.

"Are you coming?" she called over her shoulder.

Pride was an inappropriate emotion for a Serenian. But

pride spurred him into moving. Quickly, he averted his eyes from the view below and crawled into the passageway.

Jessica turned as far around as she could to look back at him. "Do you know where we are?"

"The conveyance shaft to Engineering should be at the end of this tunnel."

"Good." She began crawling. "That's where I wanted to go in the first place. We can climb down the shaft and pull open the doors at the bottom."

"There is one problem." He waited until she looked back. "A security force field surrounds Engineering."

"Oh, boy. How do we turn it off?"

"*We* do not. I could if my *link* was operational. Only authorized personnel can use the conveyance. Their *links* disengage the field before the conveyance doors open at either end—the central part of the ship or the main floor of Engineering."

"Looks like we're going to have to play this one by ear, Captain." She started crawling again.

The passageway was so narrow his shoulders often scraped against the side walls, and frequently he bumped his head when he looked up to see how far ahead she was. Each time he looked, he felt a kick low in his belly at the sight of her wiggling hips.

"Why did you wish to go to Engineering?" he asked. "To see the ship's engine?"

"Sure, I'd like to see how the engine works, but first I want to tell your Chief there's a problem with it."

He stopped. "How do you know that?"

"There is a problem, isn't there?" She kept crawling.

"Yes, but you could not know that. Who told you?"

"Nobody had to *tell* me," she said with exasperation. "I can *hear* that something is wrong." She stopped and cocked her head. "Wait. Did you hear that?"

He listened, hearing nothing more than the normal sound of the ship's main engine—the steady hum everyone on board grew accustomed to within a short while.

"What am I supposed to hear?"

"There's a miss, a hesitation in the sound. Not often. Just every once in a while. Listen again."

He waited. "I hear nothing out of the ordinary."

"Never mind then. I need to talk to your Chief. He'll believe me." She started forward again.

Her wiggling rear was doing unusual things to his libido. Irritated with his reaction, he employed a Serenian meditation technique to exert control over his body. The mental imaging had little effect. How did Terrans tolerate bodies that refused to respond to their mind?

He took a deep, cleansing breath. "I did not say I disbelieve you. I merely indicated that I do not hear whatever it is you hear. Or do not hear."

She stopped and waited for him to catch up. Difficult as it was given the confined area, she turned enough to look back at him. "Right."

He was affronted by her tone. "I do not lie."

She resumed crawling. "Whatever."

He stiffened. His word was never challenged. Jessica Marie Wyndom evoked too many reactions from him. When had any person perturbed him the way she did? A lifetime of rigid self-discipline in order to prove he was a true Serenian disappeared around this Terran female.

When he had first found her in the transport room, she unsettled him. Her insouciance, her emotional outbursts, her lack of restraint were so...Terran. A reminder of what he could have become if not for his Serenian upbringing.

As they crawled past the vertical shafts, he kept his eyes averted from the bottom of the ship below. At every shaft, they tried the hatches on each level. They pounded and shouted, as distasteful as that was. Was privacy worth soundproofing if one could be trapped, helpless? Then, they resumed their crawl toward the conveyance shaft.

"I think we're at the end." She leaned over the opening.

His stomach lurched as he watched her perilous position. Fear froze him in place. If she started to fall, he would never be able to save her.

"I can see the top of the elevator about four levels down.

It looks like it's at the bottom of the shaft." She paused. "Wait a minute. We're a level below your quarters. That would make the elevator lower than where we were before."

He swallowed the fear clawing at his throat. He could not reveal this weakness to her. *Think about her question.* She wants to know what the ship looks like. He cleared his throat. "You have a good sense of perspective. Imagine, if you will, the ship looking like a saucer with a swooping tail assembly. The area you toured earlier was in the saucer: the bridge, transport room, crew's quarters, laboratories. Engineering with the propulsion units, fuel source, and environmental controls are all in the tail section. This conveyance shaft goes between the two areas."

"Thanks, I think I've got the picture." She leaned over farther.

His terror returned. "Jessica, stay back," he shouted.

"I'm hanging on. Don't worry."

He forced his stomach to calm. He willed the panic to abate.

"It looks like there's a hatch in the top of the elevator," she called out. "What if we climb down, open the hatch, and jump into the elevator—er, conveyance? Then, we could come out into Engineering. Think that'll work?"

Climb down the shaft to the top of the conveyance. Four levels. He closed his eyes and drew on an inner strength that had previously eluded him. He *would* be able to climb down. He *had* to climb down.

"How often do they use this elevator, Captain?"

He looked up and banged his head. He rubbed the spot that had taken quite a bruising during their excursion through the narrow tunnel. "Marcus," he corrected. "I do not know. Engineering is self-contained. The crew's quarters are there. Some come up to the dining area for meals and to socialize."

"Meals? Didn't you say that dinner was soon? When?"

He squinted in the dim light to read the time on his *link*. "I apologize. You will miss another meal."

"Forget that. I could stand missing a few meals." She patted her rear. He stared, wanting to do the same. She seemed oblivious to his discomfort. "We'd better hurry. If the crew goes up to dinner, we'll probably get squashed between the top of the elevator and the top of this shaft."

"A pleasant thought."

"Why, Cap— Marcus. Was that sarcasm?" She smirked. "Okay, let's get it in gear." She inched forward. "The good news is there's a ladder."

He groaned. Another ladder. He had known all along he would have to do this. She rolled onto her back and reached to her right for a rung of the vertical ladder. She pulled her body through. His heart stopped as her foot slipped, and she dangled by one arm. Chills raced through him.

"Oops."

Her athleticism, given the softness of her body, surprised him. She grasped the rung of the ladder with both hands then found purchase for her foot.

He groaned again. He could not do this. Bile rose in his throat. He scooted back.

"Hey. Are you all right?" She looked at him, cringing near the opening.

This weakness humiliated him.

She nimbly clambered down a level and looked up. "Come on, Captain, get the lead out. Those guys are going to use that elevator any minute now."

He would not look down.

"Do what I did. Lie on your back. Slide your shoulders out farther. Now, look this way. You can reach the rung. Pull yourself out using that." She guided him until he reached the rung. "Now, swing out."

Swing out? His stomach clutched in terror remembering how she had dangled four levels above the top of the conveyance. Ice filled every vein. He could not do this.

Pride was not such a bad emotion. If a Terran female could do this... He pulled himself out of the tunnel.

"Marcus, damn it, hurry up. Look down so you'll know where to put your feet."

Not even her urgent call would induce him to look down. Once he worked his lower body out of the passageway, he would feel for the rung with his foot. With thanks for the strength in his arms due to the upper body workout he performed every other day, he pulled himself entirely out of the passageway. She must have superb upper body strength, also. Amazing. He had not thought that possible, given the soft condition of her body. He had underestimated her.

He hung in space, his feet scrambling to find the rung. "For God's sake, Marcus, look what you're doing. Lift your foot. Up five inches. There."

He closed his eyes. Relief swept through him as his foot found the rung and gave respite to his arms.

"Quit dawdling. Get down here." Her voice became more urgent. "If that elevator starts up, we'll be dead meat."

He clung to the ladder, icy dread snaking down his spine. His fingers prickled, numbness threatened to loose their grip. Childhood nightmares of falling, falling forever swamped him. *Dead meat.* An appropriate analogy.

"Marcus, c'mon."

Her command snapped him out of his panic. He willed his lungs to breathe again. He started down the ladder.

"Okay, let's hustle." Her voice came from far below. She must be almost to the top of the conveyance.

His knees started to shake. On the third step, his foot slipped off the rung. He dangled in space once again. His right hand gripped the rung with all his strength.

His foot found the rung and he stayed where he was. His heart dropped out of his throat and tried to find its normal position in his chest. The thudding in his ears grew louder as his heart notified him of its terror.

"Marcus, somebody just got in the elevator. Move your ass, damn it."

The conveyance bounced slightly. Someone, indeed, had gotten in. He moved. She dropped onto the top of the conveyance and was trying to pry up the access hatch.

He dropped to his knees next to her.

She shot him a glance. "About time you got here."

The motor on the conveyance started up.

He wedged his fingers under the hatch, and together they

pulled. The conveyance began to move.

"Help! In the conveyance," she yelled. "Open up." The top of the shaft came closer. "Marcus, hurry."

The hatch was secured from inside. "Stop the conveyance," he shouted while pounding on the hatch. They were nearly to the top. "Open the hatch."

The conveyance continued moving, but he felt the hatch loosen. Together, they ripped it off.

"What in the seven moons of Tarsus!" The voice came from inside the conveyance. It was Luqett.

"Look out below," Jessica called as the conveyance stopped with a sudden jerk, toppling him then Jessica through the access hatch. She clutched his shoulders as she fell.

Before they landed on the floor of the conveyance, he twisted his body to cushion her fall. Once again, she lay draped across him.

"What is the meaning of this?" Luqett shouted.

Her hair had come loose from its fabric elastic to tumble into his face. Marcus looked up through the reddish haze into his Chief Engineer's astonished face. The flowery scent of her hair reminded him of a meadow in the foothills near his uncle's farm. Yes, the meadow after a cleansing rain.

For several seconds, no one moved. Her body continued to sprawl the length of his. Her hand rested on his bare chest where his uniform had spread open when she clutched him as they fell. He did not want to experience the sensations she caused. Yet, he did not push her off. What did this conflict say about him?

She scrambled to her feet. "Hi, guys," she said brightly. "Thought we'd drop in and see what you all are doing."

Marcus stood up and rearranged his uniform. He glanced at the occupants of the conveyance. They appeared so dumbfounded by their commander and the Terran woman sprawled on the floor that they had backed into the corners.

"Sir, you do not appear ill." Luqett edged into his corner.

"No, I am not. Why would you think so?"

"We were told you had become infected by the Terran." Luqett shot Jessica a glance. "You instructed everyone to keep away from your quarters."

Marcus raised an eyebrow. "As you can see, I am in perfect health." He looked at the other crewmembers. They were not dumbfounded by the sight of him and Jessica, they were terrified. Terrified of Jessica.

"The Terran is not contagious," he spoke to the two cowering as far away as possible. "Chief, a moment alone in your office?"

Once the conveyance returned to Engineering, Luqett led the way to his office. Marcus beckoned to Jessica. "Come." When she did not immediately respond, he said, "Now, please. Get the lead out."

Jessie jumped. His cocky grin galvanized her. He thought he was so cute throwing her words back in her face. She had been terrified when he hadn't moved on the ladder. What had happened to him out there in the shaft?

And what was wrong with these people? They all looked at her as if she had the plague. She scurried after Marcus and into Chief Luqett's office.

Marcus closed the door and indicated she should sit. He was all prim and proper again, not looking the least bit disheveled while she was rumpled and dirt-smudged. You'd never know *he'd* been crawling around in tunnels. Worse, he'd fastened the front of his uniform. Too bad. When they were lying on the floor of the elevator, her hand had rested on his bare chest. Well-muscled and, she'd guessed right, no chest hair. If she thought his buns were great, his pecs were better.

Luqett edged away, eyeing her with apprehension.

"Hey, I don't have cooties."

"Chief, an unusual situation has occurred. I—"

"I'll say it's unusual." She jumped up. "We were locked in his quarters and couldn't get out."

Marcus shot her a glance that said 'shut up.' Not that *he* would say such a commonplace thing. So proper. So formal. She'd shaken him up, though, during their escape. That gave her the right to be a bit cocky, too.

"Please, do not interrupt," he said.

Oh, boy. Marcus looked ready to spit nails. She sat down

again. He turned to Luqett. "What were you told?"

"That you had become infected by the Terran. A mysterious ailment. You ordered your quarters sealed and no one was to contact you."

"Who made the announcement?"

"Mr. Klegznef, sir."

"See. I told you." She couldn't resist, even though her outburst put her on the receiving end of Marcus's sharp glance.

"I will speak to Mr. Klegznef. Call Chief Hrvibm. We need to discover who entered the command to seal my quarters and disengage my *link*."

"Your *link* was disengaged?" Luqett looked horrified. "But, sir, you are the only one who can disengage it."

"Nevertheless, my *link* as well as my spare, which I gave to Jessica, were disengaged. I believe Jessica would like to talk to you about our engine problem."

Luqett gave her a wary glance.

"Do not worry, Chief. She cannot infect you with some mysterious illness. You know as well as I do that our transporter decontaminates everyone who comes aboard."

"Maybe, maybe not. Perhaps our decontamination charge is not strong enough."

Marcus laid his hand on Luqett's shoulder. "Fear not, old friend. I have been in close contact with her and have had no ill effects."

Heat flared in her face at his mention of their 'close contact.' Damn her fair complexion. It revealed too much.

"Jessica, explain your concern about the engine while I go up and talk to Mr. Klegznef."

"Marcus, be careful. If he's the one responsible—"

He held up his hand. "Be careful what you say. To accuse Mr. Klegznef of—"

"Captain," Luqett exploded. "That would be mutiny."

"Precisely. It is imperative we proceed cautiously."

"Do not go alone, sir. I will call Security to accompany you."

"No, Chief. I do not want to precipitate an event. This could very well be a misunderstanding."

As he passed her, she jumped up and grabbed his arm. "Marcus, you can't go alone. Please, take someone with you. I don't want anything to happen to you."

When Luqett cleared his throat, she realized the inappropriateness of her actions. And the way she had addressed Marcus...Perhaps he had never meant her to call him by his first name in public. Surely, she was not showing him respect in front of his crew.

She released her grip on his arm and stepped back. "I apologize, sir. I am worried about your welfare." Good grief, she was starting to sound like him.

"The lassie is right, Captain. Ye canna go runnin' off without protection." Luqett's voice had changed.

"Wow. You sound just like Scotty on *Star Trek*. Cool."

While Luqett looked pleased with himself, Marcus stared up at the ceiling.

"Are you praying for guidance?" she asked. "Divine intervention? Patience? All of the above?" At Marcus's sharp look, she grimaced. "Sorry. Look, Captain, why don't you stay here where you're safe?"

"Good idea, lassie," Luqett said. "Captain, call Mr. Klegznef. Use my office while the lassie and I have a little chat about my engine."

She snapped her fingers. "Better yet, Chief, why don't *you* call the Vulture down here. We don't want to tip him off that Marcus—I mean, the Captain—has escaped."

"Vulture? Ah, you mean our First Officer." Luqett grinned. "I'm beginnin' to like ye already, lassie." He tapped his *link*. "Mr. Klegznef to Engineering. Regulation two-seven." He disengaged the *link*. "That'll bring him runnin', I think." Luqett looked very pleased with himself.

"Was that some kind of emergency code?" she asked.

"Chief Luqett informed Mr. Klegznef that an incident has occurred requiring utmost secrecy and urgency. Very well." Marcus sat in Luqett's chair. "I will meet him here. You will see there is no cause for alarm."

Luqett nodded with approval before turning to Jessie. "Now, what do ye know about starship engines?"

She gulped. "Not much. But, I can hear something. A miss. Or hesitation. Something doesn't sound right. Not right now. It comes and goes." She cocked her head and held up her hand for silence. "There. Did you hear that?"

Luqett shook his head. "Come. Let's look at the instruments." He opened the door for her to precede him. Then he looked over his shoulder and nodded. "Captain."

Marcus nodded in return. "Chief, there is no cause for concern. You will see."

Out in the main room, Luqett raised his voice to the crew seated or standing at various stations around the room. "Did the instruments pick up a disturbance just now?"

Their responses included several 'No, sirs' and shaking of heads. They still regarded Jessie with suspicion.

Luqett asked her to signal when she heard it again. She waited. The sound of the engine was much louder here. At first, it sounded smooth, just the way it had when she first arrived on board. She closed her eyes. There it was. She opened her eyes and signaled at the same time.

Again, Luqett had his technicians check their instruments. Nothing out of the ordinary had appeared on their screens.

"I'm a firm believer in trusting our instincts." The Chief placed his hand on her shoulder. His touch conveyed reassurance, strength, and acceptance. As the crew glanced from their Chief to her, their faces changed from suspicion to wariness. "I understand ye and I are in the same business, lassie. We repair what others break."

She grinned. "I just fix small things."

"It's always the small things that gum up the works of big things. Yer hearing must be very good. The young ones here—" he swept his hand around the room "—rely too much on instruments. They have let their ears grow lax. Mine?" He tapped his left ear. "I used to hear perfectly. I was s'posed to be fitted with a cochlear enhancer a while back, but I just couldna take the time." He gave her a sheepish grin. "Follow me, and we'll find what yer hearin'."

SIX

"Ah, there, lassie, did that do the trick?"

Marcus looked past Luqett, who was standing outside an open hatch. Jessica was squeezed into a narrow tunnel amidst pipes and the tangle of wires.

"For now," she called out. "I jerry-rigged it, but I don't know how long that will last. Sure wish you had a spare snap ring."

Marcus had just completed the confrontation with his First Officer. Klegznef denied all knowledge of Marcus's inability to access the main computer. In fact, he appeared surprised to see Marcus so healthy.

The computer replayed the message Klegznef had received. In disbelief, Marcus viewed himself turning the ship over to Klegznef and ordering his quarters quarantined. When Security Chief Hrvibm arrived, Marcus instructed her to discover who had over ridden his access to allow the input.

Now, he had more questions. He found Luqett on a narrow platform on the third level of Engineering. His admiration for the Engineering crew rose. Never had he appreciated the agility needed to access the controls. To navigate the tunnels and shafts, the crew needed to be part melarang. Why had the designers not planned better access to the ship's controls?

His reason for climbing up to this level was concern for Jessica. From the whispers he overheard, the crew was more than just wary of her. They feared she would, indeed, infect them with a fatal ailment from Earth.

She was his responsibility as commander of the ship. While he trusted Luqett with his *own* life, Marcus needed assurance she was not in danger. Consequently, he swallowed his fear of heights and now stood on a platform barely a meter wide with an open-weave floor and a single rail for safety. With his hands behind his back, he clutched the rail and looked straight ahead. His heart thudded and his palms slicked in anticipation of climbing back down.

"That did it, Chief." On her hands and knees, Jessica backed out of the crawlway.

He felt a gut-wrenching twist and an instant fullness in his groin at the sight of her well-rounded rear. That same enticing sight had tormented him during their escape.

By the Intrepid Ones, how could he be attracted to her? So opposite from the Serenian female. Jessica's boisterous enthusiasm, her outbursts—though often entertaining—were what he had to tamp down in himself. Such displays of emotion were not appropriate for a Serenian.

A Serenian remained calm, in harmony with himself and others. Submerging emotions that threatened his inner peace had always been Marcus's greatest trial.

In less than one Earth day, his carefully controlled equilibrium had been turned upside down by Jessica Marie Wyndom.

"Take care, lassie. Let me help ye." Luqett put his hands on her waist and lifted her out.

Marcus nearly yelled at the Chief to remove his hands. Yelled? Marcus was stunned. He never raised his voice, let alone *yelled*.

"Thanks." Still in Luqett's arms, she twisted around and looked past his shoulder. "Hi, Cap, how's it going?"

Luqett released her and spun around. "Captain, I dinna know ye were there."

Marcus stifled the surge of anger at having seen Luqett's arms around Jessica. "What did you find?"

"The lassie just fixed the acceleration enhancer. A fine mechanic she be."

"No big deal." She stepped aside. "It was a missing snap ring. I'm amazed your technology is so similar to ours—Earth's."

"Physics laws are physics laws." Luqett grinned.

"Please explain," Marcus said quietly, suppressing his irritation at her ease in Luqett's company.

"The solenoid operates the valve that restricts the flow of fuel. So without the snap ring to hold it in place, the solenoid moved back and forth. The movement of the solenoid caused intermittent operation of the valve. That's why the sound I heard wasn't regular. Such a small thing."

"Large problems often stem from small things," Marcus observed.

She brushed her knees and took a swipe at her seat. He swallowed at her attention to her rear.

"A real miracle worker she is, Captain. Instruments canna compete with a good mechanic's ear."

Marcus struggled to pay attention to Luqett's words when his mind was occupied with Jessica's body. "I thought Miracle Worker was your title, Chief."

Red crept up the side of Luqett's neck. "I try, Captain. I try." He slung his arm across her shoulder. "Y'know, sir, with Lieutenant Qilana gone, I am short-handed. May I keep this lassie?"

Marcus could not believe the rush of jealousy streaking through him. *Jealous? Him? Never.*

Oblivious to Marcus's distress, Luqett continued, "A fine crew member she'll be, Captain. She has a gift."

Marcus marshaled his thoughts. "Gift?"

"Aye. She's worth ten of those fancy instruments. Would that my hearing was as acute as hers."

She beamed at the high praise. "It wasn't much."

"Aye, but ye heard it, lassie. The rest of us dinna, and the blasted analyzer dinna catch it, either."

Luqett was certainly taken with her. Marcus fought his irritation. "Chief, weren't you scheduled for a cochlear enhancer?"

"Aye, Captain, but there was too much—"

"There is always too much to do. When we arrive home, see that the procedure is done. No procrastinating, Chief."

"Aye, sir." Luqett gave him a mock salute.

Marcus ignored the cocky gesture. "What did she repair?"

"The acceleration valve," Luqett answered. "It controls fuel to both the main engine and the hyperdrive."

"We have hyperdrive capacity now? We can return to Earth's orbit and transport our guest back to her home." The sooner she returned home the better. She disturbed him more than he wanted to admit. She made him experience emotions. Ridiculous Terran emotions.

For a moment, he thought he saw a flicker of regret cross her face. That could not be. She must be anxious to return to her home.

"No, Captain. 'Tis but a temporary fix. The lassie is good, but both engines need a complete overhaul. That blasted analyzer needs a thorough exam. It should have detected the problem. We are proceeding to Serenia with as much power as possible. I'd appreciate it if the lassie could stay here."

Now, she looked relieved. How could that be? She had made no pretense about her desire to return to her home.

"Ms. Wyndom is free to do whatever she wishes. As you can see, she has no illness with which to infect the crew." He looked at her. *Was that a question in her eyes?* "Do you wish to stay with Chief Luqett?"

"Really? Can I stay here?" Her eyes lit up.

"Ms. Wyndom might appreciate a proper uniform," Marcus said. "One befitting a member of the Engineering crew instead of a researcher. And her own quarters."

"Aye, sir. We'll kit her out. That is, if ye want to be working here with me, lassie."

She looped her arm around Luqett's and squeezed. "Of course, I want to stay. I'd love it."

Looking at how she laughed up at Luqett, Marcus swallowed his annoyance at their closeness. Gone was the fear he had seen in the conduit when *they* had been physically close. He should be relieved.

He was pleased, he told himself, that she was at ease with Luqett. She was in Luqett's capable hands and no longer Marcus's responsibility.

He swiveled around to return to the stairs, dreading that once again he would have to descend a vertical ladder.

"Captain?" She halted him with her hand on his arm. The touch of each finger burned through his uniform. "Are you sure it's all right for me to work in Engineering? I understand your need for security."

"It would not be in your best interest, Ms. Wyndom, to sabotage this vessel. You would then be unable to return to your home." He removed her hand from his arm.

Her eyes—so expressive—reflected hurt. *Why would she be hurt? What had he said?* "You have proven yourself to be trustworthy."

She brightened at his words. She had pride. Obviously, trust was more important to her than practicality. He would remember that in his dealings with her. A troubled look continued in her eyes. Later, in private, he would ask what worried her.

Now, he needed to descend the vertical ladder without her observing his hesitation. Before stepping across the opening, he glanced down for the handrail. He knew better. The queasiness started in his stomach and spread outward. He clasped the railing and waited until the vertigo subsided.

"Are you all right?" Concern edged her voice.

Why did she have to notice? She had not paid this much attention earlier. He should have told them to go on ahead.

"I forgot, Marcus." Luqett cleared his throat. "Let me go first."

Marcus forced a little laugh. Luqett was one of a very few who knew he hated heights. "That is quite all right, Chief. I am fine." Not wanting Jessica to speculate on his reluctance, he backed down the ladder. Once again, he thanked the Intrepid Ones for his pride. Such a human emotion, but one more powerful than his fear of heights.

Once he started down, Jessie stepped gingerly across the opening to the first step. She knew many people had a hard time with this type of vertical stairs in an open manhole. Was acrophobia the cause of his dithering when they'd been trying to escape from his quarters? No wonder he had frozen in the elevator shaft. He was terrified of heights.

She gulped. Guilt reared its ugly head as she realized she'd yelled at him. But, there'd been no choice. His dawdling could've killed them.

She scrambled down the steps. He must be horribly embarrassed by his debility. Before going down just now, his hands had been shaking when he clasped the railing. In the dim emergency lights of the passageways they'd traveled earlier, she hadn't seen his fear. He was probably cursing the bright light here that made his terror visible.

That small weakness made him more likeable—more human. Not quite so superior. She glanced over her shoulder. He was standing at the bottom of the vertical ladder, staring at her rear. Had he been staring like that all the time she was crawling in front of him?

Well, he could just get his eyes off her butt. He'd made it perfectly clear he wasn't interested in her as a woman. Those moments lying on top of him had been horrible, and wonderful. She'd wanted him to kiss her. To hold her tight. To make love to her.

She had to get home. She had to get away from this alien before she begged him to have his wicked way with her.

What was it about the Captain that made her lie to herself? Why did he intrigue her? After the condescending way he talked to her, she should be running in the opposite direction. Hadn't she had enough of that from her dad?

She willed her stomach to stop jitterbugging. All he had to do was come near her and her skin began to tingle.

He seemed so human and yet— If she had to be abducted by aliens, it sure was a little easier when the alien looked as human and as handsome as Marcus Viator. Not that some of the others on board weren't as good looking as he was. A couple of the younger ones who'd danced with her in the lounge could give *GQ* models a run for their money. They had the same distinctive silver eyes and smooth cheeks as their Captain. But none of them sent shivers down her spine or quickened her breath like he did.

He stooped to exit the shaft out to the main floor of Engineering. Before he turned away, she caught a glimpse of the whiteness around his lips. He hadn't gotten over his fear.

Her heart softened as she recognized the facade he'd put on. He didn't want anyone to know how badly affected he was by heights. She had to admire his determination.

Once the Chief replaced the hatch cover, Marcus said, "Ms. Wyndom has not eaten a proper meal since she came aboard. Please see to it, Chief."

"Aye, sir. I forgot myself." He patted his ample belly. "Of course, it wouldna hurt me to miss a few meals."

"Hey, you look pretty good, Chief." She playfully patted his belly.

Marcus turned and walked toward the conveyance. She needed to go after him, to tell him acrophobia was nothing to be ashamed of. That she didn't think any less of him because of his fear.

"I'll be right back, Chief. I need to—to ask the Captain something."

Luqett waved her on. "Go ahead, lassie. I have a few things to do myself. We'll have a fine meal together when ye come back."

She hurried after Marcus. For some crazy reason, she needed to reassure him she didn't hold his weakness against him. On the contrary, it made him more human.

If she told him that, would he be offended? It didn't matter. He'd shrugged off her efforts to talk to him. Now, she had to practically run to keep up with him. However, she was determined, and when Jessica Marie Wyndom set her mind to something, look out.

She narrowly escaped the closing doors. Along with Marcus, two crewmembers occupied the eleva—conveyance. If she was going to work here, she'd better start referring to things on board the ship by their proper terms.

His stony expression silenced her. He'd be humiliated if she spoke of his fear in front of the crew. The other two occupants practically hugged the back corner.

"I am *not* contagious."

They still eyed her nervously.

"Crewmen, I will assume you did not hear my latest announcement." Marcus stared at them. "Reports that the

Terran can infect the members of this crew are incorrect. You will accord her every courtesy."

She smiled her gratitude for his defense. Then, the doors opened. He didn't wait for a response from the embarrassed crewmen. He strode down the hall. She waited for the others to leave before taking off after him.

She recognized this area. The main corridor. Was he heading for his quarters? With all her traipsing around, she had pretty much figured out the layout of the ship.

Ship. A spaceship. Hard to believe she was hurtling among the stars. She always figured it would be her brother who would go up into space. Tim was the scientist, the adventurer, the dreamer. She was the down-to-earth, practical one.

Tim's obsession with space and science had led him through double undergraduate degrees in aeronautical engineering and physics by the time he was sixteen. In the eight years since, he'd gotten his Ph.D., had a successful consultant business, and taught physics at the University of Michigan. Meanwhile, Jessie had barely squeaked through two years of community college with an associate's degree in electrical technology.

As a child, she'd loved to take things apart and then put them back together, often better than new. Her folks had never understood her fascination with machinery. As learned academics barely capable of changing light bulbs, they hired someone to do that sort of thing. Which was exactly where she had gotten the idea for her business.

Gram had encouraged Jessie to go into business for herself and made it possible by giving her the farm. Gram knew how much the farm meant to Jessie. Gram also knew if she left it to her son, Jessie's dad would sell the homestead which had been in the family for over a hundred years.

Her parents expected Jessie to follow them into academia. But she just didn't have the aptitude. *They* thought she didn't try hard enough. Her teachers agreed. 'If only Jessie would apply herself.' 'If she just studied harder.' She did study. She did apply herself. It made no difference. Little wonder she hated school with a passion.

She just wasn't cut out to be a scholar.

For Tim, on the other hand, school came so easy. If his eyesight had been better, he could have gotten into flight school and from there to NASA. So he made do with playing fantasy adventure games with his nerdy buddies.

And here she was. Jessie Wyndom, repairperson, *magna cum stupido*. Space Traveler.

Coming around a curve in the hall, she caught sight of Marcus entering his quarters. By the time she got to his door, it was gone. She checked the keypad of her *link*. Had it been turned back on? Was that the symbol for 'doorbell'? She tapped the button, and the door whooshed open. She hesitated in the opening.

"Enter." Marcus's disembodied voice startled her, but she obeyed his command. The door closed behind her.

She looked around the empty sitting room.

"You have followed me this far, Ms. Wyndom. What is it you want?"

Despite the iciness of his voice, she came closer. She paused at the entrance to his sleeping area. Glancing at his bed, she realized she should have straightened the covers after her nap. The unmade bed, rumpled from her restless sleep, made the room more intimate. Funny how she hadn't thought of that when they were locked in here before. Then, she'd been too busy trying to figure how to get out.

With his hands clasped behind his back, Marcus stood in front of the clear bubble, staring into space. "You are persistent, Ms. Wyndom." He didn't turn around.

She placed her hands on her hips. "Who put a bee up your butt?"

Finally, he faced her. "Your expression is unclear."

"Hey, c'mon, Marcus. What's the matter with you? You sure didn't act all stuck up and snotty while we were crawling around under the floors. Are you mad at me?"

He rubbed the bridge of his nose. "I have no reason to be angry with you. You rescued us."

She raised her eyebrow. She could take lessons from this guy in haughtiness. "Is that your problem? Me, a girl, rescuing

Macho-Man?"

"I am happy you discovered a way out."

"Gee, Cap, try to control your excitement."

He didn't react to her sarcasm. "It is good that you are adventurous, full of courage," he said thoughtfully.

"You think I'm adventurous? Courageous?"

"Yes. Why does that surprise you?"

She stared at the floor. If she had been a kid, she'd be digging her toe in the dirt. "Nobody's ever said that to me before." She looked up. "Well, if you're not mad at me, why do you keep referring to me as 'Ms. Wyndom'? You called me 'Jessica' before."

Surprise flashed in his eyes. "It would not be proper to address you in so familiar a manner in front of the crew. You do not have a rank. 'Ms.' is a respectful title in your culture, is it not?"

She took a deep breath and blew it out. "Well, that's a relief. I'll get the hang of things around here. But that wasn't why I followed you. I want to apologize for yelling at you in the elevator shaft when you didn't hurry and we were going to get squashed. Anyway, I wanted to say I was sorry. Are you okay? I was worried about you."

"There is no need."

"Hey, I've seen bigger men than you paralyzed by a fear of heights. There's no need to feel ashamed."

"Your concern is misplaced." The chill in his voice made it clear that he didn't want to talk. He turned his back on her.

She walked up behind him. "Why did you climb up that shaft just now if heights bother you so much? You couldn't help it before because we had to get out of here. But this time, you could have just waited until the Chief and I came down."

There was a long pause before he responded. "I was concerned about you."

"Me?" She gulped.

"The crew is still fearful, as you saw in the conveyance. I needed to be certain you were in no danger."

That flustered her even more. "You could've sent someone. You didn't have to come yourself."

"I am the Captain. You are my responsibility."

She wrinkled her nose. *A responsibility.* Ugh. "You make me sound like an unpleasant task."

He shrugged his broad shoulder. "Not unpleasant."

"Not unpleasant, hey? Glad to hear that." She playfully touched his arm. "You gonna stare out into space or look at me while we're talking?"

The muscles of his forearm clenched under her hand. When he turned around, his silver eyes made her forget playfulness. She forgot concern for his weakness. Forgot everything but the way his eyes pierced her soul. What did he see? Her insecurities, her fears, her desire for him? Her heart thumped so loudly she was certain he heard it. Heat flowed through her body.

For one brief moment, she wondered if he was hypnotizing her. Then he reached for her. His arms encircled her waist, drawing her close. Her mouth parted. In surprise? Anticipation? She licked her lips and saw his gaze drop to them. He bent his head and kissed her.

Dear God. At first soft and questing, his lips turned hard and demanding with passion. She clutched his shoulders and held on while he devastated her senses. *Oh, wow, what a kisser.*

He withdrew, looking as shaken as she felt. He ran his fingers through his perfectly neat, always in-place hair. The disheveled look made him even more appealing.

"I should not have— I should never— I apologize."

Her heart sank. He regretted kissing her. She must not have done something right. Her kisser was rusty with disuse. He must be disappointed she was so inept. As she often did, she buried her embarrassment.

"Hold it right there. First, you tell me I'm no Cindy Crawford." She placed her hands on her hips and gave him a droll look. "Now, you're telling me it was a mistake to kiss me? You gotta work on your technique, Captain. I don't know about girls on your planet, but on mine that was an insult."

Instantly, those silver eyes clouded. "I did not intend—"

She gave him a light punch on his upper arm. "Hey, lighten up, big guy. I know I'm no Siren whose devastating charms lure men against their will." She waggled her eyebrows before bolting out of his bedroom. She had to get out of here. His kiss made her too vulnerable. His apologies made the situation even worse.

Marcus caught her arm before she reached door to the outside hall. Never had he experienced such intensity as when he kissed her. Now, he had unwittingly insulted her. Despite her bright smile, her joviality seemed false.

"I did not intend to insult you." His voice came out too rough. *What was wrong with him?* Was she a Siren luring him into making a fool of himself?

She looked up at him. Although her mouth was smiling, her deep blue eyes held a hint of hurt. "Not a problem. You're a great kisser, by the way. You could give les—"

"Jessica, I have wanted to kiss you since you fell out of the ceiling in my sanitary room. Now, be still." He bent his head and covered her mouth with his own.

Kissing was much better than explaining why his personal ethics did not allow him to indulge in such behavior. The intensity was still there. He had thought it was an aberration, but it was even greater than before. Never had he experienced such an overwhelming rush of passion. Ignoring the hair ornament, he threaded his fingers through her hair. It was as soft and silky as he had imagined.

Her lips softened under his. Her acquiescence thrilled him. Then, she kissed him back. She wanted him. This time he was not mistaken. Her desire was apparent in the way her fingers clutched his arms, the way her breasts swelled against his chest, the way she pressed her lower body even closer to his. She wrapped her strong arms around his neck and pulled him tighter against her.

She was not afraid of him. Inordinate pleasure filled him.

When she opened her mouth, their tongues engaged in a delightful duel. The slide of her tongue against his sent an involuntary shiver through him. This woman incited him to throw away all caution, to toss aside a lifetime of rigid control. His resolution never to indulge in casual intercourse with an inferior species wavered.

Inferior species? What was he thinking?

He gripped her arms, but she tightened them around his neck and would not let him break the kiss.

He admired her strength. Her soft curves fit against him, as if her body had been made for his. She belonged in his arms. She belonged in his bed. In his life.

His life? What was he thinking? She belonged on Earth. This time he would not permit her to stop him. He broke off a kiss he should never have started.

Several moments passed while each of them caught their breath. He was pleased that she, too, found it difficult. He had not felt this light-headed, this out of breath, since he climbed to the summit of Mt. Placid in a futile attempt to conquer his fear of heights.

Jessica gazed up at him with eyes darkened by passion. Their slumberous quality made him regret halting the kiss. All his life he had striven to conquer the sensual side of himself. The side that made him an outsider, an alien, on Serenia.

"Say you regret kissing me, and I'll deck you," she said in a shaky voice. "Guess the few dates I've had were wrong. Frigid, I am not." She bolted out of his quarters.

He picked up the yellow hairband. The men she had dated were fools.

***

The Accomplice keyed in the code. Moments later, the Leader's face appeared in the monitor.

"You have control of the ship?"

"Not yet."

"How can that be?" The Leader's face darkened in anger.

The Leader would never believe the Terran enabled Captain Viator to escape. "Our enemy is more resourceful than we thought."

"Eliminate him."

"But—"

"Your devotion to our cause is wavering?"

"No. But if we eliminate him we will never learn—"

"You must gain control of the ship before it reaches Serenia. Do not fail."

SEVEN

"You are not my sister."

Veronese Qilana held perfectly still. The young man stood in the open doorway, not the overhead door which she kept closed ever since her unexpected visitor, but the smaller door. Bright sunlight behind him kept him shadowed.

Once again, someone had surprised her in Jessica's workshop. Oblivious to her surroundings, Veronese had centered all her concentration on trying to repair this small appliance—a mixer, the frantic woman had called it this morning. Veronese often became so involved in her work that she blocked out her sense of hearing. And had been reprimanded frequently for not paying attention. 'All things in moderation' was the Serenian Code. Until recently, she had not understood why moderation was more difficult for her to achieve than those around her.

All her life she had tried to adapt while feeling like an outsider. With her Serenian mother's revelation, Veronese finally knew why.

"I called you three times. You didn't answer." The man with dark auburn hair, so similar to her own natural color, walked closer to the workbench. Timothy Wyndom was a little taller than she, with a wiry build. Anyone looking at the two of them together would instantly see the resemblance.

She set down the screwdriver. She had hoped to quickly discover what was wrong with the appliance. While she had exceptional mechanical abilities, working with primitive tools proved more difficult than she imagined.

Her brother looked quite angry. She had planned to see Timothy before she returned to the *Freedom*, but not in this fashion. Had he been at their parents' home yesterday, as she had expected, this confrontation could have been avoided.

"You may look exactly like Jess, wear her clothes, even fix your hair exactly like hers, but you are *not* my sister. Who are you and where's Jessie?"

Was it my inattention that gave me away?

From the research she had done before devising her plan to switch places with her twin, she knew Timothy and Jessica were close. She had practiced Jessica's mannerisms, most of which were quite similar to her own. She had listened to her speech patterns and was an excellent mimic. Nothing should have gone wrong. Yet, it had, right from the start.

She had only planned to switch places with her twin for less than one Earth day, just long enough to see her biological parents. Then, she planned to visit with her sister, saving the best for last. Delayed gratification, so highly prized on Serenia, meant she had not accomplished her dearest wish: to meet face to face with her twin.

She was still out of contact with the *Freedom* or any other Alliance vessel. Something very strange was happening out there in space. If contact was not restored by tomorrow, her ruse would be revealed. At most, GND—genetic nucleotide duplication—only lasted seventy-two hours.

As if that was not enough of a trial, this morning a woman pounded on the front door demanding 'Jessie get her butt in gear' and open the repair shop. Switching places meant Veronese must perform Jessica's tasks.

Of course, she did not expect her twin to take her place in Engineering. After all, of what use could Jessica be with her primitive skills? However, she did not fear for Jessica's safety. Guests aboard an Alliance vessel were always treated with respect. Jessica's safety was assured—unlike her own.

She decided the best way to diffuse this hostile situation was to bluff. "Hey, Timmy, whaddaya mean I'm not your sister? Get outa here. I got work to do."

For a second, he appeared startled. Then his eyes narrowed. "Uh-uh. You're good but not that good."

She twisted a strand of hair around her right index finger.

She found it difficult getting used to such length as well as the color. She also found, with distaste, the sight of hair on her body. Veronese and, she assumed, the rest of the transplanted Terrans, took daily depilatory pills. Until recently, she'd thought the reason for the pills and the silver lenses had been a genetic error. Since her plan had been to return to the ship within a day, she had not brought along her pills. Even so, she had not expected the growth of hair to be so sudden.

Realizing she had reverted to the nervous habit of twisting her hair, she removed the stretchy elastic and refastened her hair off her neck.

Her delaying tactics were not working. Timothy still looked angry. While researching the inhabitants of Earth, she recalled how easily they resorted to violence. From all she had learned about her brother, he did not seem to be the type whose fury would cause him to lose control. Yet, she remembered her unexpected visitor from yesterday and the uneasiness she had felt.

Timothy grabbed her upper arm. "Where is my sister?"

Ice needled down her spine. She wiped her sweating palm down the side of her pant leg. *This is what fear feels like.*

Her entire life had been spent in a sheltered atmosphere. Her pacifist Serenian parents had sought sanctuary during the Great Intergalactic War. She had not even been aware of the greatest conflict her society had known until history classes at the Academy. Despite her parents' protests, she did not apply for dispensation from the Elders' mandate. She had enthusiastically trained at Space Fleet Academy, knowing full well that she might be called into battle.

She had never encountered such anger as emanated from her brother. She was surprised she could still stop and analyze her feelings while facing someone who was trying to shake her into confessing.

She drew herself up tall and used her own voice. "You will stop this instant."

He released her arm and stepped back.

"Jessica is well. She has not been harmed."

"Where is she?" While he was not touching her, anger

vibrated from his body.

She closed her eyes. He was not going to believe what had happened to Jessica. "How did you know?"

"You didn't hear me drive up."

She looked beyond him. A black sports car was parked in the driveway.

"I called you three times, and you didn't answer. Jessie can be a space cadet at times, but she never ignored *me*. For a minute there, I thought you were starting to act like the folks. When they're involved in their work, a tornado overhead wouldn't faze them." He chuckled.

Then his expression turned grim. "The give-away was your hands. Jessie's not left-handed." He grabbed her hands, streaked with grease. "Your hands aren't used to hard work. What've you done with my sister?"

She pulled her hands out of his grasp. Surprised that he released her, she rubbed her wrist. If she spoke in a quiet, calm voice, maybe he would control himself. "Let us go into the kitchen. Perhaps, an alcoholic drink will calm your nerves." Glancing over her shoulder to see if he was following, she walked on the well-worn path to the back door of the old farmhouse.

"I don't drink alcohol. But then, since you're not my sister, you wouldn't know that. Quit frogging around. My sister is missing, and you're a dead look-alike."

She held the door open behind her for him. "I hope not a *dead* look-alike," she quipped in Jessica's voice, hoping the jocularity would make him less suspicious.

"You will be if you don't hurry up and spill your guts." He barged past her, reached into the refrigerator, and pulled out two cans. He tossed one to her.

"Spill my guts? What a quaint phrase." She fumbled with the can and then caught it. Yesterday, she had tried this unusual beverage. She liked the sharp, fizzy taste of ginger ale, especially the way the bubbles tickled her nose. She pulled the ring on top. Instantly, amber liquid spurted from the small opening. A sticky substance deluged her hand, forearm, face, even her hair.

"Wh-What happened? It did not do that the last time I opened one."

He narrowed his eyes. "Everybody knows you lift the tab slowly after the can's been shaken. What planet have you been living on, sister?"

She walked over to the sink. "You got two out of three right, kiddo." She rather liked Jessica's turn of phrase. "You'd better sit down." She ran a cloth under the faucet and wiped off the sticky residue.

Meanwhile, he sprawled in a chrome and red chair. She joined him at the table and placed her elbows on its shiny gray top. Using her own voice, she explained, "First—" she ticked off on her fingers "—not *everybody* knows about spraying cans. I did not. Second, I *am* your sister."

"No way. You're not Jessie."

"Please hear me out. I am Jessica's twin."

He sat up straight. "No. My mom never had twins."

"Would you believe," she used Jessica's voice "your parents adopted her, and I was sent to live with another family?"

He gave her a hard look. "My mama didn't raise no dummies. Jessie looks just like her."

He was correct about that. Veronese had been surprised at how much she and Jessica looked like their biological mother.

What should she tell him? Was he as open-minded about space travel and extra-terrestrials as her research indicated?

"You are correct, Timothy. I should—"

He snorted. "Only my mother calls me Timothy. If you were my real sister, you would know that."

"Yes. Tim. I should treat you with more respect for your intelligence. The adoption story was too easy, and it is not exactly true. Jessica was not adopted. I was. You asked what planet I was living on."

She stared into his blue eyes, so similar to hers without the special silver lenses. "I *have* been living on another planet. My home is Serenia, in what you call the Andromeda Galaxy."

He did not blink. He just stared back at her.

"Timothy—Tim." She reached across the table to touch

his arm. "Please believe me. I am your sister. Jessica and I were separated before we were born."

He pushed her hand away and stumbled to his feet. "I gotta hand it to you. You're good, lady. Real good. What the hell kind of idiot do you take me for? Separated *before* birth? From another planet? What's next? My sister—my real sister, Jessie—has been kidnapped by aliens?"

She did not blame him. Her story must sound far-fetched.

"I did not mean for her to think she was kidnapped but, yes, that is what it must seem like. You see, I have switched places with my sister. I wanted to meet our—"

"No way." He shook his head. "Have you been smoking that stuff he sells across the road?" Then he smacked his forehead. "Does this have something to do with that guy? Jessie wanted to call the cops, but I told her not to mess with him. Not to get involved. That's it, isn't it? You've had her kidnapped so she won't talk to the cops."

Veronese walked to the sink where he stood with his back against the counter, his arms folded across his chest.

"What did you mean about the man who lives across the road? Is he not a baseball player? A Detroit Tiger?" she asked.

Tim snorted and rolled his eyes. "Not hardly."

"He was here yesterday."

"Here? He came over here?" He looked more upset about that than about her taking Jessica's place.

"Yes."

"He's never done that before." Timothy—Tim began to pace. "When he moved in, we didn't think there'd be any problems. Just a guy trying to fix up an old farmhouse. But all the cars coming and going late at night—" He shook his head. "That guy is into some nasty business."

"He acted like he was a friend of Jessica's, but I was uncertain if I should believe him."

"Did he put the moves on you?" Without waiting for an answer, Tim went on, "I'm calling the cops, and you're coming home with me. I don't want you anywhere near that guy. Where's the dog I told you to get when old Whiskey died? I hate it that you're out here all by yourself. What was Gram thinking when she left you this place?"

"I have to stay here." If she left, how would the *Freedom* find her? She had to get back to the ship and switch places again with Jessica before GND wore off.

"You never listen to anybody," he continued. "I supported you with the folks when you started up your business. I'm the one who told them you'd be okay by yourself. I'm going to be worried sick about you alone out here in the boonies. For once in your life, will you think about somebody besides yourself?"

His protectiveness surprised her. No one had ever shown that much concern for her well-being.

He stopped pacing and scrubbed a hand down his face. "You're not my sister. Why the hell am I worried about *you?*"

She waited at the sink, holding her own emotions in check. He was not worried about *her*. He thought he was talking to Jessica. A heaviness settled in her chest.

He was angry for confusing her with Jessica. It was very disconcerting to face such strong emotion. In surprise, she realized she wanted to lash out in kind. Instead, she took a deep breath and slowly released it.

"I am your sister. I came from another planet in another galaxy. I work on a starship, an Intergalactic Alliance research vessel. Jessica is on that starship. She is learning about my world while I learn about hers."

"Jess agreed to this? No way. She would've told me first. No." He kept shaking his head. "No. You've done something to my sister. I'm gonna call the cops." He headed toward the yellow telephone attached to the wall.

Calling the authorities could lead to disaster. She had gone against regulations. The Alliance forbade interference in primitive societies such as Earth. She could quite possibly change Earth's history by her actions.

Worse was the danger to herself. If the authorities even suspected she was not from Earth, they might take her away. Away from Jessica's house. Then how could she return to the *Freedom?* The authorities would confiscate her *link*. They might even—she shuddered just thinking about it—do to her what they did to the Cardijians when their starship crashed in

New Mexico five decades before.

She could not allow Tim to call the authorities. "And tell them what? Your sister is missing? They will not believe you. I am right here. Our parents think I am their daughter. Do you think you can convince them I am not?"

Yesterday, her visit with her biological parents went very well. They did not notice how nervous she was or even suspect that she was not Jessica. Driving Jessica's pick-up truck to her parents' house had been more of a challenge.

Tim gave her a scornful look. "You could've dressed up in a Halloween costume, and the folks wouldn't notice. Mom's been grading essays all week, and Dad's working on some top secret project. It's a wonder they even knew you were there."

"We had a delightful chat," she said with a smugness she could not resist. "They smiled and laughed and told me to stay for dinner. I wanted to help *Mom* prepare it but *Dad* called out for pizza. I was uncertain what it was, but the taste was quite...unusual. If the police question them, they will say I am Jessica."

Defeated, he sat down. "You got it all figured out, don't you?"

"Please listen to me." She forced herself not to pace the small kitchen. How pleasant it would be to expend emotion. But, Serenian discipline was too strong to allow her to indulge in such a release.

"I will tell you the truth, Tim. Our mother was expecting twins. An unscrupulous scientist from Serenia separated us before Mother even knew it. I was transplanted into a host mother who gave birth to me."

"That is too weird." He still looked suspicious, but at least he was listening. She told him the rest of the story.

"If—I'm not saying I believe you but—if what you say is true, when is my sister, when is *Jessie* coming back?"

She sank into a chair across the table from him. "There appears to be a problem. I do not understand. I planned everything down to the last detail."

"So what detail did you leave out?"

Though pleased with herself for recognizing sarcasm this time, she closed her eyes for a moment in chagrin. "I cannot contact my ship."

He folded his arms across his chest and glared at her. "What did you do, forget your communicator?"

"No. I brought my *link*—my communicator. I spoke to Jessica and the Captain of the *Freedom* after I transported myself here, but our communication ended abruptly."

He straightened. "You talked to Jess? Is she okay?"

"Of course. How could she not be? Our transportation technology is quite superior. She seemed angry with me, though, for not giving her my body."

"What?"

"My twin does not take appropriate care of her body. You might call her fat."

"*I* wouldn't call her that. A little pudgy, maybe," he admitted with a sheepish look. "You'd better watch out if you even mention the word 'fat' around Jess."

"Physical fitness is prized on my planet. In order not to arouse suspicion, I had to change the way I look." She explained how she came to look exactly like Jessica.

"You had a lean, hard body, huh? No extra, uh, curves? No wonder she was mad at you." He chuckled. "Why didn't you do this genetic nucleotide thing on her? She's always trying to diet. She'd love it if you waved your magic wand and made her thin."

"GND is not magic. It is a difficult procedure that can only be performed on oneself. I could not do it to her. And, it is, uh, not exactly legal."

"So, you did something illegal *and* you lost contact with your ship?"

"I have tried to ascertain the problem with my *link*. I have not been able to communicate with the *Freedom*. I cannot hail any ship in this quadrant, and there are supposed to be at least two others." She fought the panic that she had been left behind by her ship. "I do not understand."

***

"Hey, Aurelia," Jessie hailed her guide from the day before.

She caught up with Aurelia Melora in the main corridor. This was Jessie's off-time from Engineering. Chief Luqett had taken her under his wing and put her to work. As long as she was stuck here, she was grateful to have something to do. She couldn't abide idleness.

After the spectacular—and disastrous—kiss in Marcus's quarters yesterday, she had fled back to Engineering. His kiss thrilled her clear down to her toes. She was right, no whisker-burn. But his obvious regret wounded her more than she thought possible. She never got used to rejection. Why did she set herself up? Why had she leapt so eagerly into his arms? Why had she returned his kiss?

When would she learn to think first?

Last night, while lying in bed in Veronese Qilana's quarters, she decided to avoid Marcus. Though the ship was large, she discovered this wasn't easy. He frequently walked the corridors, checking on all operations. He treated her politely, with his usual aloofness, when she was with other crewmembers. And, she made sure she always had a companion. Like now with Lieutenant Melora.

When Jessie had called out, Aurelia appeared surprised. She even glanced quickly behind her.

"You're not afraid I have some infectious disease, are you?" Jessie laughed. "Somehow that crazy rumor got started. But, I don't. You don't have to be afraid."

"N-No. I am not afraid." Aurelia's glance darted from Jessie's face to behind her again. Then, she appeared to relax.

"Are you off-duty?" At Aurelia's nod, Jessie continued, "Want to join me for something cold to drink?"

Aurelia hesitated.

"I don't know very many people here yet." Jessie hated to plead. "You were my first friend. But if you don't have time, I understand." She shrugged.

"I have time."

From her earlier friendliness, Aurelia seemed to be Jessie's best bet to find out about her twin. Jessie retrieved drinks. After she and Aurelia sat down in a padded booth in the quiet officers' lounge, she said, "Have you been on this ship long?"

"No. Most of the crew have been here much longer. Captain Viator is a very good commander. It is difficult to transfer here because no one wants to leave. I replaced a researcher who retired."

Jessie savored the taste of iced xephod tea, even better cold than hot. While hot, it brought tranquility. Cold, it refreshed without stimulating. "What about Veronese Qilana? Wasn't she recently assigned to the *Freedom*?"

Aurelia nodded slowly. "I heard she bribed an officer in Engineering to transfer to another vessel so she could take his place." A pained look crossed her face. "I should not talk about her. It is unseemly to gossip."

"Since she's the reason I'm here, I'm trying to understand her. Wait a minute, if she's an Engineering officer, what was she doing in the transport room?"

"That is most strange. She often volunteered to work in the transport room while off-duty to give the assigned officers personal time. Most uncharacteristic of her. She was not the type to do favors for anyone."

It made sense. Veronese probably volunteered in the transport room to be ready to switch places with Jessie. She must've been plotting to do this for a long time.

They chatted a while before Aurelia excused herself. Jessie stayed and thought about the picture Aurelia had painted of Jessie's twin. Veronese Qilana was haughty and oft-times difficult to work with. She definitely wanted things her own way. She was aggressive and determined. The determined part was not so different from Jessie.

She'd moved to the country despite many confrontations with her mother. Mom never argued. Instead, she had 'heated' discussions. Dad actually paid attention long enough to side with Mom. They were horrified over Jessie's decision to quit school after community college.

They insisted she was throwing away her abilities on a repair business and the Centennial farm she inherited after Gram died. Gram knew how much Jessie valued family traditions. Gram also recognized how difficult studying was for her and what her talents really were. Other than Gram, only Tim supported her. Those two accepted Jessie as she was. They didn't try to make her over into what they wanted her to be.

She was surprised her mother had taken the time to concern herself about Jessie's welfare. As head of the English department at a small, private university, Mom lived in her head most of the time. So, Mom's actually thinking about Jessie long enough to object to what she wanted to do with her life had been a shock.

Of course, his head was Dad's second home, too. He did research in biology at the University of Michigan. He was always working on a project in his head when he wasn't actually in the lab itself. Jessie and her brother didn't call him the absent-minded professor for nothing.

Dad didn't care about his mother's property. Having been in the family since the 1830s, it was designated a Centennial Farm by the Michigan Historical Commission. Jessie was only too happy to carry on the Wyndom tradition.

Tim, the heir-apparent to their parents' way of life, was five years younger than she. They'd graduated from high school the same year, which had been humiliating. It had taken a while, but she'd reconciled herself to the disparity in their intellectual abilities.

Brilliant, ultra-serious Veronese Qilana sounded like she would've fit into her family just fine. Jessie hated her. Another sibling to be compared to. Or, maybe, she'd have taken the heat off Jessie.

Surely her folks would see through this impostor. Would they recognize she wasn't Jessie? Or would they be so self-absorbed that they wouldn't even notice?

Veronese Qilana had better see what she wanted to see on Earth and then make that switch back. Soon.

"I wish to speak to you."

Jessie snapped out of her musing at the voice of Darth Vader with a cold. The *Vulture* must have swooped down on her while she was daydreaming. First Officer Klegznef wedged his large body into the recently vacated seat.

Prickles ran down her arms and settled in her fingertips.

Her heart sped up. Though she'd always loved the sound of actor James Earl Jones's voice—even as Darth Vader—this alien's deep rumble induced terror.

Determined not to let him see her fear, she lifted her chin. "Yes, sir?"

"You enabled the Captain to escape."

Oh, dear God. He was going to punish her for thwarting his plans. He'd wanted Marcus incommunicado and now, because of her, Klegznef wasn't in charge of the ship. What would he do? Surely, Marcus wouldn't let him lock her up. Would Klegznef torture her? Some kind of mental probing that would leave her a vegetable, unable to identify her assailant?

He stared at her with piercing black eyes. All she could say was, "Yes, sir."

"Thank you."

She was so stunned by his words his action didn't register. She stared at the gray hand with six fingers thrust across the table at her.

He cocked his large, gray head with its bristling quill-like hair. "It is the custom on your planet to shake digital extremities upon congratulations."

"Y-Yes, it is." Cautiously, she extended her hand. She expected his to be cold, clammy, like a corpse. Instead, she found it smooth and mildly cool. Not warm like Marcus's, but not clammy, either.

He shook her hand once and dropped it. He stood but didn't immediately leave. "You have proven yourself to be inventive and courageous."

Praise from the Vulture? "Th-Thank you." *I think.*

"Terrans still should not be aboard this ship." He did a military turn and departed.

Now that sounded more like him. Since he didn't want her on board, she was surprised he had sought her out.

"Ms. Wyndom, may I join you?"

She spun around on the bench-like seat. Marcus stood just behind her left shoulder. *What's with me today?* She hadn't heard him approach. With her back to the entrance, she hadn't seen him come into the lounge.

"Sure." She waved her hand across the table. "That seat doesn't even get cold."

He sat down and raised his eyebrow in question.

"You're the third person to sit there in the last half hour. Geez, I'm Miss Popularity," she muttered the last.

He eyed her with caution. "That is a good thing on your planet? To be popular?"

"Yeah, if it's for the right reason. Never mind me. I still haven't recovered from the Vulture's visit."

"I passed Mr. Klegznef as he exited the lounge. I was not aware he had talked to you. Did he accost you? I will make certain he does not bother you again."

She was surprised at Marcus's vehemence. Though his voice was calm, his eyes told a different story.

"Please don't say anything to him. He was very polite. He even congratulated me on rescuing you."

"He did?"

"Yeah. Surprised the heck out of me, too."

"Hmm." He paused for a moment, as if thinking. "Will you wait while I procure a drink for myself?"

"I should get back to my quarters. I have things to do and..." She let her voice trail off.

"I wish to speak. About yesterday." His silver eyes engaged hers, holding her in thrall. Daring her to refuse.

"Of-Of course." Her heart sped up at the intimacy of his gaze. Her palms began to sweat. She didn't want to talk to him. She didn't want to hear him reiterate how kissing her was some big mistake. Damn it, why couldn't he just leave well enough alone?

EIGHT

Before rising, Marcus looked at Jessica. Her long auburn hair, twisted into a braid, hung over her shoulder. Tiny wisps framed her face, softening the severity of her hairstyle. She wore the Engineering crew's dark blue uniform. It did not cling to her generous curves as the other had. Much to his surprise, he was disappointed. While she appeared more comfortable in this uniform, he would not soon forget the enticing sight of her hips swaying before him as they crawled through the access tunnels.

She glanced from him to the entrance of the lounge, as if gauging the distance. Was she ready to bolt?

"Would you like a refill?" He pointed to her empty tumbler of xephod tea.

"No. I'm fine." She would not make eye contact.

"Please wait."

She bit her lip before nodding. He walked to the replicator and ordered a cup of hot seleria. He needed the bracing liquid to fortify himself to speak to Jessica. Although chemical mood enhancers were available, he abhorred ingesting artificial substances. Seeking even natural fortification indicated the effect she had on him.

This quiet lounge was not the appropriate location for the business he wished to discuss with her. He could have called her into his quarters or his ready room. However, he did not want to be alone with her again. After the spontaneous passion yesterday, he was uncertain if he could maintain control.

He did not blame her for his weakness. He *never* acted

impulsively. Only with her. Were Terrans at the mercy of their emotions all the time? He despised this breach in his self-control.

She gave him a wary glance as he returned to the booth. "What's wrong?"

"Why do you ask?"

Her mouth curved up into a wry smile. "Answering a question with a question is not allowed. You look mad."

Now she sounded normal. As normal as possible, he imagined, given the circumstances of her being trapped far away from home.

He admired her playfulness in spite of adversity. Not for the first time, he wondered how he would react to being out of his element. If he had been transported to a world so alien from his own, would he maintain his composure? "I am not angry. I have had much to think about recently."

Her playfulness disappeared. "Yeah, like how to get me home and who has it in for you?" She leaned back against the padded seat with her arms crossed in front of her chest. A very defensive position, he noted.

Carefully, so as not to burn his tongue, he took a small sip of the seleria. His tongue tingled as the hot liquid flowed across it. With another sip, the seleria charged through his system, invigorating him. He kept his voice low. "I would like to discuss the second matter with you."

"You're finally admitting you have a conspirator aboard?" She raised her eyebrow.

Is she imitating me?

He glanced around the almost vacant room, assuring himself that no one was within hearing distance. "You may be correct about the Praetorium. I suspect someone aboard wants to jeopardize the peace of the Alliance. Please be alert while working in Engineering. Observe your co-workers."

"You're asking me to spy?"

"I am uncertain whom to trust." That was difficult to admit. Until now, he had never had cause to question his crew's loyalty. "Someone programmed the ship's computer to confine me to my quarters. Someone impersonated me to turn the ship over to my First Officer."

Her eyes widened. "Someone impersonated you? Why do you think that? Couldn't it have been a hologram or a computer-generated image?"

Though her voice was low, he still glanced around to see if anyone had heard. "To prevent tricksters, the computer has a safeguard that notifies the recipient if the image is not real. Someone who looked exactly like me informed Mr. Klegznef—who, in turn, informed the crew—that I had contracted a highly contagious disease—"

"From me."

"Yes. Apparently, no one wanted to personally verify this, even the ship's medical officer. I have already spoken to her." He did not often have to discipline his officers, but after this crisis, he had to insert an unfavorable comment in Dr. Rindor's personnel record.

"But the Vulture took command. Doesn't that mean he's at the bottom of this?"

"Mr. Klegznef believed I gave the order to seal my quarters. He swears, on his honor, he did not alter my access code in the ship's computer. I should still have had contact with the crew and the computer."

"You believe him?"

"A Zorfan's honor means more to him than his life."

She thought for a moment. "Hey, I know. That genetic whatzit. How my twin changed her looks. Maybe somebody did that to look like you."

"Impossible. Only a blood relative can use genetic nucleotide duplication to transform into another."

"Omigosh." She clapped her hand over her mouth. "Aurelia. Lieutenant Melora. Isn't she a cousin or something?"

"I have no blood relative on this ship."

"I thought— I must have misunderstood her." She looked puzzled. "You don't have a twin, do you?"

He held himself perfectly still. She could not know. "Jessica, please be alert in Engineering."

She sat back and twisted her mouth in a way he had come to associate with her pondering. Since she usually said what she thought, that did not bode well. He took a sip of his seleria. Almost absent-mindedly, she pulled her braid over her left shoulder and twisted the end around her finger. For some obscure reason, he had not returned the yellow fabric band she had dropped in his sitting room yesterday. He should, perhaps, mention it to her so she would know what happened to it.

"Has Chief Luqett talked to you?" After he shook his head, she dropped her braid and leaned closer. "The problem with the hyperdrive was not caused by normal wear-and-tear. At least, I don't think so."

He set down his drink. "What do you mean?"

"The snap ring that loosened up and fell off? I'm not absolutely sure but..."

He nodded for her to go on.

She blew out a breath. "I think someone removed it."

"Why would you think that?"

"If the ring fell off, it would still be on the floor. I went back and looked. I couldn't find it. I told the Chief about my suspicions. He's running diagnostics on the analyzer because the problem should've shown up there."

"So." He leaned forward, resting his elbow on the table, and he rubbed his upper lip. "Someone in Engineering could be responsible."

"Or more than one person is involved."

"That, too, is a possibility." He had not considered a conspiracy. A lone renegade, perhaps, but the chance of more than one person keeping a secret on a ship this size was highly unlikely. "Be alert."

Three young officers walked in, nodded to him, and sat at a table nearby. He wished they had chosen one of several empty tables across the room. They had just come off duty and their spirits were high. More and more, he realized younger Serenians did not exercise what he considered sufficient self-discipline. He wondered if that made him—what was the Terran expression?—an old fogie.

Under cover of their boisterous talk, he said softly, "I wish to speak of another topic." He cleared his throat. "You do not need to jump into supply closets when I walk down the hall." She grimaced. "I didn't think you noticed."

"I wish to reassure you. I do not plan to 'jump your bones,' as your saying goes." He allowed the corner of his mouth to curve up slightly.

She snapped her fingers. "Darn."

He choked on the seleria. Her flippancy confused him. He suspected she used it to avoid embarrassment. "I apologize for my lack of control yesterday. You are a guest aboard my ship. It is my duty to protect you. Not attack."

A spot of red bloomed on her cheeks. She rested her forearms on the table and leaned forward. "Are you referring to that kiss as an attack? No more apologies. Forget about it." She licked her lips. "I have."

That stung. And the fact that it did amazed him. Since he had met this Terran, he had dealt with more volatile emotions than he had as an adolescent. He thought he had submerged that part of himself and developed the strong discipline so prized on Serenia.

From the way she avoided his eyes, he suspected she was lying. Perhaps he needed more education on dealing with Terrans. "We will not discuss it again."

"Good," she said with false brightness. "Am I free to leave?"

"You are always free to leave."

She stalked off, head high, back straight.

He had offended her. He took a deep breath and blew it out slowly. Terrans were such complex characters.

That evening, an unusually quiet Luqett approached him outside the bridge. "A moment alone, Marcus."

He nodded. "In my ready room."

They entered the Captain's private office next to the bridge. "What is it, Chief?"

"The analyzer was re-programmed to ignore warning signals. If it hadn't been for Jessie, we would never have been alerted. Marcus, we have more problems with the engines. The crew is repairing them, but I fear even the analyzer is not sufficient to discover everything."

"Is the analyzer controlled through the ship's main computer?"

"No. It is an independent safeguard."

"Where are the controls for the analyzer?"

"In plain view of everyone working in Engineering."

Luqett gave Marcus a long look full of import. "Your next question will be who can access the controls."

Marcus gave his Chief a small smile.

"Only officers."

This confirmed his suspicion that the saboteur was an officer, had full access to Engineering *and* the main computer, as well as the ability to don a convincing disguise.

"Have you shared this information with Security?"

Luqett shook his head. "I came to you first."

"Inform Hrvibm. This will help with her investigation."

Marcus pondered the possible suspects as he paid a last visit to the bridge. Luqett's crew could usually repair anything that went wrong with the ship. But this sabotage went beyond their abilities. How could they repair what they could not detect? When the very instruments that indicated malfunctions were malfunctioning. They needed to return to Serenia quickly. Yet, without full power, if nothing else went wrong, it would take at least five days.

Days? As he opened the portal to his quarters, he realized he was thinking in Earth terms. How easily he had slipped into his guest's vocabulary. Barring unforeseen difficulties with repairing the hyperdrive, the ship would be ready to leave port six days after that. Jessica would return to her home nearly two Earth weeks after she left.

Could Veronese Qilana keep her identity a secret that long? The effects of GND had probably worn off already. She would have to hide. Jessica had suffered enough being brought aboard against her will. She should not have to face more difficulties when she returned home.

The fact that he worried about her irritated him. He would be pleased when she left the ship. She was a disrupting influence. Her lack of emotional restraint reminded him too much of what he fought against. She was a reminder of what he was.

As he prepared to retire, he opened the hidden drawer in the sanitary room that held his tablets. When he approached adolescence, his mother had given him the depilatory tablets for the first time. Less than one percent of Serenians were throw-backs to earlier generations, before body hair had been bred out. Pills had been developed to prevent embarrassment to a family having a hirsute offspring. In order to avoid detection, he took one tablet each night.

Then, he removed from his eyes the silver lenses he had worn all his life. He blinked several times before looking into the mirror. As he did each night, he searched the jade green eyes. Who was he? Where did he belong?

***

Damn, damn, damn. Jessie lay in bed wide awake. She knew their kiss had been a mistake. Why did she mention it? Why couldn't she have just left well enough alone?

With a start, she realized she was sounding like her dad. Richard Wyndom could have invented 'Don't ask, don't tell.' It was his way of dealing, or not dealing, with anything unpleasant. Even when her mother had gone ballistic over Jessie's choice of profession, Dad had zoned out. Mom had had to drag him into the discussion.

When they were young, Jessie and her brother attributed their father's vagueness to his concentration on his work. The old 'absent-minded professor' routine. As they grew older, they knew better. His disinterest hurt.

Gram had tried to help Jessie understand. Having had a father with a volatile temper, Richard kept his emotions bottled up inside, perhaps afraid they would rule him as his father's had. If he ignored a situation long enough, he wouldn't have to deal with it.

Jessie hated that withdrawal. It was as if she didn't matter enough for her father to notice. Marcus's refusal to recognize the passion between them smacked too much of her father's avoidance techniques. She recalled her comment about forgetting the kiss. By pretending she had forgotten about the kiss, she sounded just like her dad.

She rolled over and punched the feather pillow. Why had she pushed Marcus about the kiss? Probably, she thought with disgust, for the same reason she pushed her father. She wanted a reaction. An acknowledgement that she existed. That she was important.

She knew her outbursts bothered Marcus. He could be such an old stick-in-the-mud. So disapproving. Hadn't she had enough of that from her parents? Why did she keep egging him on? What perversity made her want to shake up the prim and proper Captain? Make him acknowledge her and his attraction to her?

He *was* attracted to her. She didn't have much experience, but she saw it in those spectacular silver eyes. Shivering at the recollection of their intensity, she pulled the covers up to her chin.

Similar to those in Marcus's quarters, the bedclothes were made of a delicate yet sturdy material. As soft as silk, the sheet was cool against her body. A feather-filled comforter provided warmth without heaviness.

She snuggled down in the narrow bunk, wishing she had a bubble like Marcus's where she could watch the stars. Instead, her bed had been built into an alcove with storage drawers below and cupboards above. Utilitarian, compact, the room was not much bigger than her bathroom at home.

These were Veronese Qilana's quarters. Her sister had lived here, slept here. Last night, Jessie explored the room. Veronese's clothes—uniforms and underwear—were lined up in precise rows, nothing out of place. But, she had left nothing to indicate her personality. No family pictures, no knick-knacks, no collectibles. That in itself made her opposite Jessie, whose home was filled with treasured photographs and family memorabilia.

Bookdisks next to an electronic reader indicated her twin's educational interests. Even though she couldn't read the language, Jessie could tell scientific books by the diagrams and mathematical equations. Her twin appeared single-minded in her quest for academic excellence. Jessie's parents' dream come true. Too bad she couldn't tell them.

She'd be glad to get home. Back where she belonged. Away from Marcus and his disapproval. Away from the first man to make her heart skip and her nerves go into overload. Whose kiss set her skin on fire. A man who clearly regretted his attraction to her.

It was her ego he wounded. Certainly not her heart.

***

Four days and no contact with the *Freedom*. No contact with any Alliance ship. While the concept 'abandonment' was in the Serenian vocabulary, Veronese had never comprehended its full impact. When she allowed herself to think about her situation, a crushing sensation rested heavily on her chest. Tears formed in her eyes. The longer she remained on Earth, the stronger her emotions became.

Was there something noxious in Earth's atmosphere that intensified one's feelings? Fear of discovery preyed on her mind. GND had worn off. She had awakened this morning with short black hair and her own fit body. Jessica's baggy shirts did double duty. Both she and her twin used them to hide their bodies.

Yesterday, Tim bought her an auburn wig. She practiced smiling often to soften the hard lines of her face. She tried to talk and act as much like Jessica as possible. When Jessica came home, no one should suspect she had been gone and someone else had taken her place.

If Jessica came home. She had to come home. Veronese had to return to the ship, to the place where she belonged.

She set aside the magazine she'd been perusing. In preparing for her sojourn on Earth, she had taught herself to read the English language with the help of an anthropologist from the research crew. Tonight, the magazine held no interest. She had accomplished her goal—meeting her parents. They were not what she expected. Gracious the first time she visited, they seemed surprised to see her the next day, as if their daughter's visits were unusual.

On Serenia, parental visitation was a pleasant duty one performed often. Apparently, Jessica rarely visited their parents, even though they lived close by. That surprised

Veronese. Did not Jessica respect her parents?

During her subsequent visit, they seemed more distracted, withdrawn. As if she was disrupting. She mentioned this to Tim, who assured her that was their normal behavior.

When she was not in the workshop, she prowled the house looking for clues to her twin's personality. She discovered two sides to Jessica. The workshop was orderly. Clean tools hung on hooks or were methodically arranged in cabinet drawers. The workbench, though stained by lubricating substances, was scrupulously clean, with works-in-progress tagged and lined up to one side.

The inside of the house revealed her twin's softer side. Though not a trained researcher, Veronese could see Jessica obviously valued tradition. The well-cared-for furniture was too old to be considered contemporary, but not old enough to be antique. From the photographs on the mantel, she saw the furniture had belonged to their grandparents. Old quilts were displayed prominently on beds in the guest bedrooms. Most surprising of all was the glass case protecting a collection of dolls dressed in costumes from countries around the Terran world. Such an odd hobby for a person with mechanical abilities.

The dichotomy of her twin's personality confused her. She wanted to think they were the same. According to Tim, Jessica hated school. How very different from her. At the Academy, she embraced education single-mindedly. Her drive to excel was very strong. Because of her aptitude, The Elders had assigned her to starship engineering.

The departure from her orderly life began with her Serenian mother's death-bed confession, when Veronese embarked on the mission to discover her origins. Well-planned, her mission should have been easily executed. In this world so different from her own, she tried to understand who she was.

Tim had dropped by yesterday and again today to check up on her. She asked if that was his practice when Jessica was there. She suspected not, and he confirmed it. When she promised not to steal the silver, he laughed and complimented her on her joke. All her life, she had been serious. To discover a tiny sense of humor pleased her.

Eagerly, Tim had pumped her for information about Serenia, its inhabitants as well as those of other planets. Space travel fascinated him. He wanted to know every detail of life aboard a space vessel. His inability to qualify for astronaut training because of his eyes still pained him. Not wanting to cause him further distress, she did not mention correcting his vision was a simple procedure on Serenia.

Would she ever see her home planet again? Where was her ship? Veronese tried to control the feeling of hopelessness. Despite the lateness of the hour, she decided to go outdoors. Maybe she could relieve the tension that gripped her.

Leaving the door open, she stepped out onto the broad porch which extended across the entire front of the white frame house. She sat on the swing to the left of the front door. A few gentle moves with her toes set the swing in motion.

The night was cool. The skin on her arms prickled. Goosebumps, Tim called them. Too agitated to return for a jacket, she hastened down the long driveway to the road. If she walked quickly, she would warm up.

Fallen leaves from the oak and maple trees that lined the driveway crunched under foot. The crisp air held a tang, a smell of organic material. A wood fire burned somewhere.

The farmer who rented the fields from Jessica was almost finished harvesting. Corn stubble dotted the land. Hay had been rolled into bales, ready to be taken to the farmer's land, adjacent to Jessica's, for his animals.

Veronese paused at the historical marker near the road. She remembered the words she could not read because of the dark. 'Michigan Centennial Farm. Owned by the same family over one hundred years.' Being an engineer and not a researcher, she had not realized family history was appreciated in this culture. Knowing her twin was responsible for keeping the farm in the family filled Veronese with pride. Her heritage was here, so why did she feel as alien on Earth as she'd felt on Serenia? Where did she belong?

She looked up at the black sky, dotted with brilliant stars.

How far away they looked. Moonlight shone brightly, illuminating the landscape. How different this one large orange disk with its eerie glow was from the night sky above Serenia. Serenia. Life there seemed so far away.

Shouting jerked her out of her reverie. The disturbance spilled out of the house across the road and into the yard. She withdrew into the shadow of a large oak tree. The loud voices raised in anger frightened her. Such conduct was unheard of on Serenia.

What would Jessica do? Would she cower in the shadows or confront the combatants? Or would she call the police? Veronese recalled Tim's caution and her own fear of the authorities.

By the time two belligerent men climbed into a car and spun off in a spray of gravel, she was shaking. The man who remained went inside. Keeping to the shadows, Veronese ran back into the house. She seized the telephone. Her fingers slipped off the buttons so much she had to redial twice.

"Tim?"

"Whazzamadder?" His voice sounded groggy.

She glanced at the yellow plastic clock shaped like a teapot hanging on the kitchen wall. Two-fifteen.

"I-I woke you. I am sorry." She took a deep breath. "I do not know what I should do. Across the road—"

"What happened?" This time his voice came out strong and clear, no trace of sleep. "Are you all right?"

"They were fighting. Yelling and cursing and hitting each other. I have never seen such violence."

"Hang tight. I'll be right over."

"That is not necessary. I over-reacted." She looked down at her hand. It was still shaking. "Y-You do not need to—"

He cut her off. "Lock the doors and don't answer for anyone but me." He hung up before she could protest.

She checked the front door, the one through which she had raced. Footsteps crunched outside. Someone was coming up the drive. She shoved the bolt into place.

The back door. Had she locked it earlier? She raced back to the kitchen. Her heart thudded in her chest. The door was closed. Was it locked? She couldn't remember. She fumbled with the handle.

A face appeared in the window. "Hiya, sweetcakes. Whatcha you doin' up so late?"

NINE

"Captain to the bridge."

At the urgency in the communication officer's voice, Marcus bolted out of bed. He pushed the button on his *link*. "What is the problem, Lieutenant Cabbeferron?"

"Captain, we are being hailed by the Praetorian rebels. The commander wishes to speak to you. Sir? They have blocked visual transmission."

"I will be right there." He pulled on his uniform as he spoke. Not bothering with shoes, he slipped his feet into soft leather slides, normally worn only in the privacy of one's quarters. He paused to insert the silver lenses into his eyes, blinking twice for the lenses to seat themselves.

On the bridge, he sat in the Captain's elevated chair facing the viewscreen. "Lieutenant Cabbeferron, hail the rebels."

"Yes, sir. Praetorian vessel, this is the *Freedom*. Our Captain is on the bridge."

Suddenly, the inside of the rebel vessel appeared on the screen. Marcus recognized it as a frigate from Tegro. Was it the same ship they had encountered before, near Earth? The commander's chair was turned away from the screen. Above the seat back, Marcus could see the top of a head covered with tightly-curled indigo hair.

A Tegror. He should not have been surprised. Though the Tegrors had a long and satisfactory relationship with Serenia, dissidents who embraced the rebellious Praetorium came from all Alliance member planets.

Slowly, the chair revolved. At the sight of its occupant, Marcus sucked in a breath. "Stasik?"

From the screen, Stasik Glaxpher, the *Freedom's*

navigation officer, smiled. "Good evening, Marcus. Did I disturb your sleep?"

Marcus gripped the padded arms of his chair. "What is the meaning of this?" He and Stasik had been friends since the Academy. They had served together on two other vessels before the *Freedom*.

"I wish to negotiate the surrender of your vessel." There was no expression in Glaxpher's iridescent yellow eyes.

In view of Stasik's fierce allegiance to the Alliance, Marcus could not believe his friend would join the Praetorium. "Have you gone mad?"

"Mad? What a quaint term. You have been around that Terran too long." Stasik stroked his goatee of curly blue-violet hair, a gesture he often used. "Your surrender, Marcus."

"Why would I surrender?"

Stasik Glaxpher grinned, exposing narrow, pointed teeth. "I have you in range of my weapons. As do three other vessels. You are surrounded. Confirm with your science officer, if you do not believe me." He looked to the right past Marcus. "Sorry for rousting you out of bed, too, Xaropa."

Xaropa hastily took over the science station from the night-duty officer. Marcus walked over to him. With his back to the viewscreen, he consulted Xaropa. "Is he correct?"

The science officer pointed to an instrument panel with the symbol of the *Freedom* surrounded by four vessels. "It appears so, Captain."

"Are our shields up?"

"Our shields went up as soon as the Praetorian vessels were sighted," the night-duty science officer reported.

"Prepare to cloak," Marcus said softly to Xaropa. "On my signal, take us out of here." He turned back to the viewscreen. "Negotiations, Stasik? What did you have in mind?"

"Surrender your vessel, and we will allow your crew to use the escape pods. We are within the pods' range of Rebad. They may await rescue by the Alliance."

"Rebad is uninhabitable. I will not surrender the vessel and send my crew to inevitable death."

"Would you rather we take the Terran?"

Not Jessica. A fierce protectiveness filled Marcus. They would never take Jessica away from him. "No."

"Come, come, Marcus. Do not be so hasty. Of what use is the Terran to you?" The Tegror who used to be Marcus's friend gave him a hard look.

"No," Marcus repeated.

Glaxpher smiled. "She is nothing to you. You Serenians do not develop emotional attachments to anyone." His smile changed to a harsh, bitter expression.

Marcus smarted at Stasik's assessment of his character. Although Marcus had friends among his colleagues and crew, he did maintain a distance from them. A proper Serenian distance.

Stasik was wrong. Jessica was important to him. He would never surrender her. By the Intrepid Ones, he would protect her with his life.

He forced himself to remain coolly detached as he faced his former friend. "The Terran is a guest aboard my vessel and as such is protected. I will protect her as I would protect any member of my crew."

"We want your vessel," Stasik said fiercely before visibly relaxing. "We could fire on you now, Marcus. It is only because of our long-standing friendship that I have not given that order."

No, if the Praetorium destroyed the *Freedom*, they would destroy the very reason they wanted it. Marcus gave a moment's thought to how they had discovered *Freedom's* secret before he looked over at his Science Officer.

"Captain, he is correct," Xaropa confirmed. "Their weapons are armed and ready. Our shields would be heavily damaged if all four ships fired at once."

"It appears you give us no choice." Marcus nodded to the Science Officer. "Is that not correct, Mr. Xaropa?"

"Aye, sir." Xaropa gently tapped a lighted square on his console. The forward viewscreen went blank, and the normal lighting on the bridge changed to red.

"Cabbeferron, sever all outgoing communication. Xaropa has control of the ship," Marcus announced at the same time

the Science Officer tapped his screen again. The ship lurched.
"Marcus, why do you play games?" Glaxpher's
disembodied voice chided. "I could easily transport your Terran
aboard."

"Force field around the Terran's quarters," Marcus ordered.

"The force field around Engineering already protects her
quarters," Xaropa reminded him.

Marcus grimaced. Stasik Glaxpher's treachery had
befuddled his mind. Or was it the danger to Jessica? Thank
the Intrepid Ones, Xaropa did not point out that while they
were cloaked, no one could be transported on or off the ship.

"We are now out of their target area," Xaropa announced.
"May I suggest, Captain, we remain cloaked?"

"Yes." Marcus strode to the front of the bridge. He clasped
his hands behind his back, forcibly controlling his fury at being
caught unawares by an enemy. He stared hard at his crew.
"Would someone explain how we fell into that trap? Was no
one minding the store?"

Their faces reflected a moment of amusement at his use
of Terran colloquialisms. Then, discomfiture took over as they
recognized his seldom-used sarcasm.

"Captain." Lieutenant Jherzik, the night-duty science
officer and a Tegror like Glaxpher, stood at attention. "It was
my responsibility."

"I will deal with you shortly." Marcus turned to the night-
duty navigation officer. "Engage the hyperdrive. All possible
speed to Serenia. Mr. Xaropa, call for a replacement and bring
Mr. Jherzik to my ready room. Lieutenant Cabbeferron, eyes
and ears sharp. If the Praetorium is even in the same quadrant,
I want to know about it."

"Yes, sir," she said with quiet chagrin.

"And apprise Security Chief Hrvibm of the situation."

"Aye, sir."

Marcus stalked off the bridge, nearly bumping into Luqett
who charged through the portal.

"Captain, we canna use the cloaking system *and* the
hyperdrive at the same time." Luqett looked as hastily thrown
together as Marcus and Xaropa. His graying hair stood up in

tufts, and his dark blue uniform was not completely closed at the throat. None of them wore appropriate footwear.

"We must. Perform your miracles, Chief."

"It'll take more than a bloody miracle," Luqett muttered. "It'll take Divine Intervention."

"Then, I suggest we all start praying." Marcus brushed past Luqett and strode into his ready room where Xaropa and Jherzik awaited.

Xaropa closed the door. "This is my responsibility, Captain. Lieutenant Jherzik—" he nodded to the night-duty science officer "—is under my command. I will deal with him. We have a more pressing problem than determining why he neglected his duties and did not warn of the Praetorian vessels' approach."

Marcus raised his eyebrow.

"Sir," Jherzik protested, standing at attention. "I did not leave my post. I *was* alert. I do not know where the ships came from. One moment the radar screen was blank and the next, they had us surrounded. Besides the Tegrorian frigate, I identified two Fleurian destroyers and a Stygian scout. Sir, those vessels do not have cloaking capabilities. Yet, they were invisible until they had us surrounded."

Marcus stared hard at the young officer. "How could you not see them approach?" He paused, rubbing his upper lip. "Could Glaxpher have tampered with our sensors so the Praetorian vessels could get into position?"

"That is a possibility," Xaropa conceded. "Security would be able to answer that question."

Marcus thought for a moment. "You said we have a more pressing problem, Mr. Xaropa?"

"Captain, while you were conversing with Stasik Glaxpher on board the Praetorian vessel, I checked the identification sensors. He was in his quarters."

***

"C'mon, sweetcakes. Don't be unsociable." The man from across the road pressed his cheek to the window of the back door. His dark-blond whiskered flesh spread against the glass.

Veronese stood rooted in the kitchen, her hand clutching

the doorknob. Her heart slammed against her ribcage. Fear clawed at her throat.

She could not move. Like a terrified rumiduck caught in the headlights of a speeder, she could only watch in horror as the man taunted her.

"Swe-e-et cakes," he called in a singsong voice. "You should be in bed."

The doorknob, jiggling beneath her sweat-coated palm, snapped her out of her trance. "Go away."

"*I'll* put you to bed." The corner of his mouth, still pressed against the window, curved up in a mockery of a grin.

At the sound of an approaching vehicle, she turned her head. Yesterday's rain had washed away much of the dirt road's surface. The vehicle's wheels clattered on the deep ruts.

The man jerked away from the door. "Later, sweetcakes." He gave her a mock salute before disappearing.

Headlights flashed through the front and side windows of the house as the powerful vehicle roared up the driveway. Then she heard running footsteps.

"Neesie, let me in." Tim pounded on the back door.

Thank the Intrepid Ones. With fingers still numb from fright, she fumbled with the lock.

Her brother rushed inside and slammed the door behind him. "Neesie, what happened?" He grasped her arms. "You're as white as a sheet."

"You missed him. He ran around the other side of the house." When Tim turned to race out, she grabbed the back of his jacket. "Please, do not go. Do not leave me."

She started to shake. Her knees buckled. He wrapped his arms around her and held her against his chest. She, who had never depended on anyone but herself, sobbed in relief.

"Aw, geez, Neesie. Don't cry."

His soothing voice penetrated her terror. Slowly, his comforting presence erased her fears. Her trembling stopped. She struggled to regain her composure.

"I feel silly." She brushed the tears off her cheeks.

"Was it the guy from across the road?"

"Yes. He terrified me. I could not move. I felt as helpless

as a stupid rumiduck."

He handed her a tissue. "A rumiduck?"

She wiped away the rest of her tears. "A large animal on Serenia with antlers like a deer and a duck's bill and not enough sense to flee danger," she said in self-disgust.

"Where could you go? Outside? He might've caught you."

"I feel so—so foolish." Such a ridiculous Terran emotion. "He must have seen me when I was outside. After that fight broke out, I ran back into the house."

"Good God, Neesie. What the hell were you doing out there at this time of night?"

"I couldn't sleep. The house was closing in on me." She laughed shakily. "I work on a star vessel and never felt as claustrophobic as I did tonight."

Tim grabbed the doorknob. "I'm going over there."

She clutched his arm. "No. It will make matters worse."

"How much worse can it be if you don't feel safe?"

"Please, Tim, do not go."

"Then, I'm calling the cops."

Not the authorities. She had to deter him. "If he sees a police vehicle here, he will know I called them."

"You're right." He slowly turned away from the window. "But, you can't be held hostage by fear of your neighbor."

"We could go to the police and report what happened."

He gave her a speculative look. "That might be better."

"Then the cops could stake out the house and catch him selling dope."

"For an alien, you're getting pretty good at the slang." He gave her a small grin.

His praise meant a lot to her. After four days, she had resigned herself to remaining here longer than planned. She had to fit in so as not to arouse suspicion. Though she disliked wearing the wig, she kept it on except when sleeping.

Through television, she was beginning to understand colloquialisms, as well as how Terrans interacted. Her confidence in her ability to impersonate Jessica increased daily. Perhaps going to the authorities would not be as difficult as she had originally thought.

"Let's go," Tim said. "You're out in the country, so we have to go to the sheriff's office instead of the Ann Arbor police. Afterwards, you can spend the night at my place."

She was certain she would not sleep if she stayed at the farmhouse alone. Yet, what if the *Freedom* returned? "I need something."

"Get your purse and let's go."

She ran to her bedroom. She grabbed her *link* off the top of the nightstand and dropped it into Jessica's oversize purse. Recalling a TV commercial, she released a shaky laugh. Her *link*. She couldn't leave home without it.

They spent over an hour convincing the sheriff's deputy something mysterious was going on in the old farmhouse.

"He did not believe me." She buckled the seatbelt.

Tim paused, the key barely in the ignition of the Camaro. "The deputy wrote down everything you said."

"That is not what I meant. He said he would check it out. What does that mean?"

Tim started the engine. "It means what he said. He'll send a patrol car out and check the house."

"They aren't going to find anything now. You can bet your bippy he's closed up shop." She folded her arms in front of her.

He chuckled. "God, you sound like my sister."

"I *am* your sister."

He sobered. "Sorry. You sounded so much like Jess."

She clasped her hands in her lap. "You miss her."

"Yeah." He gave her a lop-sided grin. "She can be a pain in the butt, but yeah, I miss her. I don't know what I'd do if she was gone for good."

Anguish stabbed deep in her chest. He wanted her gone so Jessica could return. Veronese was allowing herself to feel so many emotions. Fear, betrayal, desolation. Perhaps it was better to shield oneself, as she had learned on Serenia.

After a moment of silence, he glanced over at her. "Nothing against you, Neesie."

She swallowed past a lump in her throat. "Of course."

"Seriously. I really like you, kid." He cast her a quick grin and patted her leg.

Warmth spread through her chest, nearly displacing the earlier hurt. "I like you, too. *Kid.*"

"I want Jess to come back," he continued, "but it would be really great if you could stay, too."

"This is not my home."

He drove in silence through the quiet Ann Arbor streets. At this hour—so close to dawn—even the university students were asleep.

"You still haven't heard from your people, have you?" he asked.

She stared out the side window for a moment before lowering it. The crisp night air smelled different here in the city. At the farm, it was fresher, cleaner. She caught herself twirling the ends of the wig. It didn't have the same feel as her own short hair.

"I keep trying to reach any Alliance vessel," she said. "I call three times a day. All I get is static."

"Maybe you dropped that communicator and something loosened up."

"I did *not* drop the *link.* Even if I had, its protective casing is built to withstand abuse. Nothing is wrong with the *link.* If the *Freedom* was up there—" she nodded toward the sky "—they would answer. Any Alliance vessel would. Only a direct order from Space Fleet Command could recall all research vessels. And then for only the most urgent reason."

Tim parked in front of his apartment building. "An urgent reason? Like what?"

"The Alliance could be at war."

***

"Stasik?" Marcus stood in the open portal to Glaxpher's quarters. Security Chief Hrvibm and Science Officer Xaropa waited behind him.

The Navigation Officer rolled over in his bunk and pressed a button to illuminate the room. Blinking, Glaxpher leaned up on one elbow. "Marcus? What are you doing here?"

"May we come in and speak to you?" Marcus worded it as a request instead of a command.

When the short Security Chief moved from behind Marcus where she had been hidden, Stasik Glaxpher's eyes widened. "Of course."

They entered Stasik's quarters and waited while he donned a robe. He scrubbed his eyes and yawned widely as he gestured for them to be seated. They stood.

Stasik appeared surprised. "This does not look like a social visit, my friend."

Marcus shook his head. "There has been an incident." He explained about being caught off-guard by the Praetorium.

"How could this be? Our external sensors should have registered the ships as soon as they entered our quadrant."

Stasik looked genuinely puzzled. *Was it all an act?* Marcus had seen Stasik seated in the commander's chair of a rebel ship. He had heard Stasik's distinctive voice.

"I spoke to the Praetorian commander." Marcus paused. "He was you."

Stasik Glaxpher stared in open-mouthed amazement. "You cannot be serious. Me? A member of the Praetorium? Why, that is— Marcus, are you accusing me of treason?"

Stasik's outrage appeared genuine. Marcus held up his hand. "Mr. Xaropa, tell him what you discovered."

"While the Captain conversed with the Praetorian commander, the identification scanners indicated you were here, in your quarters."

"Of course, I was here."

"I checked the transport room," Security Chief Hrvibm said. "The officer on duty had been tranquilized. According to the log, someone transported away right before the ship was surrounded."

"You think it was me?" Stasik stared in horror at this information. "Marcus, my friend. You must believe me. I have been here. Asleep."

Marcus said nothing.

"If you think I transported away, how could I be here? Did the log say I transported back?"

"The transport log developed a malfunction shortly after that," the short, stocky Hrvibm said. "It stopped or was turned off."

Stasik turned from Hrvibm to stare sharply at Marcus. "I could never commit such a reprehensible act, Marcus. You know I am loyal to the Alliance. Say you believe me, my friend."

What do I believe? Nothing was as it should be. His own experience with an impersonator gave Marcus pause. "Until further notice, Mr. Glaxpher, you are confined to your quarters."

Marcus walked down the hall with Xaropa and Hrvibm trailing behind. Suddenly, Marcus stopped. In all the confusion, he had not realized a member of his executive staff had not reported to the bridge during the encounter with the Praetorium. Surely, a Zorfan warrior would not ignore a Red Alert.

He whirled around and stared at Security Chief Hrvibm. "Where is Mr. Klegznef?"

TEN

Jessie awoke to the Beach Boys singing about California Girls. She was home. Then, she stared up at the storage area above her bunk and realized she was still on board the *Freedom*. She tapped her *link* to turn off her wake-up call.

Chief Luqett had given Jessie her own *link* while Security examined both of Marcus's. After four days, they still couldn't figure out who had disabled the *links*. Nor had Chief Hrvibm traced the source of the fake "Marcus's" transmission. That bulldog-shaped female reminded Jessie of one of Tim's old girlfriends. Both had the social skills of a rhinoceros.

Jessie rolled out of bed and staggered to the mini-replicator. Inside the little box, programmed last night by her *link*, she found her morning cup of seleria. Better than a cup of coffee to kick-start her into action. She didn't need to report to her post in Engineering until mid-afternoon. After breakfast, she normally followed Chief Luqett, learning the ship's technology.

Luqett was a terrific teacher, the best she'd ever had. He treated her with respect, even though her technological knowledge was very primitive. Her eagerness to learn pleased him. He often praised her quick grasp of basic principles and her ability to extrapolate the information and then apply it to his hypothetical situations. What would have happened if she'd had teachers like Luqett? She might have even enjoyed school.

She stepped under the sonic shower. This was one advanced technology she didn't like. Even though she knew water was a precious commodity on board a starship and the number of crewmembers prohibited everyone bathing with water, she couldn't get used to showering without it. The only good thing about it was that her thick hair didn't take forever to dry.

Before she dressed in the Engineering crew's dark blue uniform, she pulled on the one-piece undergarment. She'd had to request underwear and additional uniforms from Procurement since her twin's did not fit. All that ice cream returned to haunt Jessie when she'd tried to wear Veronese's clothing. That's when she decided to start spending time in the exercise room. Along with the good-tasting, healthy food, she'd made up her mind to get into shape.

However, this 'superior' culture needed a new fashion designer. While one-piece uniforms might be okay for males, they were a pain for women. The undergarment supported her breasts, flattened her tummy, and slimmed her hips. That was not the problem. She rather liked her appearance in the dark blue jumpsuit. No panty lines, no lacy bra showing through the silk-like uniform. The problem with one-piece garments—as every woman on Earth knew—was going to the bathroom.

After she pulled on thin socks and shoes, she braided her hair. She'd lost her scrunchie. She had a pretty good idea Marcus had it. After she'd fled his quarters following that kiss, she'd arrived in Engineering flustered and with her hair in complete disarray. No way was she going back to his quarters and ask him to give back her hair band. She'd do without it.

She finished her seleria and was ready for the day. She strapped on the *link* and hit the button for the door.

Nothing happened.

Sometimes, she didn't aim it properly. She tried again.

Nothing. No door. Nothing.

She squinted at the wall. No wavy outline.

"Not me, too," she groaned out loud. She pressed a different button. "Computer, my door won't open."

"Security has deactivated your portal."

"What!" She was locked in? At least, she wasn't cut off. "Connect me with Security."

"Security."

She recognized that voice. "Hey, Drakus, is that you?"

"Yes, Wyndom. Drakus here."

"You gonna tell me why I'm locked in my quarters?"

"Captain Viator ordered the protective measures."

"What!"

"Please, Wyndom. The *link* is quite sensitive. It is not necessary to shout. I can hear you perfectly well."

"Sorry, Drakus. What's going on?"

"I will locate the Captain, and he will explain."

"I want out of here before I go bonkers."

Drakus giggled. "Bonkers?"

"Yeah. It's a technical term, and the results aren't pretty. C'mon, you little troll, tell me what's going on."

"Ms. Wyndom, Ensign Drakus is not a troll."

Jessie stared at her *link*. "Who is this?"

"Security Chief Hrvibm."

Jessie should have recognized the deep, froggy voice. It matched the woman's bulldog shape.

"Please be patient, Wyndom," Drakus said. "I will check with the Captain."

"Well, get the lead out. My little replicator doesn't do breakfast—I mean Morning Repast. I'm so hungry, I could eat a horse."

She heard a choked sound and a giggle. "Terrans do not really eat horses, do they?"

"Drakus, if you don't hurry up and let me out, I might even eat barbecued troll."

Drakus muttered something that sounded suspiciously like 'don't even think about it' before disconnecting.

At least she wasn't stuck in here with no contact with the rest of the ship like she and Marcus had been in his quarters.

She was pacing the small room when a chime rang. Cute doorbell. She'd never heard it before. She tried using the *link*. It still didn't work. "I can't open the door."

The wall parted. Marcus stood on the other side of the threshold. "Security told me you were awake."

She planted her hands on her hips. "It's about time." She walked to the door.

"Be care—"

Something smacked her so hard she fell on her butt.

"—ful. I ordered a force field around your quarters."

Stunned by the electric shock-like jolt, she continued to sit on the floor. *Damn, that hurt.* She must have lost weight. She wasn't as well-padded as before. "I'm a prisoner?" He spoke into his *link.* "Security, turn off the field around Ms. Wyndom's quarters." A moment later, he walked through the portal, closing it behind him. He reached down to help her up. "It is important you not leave Engineering."

"Why?" As soon as she stood, she withdrew her hand from his. His touch started all kinds of prickly sensations, stronger than the jolt of the force field. She didn't need that distraction now. "I thought you trusted me."

"There was an incident last night. I ordered the additional force field to protect you from being transported aboard a Praetorian vessel."

As if being beamed aboard one alien ship wasn't bad enough, she was in danger of being kidnapped again? By other aliens? "Why would the Praetorium want me?"

"They want this ship. I wouldn't surrender. I believe they want to hold you hostage until the Alliance gives in to their demands. The Alliance would never endanger a member of a primitive species." He ignored her sharp look. "Normally, the field around the Engineering sector, including your quarters, would have protected you. However, once you left to go up to the dining area or the exercise room, you were vulnerable."

"I don't understand. I thought I had to be in the transport room to be transported off ship."

"Yes, if you were sent *from* the ship. However, the renegades could easily lock onto you and transport you aboard their vessel."

"Geez, Louise. Kidnapped again?"

He nodded. "It was possible."

"Now what? I have to stay in my quarters all the time?"

"No, just stay in Engineering. The security field around this part of the ship will protect you. You will be safe as long as you stay here. You would not be protected elsewhere, for instance, in the dining area or exercise room."

Just when she was finally enjoying exercising, it was forbidden. She could forget ever wearing Veronese's uniforms now.

"I instructed Security to maintain a special field around your quarters. The incident last night involved one of my senior officers who quite possibly could have changed the system that protects Engineering." Marcus explained what had happened with the Praetorian ships and his navigation officer.

"This is getting really weird."

He rubbed the bridge of his nose. "I cannot believe Stasik Glaxpher is a traitor. I have known him since our Academy days. He is my friend."

"You have friends?" Then, seeing the bleakness in his eyes, she was mortified at her thoughtless quip. "I'm sorry. I shouldn't have said that."

Waving aside her apology, he sat in the straight-back desk chair. "It might not have been Stasik."

"Not that GND thing again? I thought you said it's illegal."

He gave her a look.

"Okay, the bad guys wouldn't be bothered by legalities. This keeps getting weirder. People switch identities right and left around here."

"We are not certain Glaxpher was impersonated. He is confined to his quarters until Security discovers whether he actually was asleep there or transported back from the rebel ship. Our sensors indicated he was in both places."

She perched on the corner of the desk, a short distance away from him. "Geez, Captain, you've got problems. Your sensors are all screwed up. Anybody could be the imposter. How do you know who to trust?"

"Good question." He scrubbed his hand down his face. "I trust you."

A warm thrill flowed through her. Though pleased with his trust, her first reaction was embarrassment. "That's because I'm from a primitive culture and wouldn't know how to switch into somebody else's body or mess with your computers."

She looked at him more carefully. Lines creased his

forehead. The brackets around his mouth seemed more pronounced. A hint of shadow smudged under his eyes. "Did you get any sleep last night? You look whipped."

His mouth curved up. "Your expressions amuse me."

"Good, old Jess. The comedian."

He stared at her, his silver eyes probing. "Why do you belittle yourself?"

She looked away.

"You do not have a very high opinion of your abilities. Why? Chief Luqett has nothing but praise for you. He said you are the best student he has ever had."

"Probably because I have so much to learn," she mumbled.

He picked up her hand and tugged until she looked at him. "Do Terran parents not teach their children to say 'thank you' for a compliment?"

"Sometimes, parents are too busy with their own lives to teach their children anything but their expectations."

His eyes grew sad.

She tried to withdraw her hand, with no success. "Guess I should just say 'thanks' and get it over with, huh?"

He was probing a little too deep. Her reaction to serious situations had always been a wise-crack. It often saved her from misinterpretations. He didn't mean anything by his compliments.

"Jessica, according to Luqett, you have great natural abilities. In my world, this is valued. You have also shown initiative in adversity. The manner in which you found a way out of my quarters is admirable. And, you have compassion." He cleared his throat. "You realized how difficult heights are for me, yet you did not ridicule."

"Yes, well..."

He stood and pulled her up with him. "You are a very special person." He stepped closer. Then, he reached out and cupped her cheek in his palm.

His touch generated heat that spread through her body. The last time they had been this close, he kissed her. She wanted another kiss. Then, she remembered his self-recriminations and pulled away. "How do I know you're the real Marcus? You sure don't sound like him."

"Touché." He smiled.

"Ah, hah. Now, I know you're an imposter. The very proper Captain has no sense of humor." She didn't really believe the person standing in front of her wasn't Marcus. She just didn't want him kissing her and apologizing later for his lack of control.

"Jessica." The deep timber of his voice vibrated through her. He was Marcus, all right. Only the real McCoy gave her goosebumps when he spoke. "I—"

"Bridge to Captain Viator." His *link* cut off whatever he was going to say next.

"Hell," he spit out.

She couldn't believe it. "My, my, my. You know how to swear?" She wondered what the equivalent of 'hell' was in Serenian and wished the translator hadn't converted his word into her language.

He shot her a scorching look before tapping his *link*. "Viator, here. What is it, Mr. Xaropa?"

"The Tegrorian frigate we encountered last night is approaching."

"Evade. I will be right there." He tapped off his *link* and started for the door.

"Saved by the bell?" She raised her eyebrow.

He spun around, then clasped the back of her neck. He pulled her close. She stopped breathing. He bent his head and captured her mouth.

The kiss was hard, demanding. And over much too soon. He released her. Without a word, he strode out.

Whew. What had happened to Marcus? He was certainly not acting like himself. Compliments? Swearing at an interruption? And then that kiss? Holy smokes. His kiss about knocked her socks off.

She'd been teasing him before. Now, she wondered. Was that really Marcus?

***

After leaving Jessica, Marcus stopped in Luqett's office. "Chief, we need to get to Serenia at the greatest possible speed."

"But, sir—"

"Do it. I do not care what you have to do but get us home before that Praetorian ship engages us in battle."

He ignored Luqett's wary look. Marcus never talked to his crew in such an abrupt manner. He did not bother to explain. Nothing was more important than getting home to Serenia.

"Aye, sir. I'll do my best."

"Do more than your best. And keep Jessica down here. By the Intrepid Ones, the Praetorium will not take her."

Luqett sucked in a breath.

Marcus gave him a hard look. "Protect her."

"Like she was my own...daughter," Luqett hastily amended at Marcus's glare.

Ignoring Luqett's speculative look, Marcus spun on his heel then had to wait for the conveyance. Too many things had gone wrong on this trip. Starting with Veronese Qilana and her ridiculous notion of visiting her biological parents and the planet from which she had come.

What was Qilana thinking? Her parents were the people who raised her. Why would she search for those whose only contribution was her genetic makeup? Why would she want to visit such an alien planet? A society so primitive most of its inhabitants did not believe in extra-terrestrial life.

Their arrogance astounded him. Did Terrans think they were the only sentient beings in the universe?

He had no inclination to visit Earth.

"Sir?" From Drakus's tone, Marcus guessed this was not the first attempt to capture his attention since leaving the conveyance.

"Yes." He kept walking toward the bridge.

Drakus appeared taken aback by his sharp tone. "When you have a moment, Chief Hrvibm would like to see you."

"I will be there after I put out a couple of fires."

Drakus's large black eyes grew round. "Fires, sir?"

"A Terran expression, Drakus. My presence is needed on the bridge. I will be with your chief shortly."

"Yes, sir. Very good, sir." Drakus nearly tripped over his

wide feet in his haste to leave.

If he continued in this manner, Marcus would alienate his entire crew. He reached the bridge only to discover the rebel ship still pursued them. Klegznef approached.

Not again. Earlier, the First Officer had lashed out at Marcus for failing to alert him during the previous night's danger. Security found that Klegznef's *link* had been turned off as well as signals from the main computer to his quarters. Klegznef swore he had not disengaged either.

Marcus hoped Klegznef had calmed down by now.

"Captain, it is strange that the rebels found us. Following when we are cloaked should not be possible."

He, too, was puzzled by the Praetorian ship's dogged pursuit. "Your conclusion, Mr. Klegznef."

"Either a tracking devise was planted on this ship or someone on board is relaying our coordinates."

"My conclusion, also. Good work, Mr. Klegznef."

Did he detect a half-smile on the Zorfan's lips? Interesting. Klegznef never responded to a compliment.

"How do you suggest we proceed, Mr. Klegznef?"

"Sir," he ground out, "I suggest we eliminate the easiest possibility. Mr. Xaropa is searching the main computer for transmissions leaving the ship. I have instructed Security to begin a thorough physical search of the entire ship for a tracking device."

"Very good. Carry on, Mr. Klegznef. You appear to have everything under control." He noted the brief flash of pride that crossed the Zorfan's gray face. "I will be with Chief Hrvibm. Keep me informed as to your progress."

Moments later, he found the Security Chief doling out orders to her staff. She had divided the ship into sections and issued instruments that would detect a tracking device. He waited until the crew departed.

"Please sit down, Captain." Hrvibm sat at her desk.

He pulled up a chair. "You have new information?"

"Sir, I traced the transmission your imposter recorded."

He raised his eyebrow.

"We originally thought it was a live transmission. The

message was recorded from your quarters."

He nodded.

"The time of the recording was while you were escorting the Terran around the ship."

"Why do you find this significant?"

"If you recall, sir, you were interrupted. Later, you retrieved the Terran and—"

"She has a name, Chief."

"Yes, sir. You retrieved Wyndom and took her to your quarters."

He caught himself drumming his fingers on the Security Chief's desk. "Where and when the original transmission took place is irrelevant if we do not know who impersonated me."

"Yes, sir, I was getting to that."

Hrvibm's thoroughness was her greatest asset. She doggedly followed every clue in an investigation. She would pick apart each detail before she came to a conclusion. However, she also seemed to think that her report should include every detail, whether significant or not.

Hrvibm folded her stubby fingers together. "You sent Ensign Drakus to continue Wyndom's tour of the ship."

"Yes, yes."

"He overheard Lieutenant Melora say she was sent by Mr. Klegznef."

Marcus often had to control his impatience waiting for the Security Chief to get to the point. Today, he had reached his limit. "Hrvibm, cut to the chase."

She stared at him with an open mouth.

He thought the Terran expression appropriate. "Who, Chief? That is the question. Who impersonated me?"

"Uh, sir, uh—"

"Spit it out, Hrvibm. We have a traitor on board. More than one, possibly. Who is it?"

She cleared her throat. "Genetic nucleotide duplication can only be used by a blood relative."

He nodded impatiently.

She sat back with a triumphant look on her wide face. "It is my conclusion that Lieutenant Melora in conjunction with

First Officer Klegznef are the conspirators."

He shook his head. "That is not possible."

"But, sir, Aurelia Melora is your cousin."

"No, Chief, she is not. A little-known fact does not appear in my records. I was adopted."

***

Veronese Qilana was a prisoner.

After two days living in her brother's apartment, she chafed at the inactivity. At least on the farm, she had work to occupy her time. She needed to return, but her overprotective brother refused to take her back.

Did Jessica feel the same sense of imprisonment aboard the *Freedom*? The confines of the starship plus inactivity must be boring.

Veronese never appreciated more the privacy on an Alliance vessel than she did living in such close proximity to a *slob*. That word described her brother perfectly. He left newspapers, pieces of paper with notes, and his clothes strewn all over the place. And little white clumps of lint from his socks decorated the brown carpet. It was enough to drive her bonkers.

She understood another colloquialism: climbing the walls. Tim's apartment was so small she kept running into him when he wasn't at the university teaching. His 'office' for his free-lance consulting work took up a large corner of the living room.

Most of the time, instead of working, he pumped her for information about what it was like to live and work in space. She understood another colloquialism—he drove her crazy.

She needed to return to the farm. Although she had left her *link* on, there was still no contact from her ship. She was afraid when they were unable to locate her at the farm with genetic identification sensors, they would fear the worst had happened.

"Tim, I need to go back to the farm."

"We went yesterday. Do you need more tools?"

"No. I want to return to the farm to stay." She waved her hand in frustration at the pieces of a lawnmower engine littering the newspaper on top of the coffee table. "I can't work here. This place is too small."

"Don't ask me again, Neesie. That guy meant you harm."

"I don't care. I need to go back."

"Don't you get it?" he yelled. "He could kill you or worse. You'd wish you were dead after he got done with you."

Veronese stared at him. No one had ever yelled at her before. Serenians did not yell. They looked at you with disappointment, expecting you to see the error of your ways and conform.

It worked. So did Tim's yelling.

"I can't ask you to accompany me. Your work is here. I must go back. I must be ready when my ship returns."

"And what if they've left you here? What if your spaceship developed engine trouble or transport trouble or—" He paused. "What was the name of those bad guys?"

"The Praetorium."

"Right. What if the Praetorium started a war?"

"No. That will never happen. We are a peaceful coalition. The Alliance cannot go to war."

The prospect of war terrified her. After watching vid accounts of the Great Intergalactic War, she had had nightmares for weeks.

"My ship will return for me," she said with more assurance than she felt. "I must trade places with Jessica. She belongs here. I do not."

***

"Once again you have failed," the Leader raged. "We need that ship."

"I do not understand why he would not believe Glaxpher is the traitor. The transformation was flawless."

"You have underestimated him from the beginning."

"Yes." The Accomplice chose not to point out that the Leader had underestimated the enemy, also.

"And the Terran? Why have you not transported her to my ship?"

"She is guarded by a special force field."

"And *you* are unable to removed it?" the Leader asked in

disbelief.

"To do so would bring suspicion on me. I will wait until an opportunity presents itself."

"You will do well to remember that time is of the essence. We need that ship."

ELEVEN

Jessie watched their approach to the planet through the small viewscreen in Engineering. Confinement to this area had worn thin. She couldn't expend her energy in the exercise room since it was out of Engineering and the protection of its force field. She couldn't go up to the research labs to talk to Aurelia. She couldn't go to the lounge and dance with her co-workers. Climbing vertical ladders in the access conduits for exercise just wasn't fun.

At least she had a few co-workers who wanted her to join them. When she had first started working in Engineering, the crew tolerated her presence. She sensed a bit of jealousy because of the way Luqett had taken her under his wing. Some seemed wary, as if still afraid she carried some deadly disease from Earth.

Probably her worst *offense* was that she'd discovered what was wrong with the engine. That made them look bad for not finding it themselves. They were the experts. She was merely a Terran. After running the diagnostics on the analyzer, Luqett instructed her to keep to herself the fact that it had been reprogrammed. She couldn't even explain it wasn't their fault for not finding the problem.

She tried to do her share of the work. Although she learned quickly, she often had to ask for assistance. At first, help was grudgingly given. But then the crew became accustomed to her willingness to learn and her ability to laugh at her mistakes. They had just started treating her like one of their own when the Praetorium threatened to kidnap her.

Her co-workers offered sympathy that she was confined to the Engineering area. A couple of crewmembers even ate their meals with her instead of going up to the dining room, so she wouldn't have to eat alone.

More than missing the freedom of movement, she missed seeing Marcus. She knew he was busy, that one lonely Terran couldn't occupy his time. But, she hadn't seen him for two days, since he had come to her quarters. And kissed her.

She ached to feel his arms around her, yearned for the touch of his smooth lips against hers. Her sleep had been restless as she dreamed of making love with him.

She watched with avid interest as the *Freedom* approached the space station above Serenia. The station was not so different from those depicted in sci-fi movies, a long axis with a circular structure near the top. Spokes fanned out from the center to the inside perimeter of the structure.

The *Freedom* was in a holding pattern, waiting for traffic to clear so they could enter spacedock. A variety of vessels also waited, while shuttles to the surface zipped by.

"A pretty sight, eh, lassie?"

She turned around at Luqett's approach. "Like in the movies. I can't believe all the different spaceships."

"Aye, 'tis a busy place. Alliance headquarters is on Serenia, so this is a main transfer point. But, I was referring to the planet itself. What do ye think of it?"

"It reminds me of pictures I've seen of Earth taken from space. A big blue marble."

"Without the pollution of Earth, eh, lassie?"

The planet, even viewed on a small screen, had sharp contrasts of colors. The blue of the water, the brown and green of the land, even the swirls of white clouds seemed so vivid. So clean. A snow-capped mountain range rose up not far from the coast.

"If ye think it's busy up here, wait until ye see Malawea. That's the major city." He pointed to a sprawling metropolis in the area between the mountains and the ocean.

"I don't think I'll get to see it, sir. I'm still confined here in Engineering."

"I dinna think the Captain intends to keep ye down here forever. Ye'll get shore leave like the rest of us."

The ship was given permission to commence docking procedures. Once the ship was in position, a tractor beam brought it into the landing area.

Jessie waited until they were docked before asking, "You don't think the Praetorium can transport me to their ship if I leave here?"

"They wouldn't dare violate Serenian space. No, lassie, now that we're home, ye needn't worry about the rebels."

"I think I'll wait to hear from Mar— the Captain."

Luqett glanced around. Many crewmembers, eager to disembark, had left their posts as soon as spacedock took control of the vessel. The few who remained behind were across the room shutting down systems.

"The Captain has taken a liking to ye," he said softly.

Heat flared in her face. "I, uh, I'm not, uh—"

"And I think ye've taken a liking to him as well." He gave her a knowing look. "He works hard, our Captain does. This ship should not be the only thing that is important to him. Our Captain needs a home and a soulmate."

She gave a short laugh. "Playing matchmaker, are you?"

He just grinned.

"And you, Chief? Do you have a home and a soulmate?"

"Aye. And my soulmate knows that my job doesn't end once we're in spacedock. I have two days of work first, instructing the Maintenance and Repair crew what needs to be done before we head out to get ye back to yer planet."

"I'd like to help. I want to learn as much as I can before I...go back." She wasn't sure why her voice faltered. She did want to return home.

***

Veronese tried again.

Tim wouldn't change his mind. "You can't go back to the farm alone."

"Jessica will lose her business if I'm not there. I've tried to do some of the work, but I need tools that are there. Her customers will be angry when they cannot reach her."

"I don't want you to stay at the farm by yourself. Not while that guy is still across the road. I called the sheriff, and they haven't seen anything unusual. Damn. I don't want you to go back." He paused for a moment. "Tell you what. I'll pack a bag and stay there with you."

"You do not need to do that."

"I do. It's my fault that guy's harassing you. If I hadn't talked Jess out of calling the cops, he'd be history."

"It's not your fault he's a criminal."

"I should know you can't turn a blind eye to what's happening in your neighborhood. I put my sister in danger."

"Jessica would not blame you."

"I was talking about both my sisters." He began to pack up his notebook computer. "I'll stay with you."

"Your classes?"

"I'll get someone to cover for me."

"But your consulting work..."

"Have computer, will travel." He grinned. "Somebody's gotta keep an eye on you."

***

For the past two days, ever since arriving at Serenia, Jessie had worked side by side with the Maintenance and Repair crew from the space station. Most of the Engineering crew had been given leave. The few who remained, like Jessie, didn't live on Serenia. They performed routine maintenance. Larger repair work was the domain of the M&R crew.

Luqett supervised, encouraging her in her efforts to be of use. Her current job, changing the lubricant in the servo-drive gearbox, meant she was lying flat on her back in just about the smallest access tunnel she'd been in so far. Her arms ached from reaching overhead. Although she had drained the old lubricant, green residue leaked down her arms or dripped on her face.

With the back of her hand, she pushed the protective goggles up higher on her nose. No wonder the crewman had a big grin on his face when she offered to do his job. She thought his delight was because he got to leave early.

Finally, she tightened the filter in place. Now, to slide back out. She was sweaty and grimy and couldn't wait to get into the shower, even if it was only a sonic one. She'd give anything for a soap and water bath.

She scooted on her butt to the hatch opening. Once she felt her feet dangle out of the hole, she wiggled until her hips stopped her. This was the third narrow access tunnel she'd been in today. Each one had its own configuration that necessitated her twisting her body to get in and out.

"Stuck again, Ms. Wyndom?"

Oh, sugar jets. Just when she thought it was safe to come out of a tunnel. "Go away, Captain, until I get out of here."

"On the contrary. You may need some assistance."

"Are you laughing at me?"

"Moi?" He chuckled.

Was he making jokes? Captain Stick-in-the-Mud? Laughing? She wiggled to get her hips out of the opening. Then, she rolled onto her stomach and—

"I have you." His large hands encircled her waist and, with little effort, pulled her out of the tunnel. He kept his arms around her, letting her backside slide down his body until her feet touched the floor.

For several moments, she remained there, pressed back against him, feeling every inch of his hard, muscular body. After whipping off her goggles, she twisted around. Holding her breath, she searched his eyes for a sign of his intent. When he dropped his hands from her waist, she breathed out.

He stepped back a fraction of an inch. Maybe a piece of paper could have gotten between them but she wouldn't place any bets on it.

He reached toward her. Was he going to hold her neck like he'd done before? Would he kiss her? God, how she wanted to feel his lips on hers again. With nerves strung tighter than a torsion spring, she moistened her lips.

His gaze followed her tongue. Then, he touched her cheek and...rubbed. Rubbed?

"You have lubricating fluid on your face." He showed her his fingers, smeared with the green substance.

Okay, God, open up a hole and let me disappear. He *hadn't* been about to kiss her. She stepped back, banging up against the wall. An echo resounded as her head hit the hollow metal.

"Are you all right?" The concern in his voice was reflected in his eyes. He again reached for her, this time to gently rub the back of her head.

She twisted her mouth in a wry smile. "Sure. I've got a hard head." She sidestepped away from him.

"Chief Luqett said I would find you here. Are you finished?"

She bent to pick up the rag she'd dropped when he pulled her out of the tunnel. She wiped her hands then turned the cloth over until she found a clean spot. She wiped her forehead and cheeks.

He took the cloth away from her. "You have a smudge on your chin." He wiped it. "And your nose." Again, he used the cloth to remove the lubricating fluid.

He crowded her against the wall. There was no place for her to go. She glanced around. Nobody else was working on this level. Several minutes ago, she'd heard the other crewman finish up. She'd told him not to wait for her.

She was alone with Marcus and, Holy Mother of God, she wanted him with a passion that took her breath away. He stood so near she felt his intoxicating heat. Her breathing quickened. Her pulse pounded in her ears. She licked her lips again.

"Are you going to kiss me or what?" she blurted out and then closed her eyes. "Damn, damn, damn." She banged her head against the wall in time with her curses. The heat that flared in her face had nothing to do with passion. "Take me out and shoot me. With my mouth, I don't deserve to live."

She heard the rumble of a low chuckle and opened her eyes. Marcus threw his head back and laughed out loud.

"So glad you find me amusing, Captain." She started to slide along the wall to the right. He shot out his left hand, hitting the wall next to her ear.

She jumped at the sound.

When she tried to slide to the left, he blocked her progress with his right hand next to her head.

"We have unfinished business." He lowered his mouth until it was a hair away from hers. His breath smelled fresh, a hint of citrus. How clean he smelled. Unlike her.

"I take it back. Don't kiss me. I don't want you to."

"Liar." He grinned.

She shook her head. "I reek. I'm sweaty and—"

His nostrils twitched. "Eau de Engine Fluid, I believe."

He chuckled. "And hard-working woman. An intoxicating scent."

"I want a shower."

"You want me to kiss you. Your eyes are transparent."

She would have answered, but her tongue stuck to the roof of her mouth.

"Do all Terrans say one thing and mean another?"

At the word 'Terran', her tongue unstuck. "Is this where the lizard comes out of your mouth and enters my body so I become one of you?"

"What!" He dropped his hands and stepped back, nearly overbalancing against the railing behind him.

He looked so startled she started to giggle. His dark brows furrowed. He'd looked at her with many expressions since she met him. But never as furious as he did now.

"Everything is a joke to you, Jessica, isn't it?"

Quickly, he walked around the railing and started down the vertical ladder in the manhole. She'd really put her foot in it now. He must be so mad at her that he wasn't even afraid to go down the ladder.

"Wait." She crouched to reach through the railing and clutch the shoulder of his uniform. His face was level with hers. "I'm sorry. I don't know what gets into me sometimes. My mouth runs on all by itself when I don't know what to say. I was... nervous. You make me feel... I don't know. Things I've never felt before. I'm, I'm sorry. I—"

"Jessica, be still." Through the railing, he cupped the back of her neck, drawing her closer to him. "The only way I got through two days of meetings down on the surface was thinking about what I would do when I saw you again."

Then, he kissed her.

It was everything she wanted. And was afraid of. His kiss turned her knees to jelly, and her stomach resembled the agitation cycle of a washing machine.

Who the hell cared if an alien being invaded her body? *Oh, invade me. Please.*

With the lower rail between them, she held his head and kissed him back. Her fingers roamed the back of his neck, feeling its smoothness. She wanted to touch more of him. Snaking her fingers along the stand-up collar of his uniform, she reached the front clasp. Slowly, she separated it.

Would he stop her boldness? She looked into his eyes. They glittered, intense, eager, urging her to continue. She spread the uniform open wider, then worked her hands into the opening. His chest was so smooth. He didn't stop her from touching him.

Resting her palm against his heart, she felt its steady thudding begin to race. Her heart hustled to catch up. His mouth left hers, trailing down her neck. She arched her head, willing him to go lower. Cool air touched her skin. While she opened his uniform, he must have done the same to hers.

He cupped her breast, kneading it, stoking the tip. Every stroke, intensified by the silky slide of her undergarment, zinged down her belly to between her legs. Still crouched on the walkway, the railing between them, she felt his warm hand trail down the front of her. When he stroked between her legs, she gasped as something hot and wet exploded inside her.

She sat back with a thump. "Oh. My. God."

Marcus stared at her dazed expression. As soon as he realized she was stunned by her climax, he bounded up the steps and around the railing. He stooped to lift her up.

Her face burned bright red. She ducked her head, refusing to meet his eyes. He tipped her chin. "You need not be embarrassed," he said.

Standing, he drew her close. Her uniform hung open, as did his. He sucked in his breath at the sight of her creamy skin. Then, he buried his face in the crook of her neck. With his tongue, he traced the tendon along the side of her neck. How sweet she tasted.

She trembled in his arms. She amazed him. She was so free with her emotions, unencumbered by societal strictures.

His intense pleasure at her wild response surprised him. No female had reacted to him like Jessica. Was that what drew him to her? Her eagerness, her delight?

From sheer habit, he tried to restrain his body's response to her touch. Yet blazing heat tore through his blood as their bodies met. He nearly lost control.

He slipped his hands inside her uniform, around her waist. She wore the standard-issue garment all female crewmembers wore under their uniform. He cursed its one-piece construction. He stroked up her back until he reached the top of the garment. There, her skin waited for his touch. He slipped the narrow strap off her shoulder. The undergarment drooped to expose the top of her breast. He bent his head and kissed the creamy skin.

Her low moan of pleasure brought him back to reality. They were standing on a second-level walkway, in sight of anyone who ventured into the open conduit. Although the M&R crew had departed for the day, intense security—in light of the Praetorium's latest aggression—was maintained. A guard checking Engineering would certainly investigate noises.

He would not subject her to embarrassment. He stepped back. After closing her uniform, he brushed her hair, loosened from its braid, away from her face.

His own uniform hung open and she still rested her fingers over his heart. Her touch burned his skin, intensifying his pleasure. With reluctance, he gently pulled her hands away and straightened his own attire.

"This is neither the time nor the place." He gently touched her face.

"Will there be a time and a place, Marcus?" she murmured.

He searched her blue eyes, darkened with passion. "Do you want there to be?"

She bit her bottom lip. Then, she cupped his jaw in her small, capable hand, her work-roughened fingertips a gentle abrasion against his cheek. "Yes," she whispered.

His heart slammed against his ribs. He exerted every iota of hard-earned control to keep from coupling with her right there on the narrow platform. As he told her, this was not the appropriate place. Nor was his apartment in the city. She needed to know him, to know who he was. He could not talk about his deepest secret on the ship. Here, he was the Captain. A proper Serenian captain. Even his apartment reflected his proper Serenian lifestyle.

Revealing his secret could only be done in the place where he felt safe. His uncle's farm.

He took a steadying breath. "I came to invite you down to Serenia."

Her eyes grew wide. Excitement danced in their blue depths. "Omigosh. Of course. I'd love to go down there. I didn't think I should...could leave the ship."

"I passed Luqett at the shuttle bay. He told me to 'spring' you. You are not a prisoner on the ship. I heard you have been working long hours not just since we arrived in spacedock two days ago but ever since you've been aboard."

"There is so much to learn, so much to do." Her hands fluttered as she talked.

"You have been taking other crewmembers' duties and letting them go down to their homes."

She shrugged. "Yeah, well, they have families down there. I don't. Besides, I didn't want to go alone."

"I would like you to come home with me." He stared hard into her eyes. "Do you understand?"

She took in a shaky breath. "Y-Yes." She lifted her chin. "Yes, Marcus, I want to go home with you."

He breathed out in relief. "Are you finished here?"

She nodded. "Except for replacing the access hatch."

He held the cover while she tightened the fasteners. When she stood, she gave him a long look. "You came up a vertical ladder again."

He swallowed. "I must be a little bonkers."

Her peal of laughter tickled him. "Marcus, you amaze me. Stick with me, kid, and I'll have you talking like a native." She rounded the railing.

He stopped her. "I will go first."

She gave him a droll look. "You just want to look at my butt so you don't think about that ladder."

He grinned before lowering himself down several rungs. "You guessed."

"It didn't take a rocket scientist to figure that out." She followed him down the ladder, being careful not to step on his fingers. "Where have you been since we docked?"

"Meetings." He groaned, remembering. "My Commander wanted to know what I was going to do with you."

"And what did you tell him."

"Her."

"Beg your pardon?"

"The commander, General Porcazier, is female."

"Ah, an enlightened planet. There's a popular theory on Earth that if women were in charge there would be no wars."

"General Porcazier earned her rank in the Great Intergalactic War."

"Oh."

"Do not sound so deflated, Jessica. The General was also the chief architect of the peace our planet has enjoyed." He reached the bottom of the conduit. After making sure she had only a few steps to go, he ducked out of the conduit entry.

She had been correct. Watching the enticing sway of her hips and talking about his commanding officer had taken his mind off the descent. While climbing down, he felt only a mild disruption in his equilibrium because of her distraction.

"Guess everybody's gone for the day," she said as she looked around the main floor of Engineering.

"I will wait while you gather your personal items, and then we will go down to the planet's surface."

She gave him a tentative smile before starting toward her quarters. She turned around. "I really need a shower. Do I have time?"

"Would you prefer to wait and take a real shower instead of a sonic one?"

Her eyes widened. "With water?"

"Of course, we bathe with water on Serenia."

"Give me two minutes." She raced off.

He was bemused by her enthusiasm, even after a long day of physical labor. He marveled at her lack of inhibition. Her initial fright over being aboard a space vessel had been short-lived. She charged full speed ahead into situations. So unlike Serenians. She brought a freshness to his life. A vitality he craved.

He chuckled at her eagerness. He had been looking forward to showing her what he considered his true home—Uncle Cam's farm. The anticipation had carried him through two excruciatingly long days of meetings with the Alliance High Command. General Porcazier was not the only one who demanded details of his encounter with the Praetorium. And they all wanted information about his visitor from Earth.

They were less than pleased with his missing crewmember. Lieutenant Qilana would be fortunate if she had a career when she returned. Disciplining crewmembers was normally the purview of the Captain on a starship. However, because of the ramifications of bringing a Terran—not just aboard the vessel but to Serenia—General Porcazier intimated that a disciplinary hearing might be called at Space Fleet Command.

While Marcus waited, Jessie ran down the hall to her quarters. Going down to the planet filled her with excitement, but not as much excitement as being with Marcus. Oh, wow. Alone at last. She giggled.

She rounded the corner and nearly ran into a man. "Sorry."

A member of the Maintenance & Repair team in the distinctive orange uniform, he looked as startled as she was.

"Aren't you guys through for the day?" She thought the M&R team had left just before Marcus found her in the access tunnel.

"Uh, no. I'm just finishing up. I have one last job." He glanced past her and then behind himself.

"Don't let me keep you, then. I'm sure you want to get home. I'm just on my way down to Serenia. At last." She grinned. She turned away to continue on to her quarters.

"Wyndom? You are Wyndom, are you not?" he asked.

The hairs on the back of Jessie's neck prickled. She glanced back. He had followed her. The corridor was empty. She'd passed no one else. He came closer.

"Jessica?" Marcus's voice, even from the distance, was

such a reassuring sound.

"A couple more minutes, Captain," she called out. She walked around the crewman to her quarters. When she looked back, he was gone.

She quickly threw some clothes and necessities into a pouch and slung it over her shoulder. Then she raced back to Marcus. "I'm ready."

He placed his hand in the middle of her back, guiding her to the conveyance. Such a protective gesture. He had no idea how grateful she was to find him waiting.

"Did a tall Serenian crewman come past you?" she asked.

"No. No one came down that corridor except you. Why?" He waited for her to enter the conveyance.

"I ran into one of the M&R crew near my quarters. For a minute there, I thought... Oh, never mind." She waved her hand dismissively. Her imagination must have been playing tricks on her. The crewman must have wandered into the wrong corridor and was too embarrassed to say so. "I can't wait to see what Serenia looks like up close. Tell me, what do you do for excitement?"

***

"What kind of incompetents do you have working for you?" the Leader raged.

"He was told to wait until she was alone. How was he to know the Captain was waiting for her?"

"Your failures are mounting." The threat in the Leader's voice brought instant fear, and something else. Anger at the continued references to failure. "It was a stupid move, anyway," the Leader derided. "We want the ship. She is only insurance for Viator to turn over the ship to us."

"We cannot seize an Alliance vessel right out from under the noses of Space Fleet Command. It could precipitate war."

A smile curved up the Leader's mouth. A smile without humor.

TWELVE

Jessie glanced over at Marcus. His strong hands deftly controlled the shuttle as they traveled from spacedock to the Serenian surface. Those skillful hands had performed miracles on her body. Just remembering lit tiny fires deep inside her. She shifted in the seat.

She'd thought their earlier kisses had been devastating. My God. Those kisses were tame compared to the wallop he delivered when he touched her. Her climax had hit so fast, so hard. He'd barely touched her and—wham, she'd exploded.

He'd known instantly how embarrassed she was for reacting with such abandon. His sensitivity surprised her. Yet, she realized he had always been perceptive of her feelings. He understood her. As if he could read her mind.

His insight was as appealing as it was disquieting. What if her feelings toward him moved in the direction of...love? There, she'd thought it. What if she started falling for him? What if he figured that out, and all he wanted was a quick diversion? A little hanky-panky with the Terran.

"You are very quiet," he observed.

She gave him a quick smile. "Just daydreaming."

"I thought you were enjoying the splendid view of my home planet."

"What view?" The shuttle had no windows. She had to squint to even see the miniature screen on the panel in front of him.

He gave her a droll look. He was teasing again. He had changed. He seemed lighter, more relaxed. As if he'd thrown off the mantle of responsibility. She wanted to tell him he sounded almost human but was afraid he'd consider it an insult.

"We have arrived at Malawea Spaceport," he announced, shutting off the shuttle's engine.

He raised the gull-wing door and hoisted himself out. Then, he turned to help her disembark. She crawled across his seat and took his hand. Tingles of awareness crept up her arm. Her foot caught on the edge of the opening, and she tumbled into his waiting arms. Hastily, she righted herself before looking around. She groaned. With all the people getting in and out of shuttles, she was sure they'd all seen her *graceful* exit. "Klutzy Jessie strikes again."

Marcus held onto her. "Are you all right?"

"Oh, yeah. That first step is a killer, though." She quickly moved away from him, hoping no one had noticed. They were in an enclosed area, like a large hanger with several levels and one open side through which shuttles came and went. Opposite the open side were glass doors leading inside.

Marcus pointed toward the glass doors. "We will go through there. Are you sure you did not hurt yourself?"

She gave him a wry grin. "Only my pride."

The building they entered looked like any airport, with travelers hurrying in both directions. Food kiosks lined the corridor. The delicious aromas reminded her she'd missed Evening Repast. Again.

She frequently missed meals on the ship, often just catching a light snack at the end of her shift. At first, she'd plunged into work to keep busy. She'd hoped the time would pass quicker. However, the longer she worked side-by-side with Luqett, the more she basked in his approval. Though only slightly older than Marcus, Luqett could easily become the proud father she craved.

During the solitary hours after the crew returned to the planet, she had daydreamed about staying aboard the *Freedom*. The Chief wasn't the main reason she wanted to stay aboard instead of returning to Earth, though. She wanted to stay with Marcus.

He placed his hand under her elbow, and that delicious tingle of awareness slid up her arm again. He competently steered her down the concourse through the travelers. Gray-skinned Zorfans strode with military precision, grim faced and eyes straight ahead. Troll-like Trucanians like Drakus scurried on wide feet, chattering with companions. Blue-skinned Tegrors glided by, their iridescent yellow eyes darting from side to side.

A small Tegror in a long, purple gown approached them. She had the same lizard-like skin as the *Freedom's* navigation officer. Her curly indigo hair was shot through with silver.

"Marcus." She stopped in front of him.

"Madame Glaxpher." He nodded, almost bowing.

"Stasik is your friend. You must help him." Worry pleated her leathery forehead and clouded her yellow eyes.

Marcus released a long breath. "I have tried."

Madame Glaxpher drew herself up taller than Jessie. Her iridescent eyes flashed. "Try not. Do. He is your friend. Insist the authorities release him. He is no more a member of the Praetorium than you are."

"Madame, I do not believe your son is a renegade. But someone is determined to make everyone think so."

"You must convince them otherwise."

Drawing the woman to the side, he motioned for Jessie to follow. "Let us discuss this matter in private."

He slipped what looked like a credit card into a slot in the wall. A pocket door slid open, revealing a small room with a table and four chairs. He motioned for the women to sit.

After closing the door, he gestured toward a food replicator. "Would you like refreshments?"

Madame Glaxpher refused. Though Jessie was thirsty and hungry, she followed the agitated woman's lead.

Marcus sat down and clasped his hands on the tabletop. "Madame, your son has been my friend since we were roommates at the Academy. I would do anything for him."

She nodded in acknowledgement. "As he would for you."

"Someone wants to implicate Stasik. When I saw the commander of the Praetorian vessel, I believed he was Stasik. The voice was Stasik's. The appearance and gestures were his."

The woman twisted her hands before looking up at Marcus.

"You know in your heart it was not my son."

Jessie ached at the anguish in the woman's voice. The same anguish was in Marcus's eyes. He must be torn between his loyalty to the Alliance and his inability to help Stasik. Jessie touched his hand. "You must do everything you can to help your friend."

He nodded. "Madame, is Stasik your only child? What about cousins?"

"Tegrors have only one offspring. He is the last of our line." She paused. "You are considering genetic nucleotide duplication."

"If it was not GND, then the disguise was flawless. Even our identification scanners indicated the commander of the rebel ship was Stasik."

"You must uncover the real traitor." Madame Glaxpher rose with stately grace.

Marcus and Jessie followed suit. The anguish had disappeared from Madame Glaxpher's face. Her eyes shimmered until they gave the appearance of yellow flames shooting out.

"It is your sacred duty, Marcus Viator, to discover who impersonated my son. Who it was who brought dishonor to our name." She pointed a long, narrow finger at him. The yellow stone in her ring glittered like her eyes. "You must expose this traitor. Only then will my son be vindicated."

She exited the room with a swirl of her gown.

"Whoa." Jessie let her breath out in a whoosh.

"She has reason to be upset."

Jessie grasped his hand. "It's not your fault."

He gave her a rueful look before breaking their contact. "Madame is correct. It is my duty as Stasik's friend to exonerate him. Come." He ushered her out into the corridor.

From his implacable expression, she figured it was wise to drop the topic. His relaxed attitude had disappeared.

"Was that your own room?"

"The room may be used by anyone in need of a quiet place."

"What was the card you used to open the door?"

"It entered my code and charged the fee to my account."

"Cool."

He handed her the card. "We do not use currency as you do on Earth. You may use my card for anything you need."

"But, won't you—"

"I have another."

A warm glow filled her at his trust in handing over his credit card. "How did you know I live to shop?" She grinned at the lie. She hated shopping.

He chuckled. "Then, I will have to see that you have the opportunity to enrich our merchants." Perhaps Madame Glaxpher hadn't completely destroyed his relaxed mood.

They exited the spaceport. Vehicles of various shapes and sizes crowded the space next to the walkway between the building and the pavement. They zoomed low to the street as well as overhead. Some vehicles could only hold one person. Others looked like public conveyances—buses, taxis. An elevated tramway ran quietly above. Despite the abundance of vehicles, she noticed no smell of exhaust and recalled Marcus's disparaging remarks about Terrans polluting the environment.

He hailed a cab. "My home is not far. We will be out of this congestion shortly. With the influx of inhabitants and the abundance of commerce, our city engineers need to design more thoroughfares."

She merely smiled. "Guess all cultures, superior or primitive, have some of the same problems."

"Perhaps I was hasty in my...unkind remarks about Earth."

"Unkind remarks?" She snorted. "You were pretty arrogant when I first came aboard your ship."

"Arrogant?" He raised his eyebrow before closing the door of the vehicle.

"There you go a—" She stopped at the twinkle in his eyes. "You're teasing me."

He gave the Trucanian driver his address and the cab took off. Literally. She gasped as the taxi gave a hiss then shot straight up about ten feet in the air. Then, it zoomed ahead. The driver jockeyed for position among other vehicles at different levels above the ground.

Once she caught her breath from the unexpected takeoff, she said, "You certainly don't have to worry about potholes or road construction."

Marcus smiled. "We have a few primitive land-based vehicles. Away from the heart of the city, the traffic lessens. Tomorrow, you will see the true beauty of Serenia—the mountains and valleys. The rivers and forests."

"Waxing poetic, Marcus?" She grinned.

He pointed out the headquarters of the Alliance High Command, a white building about ten or twelve stories high. A huge blue and yellow flag flew above a fountain out front.

"University of Michigan colors. Go Blue." She pumped her fist in the air. "My brother and my folks would be pleased."

"Will your family recognize that Veronese is not you?"

She rolled her eyes. "You've got to be kidding. My brother might, but my folks wouldn't notice if she looked like our Trucanian driver."

Marcus's sad look made her uncomfortable. How could she explain her parents' insensitivity without complaining? Or defending?

She leaned closer to whisper, "How does our driver see over the steering wheel?"

Marcus looked like he wanted to question her further about her parents but acquiesced to her change of topic. "He does not need to. Once he put in the coordinates for my home, a computer navigates. We could have used a self-automated vehicle, but I did not want to frighten you on your first day here."

His infectious grin amazed her. Yes, he had changed. He leaned back against the seat and stretched out his long legs. She gulped at the near-physical punch she felt at seeing how tightly his uniform molded his legs. If she ran her fingers up the inside of those muscular thighs, would he tremble with delight, as she had when he touched her? Or, would he give her that long, hard look for being so bold? Not willing to risk his rebuff, she stared out the side window.

Malawea resembled a large metropolis on Earth with

buildings of various sizes. Lots of people, many of differing species, surged along the walkways. The biggest difference, besides the inhabitants, was the cleanliness of the city. No litter, no smog. The buildings gleamed in the late afternoon suns, parallel to each other at about eight and four o'clock.

"Two suns? It's a miracle this planet doesn't burn up."

He blinked as if she'd interrupted his thinking. She sure hoped he wasn't still thinking about their encounter in the maintenance conduit. Heat filled her face, as she recalled her abandon on the stairway. Maybe she had embarrassed him. She really didn't want to know.

"Yes, a miracle." Then, the most amazing grin creased his face. He had grinned more today than the entire time she'd known him. "Wait until you see our night sky."

She waited. "What? You're going to leave me hanging?"

"We have arrived."

She looked around. The taxi had stopped outside a tall red building. She hadn't even been aware that they had dropped down to the curb. Marcus had such an effect on her she lost all sense of time and place.

"You need to pay the driver." He showed her how to swipe his card through a slot in the back of the driver's seat. As soon as Marcus closed the door behind them, the taxi shot up in the air and was quickly gone.

They walked into a lobby that would do justice to a five-star hotel. Or, what she thought a five-star hotel would look like since she had never been in one. "You live here? Oh, wow."

A mosaic on the floor depicted people emerging from a primitive spacecraft. The small group of travelers stared steadfastly ahead at the barren landscape, their expressions grim yet hopeful.

Marcus noticed her fascination with the floor. "That is a depiction of Serenia's early colonization. The first settlers, whom we call the Intrepid Ones, came from a system far away whose sun was dying. These pioneers escaped before their planet froze, the only survivors of a doomed civilization."

"Wow," she breathed.

He steered her toward a bank of elevators while pointing at paintings on the walls. "The panels represent the early expansion. The Intrepid Ones faced many hazards in their efforts to colonize Serenia."

She glanced from panel to panel. His ancestors had fought ferocious beasts, tornadic winds and blizzards, and harsh soil conditions.

"In light of all the violence they encountered," she observed, "I'm surprised they named this planet Serenia. It was definitely not a serene place."

"The name was their hope for a better way of life. Through fierce determination, they tamed the planet."

She pointed to a final panel where the pioneers looked out over vast green fields instead of the earlier harsh desert, houses and cities where wild beasts had roamed. "I can understand taming wildlife, but the weather? Chief Luqett said Serenia has a temperate climate all year round."

"We devised a method of controlling the weather. Now, enough history lessons. You have had a long day."

She tore her fascination away from the paintings. He was holding open a door, waiting for her. "Sorry."

Once she entered the small room, he instructed her to insert his card to activate the elevator for his floor.

"That's some handy-dandy card," she observed.

"It has many purposes. Without it, the conveyance would not move."

"Sort of a security system, too, huh?"

He nodded.

"If you need security, that means you must have crime."

"There are always those who desire what they do not have."

The door opened.

She raised her eyebrow. "Even in superior cultures?"

With his hand in the middle of her back, he guided her down a short, carpeted hall. His touch conveyed strength and reassurance. "I believe you are throwing my words back into my face. Is that not the correct expression?"

"You got it, buster." Then, she grinned up at him to let

him know she was teasing.

He smiled back, and her heart did its little tapdance.

He stopped in front of a door and instructed her to slide his card into the handy-dandy slot. The door clicked open. Motioning for her to wait, he took two steps into the room. A brief white light passed over him.

"Welcome, Marcus," a feminine voice proclaimed.

Uh, oh. Someone was here? A wife? He never mentioned being married. She'd never even asked. After that devastating kiss, he brought her home to his wife?

"Come." He motioned to her.

She took two steps into the room. Suddenly, the light passed over her.

"This is Jessica Marie Wyndom," he announced.

She looked around to see to whom he was speaking. The room was empty. Shades of her arrival on the *Freedom*.

"Welcome, Jessica Marie Wyndom." It was the same feminine voice who greeted him.

"Who is that? Where is she?"

"That is Security." He showed Jessie a small silver panel on the wall, the source of the scanning light and the computer-generated voice.

He placed his hands on her shoulders. "Now, it is my turn. Welcome to Serenia, Jessica." He lowered his head until his lips were mere millimeters away from hers.

She held her breath, waiting for his kiss. Aching for his kiss. First, though, she needed to get something straight. She leaned back and stared into his silver eyes. She was not going to be distracted by their intensity. He was not going to mesmerize her. "Are you married?"

"I beg your pardon?" He looked confused, and then offended.

She stepped back. "Do you have marriage in your superior culture?"

He released her. "Of course we do."

"Well, how was I to know?" She flung out her hand defensively. "Maybe superior cultures don't need marriage."

"On Serenia, a male and female commit or bond to each

other. For life."

"No divorce?"

"No divorce. We do not rush into commitment. Our mates are selected for us by the Elders."

"You have no choice?" She was horrified.

"Only radicals ignore the selection of the Elders."

"And you? Are you 'committed'?"

He rubbed his hand around the back of his neck—a gesture she'd never seen him use, even when he was disturbed. She didn't like the feeling she was getting.

"Not yet."

Marcus wondered how Jessica managed to pinpoint the very topics he did not wish to discuss. Commitment to a mate, like his career, was determined by the Elders. Like his increasing dissatisfaction with his career, he was not able to stifle his adverse reaction to their choosing his mate. Especially now that he had met Jessica.

"What do you mean 'not yet'? Listen, mister, I don't fool around with married guys. Being engaged, as far as I'm concerned, is practically the same as being married." She walked across the sitting room. "How could you bring me here if you're engaged to somebody else?"

Her insult to his integrity knifed through him. Anger welled up like acid in his throat. He fought to control his reaction and realized he had clenched his fists. He took a long breath, willing himself to relax. "Perhaps you meant no disrespect. A man of honor does not put aside his vows."

She stood at the window—arms around herself, hands clasping elbows, back stiff. That posture had been his first impression of her vulnerability when she arrived on his ship. Perhaps her vulnerability was what appealed to him.

No, it was her strength despite the vulnerability. Now that he had his own emotions under control, he realized she needed reassurance, as when she realized she had been transported aboard an alien spacecraft.

"I am not engaged, married, or committed to anyone. The Elders believe it is time I choose a soulmate. They have recommended three candidates, females best suited to my temperament and occupation."

"An arranged marriage." She did not turn around.

"Yes, similar to arranged marriages which many societies on your planet have found successful."

She snorted.

He walked up behind her. Sliding his arms around her, he leaned in close and nuzzled her neck. "If I was committed to another, I would never have kissed you." He kissed the side of her neck. Her pulse raced beneath his lips. "Or brought you here." He took her ear lobe between his lips, nibbled gently, and enjoyed her slight tremble. "I believe in fidelity." He placed light kisses along her jaw. Though his body reacted to her closeness, he was still in control. He could kiss her and not let things get out of hand.

"I'm sorry. At first, I thought the voice, your Security Babe, was your wife and I guess I over-reacted." She twisted around in his arms. Cupping his face between her work-roughened hands, she stared into his eyes. "Marcus, you scare the hell out of me."

He released her. He wasn't as strong as he'd thought. "And you...frighten me." He instantly regretted his admission.

For a moment, he thought she would probe deeper. Instead, she rubbed her hands together. "Oh, goody." She looked around. "Nice place you got here, Captain."

"How quickly you change the subject." He should be grateful. He did not want to explore his emotions. A proper Serenian concealed them. Yet, he wanted to probe hers. "You keep part of yourself hidden, do you not, Jessica? You wish everyone to see only a sassy, impudent person. Not the vulnerable one underneath."

Before she looked away, her bottom lip quivered. She examined the wildflower prints on the wall of his sitting room as if they were masterpieces. He did not have to wait long for her to regain her composure.

She gestured at her navy uniform, streaked with dark stains from lubricating fluid. "You promised me a shower."

"One moment." He would reassure her and, at the same time, test his self-control. He held out his arms. "Welcome to

Serenia, Jessica."

With relief that he wasn't married or engaged, Jessie forgot about her shower and walked to him. She slid her arms around his waist then rested her cheek against his chest. His steady heartbeat was reassuring, as if she belonged there. "This is very nice," she murmured. Peace surrounded her at the same time her body pulsed at being so close to him.

"Only nice?" Marcus asked. "That is an insipid word." He tipped up her chin and planted a light kiss on her lips.

"I agree. More than nice." She closed her eyes, a small sigh parting her lips and willed him to kiss her again. When he placed his hands on her shoulders, she knew her powers of telepathy hadn't worked. Disappointment jabbed its tiny needles at her.

"Allow me to show you my residence."

With reluctance, she let him give her the Grand Tour. His apartment reminded her of his quarters on board ship. Sparsely furnished. Utilitarian.

Two pictures graced a low table in the sitting room. She leaned closer to examine the people in the first picture.

"My parents," he said in a voice devoid of feeling.

The small man and woman looked young, perhaps in their twenties. They stood in front of a vehicle similar to the taxi, giving her perspective to judge their size. Aside from dark hair, Marcus looked nothing like them. Even his height hadn't come from them. "I don't see a resemblance."

He stiffened at her words.

"Oops. I shouldn't have said that. Sorry."

He took a deep breath. "I was...adopted."

"Well, that explains it."

Something wasn't right. She looked up at him only to find he was staring past her, as if remembering something unpleasant. Not wanting to spoil his relaxed mood, she decided not to probe further about his parents.

"Who's this?" She pointed to the second picture. It was of an older man, standing in a field of purple wheat-like plants. In the midst of a weathered face, the man's smile crinkled the corners of his eyes.

"My uncle." Marcus's voice softened. "He lives out in the country. We will visit him tomorrow."

He loves this man, she thought. Something she hadn't sensed when he talked about his parents. "I'd love to meet him. What about your parents? Do I get to meet them, too?"

His eyes hardened. "No. They are dead." The soft tone had completely disappeared.

She reached out to touch his forearm. "I'm sorry."

He brushed off her hand. "It was long ago."

Confused by his abrupt refusal of her expression of sorrow, she was determined not to let this go. After all, he'd tried a little psychoanalysis on her a few minutes ago. Turn about was fair play. "Why do you stiffen up when I mention feelings? Why do you deny your emotions?"

He drew up ramrod straight. Here was the Captain of the *Freedom*, not the relaxed companion of just a few moments ago. "Serenians do not have emotions."

"Bullshit."

His eyes widened at her crude response. "I beg your pardon?"

"That is bullshit." She didn't care if he thought her crude. Maybe he would wake up and listen to her. "You feel emotions. I've seen you."

"Perhaps I did not phrase it correctly. Proper Serenians do not allow their emotions to rule them."

"And you're a proper Serenian."

He gave her an odd look. "I try."

"Suppressing your emotions can give you ulcers."

"As youngsters, we learn self-control. Meditation brings serenity and enables us to be clear in our thinking."

Maybe he was just afraid of expressing his emotions, afraid they would swamp him. The old cartoon lightbulb went on over her head. Could it be the same for her father? Was Dad's seeming indifference the result of his struggle to control his emotions? Was Gram right? Did he fear he had a volatile temper like his own father? Was it possible her dad felt more than she gave him credit for? Like Marcus?

Still confused over her insight into the two men, she

followed Marcus into the small but efficient-looking kitchen. It even had a food replicator. Then, they walked down a short hall to his bedroom. One bedroom. With one large bed.

He caught her staring at the bed. "The couch in the sitting room opens into a bed."

She nodded. "Like a sofa-bed. Will one of us need it?"

Way to go, Jess. Nothing like propositioning the guy.

"Yes, tonight."

She snapped her fingers. "Oh, darn."

"You are amusing."

"A real barrel of laughs."

"You are relieved."

As always, his insight surprised her. On board ship, she thought she was ready to share a bed with this man. With him running hot and cold, she was having second thoughts. Intimacy with a man—any man, let alone this alien—frightened her. Making love was such a big step for her with someone she barely knew.

"Come," he said, clearly reading her hesitation. "This is what you wanted to see."

The tour ended in a well-appointed bathroom. Sanitary room, she remembered to call it. The glass-enclosed cubicle with criss-crossing showerheads caught her attention. Marcus reached into a cupboard and brought out two large towels.

"I will bring your belongings."

He returned shortly with her pouch. "While you are taking your shower, I will order our evening meal. Do not hurry."

She luxuriated under the water, feeling truly clean for the first time in over a week. First, pulsing jets pummeled her back, shoulders, and neck, erasing the strain of long hours in cramped quarters. Then, she twisted the control, and water as soft as rain cascaded down her body. So relaxing was it, if she stayed much longer, she'd fall asleep.

With reluctance, she left the shower. After towel-drying her hair, she reached into the pouch for a clean undergarment.

"Nuts," she muttered, holding up the one-piece garment. It slimmed her down, held her in and shaped her body, but she wanted her own clothes. She put on her bra and panties.

Dispensing with the clean uniform she'd packed, she pulled on the jeans and T-shirt she'd last worn on Earth. The jeans zipped up easily, with room to spare. She twisted to look in the mirror. They weren't nearly as snug in the butt as they'd been when she last wore them.

She was surprised at how loose they were. Looked like the exercise was paying off. Skipping meals might have had something to do with it, too. What was it about the food on board ship? It satisfied her hunger yet she never felt like eating more than small quantities. No wonder the Serenians looked like poster children for fitness and good health.

She lifted her T-shirt to tuck it in. Her jeans were loose enough she could slip her hand between the snapped waist and her tummy. The image of Marcus's hand replacing hers, slipping inside her jeans, sent tiny shivers along the nerve endings of her skin. *Whew.* She blew out a breath.

This is what she wanted, wasn't it? By coming home with him, she wanted more than a sight-seeing trip on a planet in a galaxy far, far way. She wanted Marcus. She wanted to make love with him. There, she'd decided. Before, it had been a decision made in the thrall of overwhelming lust. But now, she was sure. Yes, making love with Marcus was what she wanted.

She gripped the edge of the counter and looked at herself in the mirror wearing her own clothes. Her damp hair curled around her face. She was Jessica Marie Wyndom, from planet Earth. What was happening to her? Would she ever return to her home?

Did she want to?

Or did she want to explore the tentative relationship with Marcus? He attracted her. Attracted, hell. She straightened away from the mirror. She'd never felt so physically drawn to a man before.

And something beyond the physical.

Yes, he made her skin sizzle, her nipples harden, and her panties embarrassingly wet. Just seeing him walk down the corridor of the starship made her heart thud in her chest like the drums she'd played in her high school marching band. So, she hid behind her usual flippancy, afraid to reveal her feelings to this emotionally-challenged alien.

Now, who was the one denying emotions?

Except for the lack of grief over the loss of his parents, she'd seen him express more emotion in the past few hours than in the entire time she'd known him. His simmering excitement over tomorrow's trip to his uncle's, his relief at being away from the *Freedom* and its responsibilities, surprised her.

He had deep feelings. Feelings he fought to control. He seemed so...human. Could she forget he was an alien, an extra-terrestrial? Did that really matter?

He captivated her. And it scared her to death.

"Jessica?"

His knock brought her back to reality. She glanced quickly at the mirror then wished she hadn't. That wasn't her, was it? She looked back. A deep flush rose from her neck to her face. Her eyes had darkened. Her tightly beaded nipples showed through her shirt. Damn it, her underpants were getting wet. She desired him with an intensity that scared her at the same time it thrilled her.

"Our Evening Repast will be here shortly," he called through the door. "Do you need more time?"

She took a deep breath. *Time's up.*

THIRTEEN

When she finally ventured out of the bathroom, she saw that Marcus, too, had changed clothes.

"Will wonders never cease," she exclaimed as she walked into the narrow galley kitchen.

He arched his eyebrow.

She let out a deep sigh. "Well, some things never change. I'd like to tape that eyebrow to your forehead." He looked confused so she said, "Never mind. I was referring to what you're wearing. You *do* own casual clothes."

Black slacks made of a shimmery material clung to his rear. She still got a thrill at the sight of his buns. His sage green shirt bloused out from the waistband of the slacks. He'd even rolled up the sleeves to reveal his bare forearms. Though the shirt didn't mold his body, the broadness of his shoulders and chest wasn't diminished. Not by a long shot.

"I do not wear a uniform when I am off-duty. However, I am sorry you find my eyebrow offensive."

"I'm not complaining about the eyebrow, it's what you do with it." She waggled her own eyebrows, Groucho-style.

He chuckled. "I will try to control my errant eyebrow." He reached for a tendril of her hair. "You should leave your hair loose like this. Not bound so severely away from your face." He slid his hand around her neck, urging her to him.

She held her breath. *Kiss me. Please, kiss me.*

Chimes rang. The Security Babe announced a delivery person. For a second, Marcus's face revealed the same disappointment coursing through her. He stroked her cheek before going to the door.

"This sure beats the pizza guy," she said as he pushed a white tablecloth-covered cart into the room. The cart held several serving dishes. "Wow, it's like hotel room service."

"It is a service offered to residents in this complex. I ordered a variety of entrees to give you the opportunity to sample Serenian cuisine." He carried the covered dishes to a dining area where he'd set the table with linens, silver, and china. "Please sit." He held a chair for her.

"Thank you, kind sir, but I feel rather underdressed for the occasion." She shook out her napkin and placed it on her lap. "What would Miss Manners say?" She gave him a rueful grin.

He sat across from her. "Your reference escapes me. I do not have my *link* to consult."

"You don't wear your *link* when you're not on the ship? I brought mine since I wasn't sure if I should leave it in my quarters. I mean, my sister's quarters."

"Until you return to your home, they are your quarters."

Return home. That was what she wanted. Wasn't it? *Don't go there, Jess. Don't even think about the future. Enjoy the here and now.*

Marcus uncovered the serving dishes. Though she'd had many of the items at meals on board ship, the colors of the food still disconcerted her. Purple breads, blue vegetables, even a pink rice-like concoction. She'd learned that Serenians did not eat the meat of animals. Not that she had any objection to a good steak, but she'd enjoyed her foray into vegetarian eating. Most of the food was grown hydro- or aeroponically on the *Freedom* or was replicated synthetically.

She savored the taste of the rice and veggie casserole. "This is delicious."

He smiled in acknowledgement. "Better than—what did you call it—ice cream?"

She laughed. "Ice cream is a dessert. And nothing beats ice cream. This comes pretty close, though." She took a sip of the exquisite wine. Not that she was a connoisseur of wines or even had much experience with wine tasting, but this stuff was great. "Don't you have to wear your *link* all the time? Even when you're not on the ship? What if there's an emergency?"

"I do not wear the *link* in my residence. It is in my sleeping room. I will wear it again when we leave because, as you say, Space Fleet Command must be able to reach me." He ate two bites before looking up. "I believe I understand your reference to Miss Manners. You do not think you are properly dressed. You need not worry. Your attire is...fetching."

"This old thing." Her jeans were velvet-soft from wear. Her T-shirt was an advertisement for her business. "For such a fine dinner like this, I should be wearing a classy dress, nylons and heels, jewelry. Not jeans and sportsocks."

"Perhaps the next time. For now, enjoy your meal."

She figured it was his polite way of saying 'shut up and eat.' So, she did.

***

Jessie had been lying awake for more than an hour. In Marcus's bed. Without Marcus. She frowned, recalling the evening.

Throughout dinner he was polite, gracious even, but no longer relaxed. He'd distanced himself from her again. Where was the man who'd kissed her so thoroughly on the platform in Engineering? Whose touch set off explosions inside her? Who had brought her to his home to make love with her? Or so she thought.

When it was time to retire, she decided to give it one more try. She'd stood at the end of the sofa in her sister's nightdress. The white, shimmery material clung to her breasts and swirled around her ankles. She'd found the nightdress stuffed at the back of a cupboard in Veronese's quarters. It was so unlike the rest of her twin's clothing. A minor indulgence? A feminine desire to have a man see her in it? Wishful thinking?

Just as Jessie was wishing, and hoping. "Marcus, I can't take your bed."

Having Marcus see her in the slinky gown was the reason Jessie had thrown it in her pouch, and the reason she'd come out to the sitting room wearing it. And what a reaction she got.

He'd looked up from preparing the sofa-bed. His long, slow perusal nearly buckled her knees. Good God, she'd never seen such a smoldering look on *any* man's face when he looked at her.

"Jessica."

That one word, her name, pulled her to him. One step. The desire in his eyes lured her. Another step. The air sizzled between them. She only needed to take one more step. Did she dare? She licked her lips, dithering.

He solved her dilemma by taking that step himself. He dragged her hard up against his body, anchoring her with one strong arm. He vibrated with tightly-controlled tension. She felt every inch of his muscular thighs...and the throb of his sex. His slacks and her sheer nightgown provided meager barriers between them.

Spearing his fingers through her unruly hair, he cupped the back of her head. Slowly, despite the urgency of his body, he carefully captured her mouth.

The kiss was searing. Oh, God, this is what she wanted. She parted her lips for his tongue, welcoming him into her mouth, silently conveying her willingness to welcome him into her body.

Hungrily, he trailed his mouth down her neck. He nudged the tiny spaghetti strap out of his way then buried his face in the softness of her shoulder. She held his head, stroking his silk-like hair. So thick, so soft.

With an urgent moan, she pressed her lower body closer. He slid his hands slowly, oh, so slowly down her back. He cupped her bottom and ground his hips into hers. She arched on her tiptoes, trying to bring him even closer.

"Make love to me, Marcus," she whispered.

Abruptly, he pushed her away. Bereft, she could only stand there in shock at his rejection while he strode over to the broad window. He jerked the curtain open and stared out into the night. Trembling, she wrapped her arms around herself.

He didn't turn around. "I apologize."

She sucked in a shaky breath. "Why? I wasn't exactly resisting."

"Please go to sleep. We will talk tomorrow."

"Why not now?" She took two steps toward him and

stopped. "You think I can sleep after that. What happened to you? Damn it, Marcus. Don't turn away from me. Talk to me. What did I do wrong?" Her chin quivered. She blinked rapidly. He would not make her cry.

"You did nothing wrong."

"I don't understand." She thought they would pick up where they left off earlier on the platform outside the access tunnel in Engineering. She'd thought that was the reason for coming with him. Maybe he'd changed his mind. Damn it, she wouldn't beg him to make love with her.

"Please, go to bed." He continued to stare out the window, dismissing her, refusing to even look at her.

Hurt, confused, she'd gone to bed. And she'd been right. She couldn't sleep. She rolled on her side. Her nerves were strung so tightly she thought they'd snap. She wanted him. He'd made it clear when she first came aboard his ship that he didn't take advantage of guests. Was that the problem? Damn it, she wanted him to take advantage of her.

She didn't understand him. She wasn't so naive that she couldn't tell if he was aroused. He wanted her even though he held himself back. While chafing against it, she admired his restraint. She flew off the handle too easily. Her mouth frequently got her into trouble.

Another thing she couldn't understand was why he fought to control his humor. Several times on board ship, she caught him about to laugh at something she said. Then, his face would close up, as if tamping down his enjoyment. But, once in a while his grin would pop through, as if he couldn't contain it. That grin nearly brought her to her knees.

Just as his kisses did.

He hadn't been so controlled tonight. Before he put her aside, he'd struggled to catch his breath. His hands had shaken, ever so slightly, but still they'd shaken. He *was* affected by what was happening between them.

Still, he hadn't followed through. From the Serenians she worked with in Engineering, she'd learned about this obsession they had with self-discipline. Marcus was taking self-control to its extreme. More like self-denial.

She rolled over for about the fiftieth time. Punching the pillow didn't help. She was too restless to sleep. Maybe, a good dose of hot xephod tea would relax her.

On tip-toe, she crept out to the kitchen. Marcus had left on a small light above the counter so she wasn't stumbling in the dark. She programmed the replicator, and seconds later the soothing tea—warmed to just the right temperature— appeared. Clasping the handleless cup in both hands, she inhaled deeply.

The fragrance of cinnamon and citrus filled her nostrils, beginning the tea's magic work. With her first sip, her tightly-corded muscles relaxed. A second sip, and her edginess disappeared.

Quietly, she walked back through the sitting room. She nearly dropped the cup when she saw that he was awake. He lay on his back, watching her.

"Can you not sleep?" His voice resonated inside her.

She froze in place, two feet from where he lay. "I-I'm sorry for disturbing you."

"I was not asleep." He'd propped himself up on the arm of the couch. The covers pooled near his waist. She wondered if he slept in the nude.

He had left the window coverings open. Moonlight shone on his broad, smooth chest. Though his face was in shadow, his eyes seemed different. He raised his arm and rubbed the back of his neck. So telling a gesture. Was he as frustrated as she?

She just realized he had no underarm hair when he said, "This afternoon, I mentioned an appropriate time and place."

She nodded. This topic was much more interesting than trying to analyze his absence of body hair.

"This is not it."

How was she supposed to respond to that? There *would* be an appropriate time and place? When? Where?

She couldn't ask. What if this was just his way of backing off? She stiffened her wet-noodle spine. If he didn't want her, she certainly wasn't going to beg him to take her. Why couldn't she get her signals straight?

"Sure thing." She gave him a flippant grin before heading back to the bedroom.

"Jessica?" he called after her.

She stopped in the doorway to his bedroom.

"Tomorrow I want to take you somewhere very special. Then, you and I will discuss our situation."

Did he mean what she thought he meant? Their *situation* surely referred to the physical attraction between them. What if he didn't want a relationship with an inferior species? What if he just wanted to let her down easily?

"Go to sleep, Jessica. You must not worry about this."

"Yeah, yeah. Easy for you to say."

Marcus watched her close the door behind her. Easy for him to say? His jaw ached from clenching it. His muscles spasmed as he restrained his urge to follow her into his sleeping room. Earlier, he had nearly lost control. When she had walked out in that white garment through which he could see the outline of her body from the light behind her. When he kissed her. When she had begged him to make love to her.

Marcus had never experienced such an overwhelming desire to mate. Harsh, primitive, animalistic urges. Terran urges.

Only with Jessica.

He had to restrain himself. Not because of his Serenian reticence over strong emotions. He could not couple with Jessica until he told her the truth. She deserved to know everything. Then, it would be her choice. In order to make that choice, she had to know all the facts.

This would be no casual coupling. He had told her he believed in fidelity. Once he made love to her, he was committed. No power on Serenia, not even the Elders, would be able to separate them. She could not leave him. She could not return to Earth. He would not let her go. Making love—he used the Terran phrase—would be a commitment. Once he committed himself to her, he would be bound forever.

First, she had to know who he really was. Only at his uncle's farm was he secure enough to reveal his past before exploring their future.

FOURTEEN

The next morning, Marcus fairly sizzled with excitement. Jessie had never seen him like this. He stood at the kitchen counter, mixing a violet-colored batter. A bowl of julienne-style vegetables stood nearby.

"Did you sleep well, Jessica?"

Sleep? What was that? She'd tossed and turned all night. Before she straightened the bed this morning, it looked like two dogs had fought in the covers. Or two people had made love. She gulped. She didn't want to go there, even though thinking about making love with Marcus had been the reason for her restlessness. "Fine. You're cooking?"

"I enjoy preparing the morning meal."

She looked askance at the batter. "Purple pancakes?"

"Have you lost your adventurous spirit?" He deftly sautéed the vegetables. "You were willing to try different foods on the *Freedom* and again last night."

She released a deep sigh. "I've had new foods for over a week. I'd give anything for a cheeseburger or a pizza."

He covered the veggies then heated a flat, round-bottomed pan. "This batter is made from cassana, similar to your wheat." He dipped the bottom of the pan into the batter and quickly turned the pan upside down over the heat.

"You're making crepes." She smiled in amazement. "You are very brave. I'd never attempt that. I'd either drip batter all over the stove or burn them."

"You have other talents, Jessica." His praise sent a warm thrill through her. He probably didn't even realize how much she appreciated his off-hand compliment.

Because he'd mentioned it yesterday, she'd left her hair

unbound. She pulled a curl over her left shoulder and started to twirl it before she realized she'd reverted to her nervous habit. She tucked her hair behind her ear.

He continued making several crepes while talking. "You will need more comfortable clothes." He nodded toward the jeans and T-shirt she'd put on from last night. As much as she disliked wearing the same clothes again, she hadn't wanted to put on a uniform this morning.

"I took the liberty of ordering appropriate attire for you, which should arrive before we leave."

"You take all the fun out of shore leave." She gave him a mock pout. "I wouldn't have minded shopping for clothes. Especially with your credit card." She kept her face as straight as possible.

"I apologize. We have much to do today. Before we return to the ship, I will make certain you have the opportunity to—"

"Marcus, I was joking."

He gave her a look of chagrin before announcing that breakfast was served. The vegetable-filled crepes tasted wonderful. She recognized the vegetables from meals she'd had on the ship. The crepes had a slightly nutty flavor and a grainier texture than ones she'd had in restaurants.

They were just finishing breakfast when a courier arrived. Jessie opened the package with anticipation. Nothing could prevent her small squeals of excitement as she pulled out slacks and shirts of the same soft, shimmery material as his. The jewel colors of sapphire, emerald, and topaz were gorgeous.

She threw her arms around his neck, nearly bowling him over with her enthusiasm. "Oh, thank you, Marcus. You are so sweet." She gave him a noisy kiss.

With a look of regret, he disentangled himself, instructing her to change quickly and pack the rest of her new clothing.

She stopped at the door to his bedroom. "How did you know what size to order?"

He pointed to the small silver panel on the wall near the front door. "When you entered, the computer scanned you."

"Oh, great. The Security Babe knows how big I am."

"Jessica." He laughed. "You are just the right size. Quickly, change your attire. I wish to leave as soon as possible."

She gave him a snappy salute. "Aye, aye, Captain." She ran into the bedroom with the new clothes before he gave her a lecture on proper Serenian behavior.

The Security Babe was right. The clothes fit perfectly. There were even bras and panties in a delicate material that slid sensuously against her skin. And shoes, even more comfortable than the ones she wore on board ship. A tiny package inside one shoe revealed ribbons of the same jewel tones as the slacks and shirts. Such a thoughtful gesture, especially since he liked her hair loose.

When she walked back to the sitting room wearing the topaz outfit, he gave her a long, hungry look. Disconcerted by his appraisal, she took a deep breath. "Thank you again for the clothes, Marcus."

He nodded then picked up her pouch and his own bag. Before ushering her out of the apartment, he showed her how to set the security system.

"Good-by, Marcus," the Security Babe drawled. "Good-by, Jessica."

Maybe it was her imagination, but Jessie thought the voice sounded warmer to him. She rolled her eyes. Jealous of a computer-generated voice? *Get a grip, Jess.*

He led her to the conveyance. She was surprised when they went up. "I thought we were going on a trip. Don't we go down to the street?"

He merely smiled as he held the door for her to exit the conveyance. They were at the top of the building. Several pillars supported the roof, but all four sides were open.

"Oh, you have covered parking up here." She followed as he strode between the various vehicles. He came to a stop at a candy-apple red, low-slung one. The color surprised Jessie who assumed with Marcus's prim-and-proper decorum he'd have a sedate black or gray car.

"Do we have to wait for a valet?" she asked. All the vehicles were packed end-to-end as well as side-by-side, with just enough room to walk between them.

"No." He loaded their bags into a compartment in the front of the vehicle.

"This reminds me of my first car, with the trunk where the engine should be." She sat down in what she hoped was the passenger seat. The control panel stretched nearly across the entire dashboard, but the largest display was in front of the opposite seat.

He helped her fasten the criss-crossing safety harness which held her shoulders and her rear firmly in the seat.

"A little overkill on the safety, don't you think?" she asked.

"You will see." He touched the display screen.

"Welcome, Marcus. Where do you wish to go today?" It was the same feminine voice from the apartment. Soft, throaty, sexy. Jessie hated her.

"Uncle Cam's farm."

"Very good, Marcus. Sit back and enjoy the ride."

"Isn't she sweet."

Although Marcus ignored Jessie's sarcasm, the vehicle gave a little hiss. For a moment, Jessie wondered if she'd insulted it. Then she realized that with the hiss, the vehicle was rising straight up until it nearly touched the high ceiling.

"Well, that explains how you can pack the cars in like sardines. What do you call this?" She waved her hand, indicating the vehicle.

"A speeder."

"For obvious reasons?"

"You might say so." He flashed her a mysterious grin. Her heart did its little tapdance. God, she loved that grin.

Once the speeder cleared the surrounding vehicles, it leveled out then slowly moved forward.

"Where's the exit?" She looked at the open sides of the building. "We aren't headed there, are we?" Sure enough, the vehicle sped through the opening. "Oh, no. O-oh—"

She closed her eyes as it cleared the building. Then, she couldn't stand not knowing. She had to look. The walkway below was a long way down.

"We will be out of the metropolis soon." He stared straight ahead, a muscle ticking along his jaw. His clenched hands rested on top of his thighs. "Then, we will not need to be so high."

She reached across to clasp his hand. "With your acrophobia, I'm surprised you even attempt this."

He withdrew his hand. "The speeder is self-automated," he said stiffly. "I have programmed the coordinates of places I visit often. There is no need for concern."

She shouldn't have reminded him about his fear of heights. He was a proud man, a leader who resented anything that reminded he was vulnerable.

As they traveled at moderate speed, she found it a little unnerving to see Marcus's hands remain in his lap. The vehicle steered itself through the morning traffic. She looked around. The mountain range remained on her right.

"Will we cross the mountains?"

The knuckles on Marcus's hands turned white. "Yes, we will go through a natural pass outside the city. In recent times, since the Intergalactic Alliance headquarters were located in Malawea, it has spread much farther along the coast. The mountains and the sea are natural barriers." He stared straight ahead, never looking down. "Like Earth, the land over the mountains was barren. Our prevailing wind crosses the sea, bringing with it rain."

What's with the history lesson? A cover-up for his embarrassment over his fear of heights?

"Consequently," he continued, "this side of the mountains was lush with vegetation, as it is today, while the other side was desert. With advanced weather technology, our scientists have tamed the desert and enabled it to support food crops. My uncle's ancestors were among the pioneers to establish farms in what once was desert."

"So, the farm has been in your family for several generations? Wow, that's just like mine. My ancestors were pioneers, too. They came from New York to Michigan before it even became a state, back in the early 1830s. While Gram was alive, she got it designated a Centennial Farm by the state of Michigan. We even have a sign out front that says—" She gave a little laugh. "I get carried away sometimes."

"You are proud of keeping the land in your family."

"Yes." She was surprised that he understood. She realized that though he was an alien—something she frequently forgot—they were more similar than they were different.

As soon as the metropolis and traffic thinned, the vehicle descended and abruptly picked up speed. The force of acceleration slammed her against the seat.

"Guess all these seatbelts *are* necessary," she gasped.

Though they were traveling very fast, the interior of the speeder remained quiet, just the steady hum of a finely-tuned engine. When they got to his uncle's, she'd look under the hood. She just had to see what kind of engine made this baby go.

They sped barely above the ground, and she wondered if the vehicle would skim the plants. Dusty gray bushes and reddish shrubs covered the desolate area close to the ocean. The farther north they traveled, the rockier the coast became.

North? She had no idea if this planet had compass points. The land reminded her so much of the West Coast of the United States it seemed natural to think in Earth terms.

Gradually, the speeder turned toward the mountains. They crossed sprawling farms nestled in the foothills. Then, the speeder entered a natural passageway through the mountains. Towering peaks rose on either side. Soon, they cleared the pass.

"Wow." A dazzling array of farms spread before her. Miles and miles of farmland stretched to the horizon, broken periodically by clusters of buildings. Stands of umbrella-like trees formed natural boundaries between farms, maybe even serving as windbreaks as they did on Earth.

"Cassana," he identified fields of purple vegetation, waving gently in the wind.

"What you used for the crepes this morning?"

"Yes. My uncle's farm begins there." He pointed to a line of demarcation formed by tall trees with reddish-brown bark. "Xephods. The source of the tea you like so well."

The speeder slowed down. Several minutes later, they approached box-like buildings made of a shiny gray substance, utilitarian, sterile. The house looked more like an apartment building, lacking the character of her home.

At their approach, an older man stepped off the porch and onto the lush green lawn. He was the man in the picture in Marcus's apartment. The uncle Marcus had great affection for. A smile creased his uncle's face as the speeder came to a stop several feet away.

When Marcus got out of the vehicle, the man came closer. "Marcus. It is pleasant to see you." The welcome in the man's voice matched his expression. Yet, he seemed to be waiting, perhaps for a sign from Marcus.

Jessie saw hesitation in both men. Marcus grinned and took a step closer. Then both men laughed and embraced.

She just knew her mouth was hanging open. On board ship, mostly populated by Serenians, she had seen no physical contact between them. Except for Luqett. Although he was Serenian—she knew because she'd asked—he certainly wasn't like the others. His crew seemed to accept his pats on the back and his exuberance.

The other Serenians held themselves slightly apart. Their personal space was always respected. Marcus hugging his uncle blew her away.

Marcus returned for her. After drawing her out of the car, he put his arm around her shoulders. Curiouser and curiouser.

"Uncle Cam, this is ...a friend. Jessica Wyndom. From Earth. Jessica, my uncle Camelius Eltima."

Cam Eltima raised an eyebrow. Just like Marcus. "Earth? How...interesting." He nodded once, almost a bow. "Welcome, Jessica."

"Thank you." She nodded back. She'd learned her lesson about not shaking hands when she first came aboard the *Freedom*. "You have a very prosperous looking farm."

"It meets our needs."

She chuckled. "Never met a farmer yet who bragged."

A small smile curved Cam's lips. "Perhaps we, too, realize our hold on the bounty our soil provides is tenuous."

"Back home, I live on a farm. Actually, I inherited my Grandmother's. From what I could see as we flew over, it's nowhere near as big as this."

"After you freshen up, Marcus will take you on a tour." Cam turned and walked back to the house. "Come."

***

"I'm surprised your uncle didn't want to show me around. After all, it is his farm."

Marcus took a deep breath, inhaling the scents he missed during long flights in space. Filtered, recirculated air, while technically pure, could not match nature's own smells. He and Jessica stood on one of several small paths separating the different crops. Fields of green, purple, and yellow spread out before them. In the distance, he saw the harvesting vehicles where Cam and his crew were working.

With a long exhale, he thought about the meeting he had had early yesterday with the Elders. Once again, he asked to be relieved of his command, to be allowed to follow his dream. Even his uncle's aging, with Marcus, technically, his only next-of-kin, had not moved the Elders to change their minds. They needed his leadership should the skirmishes with the Praetorium escalate.

According to General Porcazier, Commander-in-Chief of Space Fleet, the Praetorium grew stronger. Marcus's report of his encounter with the rebel ship added to the General's conviction that the Alliance could no longer ignore the Praetorium's threat to peace. Marcus's orders were to return to space as soon as the *Freedom's* engines were repaired.

He stooped and gathered a handful of soil, allowing it to sift through his fingers. He knew where his duty lay. The tightness in his gut reminded him his duty was not here.

"I often came here as a child. This was my refuge away from the turmoil of my parents' marriage. My uncle allowed me to follow him and help with chores. I even studied soil management and farming techniques. He knew I would like to show you the farm."

Jessica brushed back a lock of hair the gentle breeze had loosened. "I assumed you studied science and space travel."

He stood and dusted his hands. "Of course. My other studies were done independently."

"I don't understand. You wanted to be a farmer? Why did you go into the military?"

Climbing to the top of a knoll, he led her to a small stand of xephod trees. "Let us be comfortable. There is much you need to know about our culture to fully understand." He sat on the ground and, before leaning back against the trunk of a xephod, tugged her hand. He drew her between his bent knees.

After she settled back against him, he wrapped his arms around her. His chest swelled at the rightness of her in his arms. She belonged there.

"When ours was a primitive society, Serenians chose their professions, as well as their mates, on such whimsical notions as what they liked. Often emotions clouded their reason. Their choices were not always appropriate or satisfying. People often became unhappy with their choices. Discord arose. Our leaders agreed that only through objective reasoning could one be at peace. Being at the whim of emotion brings turmoil."

"Ah ha. Logic is good; emotion is bad. The Vulcan Creed."

He smiled. How like her to make reference to the science fiction of her culture. "An over-simplification but accurate."

"You miss out on an awful lot by denying your feelings." She rubbed the top of his knee. "What about a happy medium?"

Was her warm touch absent-minded or deliberate? Either way, it was stirring up a reaction. He shifted on the hard ground. "Compromise is not possible. Not here, not now."

"What does all this have to do with choosing your career?"

"After a time of violent turmoil, our leaders enacted laws appointing a group called the Elders who determine a Serenian's career and mate."

She twisted around and knelt to face him. "You had no choice but to go to the Academy and prepare to be a soldier, even though you wanted to be a farmer?"

"When one works in the field in which one is best suited, one is content."

Clasping his face between her palms, she stared hard at him. "You're parroting the company line. Are you content?"

He looked over her shoulder at fields of ripened grain.

"Look at me." She tightened her hold. "Tell me the truth.

This is where you belong, isn't it? I can see the longing in your eyes."

How could he lie to her? She probed until the nerve was exposed. "Yes. But my duty is to my ship."

"To hell with duty, Marcus." Her eyes blazed with intensity. "Do what you love."

"Has that been the philosophy by which you live?"

"Damn right. You can't imagine how hard I had to fight to do what I wanted." Her passionate response should not have surprised him. "I had no interest in academics, where my parents thought I belonged. They couldn't understand why I enjoyed tinkering with engines, why I wasn't disgusted by dirt under my fingernails."

He captured one of her hands and examined it. "I see no dirt." He allowed his mouth to curve slightly.

She tried to pull away. "That was an expression, Marcus, and you know it."

Yes, he knew what she meant. He had resorted to a comic remark to sidetrack this discussion, as she often did.

"You must follow your heart. I would never deny my heart for *duty*," she spat out the last word.

He smiled. "So vehement. So unlike a Serenian female."

"I should hope so, if Serenian females follow orders like sheep."

How pallid Serenian females seemed in comparison to her. He lifted her fingers to his lips.

"Quit trying to distract me."

He raised his eyebrow. "Am I distracting you?"

She slid her other hand around to the back of his neck. "Oh, hell." She tugged. "I'm thoroughly distracted." She leaned forward to touch his lips with her own.

"Good," he murmured. Though he had been prepared to tell her the truth as soon as they arrived at the farm, he found himself procrastinating. He never procrastinated.

He allowed her to take the lead, tortured by, yet enjoying, her hesitation. She nibbled on his bottom lip until he thought she would never move on. Controlling his urge to crush her to his chest challenged him. A lifetime of discipline was nearly destroyed by each tentative kiss around his mouth.

With both hands free, she tipped his jaw so she could more easily reach his neck. "Wow. You really shave close." She lightly brushed her lips down his throat.

His groin ached. When she opened his shirt and slid those small, strong hands along his chest, he thought he would explode. He exerted all his resources not to let himself spin out of control.

Despite the intense passion raging through his body, he would not complete their union until he explained who he was. She accepted him as an alien. What would she do when she found out he had misled her? Uncertainty—an alien concept—crept into his mind. *Tell her. Tell her now.*

He understood the Terran expression 'cold feet.' Holding her upper arms, he put space between them. Her mouth was red and pouty from their kiss, her hair tousled from his fingers. He stood, fastening the closure on his shirt. Then, he pulled her to her feet. "We should continue the tour."

She dusted the seat of her trousers. He lost the battle with his self-control. He pulled her tightly to him and cupped her lush bottom. Hunger to topple her to the ground shot through him, startling him with its intensity.

Her blue eyes widened. In passion or question?

Immediately, he dropped his hands and stepped back. "Leaves were clinging to your...trousers."

A knowing grin curved her mouth. "Why, Marcus, I didn't think you Serenians knew how to lie."

Heat rushed up his neck.

She reached behind and clasped his buttocks. "Omigod, they're tighter than I thought." She gave him a little pat and a wink. "Is that your uncle hailing us?"

***

Mid-day Repast was a boisterous affair—or as boisterous as Serenians allow themselves to be. Five farm workers joined Cam, Marcus, and Jessie for the meal. She was amazed at how Marcus fit in. The workers treated him as one of their own. He seemed more at ease here than with his staff on the *Freedom.*

She marveled at his knowledge of crops and land management, surmising he must have continued independent study well after the Academy. Even his uncle asked his advice. She was content to watch as he grew more relaxed and even bantered with the others.

Doranthus, who appeared to be the foreman, started telling stories about Marcus as a teenager. "He was a curious one. Always asking questions, following after me like a celabra."

Cam's yellow-striped celabra, lying at Marcus's feet, lifted his head. Absently, Marcus patted the dog-like creature while the other workers added their stories. What emerged was a picture of an eager youth full of passion, not the controlled Captain she knew on board ship. Serenian custom had beaten him into submission. She'd caught glimpses of that zeal earlier when he showed her the fields and crops.

He belonged here. Those Elders were wrong to deny him his choice, to forbid him to follow his heart.

Cam cut off yet another story. "While we are pleased to have you both here, our work awaits us. This area is scheduled for rain tomorrow, and we have two sections of cassana yet to harvest."

"Of course, Uncle, I will assist you." Marcus gave Jessie a look of regret. "I apologize for leaving you on your own. Uncle Cam has an EI—an Entertainment and Information system—you may use to occupy yourself."

She pushed back her chair. "I can help, too."

"You are a guest."

She ignored his protest and turned to Cam. "I've helped with harvesting before. Tell me what to do."

"We can always use another pair of hands. Come." Cam led her down the hall to the small bedroom where he'd placed the pouch with her clothes. Indicating a closet, he said, "You will wish to change into overalls so as not to damage your fine city clothes."

When she joined the others, Doranthus, the foreman whose steady patience reminded her of Luqett, was issuing orders. After a few instructions, he turned over the controls of a massive harvesting implement to her.

"This is like the machines the really big farms use back home. Only a whole lot bigger. I'll bet it could cut twice as much as they do."

Soon she was ready. By lining up the machines, they were able to cut huge swaths through the purple grain. Behind each machine, a container vehicle received the threshed grain streaming out of the chute. Marcus drove the container vehicle behind her.

"Jessica," Marcus's voice echoed in the small confines of the cab. "How do you like your machine?"

She glanced down at the control panel. *Which button activated the microphone?*

"Steady there, Jessica." That was Doranthus. "Move back to the right so you do not leave any grain unharvested."

"Push the blue button on the left side of the screen to speak to me," Marcus instructed.

"Geez Louise, guys. Give me a break."

"You are not able to walk and chew gum?" Marcus asked.

"You're a real comedian, Viator. Do you realize how big this sucker is? I can't steer and hold this damn button down at the same time."

His chuckle sent tingles through her. Just what she needed, more distraction that could send her careening across the field. Try explaining *that* to Doranthus.

"Jessica," Marcus continued, "you only needed to push the button once. Now, it is voice-activated."

"Hey, this is really awesome. I'm having a blast."

"It was very kind of you to offer to help. You did not need to do so."

"I couldn't very well sit around twiddling my thumbs while all of you guys were out here working."

"Uncle Cam appreciates your help."

"And you, Marcus?" She lowered her voice. "What do you appreciate?"

A chuckle and a snort issued from the speaker over her head. "Mar-cus, tell us what *you* appreciate." The ribald comment came from one of the younger workers.

Marcus cleared his throat. "Jessica, perhaps you are

unaware that the com system is open to all."

She gulped. "I know now."

They finished the last of the harvesting just as the twin suns disappeared behind the mountains. As she stepped out of the cab of the huge implement, Marcus was waiting.

"Look at that sky," she exclaimed. Like fireworks, red, yellow, and violet streaks shot upward until the sky glowed. Just as suddenly, the display ended.

"Wait." He turned her so she was looking in the opposite direction. Above the trees, the sky began to glow again, this time with a white light. A large white ball gradually appeared.

"Oh, wow," she said softly. "A moon."

He kept his hands on her shoulders. "Wait."

Would he put his arms around her? She didn't dare ask. The other workers were taking care of the machines nearby.

She couldn't figure out his intentions. His abrupt ending to their kiss under the xephod trees had confused her. *Didn't he want her?* She wished she had more experience. Maybe she hadn't done something right. Maybe she was so inept that he figured she wasn't worth pursuing.

His large hands massaged her shoulders as she continued to watch the sky. "Your muscles are tight." He tunneled his hands under her hair to stroke the cords of her neck. Each movement of his fingers, while easing the knotted muscles, brought a tightness to her belly. Deep inside her, other muscles contracted. She drew a shaky breath.

The moon rose steadily in the sky. And then another.

"Two moons?" she exclaimed. Anything to take her mind off his touch. "You people do everything twice?"

He pulled her back against his chest. *Oh, yes.* This is what she craved.

He slid his arms around her waist and whispered, "Wait." His breath ruffled the strands of hair that had escaped the hair ribbon. His lips nearly touched her ear.

Please kiss me, she silently begged. *Maybe I am not such a klutz, after all.*

"There," he murmured against the skin behind her ear.

Concentrating on his nearness, she would have missed

the rising of the next moon had he not spoken. Her breath caught in her throat, more enthralled by his touch than the three moons rising vertically in the night sky.

"H-How many more?"

He pressed his lips just below her ear. She shivered in anticipation. *Again, please do it again.*

"That is all." He released her and stepped back. "Cam is calling us for dinner."

She stood with her hands dangling at her sides, feeling foolish for wanting more than he would give. Even more foolish that she'd been so enthralled by the tiny peck of a kiss that she hadn't heard his uncle's call.

She took a deep breath, trying to calm her jittery insides. "Two suns and three moons. I'm impressed." She started toward the house. "Hi, Cam." She waved then ran toward the older man. Putting some distance between herself and Marcus seemed like a really good idea.

FIFTEEN

Jessie glanced from Marcus to Cam. Evening Repast was much quieter than Mid-Day. The workers had gone to their homes. Cam still sat at the head of the long oval table, she and Marcus on either side of him. A sumptuous meal was spread before them.

She had so enjoyed the talk earlier she hadn't paid attention to what she was eating. Now, she noted how fresh everything tasted.

"All the food is grown here," Cam said proudly. He'd watched her through the meal as she tasted one new treat after another. He seemed to enjoy her delight.

"Last night's supper and this? Wow. And I thought the food on your ship was great," she enthused to Marcus.

Uncle Cam gave her a disgusted look. "That is not real food. It is replicated—by a machine."

"Not all, Uncle. We grow food on board."

"Bah. Using artificial lights and no soil. What kind of farming is that?"

Because she could see this was a familiar argument, she quickly finished chewing a blue vegetable that crunched like celery yet had the sweetness of papaya. "I've said this before, but if our vegetables tasted like this, who would need candy? Geez, I'd even give up my affair with those two ice cream guys in Vermont."

Cam raised his eyebrow. "You are having an affair with two men?"

Marcus chuckled. "I believe she is referring to her fondness for a food delicacy."

Sitting back in his chair, Cam shared Marcus's laughter.

He folded his arms across his chest that, despite his age, still remained muscular. His expression grew serious. "You have talked to the Elders?" He raised an eyebrow at Marcus.

He shot his uncle a quelling look she almost missed. "What?" She glanced from one man to the other. Cam waited. Marcus's face revealed nothing. She pushed back her chair. "You two would probably like some privacy. I'll go outside and walk off this delicious meal."

"You do not have to leave," Cam said. "That Marcus brought you here signifies his high regard for you, even if you are not from our culture." He turned back to Marcus. "The Elders did not grant your request."

Marcus slowly shook his head. "My duty is to my ship and its crew."

Dismay crossed Cam's face. "I, too, have spoken to the Elders. You are the last of our line. If you are not allowed to assume ownership of the farm, the property will leave our family for the first time since the Expansion."

Pain and regret flickered in Marcus's eyes. She could see how torn he was. Quickly, he resumed his rigid control.

"Why not quit Space Fleet?" she asked. "These Elders? They can't force you to be a starship captain, can they?"

"The Elders know what is best," Marcus explained. "If everyone disobeyed the Elders, chaos would reign."

Cam glared. "You have become a better Serenian than most Serenians. The Elders are not infallible. They are quite capable of making mistakes." He cut off Marcus's protest with a wave of his hand. "Look at how they have dealt with the Praetorium. They ignored this threat instead of quelling it at the first sign of insurrection. Many have begun to question an authority that hesitates to act."

"I do not believe that is so."

"Marcus, you spend your time in space. What do you know of the mood of on-planet Serenians?"

Marcus shoved back his chair and stood. "I know my duty."

"Duty to the Alliance or to your family?" Cam countered. "It's not really *my* family, is it, Uncle?"

She had never seen Marcus so agitated. Then, as if calling

on some inner strength, he unclenched his fists, straightened his shoulders, and relaxed the tight features of his face. Despite his efforts, tension still radiated from his body as he turned on his heel and strode out of the room. The door to the outside closed with a controlled snap.

Jessie looked to Cam for an explanation, but he shook his head. "Apparently, he has not yet confided in you. I will not betray him."

"Is it because he was adopted? Is that why he thinks—"

"You must ask him about his heritage. It is not appropriate for me to explain."

"I don't understand this stuff about duty to his job."

He let out a sigh. "It has been our way for too long."

"But family should come first, over a job."

"Is that true in your culture?" He raised his eyebrow.

"Geez, what is that thing you people do with your eyebrows? It makes you look so haughty, so superior."

He chuckled. "We have evolved into a race that abhors the display of emotion. I am sure you have already noticed."

She rolled her eyes. "What an understatement."

"Raising an eyebrow is as much reaction as many Serenians reveal. At my advanced age, I have relaxed. I do not always keep such tight control of my emotions as I did when I was younger. The way Marcus does."

"Okay, you made your point. No, everyone in my country does not put family before duty to their job. But that is our choice. We may not be as *evolved* as you are but we still have our free will. *We* make our own decisions—not some old wise guys like your Elders." She stood and gripped the back of the chair. "I'm sorry. I am a guest in your home. I shouldn't have spouted off like that."

"Your candor is refreshing." Cam stood. "You wish to follow Marcus. Go to him. You...ruffle his composure."

She slanted him a look. "Is that good or bad?"

Cam gave her an enigmatic smile. "He is too rigid. He takes his obligations too seriously. You make him question himself."

Puzzled, she walked to the door.

Cam stopped her with, "Marcus is the son I never had. I am forever grateful that my sister shared him with me. I would like to see him happy, content."

She tried to figure out Cam's words as she walked outside. The night air was redolent with the smells of freshly-harvested grain. A pang of homesickness hit. She was torn. Part of her missed home so badly she ached. And another part of her wanted to be here with Marcus.

Many conflicting ideas had been tossed around the table tonight. She tried sorting out Marcus's reference to Cam's family not being his. Wasn't Cam's sister Marcus's mother? But, Marcus said he was adopted. What difference did that make? Family is family. Cam said Marcus was more Serenian than Serenians. What did that mean?

Three moons bathed the yard in a warm, white glow. Marcus stood near the animal pens. Rarely was his posture not military straight. Now, with his head bowed and shoulders hunched, he looked forlorn. She debated going to him. He made it obvious before abruptly leaving the table that he wanted to be alone. Yet, her heart ached to comfort him. Willing to risk being rebuffed, she listened to her heart.

She walked up behind him, making enough noise with her approach that she wouldn't startle him. His silence made her falter. He must know she was behind him, yet he didn't acknowledge her presence. She stepped closer. Still he made no move, spoke no words.

With a boldness she didn't realize she possessed, she slipped her arms around him. She laid her cheek against his back and felt him stiffen.

Bringing her hands up across his chest, she held on. "You don't have to talk."

He took a ragged breath but didn't pull away. "I do not wish to talk."

"Good. I am glad you brought me here, to Serenia, to your uncle's farm. Thank you, Marcus. There. That's all I have to say. I'll keep quiet now."

A low rumble in his chest vibrated beneath her hands. The vibration thrummed deep inside her. She pressed her suddenly full breasts closer against his back.

"You? Keep quiet?"

She could feel the smile in his voice.

"I like *that*," she said with mock umbrage. "I'll just be as quiet as a little— Do you have mice here?"

He straightened his shoulders but did not pull away. "We have small rodents called zoots. Even if you tried, you could not be as quiet as a zoot."

"Why not?"

"They have no vocal cords. You, on the other hand, like to use yours."

"Are you complaining?" She snuggled closer, enjoying the feel of his tight buns against her belly. What would he do if she slid her hands down his chest, and maybe lower?

He took a deep breath and exhaled through his nose. "Perhaps you did not realize I came outdoors to think."

She'd try one hand and see what happened. She could always claim it slipped. "Don't think depressing thoughts. You'll get wrinkles."

The muscles in his chest contracted as she slowly slid her hand down its hard contours. The silk-like material of his shirt whispered beneath her fingers.

"You will give me no peace," he said with resignation.

"Is peace what you really want?" She hesitated at the waistband of his slacks. He hadn't really told her to stop. Growing bolder, she slipped her fingers just under the band.

Marcus sucked in a breath. A powerful sense of futility had overwhelmed him before he deserted the dining table. He had come out into the night to be alone. Cam never intruded, knowing Marcus needed privacy to repair his self-control. Jessica's barging into his solitude distracted him from his misery. But, his self-control was not yet in place.

Too many conflicts ran rampant inside him. His frustration with the Elders, and his career, always loomed larger here on Cam's farm. Roiling inside him, too, were the effects of Jessica's presence.

He was surprised by the comfort he felt with her body wrapped around him. Fast on top of the comfort, she stirred his passion. Now, with her body pressed so close the hard nubs of her breasts poked into his back, he was no longer in control. His erection surged against his clothing, demanding release.

Cool night air fluttered against his skin. She had pulled his shirt out of his trousers. Her fingers were cold from the late evening temperature. Conversely, his skin burned as she slid her fingers along his waist. He craved her touch. Inhibited by the snugness of his trousers, she released the clasp. His sex leapt in anticipation.

She pressed her lower body into his rear as she hesitated at the now open fastening of his trousers. The thought of throwing her to the ground and mounting her like a rutting rumiduck raced through his brain.

Exerting the last iota of Serenian discipline, he clasped her exploring fingers. He had not spoken to her yet about his heritage. He could barely speak now, so strong were the escalating emotions. His heart, his throat were in the grip of passion stronger than anything he had experienced.

"No." His voice came out too strong, too abrupt. When he twisted away from her, the look of devastation on her face gave him pause. He refastened his trousers then cleared his throat. "I apologize for speaking so harshly."

In the light of the three moons, he saw her cheeks flame red. "Hey, no problem. I guess I overstepped the bounds. You know us uninhibited, primitive Terrans. We just don't know when to quit." She held up her hands and retreated.

She'd wrapped those hands that had turned his insides into a quivering mass around her own waist. An oft-used method, he noted, of self-preservation, along with her quick retorts. She dropped her hands and looked up at him. The blush had nearly disappeared. How quickly she rebuilt her own defenses. Much more quickly than he had.

Her words confirmed it. "Shoot. You take away all my fun. Just wanted to see if you were like a human underneath those clothes." She waggled her eyebrows. "You got something there you don't want me to see? Something humans don't have? Would it scare the pants off me?"

She slapped her mouth. "Oh, sugar jets, I shoulda quit when I was ahead. Don't mind me. Just call me old Foot-In-Mouth." She waved at him. "Go back to your thinking. Sorry I intruded. I know when I'm not wanted." She backed up several steps then turned and fled back to the house.

He waited until the door closed behind her before leaning his forearm on the top rung of the animal pen. *Not wanted?* By the Intrepid Ones, he wanted her. More than she knew. More than he was willing to admit.

A rumiduck wandered over and snuffled his arm. Marcus reached up to scratch behind its antlers. "I *am* human."

***

Jessie lay on her stomach, the covers twisted around her legs. She'd rolled over for the thirteenth time. She punched the pillow, whispering, "Damn, damn, damn."

She flopped over onto her back and brought her arm up over her eyes. "How could I be so stupid?"

Marcus had made it perfectly clear he didn't want her touch. Hadn't he pulled away each time she ventured closer? She kept throwing herself at him, initiating the kisses and, damn it, she just didn't get the message. Did he have to hit her over the head with a two-by-four? He didn't want to get involved with an Earthling—Terran, she corrected herself. Well, shoot.

Damn him and his rigid restraint. More than once she'd felt it slip. He had seemed so vulnerable outside by the corral. So lost, so torn between his duty and what he wanted to do with his life. His vulnerability drew her to him, just as it had when she discovered his fear of heights.

For a few moments, he'd allowed her to comfort him, and then she had blown it by turning her comfort into something sexual. Damn. How could she be so stupid?

Her self-recriminations had been going on for the past two hours. Cam had merely nodded to her when she flew in from outside and said she was going to bed. Thank goodness he hadn't asked any questions.

A while later, she heard Marcus come in. The low murmur of voices carried down the hall to her bedroom, but their words were indistinct—Cam's voice slow, controlled; Marcus's clipped, abrupt. She strained to hear their words but, without getting up and going to the door, she couldn't understand them. Gradually, Marcus's tone became calmer. The hot topic must have changed to a less contentious one.

After wadding up the pillow and shoving it under her head, she decided she'd beaten herself up long enough. Going over what she should, or shouldn't, have done got her nowhere. Tomorrow, she resolved, she'd keep her distance. She'd show him self-control. She'd show him aloofness and unflappability. She would be the soul of composure.

Sang-froid would be her middle name.

***

Veronese watched the patrol car slowly sweep its searchlight across the fields and the houses on either side of the road. She stood against the partially-closed drapes.

Tim was still asleep, snoring softly in the upstairs bedroom. Just as she had each night since they returned to the farm, she paced the darkened house. She had not had trouble sleeping at Tim's apartment. But here at the farmhouse, the threat posed by the man across the road loomed large, preventing a restful sleep. Each time she closed her eyes, she relived his distorted reflection in the glass, the twist of the knob beneath her fingers as he tried to open the kitchen door. Every little creak of the old farmhouse shook her to alertness. Was it the intruder?

In her dreams, when she finally fell into an exhausted sleep, the man broke in. He stalked her through the kitchen and into the living room. Down the hallway she would scramble, with him steadily advancing. Just as he reached for her, she would bolt out of the dream, fear clawing at her chest.

So, instead of sleeping, she walked through the house, checking each window, even though Tim checked the locks before retiring. She looked for moving shadows, her heart pounding with each bush moved by the wind or cloud passing across the moon.

All these human emotions had taken their toll. An unfamiliar edginess skittered along her nerve endings all the time. In the bathroom mirror this morning, she noticed violet smudges under her eyes. Abandoned by her ship, stalked by a crazed drug dealer, she felt helpless. Nearly hopeless.

After the patrol car's taillights disappeared around the curve, a light came on in the house across the road. A lone figure stood in the front window, silhouetted by the light. From his cocky stance, she knew it was her stalker.

***

Marcus moved his hands slowly over her body, his touch gentle and firm. With his mouth, he followed his fingers, down her throat to the valley between her breasts. She turned, offering her breast to his searching mouth. He didn't disappoint her.

He covered her nipple and, with agonizing slowness, flicked the hard bead with his tongue. She writhed against the cool sheets. Though his softly murmured words were unintelligible, she knew he was pleased with her response.

He drew his hand across her belly, circling her navel, lightly stroking down further until he reached between her legs. Anxious to please him, she let her legs fall apart. He stroked the inside of one thigh and then the other, each time coming closer to the source of her desire.

She whimpered. Heat flooded her lower body, curling inside her, waiting, anticipating, struggling for release.

His touch came closer this time. This time he would do it. This time he would—

The light tap brought Jessie out of the erotic dream. She groaned into her pillow at the loss.

"Jessica," Marcus called softly. "Are you awake?"

Torn between wanting what she had dreamed and the reality she knew was in store for her, she kept silent. She knew why he'd come. To apologize.

He tapped again.

She lay perfectly still, not up for another session that would only end in rejection. He called again. *No, damn it.* He was not going to do this to her. She couldn't take another apology.

Moments later, she heard him retreat. A stair creaked as he went up to his second floor bedroom.

Good. That was what she wanted. She closed her eyes,

recalling her 'Dream' Marcus's hands sliding across her skin, caressing her, loving her.

She froze. Her eyes flew open. Loving her?

Way to go, Jess. That's a real pipe dream.

The rain came during the early morning hours. Jessie loved the soothing sound as it gently beat against the window. Burrowing under the fluffy comforter, she went back to sleep. She would deal with Marcus in the morning. She was going to have it out with him. No more of this shilly-shallying around. Did he want her or not?

***

"Neesie, I can't leave you here alone."

"Nothing has happened since we've been back. Maybe the sheriff's car scared him." Veronese straightened Tim's tie. He had a meeting in Detroit.

"And maybe pigs can fly." He swiped his hand across the top of his head. "I gotta go. I tried getting out of this meeting, but my client insists on seeing me in person. God, I hate wearing this damn thing." He tugged at the knot of his flamboyant tie.

This was the first time she had seen him in business attire. Normally, he wore blue jeans and a T-shirt or sweatshirt usually emblazoned with the logos of the University of Michigan or the Detroit Tigers. On days he taught at the university, he would throw on a corduroy jacket. Today, he wore a dark gray suit and white shirt. His tie was the only outward sign of his rebellious nature. It was decorated with what he said was a cartoon character called the Tasmanian Devil. She thought the character bore a striking resemblance to Security Chief Hrvibm and the other inhabitants of Stygia, a planet in Sector Ten.

Tim clutched her shoulders. "Come with me."

"What if the *Freedom* returns, and they cannot find me. I will be fine."

He gave her a quick kiss on the cheek. That surprised her. Serenians did not display outward signs of affection. She found that she liked it.

"Keep the doors locked," he reminded her, as if she would forget.

Veronese stood on the porch and waved as Tim pulled into the turn-around in front of the house. He waved back before driving out to the road. She glanced over at the house across the road.

The man stood in the window, watching.

SIXTEEN

Jessie finally woke up just before midday. Her dream lover had not returned, much to her dismay. She quickly dressed and left her room, overhearing Marcus and Cam in his office as she passed. Not wanting to disturb them or Cam's housekeeper, who was preparing Mid-Day Repast, Jessie fixed herself a cup of seleria and took it outside.

Despite its resemblance to an apartment building, Cam's house had a wide porch. The overhanging roof protected her from the warm, steady rain. She breathed in deeply, enjoying the smell of damp vegetation. Homesickness swamped her again.

What was happening back home? Did Tim miss her? Had he even figured out she wasn't there? Had she lost all her customers? What havoc was her twin wreaking? At least, *she* wasn't messing up Veronese's life.

The door opened. Jessie glanced over her shoulder. Marcus walked to a support post across the steps from her and leaned his shoulder against it. He stared across the lawn to the fields they had cut yesterday, where only stubble remained.

"When I was a child, I came here each summer," he said. "Even though I enjoyed my vacation, I knew I was here because my parents wanted me out of their way."

Her heart ached for the little boy who must have felt rejected by his parents. She knew that feeling. "You mentioned your parents' unhappy marriage. Did they divorce?"

"Divorce is rarely an option here, and only in cases of extreme incompatibility. Societal pressures are such that being divorced is worse than staying in a difficult relationship." He took a deep breath and released it slowly. "They were happy once. I keep the picture you saw to remind me they were happy, before I was born. They died in a speeder accident. I was in my second year at the Academy, and I felt only relief that the strife was finally over."

The anguish in his voice drew her to him. She put her hand on his shoulder, but he continued to stare straight ahead. She began to rub small circles, first on one shoulder and then on the other. His muscles remained tight, as if he deliberately denied himself the pleasure of relaxing.

"Don't torture yourself with guilt for feeling relief. Their inability to get along was not your fault."

He spun around so quickly she dropped her hand. His eyes narrowed and his mouth tightened. She was momentarily frightened by his fierce expression. "It *was* my fault. Their arguments were always about me."

"Oh, Marcus." She stroked his upper arm. "Every child thinks that. Don't blame yourself for what you couldn't control."

He gripped her hands. "Spare me your platitudes. I heard their arguments. My father detested me because—"

"Marcus, Jessica," Cam's housekeeper called from inside the house. "Mid-day Repast is served."

She ignored the summons. Marcus's voice and posture told her he had been about to reveal something important. Something so momentous he now clearly regretted ever mentioning his parents. "Why, Marcus? Why did your father hate you?"

He shook his head. "You have not eaten since last evening. Come. We will see what delicacies Cam's housekeeper has prepared for us."

She clutched his arm. "Don't shut me out. Talk to me. Tell me what makes your eyes so sad. Why do you speak of your father with such bitterness?"

"Later. You must be hungry."

Resigned, she allowed him to lead her into the house.

The rain ended during the meal. The clouds moved on, revealing the twin suns. When she said she'd like to take a walk, Marcus joined her.

"You don't need to entertain me. I won't get lost."

He smiled, his killer smile that always kicked low in her belly. He'd shaken off his earlier torment. During lunch, he and Cam had chatted about politics. While they bantered, she pieced together a better image of Marcus.

She'd learned so much about him since they left the *Freedom*. His yearning to be a farmer, his dissatisfaction with the Elders' refusal to release him from his job as starship captain, his parents' unhappy marriage, his love for his uncle. She imagined revealing so much about himself was an uncommon occurrence. On board ship, he maintained a brick wall around his innermost thoughts. Serenian reticence? Or more?

Was it being at the farm, his place of refuge?

She knew he had been about to reveal something else before the housekeeper's summons—the reason he thought his father hated him. He had nearly trusted her with another important aspect of himself. Now, he held himself aloof. He didn't even hold her hand or place his hand on her back. She was tired of him letting her get just so close and then shutting her out. If he didn't want to reveal secrets, he should never have brought up the subject of his parents' divorce.

"Wanna talk about whatever is bothering you?" she asked after they ended up at the top of the knoll. When he didn't respond, she leaned against the reddish-brown trunk of a xephod tree. Its huge branches and wide leaves provided a canopy of shade from the warmth of the mid-afternoon suns. Heat and dampness from the earlier rain combined to release an odor from the bark. She detected the citrus-y cinnamon of the tea she enjoyed.

She plucked a long wide leaf and split it along its veins, releasing more xephod tea aroma. Several long moments passed in silence while he stared out across the fields. All right, he hadn't told her to shut up. Or stalked off away from her. She latched onto the hope—meager, though it was—that he wanted to talk to her.

Stifling her impatience to prod him along, she stooped and ran her fingers through the short grass. "Does somebody come up here and cut this? For that matter, how does it grow in the shade under the trees?" She plucked a blade of grass and examined it.

He turned around and gave her a rueful look. "Always inquisitive."

She stood and dusted her hands. "Is that a rebuke for disturbing your meditation?"

"Jessica, you always disturb me."

She was entranced by his steady stare. He slowly shook his head, as if to clear it. "That was no rebuke. Merely a statement of fact. The vegetation is called lacana. It is very adaptable, growing well in any light. This is as high as it grows, so there is no need to cut it."

"Bet that would make a lot of guys back home happy. No mowing the lawn on Saturday afternoon. Just kick back and watch the baseball game on TV."

"I am certain we can think of something better to do than discuss agriculture." The serious look was gone from his eyes. In its place, she saw a flicker of desire.

She waggled her eyebrows. "You have something in mind?"

Immediately, she mentally kicked herself for the smart-aleck comment that just fell out of her mouth. She really wanted him to talk to her about whatever was bothering him but was afraid of the rebuff.

A light flared in his eyes as he came toward her. A corresponding warmth filtered through her veins. Though part of her wanted to rush toward him and throw her arms around his neck, uncertainty made her hesitate. Could she take another rejection? She backed up until the rough bark of the tree pressed into her back.

"Are you afraid of me, Jessica?" he quietly drawled.

No, I'm afraid of what you do to me. I'm afraid I don't know what you want from me. I'm afraid my inexperience will make me do something stupid and chase you away. I'm afraid you won't want me.

She lifted her chin. "I'm not afraid."

A slow smile curved his lips. "Good." He drew out the

word.

A trickle of heat began in her stomach. Before she could blink, the trickle became a flood. Her stomach twisted. Heat shot straight to her groin. All he had to do was look at her with those strange silver eyes and she became aroused.

He bent his head and touched his firm, warm lips to hers. She promptly melted. Right there, plastered against a tree, her knees turned to jelly. She clutched his shirt like a lifeline, her insecurities forgotten in the intensity of his kiss.

Pinned between the tree and the man, she returned his kiss. Last night's dream lover had nothing on the real thing. Why, oh, why hadn't she opened her door to him when he had come a-callin' last night?

The urgency in his body transmitted itself to hers. The kiss wasn't enough. She had to touch him. While she was separating the closure of his shirt, he was opening hers. Must have been mental telepathy. She stroked his smooth, bare chest, her fingertips memorizing each muscle, each rib.

He nuzzled her neck and her throat, his mouth a devious instrument of torture. He crowded closer. With his lower body pressed so intimately to hers, the unmistakable evidence of his desire throbbed against her. He dispensed with the front closure of her bra then bent his head to capture her breast. *Oh, wow!*

When she arched her hips, his sex grew harder, throbbed more incessantly. He clasped her buttocks, holding her still as she moaned her delight.

Until he slipped his fingers down her belly, she hadn't realized he'd released the fastening of her trousers. The shimmery material of their trousers whispered as he slid his thigh between her legs, opening her to his touch.

She held his head against her breast, while he alternately teased her nipple with his tongue and teeth. Below, his fingers parted her and probed. A streak of hot, pure pleasure shot through her. She needed...something more.

Her insides coiled tighter. She wanted what he had done before, on the stairway in the access conduit. The feeling of his fingers outside her clothes was a pale imitation of what he was doing now against her bare flesh. She arched into his hand, trying to force him to...do something. Anything.

He stroked once. "Ah."

Twice. "Oh, God."

Again. She arched her back and screamed. Ripple after ripple shook her to the very core.

She opened her eyes to find him looking at her. Heat flooded her face as she realized he had once again watched her climax. She ducked her head and tried to pull away.

"You cannot imagine how beautiful you looked." He tipped her chin, forcing her to look at him. His eyes held only tenderness.

"Wow," she breathed. "Oh, wow." She pulled one of her arms out from their embrace and reached up to stroke his cheek. "You sure know how to show a girl a good time."

When he started to pull her shirt together, she stilled his hands. "Let's finish this." She reached for the waistband of his trousers.

He pushed her hand away. "No," he said gruffly.

He had withdrawn, his silver eyes gray, clouded with troubling thoughts as he stared past her into the distance. He took several steps away, reinforcing his apparent desire to be separated from her.

She slowly pulled together her scattered self. Why had he done this? Why give her such pleasure yet deny himself? What had made him change his mind about making love with her? She stood there, pondering what went wrong. He maintained his silence, giving her self-doubts free rein.

She fastened the front closure of her bra. After rearranging the rest of her clothes, she took a deep breath. Why did she keep thinking this was her fault? What the heck was wrong with *him*? Damn it, he wasn't going to get away with rejecting her again. "Is that how you *superior culture* guys get your kicks?"

With a startled movement, he shook his head. His eyes cleared as they focussed on her. "I beg your pardon?"

"Yeah." She stepped closer and poked him in the chest. "You *should* beg my pardon. What was that all about? Giving the Earthling a little thrill? Gee, thanks, guy. Maybe in your culture sex is a spectator sport, but in mine it's participatory. Well, I've had it with you, buster. No more."

She strode off toward the farm buildings. The more she thought about what he'd done, the more embarrassed she got. And the angrier. She'd dreamed of her first lovemaking experience. It was supposed to be perfect. With Marcus, it should have been. Yet, each time they got to a certain point, he quit. Why?

After she traveled several yards, she heard him call, "Jessica."

Surprised he had waited so long to respond, she glanced over her shoulder. He was striding down the slope after her. She started to run, knowing she was being foolish. Yet, she ran away from him anyway. She skirted the small, dusty gray bushes that reminded her of sagebrush.

Rocks and exposed roots littered the seldom-used path. She tripped over a tangle of roots but caught her balance.

"Jessica, I insist you stop at once. You will hurt yourself." He had nearly caught up with her.

"As if I'm not hurt already," she muttered. The next rock she stepped on skittered. Windmilling her arms, she tried to maintain her footing. "Damn."

He caught her before she went down. "Why are you running away from me? I mean you no harm."

"Why do you keep shutting me out?" she retorted. "Are you just plain dense? Where's that superior intellect?"

He snagged his muscular arm around her waist, bringing her back snug up against his chest. "Please don't go."

Damn. She didn't want to be in his arms.

She was a liar, too.

"I'm an idiot, okay? You can let go of me." At least, she had the presence of mind not to struggle. That would really cap it. She'd already made a fool out of herself by succumbing to his lovemaking skills and then running away. "I can stand by myself."

She felt his chest expand as he took a deep breath. "You confuse me, Jessica." He released her.

"What? The mighty *Captain* confused?" She turned around and backed up a few steps. Anything to put some distance between them. Having him hold her again stirred up responses better left alone. Hadn't she learned her lesson up on the knoll under the xephod tree?

It was no Blueberry Hill, but she'd certainly found *her* thrill. She bit back a nervous giggle, knowing she'd never be able to explain that to an alien.

"Did I not please you?" With the crook of his finger, he tipped her chin.

Heat flooded her face. "You know you did."

"Then, why—"

"Why did you turn away from me? Would you be contaminated if you made lo— if you had sex with an alien?" She jerked her chin away from his touch.

Concern shown in his eyes. "In your culture, you make a distinction between the act of coupling when emotions are involved. Your expressions 'having sex' and 'making love' are not the same, are they?"

She wasn't going to be taken in by his look of concern. For all she knew, it was just as false as his desire for her. "What is this? A quiz on the mating habits of Earthlings? You should ask an expert. I'm no Dr. Ruth."

He slung his arm around her shoulders and began walking back to the knoll. "You amuse me, Jessica."

"Certainly glad I can provide the entertainment." She wanted to put some distance between their bodies, but he wouldn't allow it. When she attempted to ease away, he exerted a slight pressure. She refused to struggle.

"You are embarrassed by your orgasm," he said with a touch of amazement.

Embarrassed to death by his frankness, she resorted to what she knew best. "Give that man a hundred dollars."

"You are insecure." His tone again implied he'd just figured something out.

"Psychoanalysis was another area of self-study?"

He leaned toward her and lightly kissed her mouth. "I have noticed your words become sharp when you are unsure of yourself." They reached the 'scene of the crime'—the top of the knoll. He placed his hands on her shoulders. "Let me taste your tongue to see if it is as acid as it sounds."

As he bent his head, she ducked under his arm. "With a line like that, you could give lessons in mating habits. Sure you want your uncle to see you kissing an alien?"

He glanced over his shoulder then shrugged with chagrin. "My uncle is not watching. He and the others were going into the village this afternoon. We are alone."

"Oh, swell."

"It wouldn't matter if he saw me kissing you." He gave her a long look. "You are not an alien."

"Okay. You're the alien."

He shrugged his shoulders. "No, but we will talk more on that subject later."

"Oh, we will, will we? How nice of you to ask."

He ignored her sarcasm but she knew by his breathing he was getting exasperated with her. The man certainly could control his emotions. Sometimes, she wished she had that type of self-control. Then, she remembered her father's coldness and knew she could never be like that.

And she'd be damned if she was going to let Marcus do this to her time and time again. She twisted away from him. She'd been stupid to follow him back up the hill. He was not going to get another chance to practice his seductive alien ways with her. "No more kissing."

He looked startled.

Oh, damn. She'd said the last out loud. "Never mind."

Then she thought, the heck with this. She was going to lay her cards on the table. "Did you bring me back up here for a reason? If it's to try to seduce me again, don't waste your time. I've had it with—"

"This is my favorite place," he interrupted her just as she was getting up a full head of steam. "Whenever I have shore leave, I always come to the farm and always to this spot. From here—" His sweeping gesture included the fields and the buildings. "—I can see almost all of Cam's land."

Okay, she'd talk about the land. At least he wasn't trying

to kiss her again. "This would be yours if you weren't commander of a starship, right?" She leaned against a tree.

"I have no right to this land."

What was that supposed to mean? "Cam said it's been in your family since— What did he say? Since the Expansion? I take it that's a long time."

"The land has been in Cam's family."

"Are you trying to tell me something, Marcus. 'Cause if you are, the message isn't coming through."

Without turning around, he reached behind him for her hand. Immediately, she went to him. Forget all her resolutions. Forget that she didn't want him to touch her. Him reaching out said he needed her.

"Marcus, I just don't understand you. From what your uncle said, keeping the farm in the family is important."

"Control of property is not a priority to Serenians."

She squeezed his hand. "It is to your uncle. I have a little experience in this. The farm where I live has been in my family for nearly a hundred and seventy years. My father is an academic. He hated the farm. It reminded him of the back-breaking work of his boyhood."

"Farming *is* physically challenging," he admitted.

"Gram knew how much Dad hated the place. He wouldn't even visit it. While I was little, she had to come into town to see us. But, she wanted my brother and me to appreciate the wide-open spaces, so she invited us out each summer after I turned eight. I think the only reason Dad let us go was so we'd be out of his and Mom's hair for the summer."

Marcus heard the hurt in her voice at being ignored by her father. He, too, had felt his father's rejection. And his mother's embarrassment. "Did your brother enjoy the farm as much as you did?"

"Tim was only three that first summer, but he loved the freedom. Gram wasn't nearly as strict as our parents were. She didn't care if we got dirty or tore our clothes. Or ran screaming through the fields just for the heck of it."

Marcus chuckled.

"We couldn't do anything like that at home because we

lived near other university faculty. Dad had an image to maintain, according to Mom. His children couldn't look like ruffians. I think Mom was more concerned about his 'position' than he was." She shrugged.

So, Marcus thought, *in her early life she had been forced to conform to the expectations of her mother.* Jessica had no idea how similar their childhoods had been. "Your grandmother allowed you to be free." Just as Cam had allowed him to be.

"Absolutely. Gram never forced us to try to be what we weren't." She pointed her finger at him. "Like your Elders are trying to do to you."

He had known she would probe. She had been trying to puzzle out the hints he had inadvertently dropped since they left the ship. Perhaps he had not intended to be inadvertent all along. What was it about her that made him drop his guard? "The Elders know what is best."

She put her hands on her hips and glared at him. "How? Are they clairvoyant?"

"They know our aptitude and direct our education."

"What about what's in a person's heart?" She pointed to her chest. "This is what counts. Following your heart."

"Like you did?"

"Yes." The word exploded from her mouth. "You can't imagine the grief I got when I refused to further my education. Two years of community college was enough for me, thank you very much. And my choice of subject matter? Well, that certainly stirred up a hornet's nest. Until the grades arrived, my folks didn't realize I changed all the courses they instructed me to take. Too late then. They called me a recalcitrant child. Never mind I was eighteen and an adult. When I refused to agree with them, they washed their hands of me."

"They rejected you because you did not conform to their wishes." How well he understood.

Her belligerence disappeared. Her mouth trembled, her eyes glittered with the sheen of tears. She blinked twice and sniffed. "Quit psychoanalyzing me."

He acquiesced for the moment. "Do you enjoy what you do? Do you enjoy repairing what people break?"

"You bet I do." She lifted her chin defiantly, the tears gone. "And then there was the farm. Gram knew if she left it to Dad, he'd sell it without a qualm. So, she left it to the person who would cherish the land the way she did."

"You."

She nodded. Her lower lip trembled for a moment. "Oh, God, I still miss her." Wrapping her arms around herself, she sniffed twice.

He wanted to reach out to her, to hold her, but her stiff posture made it evident she wanted no expression of comfort. He took a handkerchief out of his pocket and handed it to her. "You were fortunate to have your grandmother. In that respect, our lives have been quite similar. During my summers here, I, too, felt the freedom of which you speak."

She wiped her eyes and her nose before tucking the handkerchief in her own pocket. "Even though you want to be a farmer like your uncle, you obey the Elders and continue being a space jockey?"

He blew out a breath. "You do not understand."

She grabbed his hand. "Tell me. Make me understand how you can give up what you truly desire."

For a long moment, he stared into her eyes. "I obey the Elders because Serenians obey. This is the Serenian way. I must act like a proper Serenian."

"Why? What hold do they have over you? Why is it so important to act like a *proper* Serenian?"

"Because I am not."

SEVENTEEN

Jessie guffawed. "What do you mean you're not a proper Serenian? My God, you're the most *proper* person I know."

"You misunderstood. I am not..."

She waited for him to continue. A painful expression crossed his face. Ever since they arrived on Serenia, she'd noticed many more expressive reactions from him—as if he was gradually throwing off the strictures of his culture.

"I am not Serenian."

"What?" That was the last thing she expected.

"Do you recall the story Veronese Qilana told you about twins?"

"You mean about your mad scientist who— Omigosh. You're one, too? You're from Earth?"

He bowed his head. "Few know about this."

My God, he's ashamed of being Terran. "How did you find out?"

"My mother—the woman who raised me—told me."

"Your Serenian mother. Did she love you?"

"She was a proper Serenian. Strong emotions were never displayed. I am certain she had affection for me. She confided in Uncle Cam as he, too, knows what I am."

So, that was what Cam had been trying to tell her last night. The light bulb went on in her head. "Is that why you think your father hated you?"

"My mother was unable to reproduce. He desperately wanted a son. Since divorce is not acceptable, he took his frustration out on her by withholding his affection. Through the 'underground' she heard about a scientist looking for host mothers. She thought she would please her husband by having a child. She didn't realize the fetus implanted in her would be from Earth. When she did, it was too late."

"When did your father discover the truth?"

"At my birth." He turned away from her and bent over. He brought his hands up to his face. When he turned around, he held out his hand. In his palm lay two silver disks.

She looked up in question. And saw his eyes. Jade green. "Oh, wow," she breathed. "Your eyes are beautiful."

His mouth twisted as he dropped the lenses into his trouser pocket. "That was not his reaction. At first, he thought I was a throw-back to our pre-Serenia ancestors. My mother told him the truth. He hid her and me here on her brother's farm. He told his family I was sickly and needed the fresh country air." He snorted. "The scientist made up special lenses for the few of us who survived his experiment."

"There were others?" She couldn't take all of this in. *Marcus was from Earth.*

"I was in the first 'batch.' Dr. Cenamola made some fatal errors with my group. The second time, he had more success. During the third experiment, when Veronese was taken from your mother, the Elders discovered what he had been doing. They hastily buried all his research, but not too successfully. Your twin and I were able to discover the extent of his experiment."

"What happened to this Dr. Cenamola?"

"He was imprisoned in a penal colony on Stygia, a planet in Sector Ten, the opposite end of the galaxy from Serenia."

"Is he still there?"

"An uprising occurred a short time ago. He was among the inmates who were killed."

Though stunned by what he'd revealed, she was relieved the scientist who had wreaked havoc on so many lives had been punished.

"Now." He touched her cheek. "Let us talk about something of more importance. I apologize for upsetting you earlier. I did not intend to lose control. I could not couple with you until you knew who I really am. You deserve that. You have strong feelings for me. Is that not correct?"

Uncomfortable with this topic because of his continual rejection, she arched her eyebrow. "Confession time?" Two could play his game.

"Please do not joke. I have experienced a strong reaction to you. But, I cannot couple with you and then return you to your home planet."

"You feel strongly about me?" She gave him a rueful smile. "What? Anger? Exasperation?"

He leaned closer, cupping her face between his hands. "I asked you not to joke. You use flippancy as a mask." His fingers were strong against her cheek, yet gentle.

"You aren't exactly spilling your guts."

He looked chagrined. "Your expressions are quaint. You wish to learn if I have more than a sexual interest in you. I am...uncertain."

"I haven't figured out my feelings, either," she lied. Her mind was in turmoil. His honesty about how he felt should have been a comfort. He had strong feelings for her, but he didn't love her. Was he capable of loving her? He had little experience with that emotion. Or any emotion, for that matter. Feelings had been drummed out of him by his parents. And by his very culture.

Yet, she witnessed his affection for his uncle and Cam's affection for him. Would Marcus ever loosen up enough to express his affection for her?

He had refrained from making love with her until he revealed his deepest secret. That meant he considered her special, didn't it? He trusted her. He cared for her, perhaps as much as he could care for anyone.

She reached across the short distance between them and touched his lips. In what seemed almost an involuntary reaction, he kissed her fingertips.

"Okay, I give up," she said. "I want to make love with you. Do not give me any psycho-babble about the difference between having sex and making love. I want to make love with you. Now, what do you make of that?"

His green eyes widened at her declaration. "I am humbled."

He pulled her into his arms and kissed her. For several moments, she clung to him. When they kissed before, her physical reaction had been so strong it had nearly overwhelmed her. Now, though the physical was still strong, she opened herself totally to him. She was willing to take a chance on him. On his ability to love her. As if a dam burst inside her, that knowledge released love more devastating than a flood.

In a fluid move, he laid her on the ground. The soft grass-like vegetation cushioned her. She looked up into his green eyes, more enthralling now that she knew they were really his and not artificial lenses.

She didn't care how long she had known him. She didn't care whether this would be the only time. All that mattered was loving him.

She smoothed her fingers over his brow. "We can't do this until I tell you something."

He laid his finger on her lips. "There is no need."

"Yes. Yes, there is. Are you ready? Confession time, Marcus. I think I've fallen in love you."

He tightened his grip on her shoulders. "You do not have to tell me this."

"Yes, I do. I wanted you to know."

Marcus closed his eyes. He could not look at hers, shining so bright with love for him. All her flippancy was gone. She lay vulnerable beneath him. Before baring her body, she had bared her soul. A need to speak slammed into him. She had opened herself to him. How could he do less?

She stroked his cheek. "You don't have to say anything."

But, he did. He opened his eyes. Love still shone out of hers. Now, with a hint of apprehension, as if afraid of being rejected.

What could he tell her? "Jessica, I am uncertain if what I feel for you is what you call love. I—"

The light in her eyes dimmed. "That's okay, Marcus. I understand."

Again, he touched her lips to silence her. "Let me finish. I have never allowed myself to experience emotion as strong as I have for you. No Serenian female has affected me as you have. I have always been able to control myself. Yet with you, I no longer want to."

"Then don't, big guy." Once again, she hid behind flippancy. "I'll take what I can get. C'mon. We're wasting time. Your uncle and the others could return at any moment." She opened the front of his shirt then slipped her warm fingers inside. "You do make love the traditional way, don't you? Or has your superior culture figured out a better way?"

"Perhaps you would like to discover for yourself."

With deliberation, she skimmed her fingers along his ribs. What little control he had left was deteriorating. First, he had to reassure her. "You need not worry about protection."

Her eyes widened as if just remembering to be concerned.

The motion of her fingers along his ribs and down his belly made concentration an effort. He forced himself to continue. "Because of our interaction with other planets, our scientists developed an inoculation against diseases. I have received that inoculation as well as pills that render me temporarily sterile. All males—"

"Marcus, did anyone ever tell you you talk too much?" She pushed on his shoulders to roll the two of them over.

Tightening his hold on her waist, he allowed her to be the initiator. She urged him to lie flat on the ground. She straddled him, freer now to slide her fingers down his chest. Her eyes revealed her wonder as she explored his body. As if this was new. At twenty-nine Earth-years, certainly she had taken lovers. His puzzlement distracted him momentarily. He found her innocence bewildering.

Not content with just touching him, she leaned forward to run her lips and tongue down the middle of his chest. He slid his fingers into her thick, fiery hair, loosening it from the ribbon until it flowed over her shoulders.

With no guidance from him, she edged her way over to his left side. She must feel his heart pounding against his ribs, beneath her lips. With the touch of her tongue on his nipple, his hips surged upward. He groaned out loud, still trying to control his body, which craved completion.

Finally, he could stand it no more. He dragged her up until

their mouths merged. With a hunger that took both of them by surprise, he kissed her. He thrust his tongue into her mouth while the hardness of his body surged into her softness. Through the layers of clothing, he allowed her to feel how she affected him.

He trapped her hands between their chests. Her only movement was the tightening of her thighs against his hips. He rolled her onto her back. With minimal effort, he released the closure of her blue shirt. The color nearly matched her eyes—eyes which darkened as her need intensified.

He tasted the side of her neck before wandering lower. He opened the front closure of her undergarment. Her breasts spilled forth. Why had he been critical of their lushness before? They fit neatly into his hands. Her breasts were just right for his lips, his tongue, his teeth. He gently squeezed.

Her gasp of pleasure accompanied the bucking of her hips. He scraped his teeth across her nipple. Again, her hips surged, and he drew the tight bud into his mouth.

"Oh, God, Marcus, you can't keep doing this to me." Her breath came out raggedly. Her heart raced beneath his fingertips as he rolled her other nipple.

"You wish me to stop?" As if he could.

"God, no." She moved her hands restlessly down his chest. When she reached the waistband of his slacks, she hesitated before searching for the closure. She brushed his engorged sex, sending alarms throughout his system.

"Wait." He struggled to take a breath.

"No." She abandoned her search for the closure and slid her hands around his hips. She clasped his rear, pulling him closer to her. "You can't stop. Not now, not again."

He levered himself above her. "I merely wished to suggest we dispense with our clothing. But, I will accede to your wishes."

He brought his mouth down on hers. Eagerly, she returned his kiss. When he darted his tongue between her lips, she drew it deep into the soft recesses of her mouth. Hot, so hot, he thought he would go up in flames. Passion brought him too close to the edge.

She released the closure at his waist. "And I'm willing to accede to yours."

He rolled off and quickly dispensed with their clothing. As he stood over her, she stared at his body. "Omigod, Michaelangelo's *David* has nothing on you. You're...magnificent."

Her praise filled his chest with pride. As he knelt, he scanned her body. She, too, was magnificent.

"Don't look at me, Marcus." Her cheeks turned bright red. "Over a week without a razor, and my legs look like a hairy beast's. While you—" She waved her hand at his hairless body. He hadn't realized how she would react to what must be an unusual sight.

"I am not displeased by your appearance, Jessica." He lightly kissed her lips. "You are all the more exciting because your secrets are hidden."

As he slid his fingers slowly down her belly, her breathing quickened. When he reached her nest of curls the color of the tree behind them, he reminded himself to be gentle. He probed. She was ready.

She lifted her hips, encouraging him to explore further. He slid his finger into her. She gasped.

Her breathing grew rapid as her body tightened around his finger. Using his thumb, he grazed the tender bud at the top of the folds. She shrieked.

"Damn it, Marcus." She struggled to catch her breath. "Don't you dare stop there." She reached between them, encircling his sex with her strong fingers.

"Wait." He was losing control.

"No. Come to me, Marcus." Her awkwardness in trying to complete their union convinced him of her inexperience.

He cupped her chin, forcing her to open her eyes and look at him. "Is this your first time?"

Her cheeks burned red again. "Does it matter?"

He had been right. "You have valued your innocence. Surely you want to wait for the man you love." He had to give her the choice. He could not take from her that which she should give to her soulmate. He already knew she was his soulmate. She had no idea that once he coupled with her, he was committed to her. For life.

"I have chosen you, Marcus."

Humbled by her admission, he completed their union. Never had he experienced such rightness. Though she was tight, she eagerly took him into her body. When he hesitated at the resistance, she surged upward, gasping for a moment then adjusting to the fullness of him.

He tried to hold back, but she would not let him. The moment of his completion was near. He had to bring her with him. They started this together, they would finish together. He forced himself to slow down. She sped up her movements. He reached between them and stroked. She arched her back, as if launching herself in flight. It was he who flew.

He buried his face against her neck, holding her tightly. This felt so right. He belonged to this woman. He was committed. And she belonged to him.

Her body limp, she sagged in his arms, staring at him with wonder and amazement. "I love you, Marcus."

***

"Hey, sweetcakes. Where'd your boyfriend go? He leave you here all alone?"

The man stood in the middle of the driveway in broad daylight. Veronese stayed to the right of the window, hopefully hidden by the drapes. She felt foolish hiding, yet she had promised Tim she wouldn't go outside.

Feeling foolish was a new experience for her. Her sojourn on Earth had provided many new experiences. This was one she could have cheerfully done without. She wished she had a ziff blaster. She'd give her harasser one good jolt, enough to knock him on his rear. The thought gave her satisfaction, another new experience—even if she could not act on it. A sudden sense of guilt assailed her. What would her pacifist Serenian parents have thought of her violent reaction?

"Sweetcakes? How come them cops are watching this road? You didn't do something stupid and call them, did you?"

She clutched the small cellular phone Tim told her to wear around her neck at all times. He'd programmed the sheriff's number, so she only needed to hit one digit and the phone would dial automatically.

"I wasn't going to hurt you none."

She poised her finger over the button. If he took one step toward the house, she would call the sheriff.

"You get lonely tonight with your boyfriend gone, you call me, hear? I'll come over and keep you company." He gave the window a two-finger salute as if he knew she was hiding behind the curtains. Then, he turned and strolled back to his house across the road.

She slid down the wall and sat on the floor. Her hands were shaking so badly would she even have hit the correct button? She scrubbed her hands down the sides of her sister's jeans. Her palms wouldn't dry.

She should have called the sheriff. It would do no good now. By the time a patrol car came, the man would be in his house. He would probably deny he was ever here.

She glanced at her sister's watch. Three o'clock. Tim said he would be back no later than four.

***

"Damn." Tim slammed his fist on the steering wheel. He was stuck on I-94. And he wasn't alone. Nobody was going anywhere. He'd promised Neesie he'd be back by now. Instead, a ten-car pile-up left him and everybody else who wasn't near an exit twiddling their thumbs while emergency workers freed the trapped and tended the injured.

If only he'd listened to the radio instead of his CD player. He could've gotten off at the last exit. Cement K-rails down the median prevented him and everyone else stuck in the tie-up from turning around.

He should have insisted Veronese come with him.

***

During Evening Repast, Cam seemed to watch the two of them. Jessie squirmed in her chair, hoping he didn't know what they had done under the xephod trees. Marcus seemed pensive, more so since they'd returned to the house. She should never have blurted out her love for him. Even if it was true.

He had not referred to it. Though he was tender in his

ministrations after they made love, she was sure he regretted losing control. She'd pushed him until he had to finish what he started. Was theirs only a physical union for him?

She felt joined with him emotionally and, in some strange way, spiritually. As if they had truly become one.

She hadn't guarded her virginity the way he claimed. No man had ever tempted her to go beyond kissing and a little petting. Much to the derision of her few dates, she'd felt no need to go further, and hadn't hesitated to tell them that. Until Marcus. Now that she'd had a taste of the wonders, she wanted more. She couldn't wait until they went to bed. It wasn't just the sex—which was wonderful. She knew there would be no other man for her. She felt as committed to Marcus as if they'd exchanged vows.

The meal dragged on. She looked across the table at Marcus to try to catch his eye. When that didn't work, she slipped her shoe off and stretched her leg out. She ran her foot up his calf. Startled, he jerked back in his chair and then tried to cover his abrupt movement with a cough.

Cam looked from one to the other before continuing to talk about his trip to the village.

"Did you hear anything of interest?" Marcus asked, completely ignoring her and the foot she rubbed up and down his calf. Then he gave her a sharp look before shifting his legs out of her reach.

"People are worried the Praetorium will attack Serenia." Cam rubbed his index finger over his upper lip. "Rumor has it they are massing an army in Sector Ten. It is believed that soon we will be plunged into war."

"The Elders will not commit us to war. The Alliance will prevail, as will the peace we have enjoyed."

"The Elders may not have a choice."

Jessie gave an exaggerated yawn. "I think I'm going to turn in. You guys go ahead and talk." She gave Marcus a hard stare, willing him to abandon his interest in politics. He didn't.

Well, shoot. After she left the dining room, Marcus and Cam debated further. Their voices carried down the hall to where she was preparing for bed. They must have gone into the sitting room. She could hear them clearly. Cam was adamant that war was imminent. Marcus would not be swayed. According to him, the Praetorium would never attack a superior strength like the Alliance.

As she slipped on her sister's slinky nightgown, she realized their voices had lowered. More curious than last night, she walked to the door. Unable to distinguish the words, she opened it a crack.

"—your intentions?" Cam admonished.

"Are none of your business." Marcus's tone would ordinarily cause the questioner to falter.

Not Cam. "What of the Elders' candidates? Will you reject them and choose Jessica?"

Candidates? Had she given her heart to Marcus only to lose him to someone chosen by the Elders?

"You probe too far, Uncle."

"You must do what is best for her. How can she stay on Serenia? She will always be an outsider. Remember how you felt? Do you want that for her? What about offspring? Will you subject them to an existence of not belonging? Or will you feed them pills and have their eyes fitted with special lenses so you can pretend they are *real* Serenians?"

"I do not know." Marcus's voice revealed his weariness.

"If you love her, you will set her free."

***

Dusk settled over the farmhouse. Veronese debated turning on lights, thereby signaling she was there. Where was Tim?

Determined not to allow fear to keep her hiding in the dark, she turned on the kitchen light. Preparing dinner would keep her occupied until Tim came home. As she pulled vegetables out of the refrigerator, she thought longingly of her life on the *Freedom*. What she wouldn't give right now for a food replicator.

Switching places with her twin had seemed such a good idea in the planning stages. All she had wanted was to see her parents and her brother. Last, and most importantly, she would transport back to the ship and meet her sister. She had planned so carefully. And nothing had gone right.

Rinsing the celery under a stream of running water, she hummed along with the radio. She tapped her foot to the music, swaying to its gentle beat.

A light tap on the window above the sink brought her head up. She screamed.

***

Jessie stumbled to the bed. Would Marcus listen to Cam? Would he insist she return to Earth? Before, all she had wanted was to return home. Now that she'd found Marcus, she wanted to stay on board the *Freedom*. Would the Elders allow it?

She was an asset to the ship. Chief Luqett said so. She could pull her own weight. She was a quick learner. What did it matter if she wasn't a Serenian? Many on board were not. True, they belonged to member planets of the Alliance and she didn't. But why should that make a big difference?

She pulled the covers up to her shoulders and thought about what it would mean if she did not to return to Earth. Tim would understand. He would encourage her, the way he always did. Could she leave behind her business? A twinge of regret pierced her determination. She'd sacrificed so much to follow her dream, braving her parents' disappointment, scorn, and then their indifference. She'd poured herself into her work. But, Marcus was worth ten—no, a hundred—times more than her business.

But, what about Gram's farm? Could she give it up for him? He was willing to give up his Serenian mother's heritage, Cam's farm, for doing what he believed was right. She began to appreciate his sacrifice. She could do no less.

She would gladly give up all for him. For his love. He loved her. She knew he did. He just wasn't used to the words. No, more than that. He'd experienced little in the way of love. Not a mother's love for a child, and certainly not a father's. Without receiving love, how could he know how to give it?

Cam loved him. While Marcus never knew the love of his Serenian parents, he had Cam's love and acceptance. She would show him what the love of a woman meant. Chief Luqett talked about soulmates. What a wonderfully descriptive term. Two souls mated for life.

She would be Marcus's soulmate. He would come to her at the end of a hard day and she would love him and comfort him. She would help him get in touch with his human feelings.

A slow smile curved her mouth. When they made love, he would again find fulfillment in her. She would teach him to truly lose control. The way he had under the xephod trees.

She waited. He did not come. The voices had ceased some time ago. Where was Marcus? Surely, she hadn't missed him going up to his room. Had he gone outside?

She waited some more.

The house quieted. She slipped out of bed and reached for a robe hanging in the closet. She hadn't latched the door. Now, she opened it and peered down the hall.

Where was he?

Enough waiting. She walked down the hall, bare feet slapping lightly against the wood floor. Marcus was sprawled in a large chair in front of the fireplace, staring at the ashes from an earlier fire, seemingly lost in thought.

Silently, she sat at his feet and leaned against his legs. He stroked her hair absently, the way he'd stroked Cam's dog-like celabra. She rested her head on his knee.

He continued to stroke. "What am I to do with you?"

"Have I ever mentioned how much I hate it when somebody makes decisions for me, particularly if they're supposed to be for my own good?"

He chuckled softly. "I remember."

"I could stay, Marcus." She sat up, not bothering to hide her eagerness. "I don't have to go home—to Earth." She wanted to kick herself for begging. Yet, what else could she do? "Say the word, Marcus. Ask me to stay?"

Marcus recalled her profession of love. Again, just as it had this afternoon, the thought was double-edged. Wonderment that she wanted to be with him and despair that he would have to return her to her own planet. How could he let her go? "Jessica..."

"Are you already engaged? Never mind. Forget I said that. You wouldn't be. You wouldn't have made love with me if you were committed to another woman. I'm just nervous, I guess. I want you so much. Come to bed. Make love with me. Don't send me back to Earth. I want to stay with you. I'll be a big help on the ship. I won't get in the way. I'm babbling."

Marcus rose and held out his hand. He had done enough thinking for one night. Cam always needled him when he needed it most. He and Jessica would make love and worry about tomorrow, tomorrow. They still had two more days of shore leave. He did not intend to waste them worrying about what would happen when they returned to the ship.

He led her into her bedroom. With slow, deliberate movements, he untied the sash of her robe and slipped it off her shoulders. Her eyes shone bright with anticipation.

"Do you need this?" He hooked his finger under the narrow shoulder strap of the sleeping gown.

In answer, she shrugged. The strap slid down her arm. She dropped the other strap, then did a slow wiggle. His body tightened at the enticing little dance. The gown slithered down her body, revealing the tops of her breasts, then her nipples, already puckered and waiting for his lips.

"What are you waiting for, big guy?" She wiggled again, and he grew harder. The gown dropped further, clinging to her hips for a moment before joining the robe on the floor.

Then, she climbed into bed and held her arms out to him. "No more thinking tonight. Come to me."

***

Veronese thought her heart would pound right out of her chest. The dusk-to-dawn light hanging on the utility pole next to the driveway illuminated the man standing at the window. His cocky grin did not match the feral gleam in his eyes.

Fleeing the kitchen, she flipped open the cell phone. This time she didn't hesitate. She punched the button. She ran to her sister's bedroom, giving the sheriff's dispatcher her address. "Hurry. He's breaking a window."

"Sweetcakes," he called. "You oughten to have called the cops. You call 'em back and say you made a mistake."

Remembering Tim's instructions, she locked the bedroom door. Then, with a mighty effort, she slid the dresser in front of it. That might slow the man down.

Without turning on the light, she ran to the window. She looked outside before unlocking and lifting the lower sash. Tim had sprayed a substance on the track so the window would open easily and without noise. Grateful for his foresight, she slipped over the ledge. Once outside, she closed the window.

Veronese ran to the garage, staying in the shadows and hoping the powerful floodlight wouldn't betray her to the man rampaging through the farmhouse. His curses shattered the night and sent terror skitting down to her fingertips.

His words did not frighten her. His voice did. Its syrupy sweetness could not disguise the menace beneath. What was she going to do if he found her?

EIGHTEEN

After what seemed like an eternity, the traffic finally started moving. Tim expelled a deep breath, relieved he would soon be at the farm. Veronese must be frantic with worry.

She had seemed such a cool customer when he first met her. So poised, so aloof. Scientific in her examination of every part of the new life she had been forced to live. He was still amazed at her daring to enter an alien civilization and try to blend in.

Yet, underneath her cool composure lay vulnerability. He knew the fear of being abandoned by her ship gnawed at her. Fear seemed such an alien concept to her. She had plenty to fear, starting with that jerk across the road.

Tim raced along the main road running north from the expressway. He watched for deer, plentiful in this area with all the harvest gleanings on the ground. Dusk and dawn were the deer's favorite time to catch drivers unaware. He switched on his high beams. Where was the turn-off to Jessie's road?

There, up ahead, the end of the fence line. Braking hard, he swung the sports car onto the dirt road. The recent rains created a washboard effect. His teeth jarred at his car's bumping along the ruts. He swerved to avoid a crater the size of Rhode Island.

The hair on the back of his neck began to prickle. Something was wrong. Neesie? He accelerated, heedless of the pounding to the undercarriage of the Camaro.

Up ahead, across the field to the right, he could see the farmhouse. Lights blazed from every window. Something was terribly wrong. He felt it again. That hair-raising, gut-clenching fear.

He concentrated on avoiding the deep ruts in the road and getting to the farmhouse as quickly as possible. Out of the corner of his eye, he saw movement on the left.

Oh, shit. A deer.

***

Veronese heard the roar of a powerful sports car. Tim. She crouched between a large bush and the back of the garage. Spiky branches poked through her thin T-shirt, yet she dared not move. The cold night air raised goosebumps on her bare arms.

"Sweetcakes. You done playing hide-and-seek? I know you're out here. Why are you running away from me? We could have a good time, you and me." He had already circled the house. Now, he approached the garage.

The sports car came closer.

He jiggled the knob of the small door to the garage. "You hiding in here, sweetcakes?"

Having no success, he rattled the overhead door. "Where the hell are you?" He kicked the metal door.

She heard him try the small door again. Then, a thud. She felt the garage shudder. He must be throwing his shoulder against the door. She'd thought of hiding in the garage. But, in her flight, she hadn't grabbed the keys off the hook next to the back door.

The garage shook again with the force of his body slamming against the door. It gave way with a crash. She heard another crash and the sound of tools being flung on the cement floor. Glass shattered, and something came flying through the window to the left of where she hid. She was too frightened to move and brush the shards of glass off her shoulder.

"I'm going to find you," he yelled. "I've been real patient, but now I'm getting mad." His voice turned conciliatory. "C'mon out, sweetcakes. I'll forgive you for running away from me."

She heard a thud and a glugging noise. He'd kicked over the water cooler.

The door slammed against the wall. "Where the hell are you, bitch?"

***

Tim yanked the steering wheel. He missed the deer—a huge buck. As if the Camaro had a life of its own, it flew left, headlights first, into the ditch. The airbags deployed.

After batting aside the suffocating bag, he couldn't open his door. The force of hitting the ditch must have jammed the left front quarter panel. He crawled across the gearshift to the passenger door, batting aside the other airbag on his way. He shoved hard on the door. Finally, it opened.

His knees shook as he stood in a foot of water and surveyed the damage. The car wasn't going anywhere. He reached inside and hit the emergency flashers. He'd have to call for a tow. He started walking toward the house.

"Where the hell are you, bitch?"

At the sound of the man's voice, Tim broke into a run. He pounded across the lawn. The garage, Jessie's workshop, had been broken into. A quick glance told him no one was there.

He was heading toward the house when he heard a scream.

"Neese?" he yelled. "Hang on." As he raced back to the garage, he heard a siren.

"Tim?"

A man was dragging Neesie around the side of the garage.

"Let go of my sister, you son of a bitch."

"Look out!" she cried. "He has a gun!"

***

"Marcus." Uncle Cam rapped sharply on the door to the sleeping quarters where Marcus spent the night with Jessica.

He rose from the bed and slipped on a robe before going to the door, yawning on his way. He and Jessica had done little sleeping, and even less talking. They had time.

They had two days left before returning to Malawea. The repairs to the engine should be nearly complete. Once their brief respite was over, the crew would return. Then, he would receive his orders.

He was certain his first destination would be Earth to retrieve his missing crewmember, and return Jessica. They had not discussed this last night after she begged to stay. But Earth was her home. She had to return. Why, then, did it feel as if a knife had sliced his heart into pieces?

They would talk today.

He opened the door. Though barely dawn, Cam was already dressed. "You have a message from General Porcazier. She is displeased you did not respond to her message two hours ago. She thinks your *link* is turned off."

"I will contact her immediately."

Marcus checked his *link*. It was not operating. Odd. He used Cam's vid unit in the sitting room.

"Captain Viator, return to Malawea immediately." Despite her efforts to control herself, his commanding officer's expression held a hint of anger. "The Praetorium destroyed the trilium mining colony on Brzesch."

Marcus sucked in his breath. Trilium, a source of high energy, was used to power space vessels. Brzesch, in Sector Ten, was the Alliance's largest producer of trilium.

"I will return at once."

"Do so. I am holding up my briefing for you." General Porcazier gave him a sharp look. "Captain Viator, an Alliance officer is never out of contact with Space Fleet Command. Did you turn off your *link*?"

"No, General, I did not. I know my duty."

"Have your *link* examined by a technician when you return," she ordered.

"Yes, General."

"As soon as you are properly attired, prepare for transport."

"General, with your permission, may I have a moment to bid farewell to—" He broke off. "I wish to take my leave of my uncle."

She raised her eyebrow. "And to your Terran visitor?"

He swallowed. The General's intelligence-gathering network had no equal. Of course, she would know Jessica was with him.

"You will return the Terran to her planet. Is that understood?"

Marcus fought hard to control the pain slicing through his chest. The decision had been taken away from him. He had to obey orders. Jessica must go back to Earth.

"Signal Central Transport when you are ready. And, Captain?" She glared at him. "Do not delay."

The screen went blank as the General ended transmission. Normally, she ruled with a light touch, more conciliatory than demanding. Yet, all who misinterpreted General Porcazier's quiet strength discovered she had not risen to the head of Space Fleet Command without the ability to lead.

He did not enjoy being on the receiving end of a rebuke. The General's eyes had glittered sharply with her reprimand. Marcus had no wish to repeat the experience.

He returned to Jessica, sprawled in sleep. They had made love many times during the night. She amazed him with her passion, her total giving. Just as she had under the xephod trees, she freely opened herself to him. Would that he could capture some of that freedom of spirit, that openness.

After dressing quickly, he leaned over the bed to wake her. He delayed for a moment, gazing at her fiery hair splayed across the pillow. Memories flitted through his mind of plunging his hands into the softness of her hair, letting it flow over his fingers. She looked so peaceful in her slumber. Knowing how distressed she would be to discover he had to return her to her planet, he decided not to tell her yet. With reluctance, he touched her shoulder. Their interlude, all too brief, was over. Duty called.

Jessie opened eyes muzzy from sleep. Marcus, sweet Marcus, had such a serious look on his face. "How come you're dressed already? C'mere, big guy. Let's—"

He pulled away. "I must return to Malawea."

She groaned. "We have two more days of shore leave."

"Not anymore." He told her about the Praetorium.

That woke her up. "Looks like the price of gas just went up. Don't give me that look, Marcus. I understand the significance. No trilium, starships don't go. Or, as we would say on Earth, whoever owns the remaining trilium, rules. I'll get dressed."

"You have time. *I* do not. I must leave immediately."

"What do you mean?" She searched for the nightie she'd worn for all of thirty seconds last night after he joined her. He hadn't seen a need for the delicate nightwear. And neither had she. Now, in the cold light of early morning, with the return of the *proper* Serenian in uniform, she covered her nakedness. Wincing slightly from the night's 'activity,' she crawled across the tangled covers to the end of the bed where he'd sat to put on his shoes.

He shifted toward her. His eyes darkened. He'd already replaced the camouflage lenses. He hooked his finger under the thin strap slipping off her shoulder. His tender caress as he slid the strap back into place told her more than his stern expression.

"I must hurry. Central Transport is awaiting my signal. You will return to Malawea in my vehicle. All ships are readying for immediate deployment."

"They're going to transport you back to headquarters?"

He kissed her shoulder before standing. "Yes. Do you understand how serious this is? Central Transport is only used on-planet during an emergency."

Ignoring the tenderness between her thighs, she knelt on the bed. "Marcus?" She looped her arms around his neck. "I love you."

"I know." He pulled her tightly against him. His kiss was hard, demanding, almost desperate. And way too short.

"I will make the necessary arrangements for you to use my vehicle and to enter my home. You will need to return to the ship immediately. The crew has already been recalled. Once the General finishes her briefing, the ship will leave."

He kissed her once more and then strode out of the room. She sat back on her heels. Their love affair had barely begun. Was this how it ended? When they returned to the ship, would they go back to being Captain and crewmember? Serenian and alien visitor?

***

By the time Jessie arrived on the ship, preparations were already underway to return to space. Luqett was issuing orders in his booming voice. He gave Jessie a sharp look as she took her station. With chagrin, she realized she was the last of the Engineering crew to arrive.

When she had helped the Chief with refitting the *Freedom*, he'd assigned her to monitor the hyperdrive, making sure all systems were ready prior to take-off. The mighty main engine was already powered up. The hyperdrive was on-line.

Once the rest of the crew were aboard, they departed spacedock. After the ship cleared the portal, Marcus's voice came through the central intercom. "Chief, is the hyperdrive operational?"

"Absolutely, sir. Just give the word."

"Navigation, engage the hyperdrive on my mark. Now."

Jessie was prepared for the force of the great ship as the hyperdrive compressed time and space. She'd already widened her stance, and now she held onto the edge of her workstation. The force still took her breath away.

Luqett patted her shoulder as he watched the instruments for any sign of trouble. "You'll get used to it, lassie. The hyperdrive seems to be doing its job. You earned your keep working extra duty while the others took their leave."

She basked in the warmth of his praise. She *had* worked long hours before leaving with Marcus. Luqett never failed to make her feel wanted, needed. She could get real used to these compliments. Here, aboard the *Freedom*, her talents were appreciated.

"Attention, all crew." Marcus's voice came over the general com unit. "This is the Captain. My apologies for aborting your shore leave. You are to be commended for your prompt return to the ship. Because of the speed with which you returned, the *Freedom* is the first vessel of those in spacedock to be deployed."

A cheer went up in Engineering, even from the Serenians. Jessie high-fived the enthusiastic blue-skinned Tegror next to her.

"As I am sure you are aware," Marcus continued, "the Alliance has come under more intense attack by the Praetorium. The mining colony of Brzesch was destroyed. Military matters will now take precedence over research. You will do well to recall your warfare training at the Academy."

Several of the crew glanced around, sheepish looks on

their faces, as if they'd forgotten they were trained for battle.

"Our destination," Marcus continued, "is the Milky Way Galaxy where Praetorian ships have disrupted Alliance communication. Our mission is to restore communication and protect the trilium colonies on the moons of Neptune. And, we need to retrieve our crewmember who made an unscheduled trip to Earth."

Several people turned toward Jessie. She shrugged and ducked her head. It wasn't her fault that Veronese Qilana decided to go AWOL. Jessie didn't envy the tongue-lashing her twin was going to get when she came back. During one of their long working sessions, Luqett mentioned the possibility of the Alliance's equivalent of a court-martial.

Surely, Veronese had realized the consequences of her actions before she left on her little adventure?

***

Veronese paced the surgery waiting room, her arms wrapped around herself. No one would tell her about Tim's condition.

Everything had happened at once. The stalker had knocked Veronese to the ground, pulled a gun out of the waistband of his jeans, then whipped around and shot Tim. A patrol car rocketed up the driveway immediately after. The intruder fired off three shots, hitting the car, before the sheriff's deputy killed him.

She'd tried to stanch the blood flowing from Tim's abdomen. Paramedics arrived, shoved her aside and spoke over their radios in hurried, anxious tones. The ambulance left, sirens shrieking.

After his back-up arrived, the deputy drove her to the University of Michigan Hospital where he took her statement. Then, she waited while doctors fought to save her brother's life.

"Ma'am?" The deputy had returned. "How's your brother?"

She shook her head. "I don't know. He is in surgery. They are all so busy..." She had never felt this helpless.

"No news is good news." He gave her an optimistic look.

She nodded, wanting to believe him.

"Why don't you sit down for a minute?" He led her over to a couch designed more for utility instead of comfort. "I locked up your house. Figured you might need your keys and purse." He handed the items over to her. "I thought you'd like to know about your brother's assailant. The man—" he consulted a small notebook "—a Kirk Morris is dead. We checked his house and found enough coke and crack to make the DEA boys plenty happy."

"DEA?" She twisted her fingers, trying to concentrate, but her brain wasn't making connections.

"Drug Enforcement Agency. When you filed your complaint last week, we passed it on to them. They've been watching the house."

She looked at him sharply. "Why didn't they do something before he shot my brother?"

"Earlier this evening, they'd gotten an anonymous tip that a drug deal was going down in Chelsea. We figure Morris knew the DEA boys were out there and phoned in the fake tip. When they heard about your break-in, they beat it back." The deputy pulled at his tie. "I-I'm sorry I didn't get there sooner."

Her mind kept screaming that she should have gone with Tim to Detroit. Then this could have been avoided. No, it was worse than that. She should never have switched places with Jessica. If she had never come to Earth, nothing would have happened to Tim.

"I found your brother's car in the ditch and had it towed. Is there someone who could be with you? Family? A friend? I could call—"

Family. She should have called Tim's parents. She had accepted that *her* parents had been those who had raised her on Serenia. Not the people whose only contribution had been her genetic make-up.

"No. You may leave now." She stood, nearly missing the bewildered look on the deputy's face.

She had been too abrupt. Jessica would have treated the man better. She turned back. "Thank you for coming." She held out her hand. "I appreciate your kindness."

"Sure." He walked to the elevator.

She walked down the hall looking for a telephone. She dreaded making the call. She dropped coins in the slot and tapped in the number. When Tim's father answered, emotions so clogged her throat she could barely speak.

***

"Ms. Wyndom?" A doctor stopped her as she walked back into the waiting room after making the hardest call she had ever made.

"My brother?"

"He's out of surgery. He'll be in recovery for a while, and then he'll go into ICU."

"Thank the Intrepid Ones he's still alive," she mumbled.

"What?"

She sagged against the doorframe.

"Careful there." He held her elbow and steered her to the couch. "He's not out of the woods yet." The doctor scrubbed his hand down his face. Weariness shadowed his eyes. "The bullet tore up his insides. We patched him up, but we're concerned about his spine. I've ordered a neuro consult, but I'm pretty sure what they're going to find. I don't want to give you false hopes, Ms. Wyndom. If your brother survives all the surgery we've done tonight, he may never walk again."

***

"The hyperdrive is working properly, Chief?"

Jessie turned at the sound of Marcus's voice. It was the first time she'd seen him since he left her in the bedroom of his uncle's home yesterday. Remembering how they had spent the night before brought heat to her cheeks. She hoped the Chief wouldn't notice. She needed to learn how to guard her reaction to Marcus around the others.

"Aye. We're at full throttle, and she has more to give. This ship will take ye where ye need to go, sir."

"Will we be able to cloak and use the hyperdrive?"

"Shouldna be a problem, Captain."

"Your crew did a fine job, Chief. I have included a commendation in my report. When this engagement is over, they deserve extra shore leave."

"Aye, sir."

Jessie heard the enthusiasm in Luqett's voice. He worked his crew hard, but the Chief took special care of those under him. He would make sure they were rewarded.

"Have someone relieve Ms. Wyndom." Even though she was standing at her station, not two feet away, Marcus didn't address her. "She is to report to my ready room as soon as possible."

"Aye, sir."

She whipped around but only got a glimpse of Marcus's back as he strode out of Engineering.

"Dinna worry, lassie. He's not displeased with ye." The Scottish accent was strong in Luqett's speech. "He'll want to prepare ye for yer transport home."

She bowed her head. She wasn't ready. She needed more time. She'd thought she and Marcus would talk about her staying when he came to her room. But, he'd had other things on his mind, and then so did she. They'd made love, postponing the discussion until morning. Then, the you-know-what had hit the fan.

She relinquished her post to her replacement, and Luqett followed her to a discreet distance from the rest of the crew.

"I dinna want ye to leave, lassie." His silver eyes, like Marcus's yet without that intense, piercing quality, saddened as he lowered his head to talk quietly to her. "You have been a fine addition to my crew. If you want to stay aboard, ask the Captain. I will request you remain here in Engineering."

"Thanks, Chief. I appreciate your confidence in me."

With great reluctance, Jessie entered the conveyance to go up to the bridge-level of the ship. She leaned her head against the gray wall and closed her eyes. She just knew Marcus was going to send her back.

But what was on Earth for her? The better question was what was here, in space? That was easy. Marcus. Yesterday, during her long ride from his uncle's farm, she'd had time to think. The vehicle propelled itself automatically. She only had to tell its on-board computer her destination. His vehicle was the embodiment of 'leave the driving to us.'

During the ride, she reaffirmed her feelings about Marcus. She loved him. She wanted to be with him. If only as a crewmember. Anything to see him. To be near him.

He had never expressed his love for her. He had shown her respect, caring. During their love-making, he had transported her to a realm of pleasure she thought only existed in romance novels. Was that enough?

He had shown her a world so different from her own. A world of advanced technology where her talents were appreciated. Where she was valued.

Luqett wanted her to stay. Would Marcus allow it?

***

Veronese stared at the doctor in disbelief. "Tim will never walk again?"

"We won't know with certainty until after the neurosurgeon examines him." The doctor stood. "As soon as your brother is in the Intensive Care Unit, the nurse will come and get you. You'll be able to see him." He asked if she had any questions. When she shook her head, he left.

Numbness spread through her body. Her brother might never walk. He had saved her from the drug dealer at nearly the cost of his life.

"Where's Timothy? Where's my son?" Denise Wyndom rushed into the waiting room followed by Tim's father, Richard.

When the nurse finally told the waiting family Tim had been transferred to the Intensive Care Unit, Veronese followed his parents down the hall to the elevator.

"This never would have happened if you hadn't insisted on staying on that goddamn farm." Richard continued the harangue he'd begun in the surgery waiting room after Veronese explained what had happened.

As before, she was still completely taken aback by his vehemence.

"Tim never would have come in contact with a drug dealer if it wasn't for you. I hope you've come to your senses, young lady."

Hot tears prickled her eyelids. Veronese called upon all her Serenian discipline not to cry. She understood Richard and Denise were worried sick about Tim. So was she. Could they not have spared a moment to see if she was all right?

Tim's parents went up to the nurse's station. Veronese waited, allowing them to see their son first.

"Timothy is awake and asking for you," Denise Wyndom told Veronese several minutes later. Tim's mother sank onto one of the chairs in the waiting room. "I couldn't stay and see him like that."

Veronese rushed around the corner to her brother's bedside. Machines beeped, an antiseptic smell pervaded the air. Tim's eyes were half opened.

"Jessie? Bring Jessie back," he mumbled.

"She's here, son," Richard said.

"Neesie," Tim whispered, "get Jessie."

"What did he say?" His father came closer.

"Get Jessie."

"Open your eyes, boy. Jessie's right here." He turned to Veronese. "Say something, damn it."

"I-I'm here, Tim. Everything will be all right."

"Jess? That you? Really you?"

She squeezed his hand and leaned close to whisper in his ear. "I'll get her. I don't know how, but I'll get Jessica."

***

Marcus was waiting for Jessie in his ready room. He stood with his hands clasped behind his back, staring out into the blackness of space. When he turned around, she could see determination etched into his features. And a bleakness in his eyes.

"We will enter the Milky Way Galaxy shortly."

"I know." Her voice cracked. She cleared her throat. "Has there been any contact with my sister?"

"No. There has been no contact between any Alliance vessels since we left this system. General Porcazier believes the Praetorium is disrupting transmissions."

"It's been nearly two weeks. Veronese must be frantic."

"Lieutenant Qilana is Serenian. She would calmly analyze the situation and conclude there has been interference on the part of the Praetorium."

"Why? Have they ever jammed transmissions before?"

"No."

"Have they ever been this aggressive before?"

"No," he conceded.

"Then, my *sister* must believe you have abandoned her."

He shook his head. "Lieutenant Qilana is—"

"Terran. With Terran emotions. Just like you, Marcus. Even though you try to hide them."

"I could not hide them from you, could I?"

That stopped her for a moment. "I don't want to go back," she said quietly.

His eyes widened. She saw a flicker of hope before he shuttered his expression.

She rushed on. "I've thought about it, Marcus. I want to stay here. With you."

He closed his eyes, but not before she saw the pain reflected there. "It is not possible."

"Give me one good reason."

When he opened his eyes, all emotion had been erased. "You are Terran. You belong on Earth."

"You're Terran, too," she shot back. "Is Earth where you belong?"

He slowly shook his head. "My duty is here." He took a deep breath. "My orders are to return you to Earth."

"What? When did you get those orders?" she demanded. "Did you know yesterday? At the farm?"

"Captain," his *link* squawked, preventing him from answering.

He pressed the button. "What is it, Lieutenant Cabbeferron?"

"Sir, we just received a distress call from Earth. It was Lieutenant Qilana."

Jessie grabbed his arm.

"Relay the transmission here to my ready room," he ordered.

"Sir, the transmission ended abruptly. When I tried to call her back, I received nothing."

"Nothing?"

"No, sir."

"Navigation, all speed to Earth. Viator out."

"Is it the Praetorium? Are they jamming communication from her?" Jessie demanded.

"The General's information is usually correct."

"Even if her orders aren't?" she challenged. She was not going to let this go. She would fight to stay aboard. She'd go to his General and—

"Captain," his *link* squawked again. "Praetorian vessel approaching."

"Shields up. Red Alert." As he switched off his *link*, the lighting changed to flashing then steady red. "Wait here," he told her.

"My place is down in Engineering."

"Your place is where your Captain says it is." He opened the portal. "If you won't wait here, come."

Snagging her wrist, Marcus strode rapidly to the bridge. He wanted her by his side where he could protect her. They dodged crewmembers rushing to their duty stations.

Tension between the Alliance and the Praetorium was mounting. The negotiators needed to bring a swift end to the hostilities before they escalated into full-scale war.

"I should be in Engineering," she protested again.

"They managed without you before you came, and they will manage without you when you return to Earth."

"I told you," she snapped. "I want to stay here."

Though his heart had soared when she first spoke of staying with him, Marcus knew it was not possible. He could not disobey a direct order.

The officers on the bridge turned to him as one, then looked back to the view screen. A speck in the far left corner appeared to be moving toward them.

"Is that the Praetorian vessel?" he asked.

"Yes, sir," Science Officer Xaropa responded. "It has the same signature as the Tegrorian frigate we encountered before. Engage cloaking device, Captain?"

"No. We will not hide from these renegades. We must discover the location of their disrupter in order to restore communication in this sector. We must discover how their commander impersonated Mr. Glaxpher."

Marcus had won one concession from his commanding officer. Stasik Glaxpher was allowed to remain on board the ship, though not on duty.

"Navigation," he spoke to Glaxpher's replacement, "steady course."

"Aye, sir."

"Mr. Xaropa, I am depending on you and your scanners to discover the source of the disrupter."

"Aye, sir."

"Lieutenant Cabbeferron, are you picking up transmissions from the Praetorian vessel?"

"No, sir. Wait. Yes, sir. The Praetorian commander is hailing us."

"On screen."

The viewscreen blurred, then the picture dissolved into a zigzag pattern. They must be jamming the video.

"Alliance vessel." A familiar female voice could be heard but no picture. "This is your only warning. Surrender, or we will fire on you."

"Who is this?" Marcus demanded. "If you are not a coward, you will show yourself."

The lines of the screen swirled, then slowly a clear picture of the interior of the vessel appeared. The renegades had not bothered to alter the bridge of the Tegrorian vessel. Xaropa was correct. It was the same ship that had attacked them before. The one with Glaxpher's double on board.

"I knew that distress call from Earth would bring you to us." The female speaker stepped into view. "Viator, surrender your ship."

A gasp escaped from several crewmembers.

Only a lifetime of strict discipline enabled Marcus to contain his astonishment. "General Porcazier, what is the meaning of this?"

NINETEEN

"You underestimated the Praetorium's allies, Viator," General Porcazier said with a satisfied smile.

Marcus's astonishment lasted momentarily. He did not always agree with his commanding officer, but he had never doubted her loyalty to the Alliance. This had to be another hoax. "You are no more General Porcazier than you were Stasik Glaxpher."

"Always suspicious. An admirable quality, Viator, under normal circumstances. You are wrong in this instance. I am, indeed, Eleah Porcazier." She sat back in the commander's chair and crossed her arms with a smug air of satisfaction. "Alpha one Alpha one Omega."

The General's emergency code. Marcus rubbed the bridge of his nose. For a moment, his belief that this was an imposter was shaken.

"You are surprised. Good." She smiled. Marcus noted her smile did not reach her eyes.

Her eyes. General Porcazier's eyes were never flat. When she had reproached him at his uncle's for being incommunicado, her eyes blazed with intensity. He recalled the previous imposter. When angered, Stasik Glaxpher, like all Tegrors, made his eyes appear to shoot yellow flames. Unnerving to opponents. Yet, when Marcus angered the rebel 'Glaxpher,' the imposter's eyes had been curiously flat. Like this one's.

This rebel commander was not General Porcazier. Marcus turned his back to the screen. "End communication."

"Aye, Captain," Lieutenant Cabbeferron responded. The screen went blank. The only sound was the steady hum of the engines.

"Contact Space Fleet. That was not General Porcazier."

"Sir." First Officer Klegznef stood at attention. "She does know the General's emergency code."

"So does every starship commander and executive crew."

"While you were speaking, Captain," Xaropa interjected, "I performed a high-intensity genetic scan. Our sensors indicate the commander of the Praetorian vessel *is* General Porcazier."

"Those sensors have been wrong before." Marcus looked hard at Xaropa. "Why were they not repaired while we were on Serenia?"

Xaropa paled at Marcus's sharp tone. "Sir, the technicians thoroughly examined them and declared our sensors working perfectly."

"Captain," Lieutenant Cabbeferron said, "I am unable to contact Space Fleet Command. Our communications are being disrupted by a very powerful energy source."

Xaropa concurred. "The source of the disruption is not only powerful but close. I suspect it is coming from the Praetorian vessel."

"The commander of the Praetorian vessel is hailing you again, sir," Cabbeferron announced. "She is angry you cut off communication."

"Do not respond, Lieutenant," Marcus said quietly, his anger at the malfunctioning equipment under control again. "Are you able to contact Space Fleet through emergency channels?"

"No, sir."

"Locate that disrupter, Mr. Xaropa."

"I am attempting to pinpoint its exact location."

Marcus walked to Xaropa's side. He scanned the instruments while the Science Officer made adjustments.

"Sir," Cabbeferron called out. "The commander is ordering us to surrender our vessel, or she will fire on us."

Marcus spoke quietly to Xaropa, then he said, "Open the channel, Lieutenant."

"Viator, you will not cut off communication again." The

Diane Burton

imposter showed extreme agitation. Even though her face was mottled in anger, her eyes remained flat—convincing Marcus this was, indeed, an imposter.

"My apologies, General. Our communications officer has been experiencing difficulties with our equipment."

"Surrender your vessel at once, Viator."

"If you continue in this manner, General, we will consider this an act of war."

"Exactly." She smiled, her eyes still cold.

"It is not in our best interest to surrender. Is that not correct, Mr. Xaropa?"

"Yes, sir."

Nearly simultaneously, the Red Alert light ceased. On screen, the imposter stared in open-mouthed astonishment right before disappearing, and the *Freedom* lurched suddenly.

Jessica fell to the floor. She had been standing patiently next to the Captain's chair which Marcus had not bothered to use. He offered her a hand up.

"What happened?" She dusted off the seat of her uniform. "How come I'm the only one who falls down?"

"You must learn to anticipate sudden moves. The imposter should be in the transport room greeted by an armed guard."

Her mouth hung open. "You beamed her aboard?"

"Yes. Mr. Xaropa, have you located the disrupter source?"

"Almost, sir. There." The Science Officer touched the corner of his instrument panel. On screen, a powerful flash erupted from the Praetorian vessel.

"Did you blow up that ship?" Jessica asked in astonishment.

"We destroyed the communication disruptor." Marcus tapped his *link*. "Security, take the imposter to the Medical Center. I will be there shortly. Navigation, resume all possible speed to Earth. Communications, report what has transpired to Space Fleet and contact all Alliance vessels. Try to raise Lieutenant Qilana. Tell her we are on our way. Mr. Klegznef, you have control of the ship."

He headed down the hall, Jessica scurrying after him. They entered the Medical Center to find their unwilling visitor surrounded by Security guards.

"You cannot do this, Viator," the imposter announced.

Jessie watched as one of the guards attempted to pull a wig off the woman's head. Security Chief Hrvibm silently stood near by, her stocky arms crossed in front of her prominent chest.

"Viator, this is an outrage," the 'General' screamed.

It wasn't a wig.

"Can we interrogate her?" The little troll, Drakus, rubbed his hands together. "Please, Captain. I love a good interrogation."

Marcus glared at Drakus. "Extend the *General* every courtesy but be alert. Chief Hrvibm, I want guards posted inside the Medical Center and outside in the hall. Dr. Rindor," he spoke to the medical officer, "run the test for GND."

Genetic nucleotide duplication. What her sister used that had started this whole mess.

"Viator, you will regret this," the fake General cried.

"What will happen now?" Jessie asked.

"We will discover who that really is. I do not believe she is General Porcazier any more than I believed Stasik Glaxpher joined the Praetorium."

"You are making a grave mistake, Viator. You will pay for this flagrant breach of military procedure."

While the doctor prepared a square silver instrument, two guards secured the imposter's arms and legs in restraints on an examining table.

"I thought GND was limited to relatives," Jessie said. "Are there really people who can assume any identity? What are they? Shape-shifters? Or is this all some kind of elaborate mask and costuming?"

"Security has already determined this is no disguise."

"What if this really is your General?" She peered around Marcus to see the doctor press the square instrument against the side of the woman's neck.

"In that case, she will be our prisoner and will stand trial for treason back on Serenia. Doctor, how soon will you have the results?"

"Shortly, Captain." The doctor plugged the instrument into a unit similar to a notebook computer.

"Call me when you find out." Marcus spun on his heel and walked off. Jessie followed him out to the hall where Drakus stood guard. "Be alert, Drakus."

The little troll saluted. "Yes, Captain. Never give up. Never surrender."

Jessie groaned. "Don't tell me. You've been watching Terran movies again."

Marcus headed down the hall. She hastened to catch up. "Marcus, we need to talk. About my stay—"

"Please wait until we are alone." He nodded to crewmembers as they passed.

She hated it when he was right. She itched to talk to him, to get things out in the open. Yet, she knew this conversation was better conducted in private.

"Captain to the Medical Center. Regulation two-seven."

The urgent secrecy code. Jessie had never seen Marcus run before. Always the controlled commander, he usually strode purposefully down the hall. Not now. She caught up just after he entered the Medical Center. Drakus and the other guards stared flabbergasted at the 'General'.

Still restrained on the examining table, the imposter was...molting. Her dark hair, previously arranged in a soft pouf, had become shaggy and gray. Her face was dissolving, and all Jessie could think of was the bad guys in the Indiana Jones movies. She shuddered. What next?

The face did not dissolve into a blob of melting flesh. Instead, it contorted into the face of an old man.

Marcus's features hardened. "Dr. Cenamola."

"You know this guy?" Jessie asked. The figure on the table had shrunk. The restraints were so loose, the old man easily slipped his hands and feet through.

Marcus stared at the old man. "You are supposed to be dead."

Dr. Cenamola swung his thin legs over the edge of the table. "As a Terran writer once said, 'Reports of my demise are greatly exaggerated.'"

Marcus turned to Jessie. "This is the scientist who experimented with twins."

"You!" Jessie gasped.

"Viator. You are evidence of my failed experiment." He looked at Jessie. "As is your sister, Wyndom."

"Wait a minute," Jessie protested. "Don't blame Marcus and my sister for your screw up."

"I spent nearly your entire lifetime, Wyndom, in prison because the Elders refused to see the value of my experiment. Viator and Qilana are all that are left to remind me."

"Hold it. How did you transform into those other people? I thought that genetic nucleotide duplication stuff only worked on blood relatives." She looked to Marcus for support then back to the old man.

The scientist, whose experiments had irrevocably changed so many lives, smiled smugly. "I developed a new formula. I can transform myself into anyone I want to be. You see, I had plenty of time to work on this." His eyes hardened. "The rest of my life in prison, it was supposed to be. But, being so far away in Sector Ten, the authorities never knew I was given access to laboratory facilities. Now, they are the ones who will suffer from the chaos *I* created."

Cenamola glared at Marcus. "You spoiled my plans to capture this vessel. Why did you not believe what everyone else saw?"

"My skepticism must come with my Terran blood." Marcus's announcement drew a gasp from the guards.

"Captain?" Drakus asked. "You are Terran?"

His *link* squawked. "Captain?"

He tapped it. "Yes, Lieutenant Cabbeferron."

"We are approaching Earth. As usual, we are cloaked to avoid detection by Terran surveillance systems. We have resumed communication with Lieutenant Qilana. She sounds desperate to exchange places with Ms. Wyndom."

"Thank you. Viator out." Marcus turned to Security Chief Hrvibm. "Confine Dr. Cenamola. Keep him under guard—make that two guards—at all times." He started to leave, then turned back. "Why have you resumed your own shape?"

Cenamola dropped his head. "The formula requires frequent injections to maintain the persona," he muttered.

"It wore off," Jessie said in amazement. "You got caught because your stuff is faulty."

Cenamola shot her a lethal look, then turned it on Marcus. "Viator, you will rue the day you interfered with my plan. I will make certain you pay for sending me back to prison."

Marcus guided her out of the Medical Center. "Pay him no heed. He is insane."

She shivered. "You can say that again. That guy gives me the creeps."

They walked down the hall toward the bridge. "We will soon be in range to retrieve your sister. We need to talk."

The urgency in his voice matched his pace. She had to hurry to keep up with him. *Finally*, they would talk? Mere minutes before she and her twin would exchange places again? What was he going to say? So long, farewell, and all that? Nice knowing you, kid? Don't call me, I'll call you?

He escorted her into his ready room, which reminded her of an executive's office. As soon as the portal closed behind them, he pulled her into his arms.

"I do not want to lose you." He kissed her with a hunger she felt all the way to her toes.

Oh, God, she didn't expect that. She returned the kiss, eagerly, as hungry for him as he was for her.

"Let me stay. Talk to your General. Your real General. Explain to her that I will not be a burden."

He held her arms and stepped back. "Are you sure? What about your family?"

"My parents probably wouldn't even miss me. Sounds awful, doesn't it? They're so wrapped up in their own work, they hardly pay attention to me anyway. But, Tim..." She walked over to the transparent bubble. "Tim would understand. With his interest in space, he'd say 'go for it'."

Marcus came up behind her and placed his hands on her shoulders. His reflection shown in the bubble, his expression full of concern. "You are very close to your brother, are you not?"

She took a deep breath. "He's the only one besides Gram who encouraged me to follow my dream. He's always stood by me." If she stayed here with Marcus, would she ever see Tim again?

"Captain Viator? We are transporting Lieutenant Qilana now."

"I have to see her." Jessie bolted out of the room. She ran down the hall, heedless of bumping into people. She burst into the transport room just as a very agitated Veronese Qilana stepped down from the transport platform. She was dressed in jeans, one of Jessie's T-shirts, and an obvious wig, slightly askew.

"Jessica, you must go home," she said, her voice frantic.

Jessie ran to Veronese. "What's wrong?"

"Tim has been injured. You must go. He needs you."

Jessie's heart lodged in her throat. "What happened?"

Veronese seized Jessie's wrists in a grip that made her wince. "We need privacy."

Marcus dismissed the transport personnel, including the observers in the concealed room. "Lieutenant Qilana."

"Captain," she acknowledged without turning her attention from Jessie. "There was trouble with the man across the road. Tim has been seriously injured. He has been calling for you. Since I've been there and still he calls for you, they think he's out of his head. You must go back."

"How bad is he hurt?"

Veronese looked down at the floor before lifting her chin. Without the camouflage lenses, her eyes—the same blue as Jessie's—clouded. "The doctors aren't sure. If he lives—" Her voice cracked. "—he may never walk again."

"Oh, dear God." Jessie looked at Marcus, pleading with him. What should she do? He only stared at her, giving her no assistance. This was her decision. *Oh, God.*

When he spoke, it was not to her. "Lieutenant Qilana, until further notice you are confined to your quarters."

Veronese swallowed. "Y-Yes, sir."

"If you are going to Earth, Jessica, you need to go now." His voice betrayed nothing. She needed his understanding.

Why didn't he say something?

"Wait." Jessie grabbed her twin's hand. "Please, Marcus, give us a minute." She reached up and touched Veronese's face. "I wish you had done things differently. I wanted to talk to you."

Tears shimmered in Veronese's eyes. "I, too, wish I had done things differently. Do not hate me."

"I could never hate you. You're my sister."

"Tim nearly lost his life trying to save me. You must hurry. He needs you."

"Marcus?" Jessie turned to him, pleading with him to understand. "I have to go."

"Yes." He gave no sign that her departure would affect him. "Lieutenant Qilana, report to your quarters."

"Yes, sir." Veronese gave Jessie a long look.

She hugged her twin. "Come back with me, Veronese. We can be a family."

Veronese gave her a half smile. "No. I did consider it, but my place is here. What I did—leaving the ship without permission, switching places with you—was wrong. I have to accept the consequences of my actions." She stepped away from Jessie. Then, Veronese pulled off the wig and stood at attention. "Sir, I will await further instructions in my quarters."

A sob snagged in Jessie's throat. She had to go home. She had to see her brother. She had to leave Marcus. Would she ever see him again?

After the portal closed behind Veronese, Jessie turned to him. "Go easy on her. If it wasn't for her, I'd never have met you." She threw her arms around his waist. "I don't want to leave you."

"Stay then." He cradled her head against his chest. Despite his calm outward appearance, his heart beat rapidly under her ear. "Stay with me, Jessica. I will obtain permission from Space Fleet Command. I want you with me."

Why did he wait until now to say that? She was so torn. "My brother needs me. What if he dies? I could never forgive myself for not going to him."

Marcus stepped back, staring long into her eyes. She

couldn't read the message. "You must do what you need to do, Jessica."

"Bridge to the Captain."

He touched his *link*. "Viator, here."

"Captain, the Praetorian vessel is approaching again."

"Are we cloaked?"

"Yes, sir. We uncloaked just long enough to transport Lieutenant Qilana. Their scanners must have discovered us in that brief period."

"Maintain position."

"But, Captain, they will—"

"I said maintain position." He ended communication. He held Jessie tightly. "If you are returning to Earth, you must go now." He kissed her hard before setting her aside.

She grabbed his hand. "Come with me, Marcus. Come to Earth. You are Terran. You belong there."

For a moment she saw a wistful look in his eyes, but it was gone so quickly she wondered if she had imagined it.

He straightened his already stiff spine. "I am commander of this vessel. My duty is here."

Her eyes burned. Her throat thickened. "And my duty is to go to my brother."

"Captain, the Praetorian vessel is nearly in range."

"You must go quickly." He reached into a drawer beneath the transport control. The same drawer from which he'd pulled out the universal translator when she first arrived.

She unstrapped her *link* and handed it to him. She tried to remove the tiny patch from behind her ear. She'd been wearing it so long she had nearly forgotten about it.

"No, keep them and take this." He pressed into her hands a small box, slightly larger than a deck of cards. "It is a subspace transmitter with a longer range than your *link*. We will be able to communicate."

He pulled her roughly into his arms. "I love you, Jessica." With abrupt movements, he pushed her to the transport platform.

Her heart swelled with joy at his announcement. A bittersweet joy. She stumbled on the step to the platform. He helped her up before going back to the control console. His eyes caught hers, and she was certain she saw love shining forth. He loved her.

"I will come back for you." His solemn tone made the words sound like a vow.

"Marcus," she cried, reaching out to him. "I love—"

Everything went black. The freefall disoriented her. It was the same roller coaster ride she'd experienced on being transported to the ship.

When all movement ceased, she opened her eyes. She was sitting on her bed in her lilac and white bedroom. The exact same spot she had been when she was transported aboard the *Freedom* nearly two weeks before.

She was home. Oh, God, Marcus had said he loved her! Would she ever see him again?

***

Marcus knew the ship was vulnerable during the brief moment while Jessica was transported to Earth, but he had to send her back. He experienced a crushing sensation in his chest. He had found his soulmate, his love. And now she was gone.

Vowing on the names of the Intrepid Ones that he would return for her, he walked out of the transport room. His heart weighed as much as a giant korvapid. Jessica was gone. When she had looked so devastated by her brother's condition, he'd considered going with her. But his duty was here on the *Freedom*. He could no more abandon his ship than she could abandon her brother.

The *Freedom* jerked, and he heard a high-pitched whine. His ship had just fired a photon torpedo.

He raced to the bridge.

***

Jessie found Veronese's note lying on the pillow. In between apologies, she'd outlined the events that had happened since she and Jessie had switched places.

After stripping off the uniform, she dressed in her own clothes. She could just see the astonished looks she'd get if she raced through the University Hospital wearing something out of a sci-fi movie.

Within minutes, she had jumped into her truck and was racing to the hospital. During the twenty-minute trip, she thought about Marcus. He said he loved her, he wanted her to stay—the only bright spot in this entire horrific day. Her heart soared at his words. He *would* come back for her. *He loved her.* Why had he waited so long to tell her?

She craned her neck to look out the window, up to the gray, overcast sky—as if she could see the starship. Had she endangered the ship when he activated the transporter? She prayed it was safe.

When she reached the hospital's Intensive Care Unit, she found Tim all alone. *Where were her parents? Why was he all by himself?*

She clasped her brother's hand. "I'm here, Tim. It's me. Jess. I'm here."

His eyes fluttered. "Knew you'd come," he rasped.

"He's finally recognizing you."

Jessie whirled around. A nurse who looked like she could play left tackle for the Detroit Lions stood behind her.

"I'm his sister."

Sally, according to the name on her hospital ID tag, gave her a funny look. "I know. You've been here enough."

"My parents?"

Sally arched an eyebrow. For a moment, Jessie's heart twisted. That movement reminded her of Marcus.

"They've come and gone for the day. They strolled in, stayed their usual five minutes, and then left." The woman was in her late fifties and probably thought she didn't need to censor her words.

Jessie gave her a sharp look.

"Well, shut my mouth, honey. It's just that you've been here nearly night and day. And they—" She shook her head. "What the hell. Who am I to judge?" She returned to the nurses' station and the monitors that kept tabs on the two other patients in the ICU.

"So, the folks aren't here," Jessie mused. "Why am I not surprised?" She looked at Tim. His eyes were closed, his breathing slow and shallow through parched lips.

She walked out to the nurses' station. "Okay if I give him something to drink?"

"You give him ice chips every time you come." Sally again gave her a strange look. "I thought you were going home to get some sleep. You need it. You're getting loopy." Her smile let Jessie know she understood. From the way the irascible nurse talked, she and Veronese must have gotten quite friendly.

"I couldn't rest." Let the nurse think she was so tired she forgot. She'd have to watch what she said.

She rubbed an ice chip along Tim's lips. His tongue greedily lapped at the moisture. She slipped a chip into his mouth. Then his breathing deepened. Even though she rubbed another chip along his lips, his mouth didn't open.

"He's fallen asleep," Sally whispered from the foot of the bed. "He seems less agitated. I like this boy. He's a fighter. Glad to see he's finally coming out of it."

Jessie rubbed her forehead, her fingers icy from the chips.

"You look all in, honey. Why don't you go lie down in the waiting room? Nobody's there." Sally pointed toward the hall.

Jessie walked as far as the door before turning back to the nurse. "Tell me again how he is."

With a firm grip on Jessie's arm, Sally guided her out into the hall. "Even if he appears asleep, we don't know how much a patient hears." She kept her voice low. "The doctors have been concerned with his disorientation. Not knowing you, calling for you even though you were standing right there."

Jessie nodded. She couldn't explain that Tim wasn't disoriented. He knew which sister was which. In her note, Veronese explained that right away he had recognized she wasn't Jessie. How like him to be so observant.

"The bullet damaged his spinal cord. The docs are doing the best they can. You couldn't ask for a better neurosurgery department than ours. Your brother was lucky—if you can say anything about getting shot is lucky—he was brought here. They expect he will have full use of his upper body. Below the waist..." Sally shook her head.

Marcus should have come with her. He should have sent

the ship's medical officer. Serenia's advanced technology could save her brother from a lifetime in a wheelchair. Why the hell didn't Veronese demand help for their brother?

Then, Jessie recalled the Alliance mandate about non-interference. She sagged against the wall. Marcus would never defy the rules.

"Hey, you aren't going to pass out, are you, hon?" Sally steered her to a chair in the waiting room and pushed Jessie's head between her knees. "Deep breaths now. Take deep breaths."

***

Marcus burst through the portal to the bridge. "Did we just fire a torpedo?"

"Yes, sir. At the Praetorian vessel." First Officer Klegznef stood at attention.

"On whose orders?"

The Praetorian vessel circled around, then aimed its bow at the *Freedom*.

"Mine, sir." Klegznef eyed him with defiance. "They were in attack position. I called you twice. You did not answer your *link* or the general com unit." He lifted his granite-like chin.

"Navigation, my orders were evasive maneuvers," he said to Berea, Glaxpher's replacement. "Why have we not moved?"

Berea glanced from Klegznef to Marcus, as if questioning whose orders to obey.

"Mr. Berea, take us out of here or be relieved." Glaring at Klegznef, Marcus dared him to contradict. "Lieutenant Cabbeferron, did you not check out my *link* yesterday?"

"Y-Yes, sir."

He ripped it off his wrist and tossed it to her. "Check it again. Twice now, I have been unable to receive messages. And check the com unit in the Transport Room."

"Yes, s-sir." Cabbeferron fumbled with the *link*. The rest of the bridge crew looked askance at Marcus's abrupt manner.

A blast of light emanated from the enemy ship. The *Freedom* lurched as it veered to port. Marcus reached out for the rail behind the navigator's position to steady himself.

"Captain, they have fired on us," Xaropa announced.

"Thank you for reporting the obvious." He did not disguise his sarcasm.

"Put us out of range, Mr. Berea."

"Aye, sir."

"Mr. Klegznef, I will see you in my ready room. Mr. Xaropa, you have control of the ship." Marcus stalked off the bridge and nearly ran over Drakus. "Why are you not guarding the prisoner?"

"Chief Hrvibm said you wanted to see me."

"There must be some mistake. Report to your duty station. We are under attack."

"Aye, sir." Drakus saluted. "Never give up. Never surrender."

As soon as Marcus and Klegznef entered the ready room and the portal closed, Marcus whirled on his First Officer. "What were you thinking firing on that vessel?"

Klegznef shot him a belligerent look. "It was preparing to fire on us."

"We are not at war. Or we weren't until you fired."

"We should be! The Trucanian is right. Never surrender."

Marcus ignored Klegznef's outburst. "The Praetorium has done its best to engage us, but we have restrained ourselves, letting the negotiators reason with the renegades."

"Reason? Bah. The only reason they listen to is a photon torpedo up their—"

"Mr. Klegznef," Marcus cut him off sharply. "You are an Alliance officer. Why, in the name of the Intrepid Ones, would you risk the lives aboard this vessel to strike out at that ship? That was an act of war."

"We should be at war with the enemy of the Alliance."

"That is for the authorities to determine."

"Authorities," Klegznef spit out. "They do not have the backbone of a zoot. The Alliance has to stop the Praetorium. Is the peace you treasure not worth fighting for?"

Marcus pinched the bridge of his nose. The Zorfan had countermanded an order. He had to be disciplined.

Taking Marcus's silence for hesitation, Klegznef plunged ahead. "Sir, you abducted their commander. You fired on their ship, destroying the disruptor. How is that different from defending ourselves?"

His First Officer had a point. Were Marcus's actions any different?

"Captain?" Xaropa's voice came over the general com unit.

"Yes."

"The Praetorian vessel has followed us."

"Are we not cloaked?"

"Yes, sir. Nevertheless, they have followed us."

A large jolt hit the ship, throwing Marcus to the floor. Klegznef stared down at him.

"It looks like you just got your wish, Mr. Klegznef." Marcus stood and straightened his uniform. "We have just started the Second Intergalactic War."

"Never give up. Never—"

Marcus cut him off. "Don't say it."

TWENTY

Jessie walked out of Tim's room and stared down the hospital corridor at the man waiting for the elevator. "Marcus?"

The elevator doors opened, and he stepped inside.

"Hey," she hollered. It had been four weeks since she had left the *Freedom,* and now Marcus was finally here.

The doors began to close. Didn't he hear her?

"Wait." She ran. Marcus was here. He'd come for her.

He stuck out his hand to stop the closing door. At the resistance, the door folded back into the wall. He smiled as she barreled into the elevator. She tried to catch her breath. After all this time, Marcus was finally here.

"Just in time," he said in his deep voice. "Which floor?" He raised his eyebrow.

Now, he was playing games? "Mar-cus?"

"Sorry. Wrong guy." He shrugged and pushed the 'open door' button. The elevator lurched. "Too late. Looks like we're going down whether you wanted to or not."

His deep voice didn't vibrate through her. Something wasn't right. She stared at the man. He had Marcus's build, dark hair and chiseled features. Though he had a military carriage, he was looser limbed than Marcus was. "You're not Marcus," she said flatly.

"'Fraid not. Wish I was, though. There's nothing like having a beautiful woman chase after me." He waggled his black eyebrows. No, this wasn't Marcus. This jokester didn't act at all like Marcus.

"You look so much like someone I— Someone I know." She sagged against the wall. She was so sure Marcus would return. Ever since she returned to Earth, she'd tried contacting him. The transmitter he gave her didn't work.

All she got on that subspace communicator was garbled sounds. The *link* only had static. She'd lost contact with Marcus, and he hadn't come back for her.

"Hey, you aren't going to cry, are you? I don't do well with crying women."

She blinked back the tears forming in her eyes. "No."

"You look like you've had a bad day. I was heading to the cafeteria. C'mon, I'll buy you a cup of coffee, and then I *will* be someone you know."

She looked up at him. His green eyes twinkled. She could only stare. Those eyes were the same shade as Marcus's. So unusual. Like exquisite jade. Two men with such distinctive eyes, who looked so much alike, who even sounded the same. Could it be? Omigod. Could this be Marcus's twin?

"Speechless? I have that effect on women all the time. My pearls of wisdom just stop them in their tracks." He held out his hand. "Scott Cherella. Prodigal son."

She allowed him to shake her hand. The odds of finding Marcus's twin were too great to contemplate. His self-deprecating tone snagged her attention. "Prodigal son?"

"Ah." He held the elevator door, motioning for her to precede him. "Curious?"

"Yes. No. I mean..." She exited the elevator.

"And decisive, too. The cafeteria is this way." He waved his hand down the hall. "Although I'm sure you know that since you come here twice a day."

She stopped. So did he. Hospital personnel and visitors dodged around them. "How do you know that?" she demanded. Had this man been stalking her? Like the drug dealer across the road had stalked Veronese?

"You sit in a corner. You take your coffee black and your grilled chicken salad with fat-free French dressing. And you don't wear a wedding ring."

Now he was really making her nervous. He'd been watching her.

He gave her a reassuring smile. "Hey, don't look so worried. You've been in line ahead of me two days in a row.

You just stare straight ahead, never looking around. I promised myself that if you were here today, I'd talk to you. With all these people around, you're safe. Besides, I'm harmless."

"Yeah, right." How would she know he was harmless? Hadn't she thought the man across the road was harmless?

He gave her a comically wounded look. Then, he held out his hand again. "Hi, I'm Scott Cherella, from Houston."

Okay, not Marcus's twin. All the twins in Cenamola's experiment had been from here in Ann Arbor.

He twisted his mouth ruefully. "At least, I used to be from Houston. I'm back home for my mother's surgery."

Back home?

"Now, you know me, and we can have that coffee together. Right?"

He *was* from Ann Arbor. She had to find out more about this man. Taking him up on his offer of coffee, she walked into the cafeteria. He was right about one thing. She *had* been so lost in her thoughts lately—worrying about Tim and her inability to contact Marcus—that she hadn't paid attention to anything, or anyone, around her. It was a wonder she had even seen him at the elevator upstairs just now.

If this was Marcus's twin, what would he say when she told him? *Should* she tell him he had a long-lost brother who was passing himself off as an extra-terrestrial?

***

"Captain Viator." General Porcazier, the real General, looked at him from the vid screen. "Good job routing the Praetorium from that sector. Now, your ship is to proceed to the Fleurian system."

Marcus controlled a grimace. "We hoped to return to Sector Six."

She gave him a stern look. "Around the Terran Sun? After that disaster when your ship engaged the rebels? I think not. You may not have single-handedly started this war but, by the stars, we are in the middle of one. We are not concerning ourselves with that sector. Not enough there for the Alliance to bother with."

"What about the trilium mining colonies on Triton and

Proteus?" He named Neptune's moons.

"Having lost that sector at the beginning of the war, we have had to utilize other resources for trilium. The Alliance does not fault you for engaging the Praetorium and not protecting the mining colonies. You were out-gunned from the beginning."

He winced. His ship had been outnumbered. No one thought the Praetorium would assemble in Sector Six. With their extremely powerful disruptors, they had been able to prevent the Alliance from spotting their ships. Thus hidden, the rebels were able to prepare for a major engagement.

His destruction of the disruptor on board the Praetorian vessel commanded by Cenamola had given the Alliance only momentary communication control. Another rebel ship immediately took over, jamming transmission to Space Fleet Command. And from his ship to Jessica.

The *Freedom* had searched out and destroyed three such disruptors, temporarily restoring communication with SFC. Predictably, the amassed rebel ships scattered. Then, in what Marcus could only deduce as a stupid blunder, the *Freedom*, the only Alliance ship left, was ordered to go to another sector of more strategic importance.

Sector Six, including Earth, held nothing of value to the Alliance, other than as a species to be studied. Research into primitive cultures was a luxury the Alliance could not afford now. All resources were needed to defeat the Praetorium.

Yet, Marcus was certain the rebels still had a secret base somewhere near Earth.

"I request permission to engage the enemy in Sector Six and recover the mining colonies." He had to get back. He'd promised Jessica he would return for her.

"Your ship, Viator, is needed in the Fleurian System."

He exerted all of his self-control not to protest. He held his arms straight at his sides, his hands hidden.

"Captain, your duty—"

Slowly, he unclenched his fists. "I understand my duty, General." That duty led him farther away from Jessica.

"I am pleased to hear that. With all that has happened

since the inception of this war, I have neglected to congratulate you. The Alliance High Council extends their appreciation for your uncovering the impersonator."

"The perpetrator of the Gemini Experiment should never have escaped confinement," he growled. Dr. Cenamola, the unscrupulous scientist who had stolen fetuses from their Earth mothers, was still imprisoned on board the *Freedom*.

"You are, of course, correct, Captain. Security measures have been tightened in all penal institutions. However, he will be your prisoner a while longer."

"He needs to be in a more secure facility than what we can provide aboard the *Freedom*."

"That may be. However, until you return to Serenia, he will remain with you."

"General, I must protest."

"He cannot have the opportunity to ever again wreak havoc upon Serenians, on the entire Alliance. I trust you, Viator. You will not allow him to escape."

He merely nodded. It was futile to protest. Once the General had made up her mind, nothing changed it.

"It is to your credit you did not believe your friend, Glaxpher, was a traitor. Otherwise you, like the others, would have been tricked into believing the traitor was me."

While impersonating General Porcazier, the scientist had ordered all ships to vacate Sector Six, leaving the *Freedom* alone.

"You would never betray the Alliance, General."

She acknowledged his words with a small smile. "Proceed to the Fleurian System. We must protect our allies lest they join our enemies."

Away from Earth. Away from Jessica. Yet, he could not disobey a direct order. "Yes, General."

The transmission ended. He slammed his fist on the desk. The opposite direction from Earth. By the fires of Tarsus, how could duty be so odious?

It had been over an Earth month since Jessica left the ship. Would she think he had abandoned her? Or would her love for him give her hope that he would return?

His duty, his allegiance to the Alliance, prevented him from going after her. To abandon his post in time of war was unconscionable.

Alliance ships routed the Praetorium from one sector to another. The Praetorian ships, with their sophisticated disruptors and their ability to hide their presence from Alliance scanners, wreaked havoc on planets loyal to the Alliance. When he saw the devastation wrought by Praetorian forces, he thanked the Intrepid Ones Earth held no interest for the rebels. Jessica's people, with their primitive weaponry, would be helpless.

Being a primitive culture and ignorant of space inhabitants was not what kept Earth from being attacked by the Praetorium. Earth had nothing the rebels wanted. No advanced weapons, no energy source. Earth would be a useless conquest, a waste of time. The Praetorium had more important planets to conquer.

With little enthusiasm, he instructed Glaxpher—the navigation officer was back at his post—to proceed to the Fleurian System. Marcus would follow orders. He knew his duty.

***

Scott Cherella entertained Jessie with his non-stop observation of hospitals. She didn't have to think, just observe. His manners were more flamboyant than Marcus's. While she could never accuse Marcus of being flamboyant, she saw glimpses of him in Scott.

"Am I putting you to sleep?" Scott raised his eyebrow. Her heart lurched. He looked so much like Marcus.

"Uh, no. What did you mean about being a prodigal son?"

Scott smiled, and it was almost like being with Marcus again. "I left home at eighteen. Joined the Navy to see the world. And I did see a good chunk of it. Mostly from several miles up." At her questioning look, he explained, "I was a pilot. Then—" he beamed "—I was chosen by NASA."

"You're an astronaut?" *My God, what a coincidence.*

"*Trained* to be an astronaut." His smile disappeared. He rubbed the bridge of his nose. "I was scheduled to be the back-up pilot for a flight next year. With all the government cutbacks, the flight was scrubbed and a lot of us were let go last month. I was weighing my options when Mom had her heart attack. So, here I am back in good, old A-Squared."

She smiled at the nickname for Ann Arbor—two A's, A^2. "You were born here?" Things were falling into place. At his nod, she asked, "When?"

When he told her, she scrubbed a hand down her face. About the same time as Marcus. This was too bizarre. He had to be Marcus's twin, but the chance of her actually running into his twin was astronomical.

"Did your mother think she was having twins when she was pregnant with you?"

Scott looked at her as if she'd taken leave of her senses. Maybe she had.

***

Today was the day Jessie and Tim had looked forward to for months. He was finally coming home. A long-delayed Christmas present—in February. His rehabilitation had advanced to the point where he could go home. He would return to the rehab center only as an outpatient.

Workers had already installed his special equipment in Jessie's farmhouse. Her parents had made it clear the week after Tim was shot that they could not deal with his disability.

"I'm in the middle of a major project," Richard said. As long as she could remember, Dad was always in the middle of a major project. "I can't be running back and forth to the hospital." Yet his lab was minutes away.

"You got him into this mess, missy, you can take care of him."

Even though the blame for Tim's injuries lay squarely on the dead drug dealer, Richard continued to heap guilt on Jessie's head. If he had said all the nasty things to her twin that he said to her, she could imagine how devastated Veronese must feel.

Though her mother's reaction had been different— "I can't stand to see Timothy this way. It's tearing me apart to see him so helpless. I just can't bear it." —it added up to the same thing. Jessie immediately assumed responsibility for her brother.

When she realized Tim's recovery would be long, she brought all of his belongings to the farm. It was cheaper to break his lease than pay rent on an apartment he couldn't use, or probably ever go back to.

It tore *her* apart watching Tim struggle to sit up. It killed her to see the despair in his eyes as he realized a wheelchair would be his lifelong companion. Yet, unlike her parents, she visited him in the hospital twice each day, kept her business going, and called Marcus on the transmitter. After four months, she had nearly given up.

Marcus had said he would return, and he was a man of his word. She recalled what he'd said about her twin. He thought Veronese would understand them leaving her behind, and she hadn't. Veronese had been terrified that she'd been abandoned. Damn it, Jessie felt the same way. Wouldn't he realize how she felt? Why didn't he come back for her?

Had the encounter with the Praetorium escalated into war? Was the gobbledygook on the transmitter a jamming device disrupting communication, as the Praetorium had done before?

"Are you going to stand there with the car door open and let me freeze to death?"

Coming back to earth, she maneuvered Tim's wheelchair close to the car so he could swing himself into it.

"Give your sister a break, buddy," Scott chided. "She's probably mooning over her sweetheart."

Tim laughed. "Mooning? That's a good one."

She reached into the backseat for Tim's duffel bag with his equipment and meds. Scott pushed the wheelchair up the ramp he'd built last week.

After their first encounter, Scott had found ways to run into her. He scheduled his visits with his mother to coincide with her visits to Tim. Even after his mother went home from the hospital, he still returned to see Jessie. Many evenings he brought dinner for her and Tim, giving Tim a break from hospital food. After Tim told him what had happened with the drug dealer, Scott began to follow her out to the farm at night to make sure she was safe. His kindness went a long way to make up for her parents' neglect. And Marcus's desertion. Scott made her feel special while she poured her energies into taking care of Tim.

He looked so much like Marcus. He was a good, kind man. So thoughtful. How easy it would be to love him. So, why did she still love Marcus? Was she a masochistic fool? She'd given him her heart. She'd pledged her love to him, and she would honor that pledge. If she believed Marcus, he committed himself to her, too. Marcus said he loved her. She hoped that would be enough to sustain her in the difficult days to come.

***

"Calling the Intergalactic Alliance vessel, *Freedom*. *Freedom*, please respond." Jessie gripped the transmitter tighter. "*Freedom*, please come in. Where are you, Marcus? Please answer me."

Her hands shook, not just from the cold. "Calling the Alliance vessel, *Freedom*. Please respond. Marcus, damn it, answer me."

"Aren't you freezing out here?"

She spun around at the sound of Scott's voice. She reached for the porch post as everything swam around her.

"Hey, there." Scott steadied her. "Did the pup trip you?"

She'd gotten a mutt from the pound after she came home from space. The six-month-old Labrador Retriever-Irish Setter mix was big, goofy, and clumsy. He also helped assuage her loneliness.

"It wasn't Max. I just got a little dizzy. Maybe I was craning my neck too much." She knew why she was dizzy, and it wasn't from craning her neck.

"You know, that is just about the dumbest dog I've ever seen. Almost as dumb as his mistress." Scott grinned. "Where are your gloves? Your fingers are like ice."

He stuffed her frozen hands inside his coat and under his arms while he drew her close. He put his arms and down jacket around her, then rested his chin on the top of her head. His warmth enveloped her. "This feels pretty good," he said.

Scott made no secret he was interested in her. At first, she thought he was just fascinated by her story of travelling in space to another galaxy. He was skeptical until he talked to Tim and learned about Veronese.

Avidly, the two men had pumped her for details of her adventure. Scott insisted on drawing diagrams of the interior of the *Freedom* from her descriptions. She went along with them because it kept Tim's mind occupied.

She tried to send Scott away, but he just kept coming back. She was in love with his brother. She was certain he and Marcus were twins. She told Scott it wasn't fair to him. Yet, her responsibility for Tim weighed heavily on her shoulders. It was heaven to have someone take care of her the way Scott did.

"You're millions of miles away, aren't you?" Scott murmured into her hair. "On the *Freedom* with Marcus."

She tried to pull back.

"It's okay. I'm getting used to playing second fiddle to my brother. It still seems strange to know I have a twin. Mom was in a talkative mood last night. I asked her about her pregnancy with me. She said it was the oddest thing. At first, her doctor said she might be having twins. He thought he heard two heartbeats, and Mom got real big, real fast—much bigger than she did with my sister. Then, one month later the doc said he must have made a mistake. But, all through the pregnancy, Mom thought she was having twins. When I was born, she insisted there was another baby, and she became so upset that the doc sedated her. After that, she never spoke of it again. C'mon. Let's get you inside."

Jessie still felt a little dizzy, but she let Scott lead her back into the house.

"You need to take better care of yourself," Scott chided in his good-natured way as they went into the living room. "Tim, did your sister eat today?"

Tim glanced up from his computer. With Scott's help, she had turned the living room into a bedroom and office for Tim. "She fixed Sloppy Joes for supper. Why?"

"She got dizzy out on the porch."

Tim looked at her in alarm. "What's wrong?"

She shoved her hands into her jeans pockets—jeans that had gotten so snug she couldn't snap them anymore. Despite the healthy diet and exercise program she'd adhered to since her return from space.

"There's nothing wrong with me." She took a deep breath. "I'm just pregnant."

***

"Captain, when will we be returning to Earth's orbit?"

Marcus had been on his usual rounds of the ship, stopping for a brief tour of Engineering. He was waiting for the conveyance to return to the bridge when he was accosted by the woman who looked so much like Jessica.

Veronese Qilana waited for his response. After returning to the ship, she told him she was prepared to accept punishment for leaving without permission. The outbreak of war with the Praetorium made it necessary to postpone disciplinary action. Her engineering expertise was needed after two crewmembers were injured during the attack following Jessica's transport to Earth.

According to Chief Luqett, Qilana worked longer hours than the rest of the crew. Marcus wondered if she was trying to make up for putting the ship at risk because they had to decloak twice.

He pinched the bridge of his nose. He should be angry with Qilana, yet were it not for her actions, he would never have known Jessica. For that, he was grateful and more than willing to postpone official disciplinary action. Lately, though, her tone when speaking to him had become more insistent.

"Our orders are to follow the Praetorian vessels into the Cardijian System, where we are to engage them in battle and defeat them." He gave a short, mirthless laugh as the conveyance arrived.

She followed him into the conveyance. "You find our orders amusing, sir?"

"Redundant, Lieutenant. Of course, we're going to try to defeat them. Yet, each time we win a battle, some of the Praetorian ships slip through our fingers."

She gave him a long look. "This new assignment takes us

farther from Earth."

He slammed his fist against the wall. "Don't you think I know that!"

She jumped at his display of temper. He was tired of controlling—denying—his emotions. By the Intrepid Ones, he had them. He was only human.

"Permission to speak freely, sir?"

He nodded wearily.

"Why haven't you gone back for my sister? You love her."

He arched his eyebrow. "Perhaps I was hasty in granting you that freedom."

"Sir, we need to return to Earth," she said vehemently. "While I don't want to live there, I need to find out if my brother survived. I have tried repeatedly to call Jessica, but I receive no answer. I think the Praetorium are still in that sector and jamming Alliance communication signals."

"Alliance Command believes the Praetorium have left Sector Six and are concentrating their resources in sectors with more strategic advantage."

She shook her head. "I do not agree."

Neither did Marcus, but he could hardly express to a subordinate his disagreement with his orders.

She plunged on, "What if they left their jamming devices behind? We have had no contact with Jessica. She must think we have abandoned her."

He remembered Jessica saying the same thing. "Our orders—"

"Orders be damned, sir." Then, she gulped at her boldness.

"Repeating Terran expressions, Lieutenant?" He could not fault her. Qilana was not saying anything he had not thought himself. He clenched his teeth. "I will forget your comment. Our duty is to follow orders. We are proceeding to the Cardijian System. You may return to Engineering." He walked out of the conveyance and headed to his quarters. He needed to calm down.

She followed him, slipping through the portal to his quarters before it closed. "What about your duty to the woman you love, sir?"

"That is enough, Lieutenant." He was weary to the bone. Ever since her sojourn on Earth, Qilana acted less and less like a Serenian. She was wearing him down with her persistence. This was not the first time she'd followed him into his quarters.

"I know you love Jessica." She stopped in front of his vid unit and picked up the scrap of yellow material. "What is this?"

He snatched it out of her hand, ignoring her startled look.

"That is one of Jessica's hairbands—a scrunchie." Veronese stared at him as he twisted the fabric in his hands. It had been his touchstone, a reminder that Jessica had been real. The soft ornamentation was the only tangible he had of her.

"You are dismissed, Lieutenant Qilana." His voice sounded strained even to him.

"I know you love my sister, sir. You must not abandon her."

"Go," he said past the thickness in his throat. "We will not speak of this again."

Veronese looked like she wanted to argue further. At his fierce expression, she nodded and left. He rubbed the bridge of his nose with relief. He had given her time to start acting like a Serenian again. Truth be told, he liked talking with her. She looked so much like Jessica, it was as if a part of her remained here with him.

But Qilana was going too far. Although a diligent worker, her private disagreements with him had escalated. He knew he would have to discipline her.

It was difficult to summon the energy to discipline someone for his own thoughts.

"Computer, replay the events of 4127.633." He gave the date and time—forever etched in his mind—of the last time he saw Jessica.

***

"Pregnant?" Tim and Scott exclaimed in unison.

"Sure," Jessie said with a tilt to her head and a cockiness that was purely false. "Isn't that what happens when you're abducted by aliens?"

"Have you been to the doctor?" Scott seemed to be the

first to recover.

"Of course. If the baby keeps to an exact timetable—and no child of Marcus's would dare not conform—he or she is due the end of July." She knew exactly when the baby had been conceived. She'd had one glorious day and night with Marcus. A time not likely to be repeated.

Tonight was the last time she was going to call him. From now on, he could damn well call her. There hadn't even been static tonight. No garbled messages. Nothing. Maybe the transmitter was broken. Maybe she wasn't doing something right or, more likely, Marcus was ignoring her.

To the astonishment of the two men in her living room, she hurled the transmitter against the wall, burst into tears, and ran to her bedroom.

TWENTY-ONE

"The war is over, Captain Viator." General Porcazier grinned at him from the vid monitor.

Marcus exhaled a long breath. His duty was done. At last, he could go to Jessica.

"Your ship is to return home for refit and to give your crew a well-deserved rest. Your outstanding service to the Alliance will not go unrewarded." A secret grin curved her mouth.

"General, what about Sector Six?" Earth.

"Viator," the General said sharply, grin erased. "You are taking far too much interest in that sector. Research into primitive cultures is not needed now. We must be vigilant lest the Praetorium ignore the peace treaty and reassemble."

"Requesting permission to patrol Sector Six to be certain all communication disruption devices are destroyed." He could then return to Earth and retrieve Jessica. General Porcazier gave him a look reserved for those who challenged her. Nevertheless, he plunged on, "With due respect, General, I would like to return to Sector Six. Indications are—"

She waved her hand, a sharp gesture that cut him off. "No. Assuring that peace reigns throughout the Alliance is our primary concern. There are other planets more worthy of our interest than Earth."

Again, he stifled his frustration. No planet was more worthy of *his* interest than Earth. He had to return for Jessica.

"You will not need to concern yourself about military and political matters much longer, Viator." Again, she gave him that secret smile, as if taunting him with knowledge he did not have. "After refit, the *Freedom* will patrol Sector Ten under its new commander, Captain Klegznef."

His jaw unhinged. She was taking his command away from him? Why? She'd said he would be rewarded for his service. "You may not share that information with Mr. Klegznef. He will be told when he is here to receive his commendation. As for you, Viator, I had planned to inform you of the Elders' decision *after* your respite on Serenia. I am not pleased you precipitated this discussion."

"What decision?" Marcus clasped his hands behind his back. The better to keep from slamming them on the desk below the vid monitor. His commanding officer had always been straight forward. He had never known her to tease.

"Marcus." She leaned forward. "I know how much you have wanted this. The Elders have decided to allow you to leave Space Fleet. You may assume control of your uncle's farm."

He was stunned. They'd granted his request. His mind whirled at the thought. So much so that he nearly missed the rest of the General's speech.

"...service to the Alliance. I will miss your unswerving devotion to duty."

Devotion to duty meant he could not return for Jessica. The Elders had finally granted his greatest desire. Or so he had thought.

"You do not look pleased, Marcus. While we Serenians refrain from exuberance, I expected at least a smile. You have gotten what you asked for."

What he asked for. His chest tightened. He recalled a Terran expression. *Be careful what you ask for. You may get it.*

Later, Marcus could not recall what he said to his commanding officer. He must have made an appropriate expression of gratitude, for she questioned him no more. After concluding communication, he paced his quarters. He had what he wanted. Permission to take over Cam's farm. So, why *wasn't* he jumping for joy?

Returning for Jessica had motivated him to be more aggressive in battle so as to end the war quickly. Even his First Officer had remarked that Marcus was nearly as warrior-like as the Zorfans. He was certain Klegznef intended that as a compliment.

His orders were to return immediately to Serenia. He finally had what he wanted—Cam's farm. Yet, how could he abandon Jessica? He had promised he would return for her. His word, his integrity, meant more to him than—

He stopped pacing. Was his promise more important than duty?

All his life he had tried to live up to Serenian standards. Uncle Cam called him more Serenian than Serenians. Had he spent his entire life trying to be something he wasn't? The answer stopped him. Of course he had. He had become a military leader, not a farmer. Instead of bringing new life to the soil, he destroyed life, albeit, in defense of his homeland.

His homeland? Serenia was not his homeland. His head whirled with conflicting thoughts and emotions. He had been indoctrinated into a culture that prized suppression of emotions and free will.

Even before Jessica turned his life upside down, he had begun to question the absolute authority that ruled Serenia. Dissatisfaction with his career had niggled in his mind long before she was 'accidentally' transported aboard his ship.

He had given his word that he would return for her. Was that all that mattered? His honor, his integrity? Were those the only reasons for returning for Jessica?

He took a deep breath. A 'true' Serenian would say yes. But, he wasn't a true Serenian. He was Terran, with Terran emotions. There. He'd admitted it.

He wanted to return to Earth because he loved Jessica. He could not imagine living without her. Now, he had to make a decision that would affect both their lives.

***

"Jess?" The porch creaked as Scott came up behind her and placed his hands on her shoulders. "Don't turn around. I want to ask you a question, but I don't think I want to see your face when I do."

"Sounds ominous." She continued to stare at the sky. "It's a nice night, isn't it? After the harsh winter we've had, I didn't think spring would ever get here."

"Jess—"

"Maybe this warm spell is Mother Nature's tease," she rushed on, curious about his question yet fearful, too. "March came in all too peacefully. It can't go out the same way."

Scott cleared his throat. His hands tightened on her shoulders. "Your parents think the baby is mine."

Her parents had made a rare visit that evening. They even stayed for dinner, another surprise. Their attention had been on her burgeoning belly instead of Tim's condition. Each time she'd tried to talk about his therapy and advances, one of her parents diverted the discussion to her pregnancy. Neither one looked directly at Tim.

What a switch. After years of being ignored, now *she* was the focus of attention. She'd been furious with them. They ignored Tim, the son on whom they had showered all their hopes, as if they didn't see him anymore. As if, with his disability, he had become invisible.

She'd followed them out to their car and vented. "His mind isn't disabled. Can't you see that? He is still consulting. His clients didn't leave him. In the fall, he'll be strong enough to go back to the classroom."

At her father's snort of disgust, she said, "Even if he can't walk, he's still worthy of your love."

Her mother made a comment about elevated emotions caused by the hormonal imbalance of pregnancy before saying a strained good-night. Jessie stomped around to the backyard to cool off. She'd almost gotten her 'hormonally imbalanced' emotions under control when Scott came out.

"Don't worry. Dad won't come after you with a shotgun. I'm surprised he even took the time to say something to you."

"Marry me, Jess."

She whirled around, slipping away from him. "I don't love you, Scott. And you don't love me."

He rubbed the bridge of his nose. Her heart twisted at such a Marcus-like gesture. "We're good together. You make me laugh, Jess. We're friends, good friends. Isn't that enough for us? And for the baby?"

She rubbed her upper arms through the long sleeves of the denim maternity smock. "No." She wanted, *needed*, love. Marcus's love. Or nothing.

"He isn't coming back, Jess. If he was killed—"

"Don't say that! He isn't dead!" Her lips trembled. "He can't be dead."

"How would you know? Who would tell you? Your transmitter doesn't work. Throwing it against the wall certainly made sure of that."

She crossed her arms in front of her chest. "Well, I didn't get anything from it before, either."

"How would you know if he's still alive?" Scott repeated.

"My sister would make sure I got that message."

"Maybe the whole ship blew up."

She stopped her lip from quivering again. *How could he be so cruel?* "You'd better leave. I won't listen to this."

"Damn it, Jess. I'm trying to do the right thing here. My twin let you down. Think about the baby. Little Jessica needs a father."

"Little Marcus *has* a father." She closed her eyes and took a long, agonizing breath. "I can't marry you, Scott. Even if Marcus is dead, I won't marry you."

***

Marcus stood at the oval table in the conference room. The executive officers seated around the table looked at him expectantly.

"As I announced to the crew, the war with the Praetorium has ended. The Alliance is pleased with the performance of this ship and her crew. General Porcazier made it clear commendations are in order. Promotions, also."

Their reactions were as varied as their race. The Serenians smiled. Glaxpher's blue mouth split into a wide grin as he thumped the table. Klegznef remained stoic, acting as if this was his due. He was right. They all deserved to be rewarded for their outstanding service to the Alliance.

"Our orders are to return to Serenia. You and the crew deserve a hard-earned respite. The ship will be refitted and then will patrol Sector Ten."

They looked at him with the same measure of surprise as they did their pleasure earlier.

Except for Chief Luqett. "Sector Ten is the back of beyond, sir," he declared with vehemence. "We are going to retrieve Jessie first, aren't we?"

Marcus sat down and said nothing.

Luqett looked around at the others before pinning Marcus with a hard stare. "We have to go back for her. She only left because her brother needed her. Surely, he has recovered by now. I need her in Engineering. She is a quick learner and—"

"Marcus?" Stasik Glaxpher interrupted. "You have always urged us to speak freely in this room." He leaned forward. "My mother told me how Ms. Wyndom encouraged you to prove I was not a traitor. Chief Luqett is right. She was an asset to this ship." He gave Marcus a sheepish look. "I heard she wanted to stay aboard."

The others nodded in agreement, adding anecdotes of her thoughtfulness to them. Marcus had not realized how rampant gossip was among his officers.

"She rescued you, Marcus," Luqett declared. "Had she not found a way out of your quarters, how long would you have been there before the truth was known? How long before we would have discovered that traitor?"

"Has Dr. Cenamola ever revealed how he tricked us? Or how he accessed the ship's computer?" Xaropa asked.

Security Chief Hrvibm shifted in her seat. "He will tell us nothing."

"The lassie was brought here against her will." Luqett redirected the conversation. "Yet she made the best of the situation. She wasn't content to sit by, fearfully waiting for us to take her home. Don't forget how she pitched in and found the problem with the engine. Had it not been for her, we would not have known about the sabotage to the analyzer, either."

Glaxpher and Xaropa nodded at Luqett's fierce defense. Not the Zorfan. Klegznef sat stoically silent, as did Hrvibm. Except for himself, Marcus knew what he was about to propose would have the biggest repercussion on his First Officer— especially in light of the promotion Klegznef was about to receive.

"She had courage." Klegznef's praise shocked everyone at the table—if their expressions were any indication.

Marcus nodded. "Yes, she did."

"It would not be appropriate to leave her on that primitive planet."

Marcus closed his mouth. Klegznef, her strongest critic, defending Jessica? What had gotten into the Zorfan?

"Thank you, Mr. Klegznef. Although our orders are to return immediately to Serenia, I am detouring this ship to Earth for Ms. Wyndom."

Again, their reactions varied. From Luqett pounding the table with glee to Klegznef who stared at Marcus with no expression. Even Hrvibm had a small smile.

"What I am proposing is against orders," Marcus continued. "I asked to return to Earth, and the answer was no. I am going anyway. Now is the time to go on record if you object."

Silence hung around the room. The officers did not look at him. They did not even look at each other.

Marcus clasped his hands on top of the table and leaned forward. "I must caution you, while the responsibility is mine, as well as the consequences, you may be subjected to reprimands."

Luqett looked around at the others before staring at Marcus. "Your point? Sir," he added hastily.

No one else spoke. Everyone found the red burl of the xephod wood tabletop most fascinating. Except Klegznef, whose expression never changed.

"While I appreciate your earlier encouragement, I will note in my log that the responsibility for disobeying a direct order is mine alone." Marcus stood. "Mr. Glaxpher, lay in a course for Earth."

***

Another glorious spring day had arrived. Jessie loved this time of year when the earth was reborn. Scott was hanging the swing from the porch roof. Jessie sat on the steps to keep the puppy out of his way. Max was still all legs and clumsy feet.

Scott hadn't stayed away after she refused his marriage proposal. He'd returned this morning full of apologies and a bouquet of daisies. She'd offered a weak protest, grateful he hadn't abandoned her—like Marcus.

"It looks so different." She waved her hand at the empty land across the road. After Tim's injuries, every law enforcement agency, it seemed, had gotten into the act. Local, state, the Feds, DEA. They raided the farmhouse and arrested anyone foolish enough to come looking to buy drugs. The land was confiscated. Two weeks ago, a mysterious fire burned the dilapidated house down to the ground.

She heard the property was for sale. "I'm thinking of buying the property." She pointed across the road. "When Marcus comes, he'll need more land to raise crops."

"What if he never comes?"

"He will, Scott. I have to believe he will. It's all I have to cling to." A sob tore from her throat. "He has to come back."

Scott knelt on the step and put his arms around her. For just a moment, she let herself take comfort from him.

**

Marcus stood on the bridge, his hands clasped behind his back. The ship would soon be close enough to Earth to transport Jessica.

As often as he'd orbited the planet, he had yet to step onto Earth's surface. With the Elders granting his request to leave Space Fleet, he would never come here again. He decided to see for himself where he was conceived. He'd never had the desire to trace his ancestry, like Veronese Qilana. With time at a premium, he couldn't search for his biological family. Though Cenamola had selected his subjects only from one area in Michigan, Ann Arbor was a large, sprawling community. Marcus didn't have a hope of finding his twin in the short time he would be there.

"I have decided to go down to the planet's surface to bring back Ms. Wyndom. Mr. Klegznef, you have control of the ship." Marcus almost told him to get used to it before leaving the bridge. He walked to the transport room.

"Captain?" Veronese Qilana stood beside the transport platform.

"I will bring back your sister." Marcus stepped onto the platform.

She joined him. "I wish to see my brother."

Marcus nodded to the operator. He would not waste time arguing. He'd waited too long to see Jessica. Now that she was so close, each moment seemed like an eternity.

He felt the familiar buzz in his ears and the slight disorientation as the transporter sent him through space.

"Pin-point accuracy, Ensign Duross," Veronese spoke into her *link*. "Well done. Qilana out."

Marcus looked around. Well done, indeed. They stood on a gravel driveway in front of a white farmhouse with forest green shutters and a wide porch. The house of his daydreams. Two figures were seated at the top of the steps. The man's arms were around the woman. Jessica.

A black, long-haired dog tripped over his big feet as he raced toward Marcus. The couple rose. Marcus sucked in his breath. Jessica was pregnant. His heart lurched in his chest as the man put his arm around her in a protective gesture.

Marcus was too late. She had not waited for him. He couldn't blame her. He'd been gone nearly six months. He had promised to come back for her immediately and had not. He had promised to contact her and he had not. She must have turned to another.

Beside him, Veronese gasped. "Your twin."

Intent on Jessica, Marcus had not looked carefully at the man. There was no denying the resemblance. *How had Jessica found him? Had she found comfort in the arms of a man who looked exactly like him?* Insecurity slowed him, unlike Veronese who raced ahead. She'd certainly thrown off Serenian constraints quickly enough.

"Jessica," Veronese cried as she ran up the steps and threw her arms around her sister. "Look at you. Pregnant."

"What's going on out there?" a man—Tim?—called through the screen door. "Neesie, is that you?"

Veronese ran into the house.

Jessie ignored the sounds of the cheery reunion inside as she watched Marcus. Part of her wanted to race down the steps to him the way Veronese had raced up. After all this time, without a word, he certainly didn't seem to be in a hurry to come to her. She'd be damned if she'd make a fool of herself falling all over him the way Max was. Dumb dog.

She held herself stiffly. "What took you so long?"

"Why is your transmitter turned off?" he countered.

"The damn thing didn't work." Her restraint broke. "You left me here. You left me alone. You said you would come back and you—" She started to cry. "Damn you, Marcus. Why didn't you come back for me?"

Scott stepped protectively closer. "As happy as I am to meet my long-lost brother," he drawled, "I ought to take you behind the barn and punch your lights out for all you've put her through."

Through her tears, she saw uncertainty in Marcus's eyes. Good, she thought. Let him wonder. Just as quickly, she regretted her bitchiness.

"I take it you're Marcus. Wow, it's like looking in a mirror. I'm Scott." He held out his hand.

She sniffed. "He doesn't shake hands." When he did, she said, "Okay, make a liar out of me." She put her hands on her hips. "So, big guy, what brings you here?"

Scott looked at her as if she'd lost her mind.

"Jessica," her twin called through the open door, "it wasn't his fault. We—"

"Sticking up for him, *dear* sister?" she yelled back.

Scott grabbed her shoulders and gave her a little shake. "Why are you acting like this? He's here. Quit acting like a brat and go down there and kiss him."

Heat bloomed in her cheeks, and she cursed her fair complexion. To hide her blush, she bent to pet Max.

"You're on your own, kid." Scott went inside.

Jessie stood and stared at Marcus, willing him to come to her, too stubborn to go to him. "Why didn't you contact me? The bad guys jam the signals?"

"Yes."

"For six months?" she exclaimed. "Give me a break. The Alliance wouldn't put up with that. I couldn't raise the *Freedom,* or any Alliance ship. It's been six long months. By God, Marcus, I tried to contact you. I tried every damn night and day until I gave up."

"I take it you missed me." The corner of his mouth curved up. Despite his quip, he climbed the steps without his usual briskness. Again, she thought she detected uncertainty in his silver eyes.

"Don't make fun of me, Marcus."

She wanted to throw herself into his arms yet willed herself to control her emotions. She could do a darn good imitation of a Serenian. He wasn't the only one who could hide his feelings.

"I missed you." His soft admission tore her heart.

"Damn you," she whispered. Tears flooded her eyes. She swiped at them. So much for concealing her emotions.

He touched her cheek. "Please. Do not cry."

She swiped again at the tears rolling down her cheek, brushing aside his fingers. "I am not crying."

"You're doing a pretty good imitation." His mouth quirked.

"Making jokes, Marcus?"

When he reached out to touch her face again, she noticed his hand was trembling.

"Where's that Serenian control?" She folded her arms on top of her protruding belly. "First a joke and now your hand is shaking? Will wonders never cease."

"Scott is my twin?"

She gave him an exasperated look. "Could two guys look so much alike and not be twins?"

"Do you love him?"

"Of course, I love him." He was Marcus's brother. How could she not love him?

A pained look crossed Marcus's face. "Is that why you married him?"

"Married? You think Scott and I—" She began to laugh. "Oh, Marcus, you are so dense."

"The baby?"

"You and I had one sweet night of ecstasy, and here's the proof sticking out in front of me."

"B-But, it can't be. The pills for temporary sterility never fail."

She placed her hands on her hips. "Maybe they don't work on humans."

"We *are* human," Marcus said. "I mean, Serenians are human, with the same genetic make-up as Terrans. The sterility pills should not have failed."

"You know, for a superior culture, you sure have a lot of problems with equipment. Who designed those pills? The quack who thought it was a good idea to separate twins?"

"That quack—" Veronese stood inside the screen door "—is still imprisoned on our ship. The Alliance decided Captain Viator was the perfect jailer. He wouldn't be tricked by Dr. Cenamola the way the others were. Would you two hurry up? We don't have much time."

"C'mere, big guy. I need that kiss I've been waiting six months for." She threw her arms around his neck, bumping him with her distended belly. "Oops, forgot about Junior for a moment."

Marcus felt bewildered, then marveled at the experience. She carried his child. In awe, he touched the mound in front of her. At a sudden movement, he dropped his hands and stepped back. "What was that?"

She tugged on his neck. "Did Junior kick you? Good. About time you got to share in the fun. Oh, God, I've missed you so much, Marcus." She pressed her lips to his, erasing any doubt about the object of her affection.

His heart ached that she'd been alone when she discovered she carried his child. He let his kiss tell her how much he missed her. How he had longed for her smile to brighten up the dark days of the war when the burden of leadership weighed heavy on his shoulders.

In her arms, he was at peace.

She leaned back. "What did Veronese mean when she said you have little time?"

The reminder slammed into him. "I came for you. We have

to return to the ship. Quickly."

"Return? I thought you..." She dropped her arms. "Oh, Marcus, I can't go back with you."

"You have to. We're returning to Serenia."

"I-I don't understand. I thought you came here to be with me."

He explained about the war which had prevented him from returning for her. "I have come back for you, Jessica. To return to Serenia."

"L-Let's go inside."

As he walked into the house, he was overwhelmed by the rightness of the place. Even on Cam's farm, he hadn't felt as comfortable as he did in this room. A young man sat in a wheelchair, a hospital bed nearby. Her brother was still paralyzed. Marcus hadn't realized that the physicians had not healed Tim's injuries.

Veronese sat on the floor next to her brother. Scott leaned against the fireplace mantle, watching. Jessica motioned for Marcus to sit in a wide, stuffed chair before easing down into a straight-back rocker that gleamed as if it was new.

"Jessie refinished that rocker," Tim said. "It was Gram's and pretty beat up. She worked on it to keep her mind off you." He stared pointedly.

On rare occasions Marcus had been on the receiving end of a dressing-down. Even General Porcazier hadn't made him squirm as he did now with Jessica's brother rising to her defense and his own twin glaring at him.

"It was not his fault." Veronese scrambled to her feet. "We do not have time for past history. Our ship is waiting. We have to go back to Serenia. Marcus—uh, Captain Viator—disobeyed a direct order by coming here."

He tried to signal her to stop.

She didn't. "He put his career on the line for you, Jessica. If we have a slight delay, it could be attributed to engine problems. In fact, that's exactly what Chief Luqett is going to report. Engine problems. We came for you, Jessica. We cannot stay. You must come with us. Now."

Jessica twisted her hands on her lap. "I can't go. I can't

leave Tim."

"That's a bunch of bull," Tim blurted.

"Tim, you can't live alone. The doctors say it will be months before you can take care of yourself."

"I don't need you to babysit me," he retorted. "I'll hire a nurse. You can't sacrifice your life just because mine's messed up."

Veronese looked stricken. "It is all my fault you are paralyzed."

"Can we get on without the pity party?" Scott drawled. He received three angry looks for his interference.

"Tim, I won't leave you." She crossed her arms and rested them on top of her rounded belly. "I love you, Marcus, but I can't go with you."

Marcus was dumbfounded. She wouldn't go back with him? His heart twisted at the thought of never seeing her again. Yet, he understood. She believed her duty was to take care of her paralyzed brother. He could take care of that. He tapped his *link*. "Transport Dr. Rindor to these coordinates."

Jessica gave him a sharp look. "What are you doing?"

He smiled. "Once your brother is cured, you will be able to leave."

She eyed him suspiciously. "I thought you were not allowed to interfere in the lives of your research subjects."

Veronese gave him a tremulous smile. "Thank you, Captain. I could not ask you to disobey that mandate."

Marcus shrugged his shoulders. "What's one more disobedience?"

TWENTY-TWO

At the bright light from the transport beam, Jessie shielded her eyes. Her dog sniffed the new arrival, nearly tripping the ship's medical officer.

"Max, sit," Jessie ordered. The dog continued to circle the doctor.

Dr. Rindor, her medical equipment pouch slung over her shoulder, looked around the living room. "Captain?"

"Please, examine him." Marcus pointed to Tim.

The tall, stately doctor—a Serenian, like Marcus—slipped the small pouch off her shoulder. She opened it. Instead of the silver examining tool, she pulled out a ziff blaster. She tossed the pouch aside, spilling the contents on the floor. "Over there, Captain." She waved the weapon. "With the others."

Jessie couldn't believe this. Marcus looked dumbfounded. "Rindor, have you gone mad?"

"Viator, you are such a fool." Rindor's soft female voice changed to a harsh rasp. The stately doctor began to shrink. Her features dissolved into a different doctor. Cenamola. "My remaining research subjects all together. How convenient."

Jessie put her fists on her hips. "You again? Your fancy GND stuff wore off pretty quick this time."

"Quiet," Cenamola ordered with an angry wave of the blaster.

"Jess," Scott said quietly, "it's not a good idea to piss off someone holding a gun. Who is this?"

"He's the jerk who separated us before we were born," she said to Scott who, with Marcus, took a step toward the old man.

Dr. Cenamola flourished the weapon. "Stop right there.

Viator, you will not thwart me this time. First, you will give me what I want and then I will make certain you pay for interfering with my plans."

"No," Jessie cried, leaping to her feet. Max started to growl.

Though he watched Scott and Marcus, the old man pointed his weapon at Jessie. "Sit."

Max sat. Fine time for the dog to obey. Jessie sat, too. She gripped the rounded arms of the rocker.

"Your little side trip to Earth, Viator, has worked out perfectly for me. I will wait here until my transport arrives. But, this unauthorized trip will cost you more than a reprimand from Space Fleet Command. You four are all that are left of my experiment. I can tidy up all the loose ends right now by removing the evidence."

At Cenamola's menacing tone, a low growl emanated from Max's throat. The dog stood. A ridge of hair rose from the back of his neck down his spine.

"Restrain that beast, or I will kill it," Cenamola ordered.

"Hold it, buster. Leave my dog alone." Jessie grabbed Max's collar.

"Jessica," Marcus said calmly, as if they weren't in the worst fix they'd ever been in. "Keep quiet and hold onto your animal."

"Just a minute, doc," Jessie said, hoping to stall long enough for Marcus to come up with a plan. "Before you kill us, I want to know something."

Cenamola shot her an angry, flustered look as if he couldn't figure out why she wasn't quaking in her boots. She was but, damn if she'd let him know it. "C'mon," she wheedled. "You must have been pretty clever to escape. How did you do it?"

Cenamola preened. "The Captain thought he destroyed the new serum. I concealed enough to effect my escape. The medical officer is quite gullible. I have been biding my time, waiting for you to return to this quadrant, Viator. From what I heard from the guards and anyone else foolish enough to talk outside the room in which you imprisoned me, you are infatuated with Wyndom. As soon as the opportunity presented itself, I faked a grievous illness. Overpowering Dr. Rindor when she came to my aid was not difficult."

"How did you manage to trick everybody?" Jessie asked with what she hoped was a proper amount of awe. "The engines, the ship's computer, the analyzer? C'mon, doc, inquiring minds want to know."

"I do not have time for your silly questions."

Obviously, she hadn't exuded enough awe.

"I have planned this insurrection since the Elders incarcerated me," Cenamola muttered. "Nothing should have gone wrong. Nothing. Yet, time and again, Viator, you thwarted my attempts to capture your ship."

"The ship?" Jessie asked. "What's so special about the *Freedom*? If you needed a ship, why not just take one that was easier to capture?"

Cenamola looked at Marcus who stared back with unblinking persistence. "You know what I want. Give it to me."

Marcus continued to stare at Cenamola with no expression. "I do not know what you are talking about."

"Viator, you will pay for your interference. If you do not give me what I want—" Cenamola swung the blaster from Scott, near the fireplace, past Veronese and Jessie, and stopped at Tim "—I will eliminate these four, one by one."

Marcus stepped forward. "Take your revenge on me, but leave the others alone."

"No! It will hurt you more to watch your woman die and—" Cenamola looked at Jessie. A flash of insight lit his silver eyes. "And your child."

"No! Not my baby," Jessie cried, releasing Max's collar.

The dog leapt at Cenamola. Snarling and baring his fangs, Max snagged Cenamola's sleeve.

Fearfully, Cenamola tried to shake the animal loose. Scott and Marcus rushed forward. In the resulting tussle, the blaster fell to the floor. Veronese scooped it up. She leveled it at the old man. "Scott, Captain, step aside."

After they released Cenamola, he calmly straightened his uniform. "You will not discharge that weapon, Qilana. You are a pacifist, like your parents. Give me the blaster." He started toward her.

Jessie could see the blaster wavering. Veronese's hands were shaking. She gripped the weapon tighter. "Do not come any closer. I will not hesitate to—"

Cenamola charged Veronese. She fired. The old man froze in place and then vanished.

"My God, what happened?" Jessie cried as she rushed into Marcus's arms.

"He was vaporized," Veronese explained. "I am sorry, Captain. I did not know...I should have thought—" She started to tremble. "I did not think to change the charge to *stun*."

Scott pried the weapon from her fingers and set it aside before helping her over to the couch.

"I have never k-killed anyone," Veronese mumbled. "I w-work in Engineering. I am not a w-weapons tech. My parents were p-pacifists, just as he said. If they w-were alive, they would never for-forgive me for k-kill—"

"You did what you had to do, Lieutenant." Marcus held Jessie tightly. His *link* beeped. Without releasing her, he tapped it.

"Captain," Klegznef reported. "Cenamola overpowered Dr. Rindor and escaped. Security is searching for him now."

Marcus shook his head, ruefully. "Inform Chief Hrvibm that she can stop the search. Cenamola was here."

"*Was*, sir?"

"Dr. Cenamola is dead."

"I will inform Chief Hrvibm immediately."

"Very good, Mr. Klegznef. Send Dr. Rindor down here as soon as possible. Viator out."

Jessie buried her face in the crook of Marcus's neck. "I was so scared."

He tightened his hold on her.

"I can't believe he was really going to kill us," she said. "He came here to erase what was left of his experiment." The horror of Cenamola's plan left her shaking.

Marcus lifted her chin. "Yes. Your sister saved us all."

Jessie glanced at her twin. Scott sat on the couch next to

Veronese. He patted her hand as if he didn't know what else to do.

"Whew." Tim swiped his forehead. "Don't know about you guys, but I've had enough excitement for a while. Here, Max." He patted his knee. "You're a hero, too."

Veronese gave a shaky laugh. "He certainly was." She pulled her hand away from Scott's and stood. With agitated movements, she began picking up the items that had fallen out of the small pouch—the silver medical examining tool, a square box that Jessie had seen the doctor use to heal cuts and abrasions, and a necklace with a red oval stone. "Too bad the dog wasn't here when I was terrorized by the drug dealer."

Jessie felt a surge of guilt. "I should've listened to you, Tim. If I'd gotten a dog sooner, he could've saved—"

"Past history, Jess," Tim said. "Good thing Max was here now. What's that, Neesie?" He pointed to the necklace she was putting into the pouch.

"I have no idea." Veronese took it back out to examine. When a bright light filled the room, she dropped the necklace on the end table.

The transport beam startled Jessie again. Dr. Rindor stood in the middle of the living room. Max circled the new arrival. He sniffed and then came back to lie beside Jessie's rocker, apparently satisfied this visitor was no threat.

Rindor looked around in surprise. "T-Twins?"

Marcus released Jessie and motioned toward Tim. "Examine him and correct his condition."

Dr. Rindor raised her eyebrow. "Captain, we are not allowed to—"

"Doctor." Marcus leveled a hard stare at her. "We have interfered in the lives of these people for the past six months. Let us do some good for a change."

Rindor gulped at his harsh tone. "Yes, sir. The patient will need to lie on his stomach."

While Scott helped Tim onto the hospital bed, Dr. Rindor asked questions about his injury and current treatment. Then, she ran a small silver box over his back.

Jessie held her breath. *Oh, God, could the doctor do it?*

Could she cure Tim?

After what seemed an eternity, Dr. Rindor looked up and smiled. "Captain, I believe Chief Luqett would say 'piece of pie'." She made an adjustment to the examining tool.

"Pie?" Marcus asked.

"Cake," Jessie and Scott said in unison. Then Jessie gave a nervous laugh.

Dr. Rindor held the tool just above Tim's back. Jessie prayed as she'd never prayed before. *Let Tim walk again.*

Finally, the doctor helped Tim roll over. "Your legs will be weak from disuse. Proceed slowly. Continue with your exercises to strengthen the muscles."

"That's it? How long before he walks again?" Jessie asked.

Rindor smiled. "Very soon." She turned to Marcus, her smile gone. "Captain, I-I was remiss in my duties. I believed Dr. Cenamola posed no threat. He was old and feeble. I did not realize..." She let her voice trail off in embarrassment.

"We will discuss this later. You may return to the ship."

"Yes, sir." Dr. Rindor became the proper, emotion-controlled Serenian again. "Chief Luqett said he can give you a little more time. He has informed Space Fleet Command that the hyperdrive is not responding properly."

"Thank you. We will be along shortly."

Jessie clasped Dr. Rindor's hands. "Thank you."

Tim pushed himself into a sitting position, looking stunned, as if he didn't believe what had happened. He shifted his legs to the side of the bed then looked at the doctor in awe. "I moved my legs. I actually moved my legs."

Rindor smiled. "Of course."

"Thanks doesn't seem enough." Tears gathered in Tim's eyes.

Rindor tapped her *link*. "Ensign Duross, I am ready for transport."

She was gone in a flash of light.

Marcus clasped Jessie's hand. "We need to talk."

She gave him a watery smile. Tim wasn't the only one with tears in his eyes. "We could go outside." She pulled him toward the door.

Diane Burton

"Wait," Tim said. "He has to change his clothes. It rained last night. He can't go tromping around out in the muck." He had an odd expression, as if he had a secret.

Jessie shook off her fantasy. Tim must be disconcerted by the turn of events. *My God, after thinking he'd be paralyzed the rest of his life, he'd been given a miracle. She could forgive him for having an odd expression.*

"Change my clothes?" Marcus looked down at his uniform.

"I have some old things in the upstairs bedroom." At Marcus's sharp look, Scott gave him a sheepish grin. "I don't stay here. She's always asking me to move stuff when I'm wearing good clothes. I learned my lesson."

Scott led Marcus upstairs. "Jessie sleeps downstairs, not up here."

Marcus continued to glare at him even after they entered a small sleeping room. He knew Scott understood exactly what he was thinking.

Scott closed the door. "Okay, let's get to the point. I've never slept with her. She doesn't love me. She loves you, you big idiot."

Marcus raised his eyebrow.

"Believe what you want." Scott opened the dresser and roughly pulled out a pair of old jeans and a flannel shirt. While Marcus changed into the unusual attire, Scott pulled a pair of battered athletic shoes from the closet.

"You took care of her," Marcus said flatly as he buttoned the shirt.

"Yeah."

"Thank you."

"Before we go down, I want to know one thing," Scott said. "Do you love her?"

Marcus had told Jessica he loved her before she transported back to Earth. To make that confession, he'd had to stifle every Serenian stricture against emotion. He had no intention of confiding in this man he had just met—even if he looked exactly like him.

"Listen, buster." Scott grabbed the front of Marcus's shirt. "She's been through a lot. You'd better not hurt her again."

Marcus drew himself up straight. "You will remove your hand."

"Or what? You'll beat me to a pulp?"

Marcus continued to stare. The anger within him was almost too much to control. Scott dropped his hand.

Marcus straightened his shirt. "Your loyalty to Jessica is appreciated. I have returned for her. You need not concern yourself over her welfare. I will take care of her from now on."

"But, do you love her?" Scott persisted.

Marcus hesitated. "Yes."

"What a relief. Thought I'd have to knock some sense into you." Scott grinned. "It's weird knowing I have a brother. Jessie described you, but I never took you for such an uptight son of a bitch." He clapped Marcus on the shoulder.

"You, on the other hand, are exactly what I anticipated," Marcus said with a perfectly straight face. "A smart-ass Earthling." Then he allowed a small smile to escape.

Scott laughed. "Jessie said you called us Terrans."

"Just getting with the program. One moment, please." Marcus turned to face the mirror above the dresser. He removed the silver lenses and blinked several times. He left the lenses and his *link* on top of the dresser.

"What are you guys doing up there?" Jessie called from the bottom of the stairs.

"Shoes," Scott said, handing them to Marcus. Then, he opened the door and hollered down to Jessie, "Planning the invasion of Earth."

Once downstairs, Marcus walked outside with Jessica.

Tim sat on the edge of the bed, wiggling his feet. "God, this feels so good." He glanced through the window to make sure Jessie and Marcus were out of earshot. "Listen, guys, we got a problem here."

Veronese jumped to her feet. "Are you in pain?"

Tim brushed aside her concern. "Not me, Neesie. Those two." He pointed toward the side window.

Scott scrubbed his hand down his face. "You're right. She wants him to stay."

"He can't. The Captain has his responsibilities on board ship," Veronese insisted.

"Marcus has responsibilities here, too." Tim stretched first one leg out in front of him and then the other. This felt good. Damn good. "Listen, guys, I had a good reason for making sure Marcus changed his clothes before going outside. And it wasn't the mud. See, I've had a brainstorm." He looked hard at Scott. "How bad do you want to go into space?"

"What?" Scott and Veronese asked in unison.

Tim explained to Veronese about Scott's training at NASA. "Here's your chance, Scott. Take Marcus's place."

Scott snorted. "Brainstorm? More like a brainfart."

Veronese's mouth dropped. "Him? Take the Captain's place? It will never work."

"I don't know the first thing about—"

"Marcus left his uniform upstairs, didn't he?" Tim persisted "And his camouflage lenses?"

Scott nodded. "And his communicator."

"Good." Tim grinned, pleased with his plan so far. "Remember all those diagrams you drew of the ship when I was in the hospital and you and Jessie were trying to take my mind off my, uh, situation."

"Didn't think you caught on," Scott said.

"I was shot in the belly not dropped on the head," Tim snorted. "Get those diagrams and all the notes you took about the crew. You left them here, didn't you?"

Scott opened the bottom drawer of the roll-top desk sitting against the far wall. He pulled out the diagrams and the notes he'd made when Jessie described her adventures in space. Okay, Tim thought, steps one and two of the plan were in place. Now to step three.

He looked at Veronese. "Scott has the scientific knowledge. He's a quick learner. But, he'll need help. Inside help."

Scott rubbed the bridge of his nose. "I didn't say I'd do this."

Veronese cocked her head to look at him. "He does have many of the Captain's mannerisms. Their voices are nearly the same. He has what I believe is called a Southern Accent."

"He could work on that," Tim said.

"Would you two quit talking about me like I'm not here?"

"He would need to stay in seclusion for two or three days until the depilatory pills took effect. He is—" she grimaced "—quite hairy."

"What do you mean?" Scott and Tim asked together.

"Other than eyebrows and on the head, Serenians have no body hair."

Tim started to chortle. "Jessie never mentioned that."

"*No* body hair?" Scott exclaimed. "That would be weird."

"Do you think looking like a hairy beast is not weird?" Veronese countered. "You will have to take my advice. If you wish to do this, I could help. But, you would have to do what I say."

"Now, wait a minute. I didn't say—" Scott hesitated for a moment. Then he started to grin.

"Ya-hoo," Tim shouted. "I knew you couldn't resist. And I knew you'd help him, Neesie."

"Perhaps he should give this more thought," she said. "I am not certain he fully understands—"

Scott cut her off. "I understand. I'm going. I can't pass this up."

***

Marcus listened with half an ear as Jessica showed him her farm—her workshop, the outbuildings, the fields. He had to go back to the ship. He had to return to Serenia before his detour was detected. The repercussions from his disobedience to a direct order would land on his senior officers. Luqett and Glaxpher, for example, would insist they had supported him. How could he allow them to suffer the consequences of his actions?

Jessica's brother was cured. Now, she had no reason to stay. Yet—

She carried their child. He had never thought of offspring. Despite the Elders' repeated messages about potential candidates for commitment, Marcus had delayed. Deep inside, he must have known he could never ask a Serenian to have mixed-race offspring. He never wanted anyone to look at his child the way his father had looked at him. With disgust.

"Marcus, look at all this." She waved, indicating the green fields of new growth. "This is what you've always wanted. This farm is over a hundred acres. The land across the road will be for sale soon. We could buy it. Don't go back to the ship. Stay here."

"Jessica, I *want* to go back." With everything happening so quickly, he hadn't had time to tell her his good news. "I could not say so in front of Veronese, but the Elders have agreed to my request to leave Space Fleet. I am allowed to take over Cam's farm." He couldn't help grinning.

She gave him a half-smile as she headed toward the animal pens. "That is wonderful, Marcus. I am happy for you. It's what you've always wanted." Her tone did not match her words.

He was confused. "I thought you would express your happiness differently."

"What? You think I should be jumping up and down?" She gave him a big smile. An artificial smile. "I'm happy, Marcus, really happy."

"You are mocking me." Why was she holding back? Perhaps he needed to try a different approach. "Jessica, do you remember when you were aboard the *Freedom*? You begged to stay. You were a valuable asset to the crew. On Serenia, your work will be valued."

Placing her foot on the lower rail of the pen, she folded her arms on the top rail and rested her chin on her arms. A large animal—a horse, he thought it was called—trotted over and snuffled her arms. She rubbed the animal's muzzle for a moment. "I've learned something about myself in the past six months. I don't need anyone else to validate my worth. You and Chief Luqett helped me see that. And I am grateful."

She turned toward him, placed her hands on his shoulders, and stared into his eyes. Her blue eyes, usually so bright and clear, clouded with dismay. "Marcus, it's not just me now." She patted her belly. "I-I don't want my children raised on your planet."

He tightened his hold on her. An overwhelming

possessiveness swept through him. "That is my child, too."

Her chin quivered. "Yes. But my responsibility is to protect—"

"I cannot leave you on such a primitive planet."

She spun away from him, taking several steps before facing him. "Primitive? At least here we are able to choose our own way of life. Unlike you, who yearned so long for something you could not have until the authorities gave you *permission*," she said with contempt. "My God, you people name your ship *Freedom*, yet you don't even have the freedom to choose how you want to live."

The irony had not escaped him. He exhaled slowly. "I must return to the ship. I disobeyed a direct order to come here. If I do not return, my executive officers will suffer for my disobedience. How can I let them be punished for my actions?"

She lifted her chin—such a stubborn chin. "I cannot go with you, Marcus."

"I cannot stay. I have a responsibility to my crew."

"Yet, you will leave us behind? Even if you do not care enough about me to stay, what about this?" She pointed to her belly.

Not care enough about her? He loved her with all his being. He turned away, staring out across the land. Had he not always put duty before his own desires? Had he not always done the *right* thing, no matter what the cost? He had always served the Elders faithfully. What more could they ask of him? What more could he sacrifice?

He would rather tear out his heart than leave her. To abandon his offspring—a child he would never see—was unthinkable. He could insist Jessica come with him. He could have her transported to the ship. But, at what cost? She would never forgive him. If he brought Jessica to Serenia, their child would be an alien in an alien land. An outsider. Always feeling as if he never belonged. Was that what he wanted for his offspring?

The silence between them lengthened. Jessie stared at Marcus, her heart torn apart by his unwavering expression.

He wouldn't even look at her. He just stared ahead. He wasn't going to stay with her. He didn't want her. He didn't need her farm. He had Cam's now. She was such a fool for thinking that would entice him to stay. Obviously, his love for her—if he did love her as he said six months ago—wasn't stronger than his *duty*.

She lifted her chin. "I guess there is nothing more to say. You have your responsibilities and I have mine."

Marcus continued to stare across the field. *To hell with him,* Jessie thought. He'd made up his mind to go back to his world. Back where his officers and his ship meant more to him than she did.

As she stalked back to the house, she muttered, "Once, just once, I'd like to come first in somebody's life."

She stopped on the back porch to remove her mud-caked boots. She didn't wait for Marcus but went inside.

"Sit down, sweet sister of mine." Tim grinned as she walked into the living room. He was standing but holding onto the back of the couch. "While you and Lover Boy were making out behind the barn—"

"We were not making out," she retorted. As happy as she was to see Tim standing on his own, she didn't want to talk to him. She just wanted to go to bed and pull the covers over her head.

"Whatever. The three of us—" Tim nodded to Veronese and Scott. "—made some decisions." He looked up as Marcus padded into the room. Like her, he'd removed his muddy shoes. "Your commanding officer has been trying to contact you, Marcus. Communications is having 'technical difficulties,' but she can't hold the General off forever." He grinned again before carefully walking around to sit on the couch. "Like I said, Scott, Veronese, and I decided that *Captain Viator* needs to go back to his ship."

Jessie gasped in hurt and outrage at their betrayal. "How could you?" Tears clogged her throat.

Marcus looked at Tim in surprise. "You're right. I do need to go back. I will tender my resignation, and then I will return to you, Jessica." He clasped her hand and stared deeply into her eyes. "That is my solemn promise. I will come back. First, I must be assured my crew is not punished for my disobedience. If the Alliance will not allow a ship to bring me back, I will hire a mercenary. Either way, Jessica, I will return. Nothing will prevent me from being here when our child is born."

Jessie figured she must look as stunned as the others. Their open-mouthed expressions were almost comical. Marcus just looked very pleased with himself. He was coming back for the child. Not her. But, he *was* coming back. She could take comfort in that.

"What about your uncle's farm?" she said. "I thought that's what you've always wanted. You can't give that up."

"Jessica." He dropped a light kiss on her nose. "Given a choice between Cam's farm and you, I choose you, my dear."

Jessie couldn't believe his words. He was choosing her— over his duty, over his heart's desire. Joy washed over her. Then, she realized he was leaving. He'd promised to come back for her before. Could she trust him?

"Now," Marcus continued, "I will change back into my uniform and return to the ship. The sooner I go, the sooner I will be able to come back to you." He headed toward the stairs. Max trotted after him, followed by Scott and Veronese.

Scott put his hand on Marcus's shoulder as they climbed the stairs. "Tim didn't quite finish. We have a proposition..." His voice trailed off as they went into the bedroom and closed the door.

Jessie turned to Tim. "What's going on? Why did Veronese go up with them?"

Tim smiled. "Listen, kid. We've got this all worked—"

A bright light filled the room. Security Chief Hrvibm stood where the light had been. She held a ziff blaster.

"Hrvibm?" Jessie cried. "What's going on?"

"What did Dr. Cenamola say?" Hrvibm demanded.

"What?" Jessie couldn't believe someone else was holding a ziff blaster on her.

The Security Chief pointed the weapon at Tim. "Tell me what Cenamola said about his plans—about me—or I will..." She waved the blaster menacingly.

"Nothing," Jessie said. "He said nothing about you."

"He was going to leave me on the ship. After all I've done, he was going to leave me behind. Where is it?" She searched the room as she spoke. "There." She scooped up the necklace with the red stone and slipped it around her neck. "He was never going to take me with him."

"Chief, what are you talking about? Why would Cenamola..." Jessie's voice trailed off as something dawned on her.

"She was his accomplice," Tim said. Their minds must have gone down the same path and arrived at the same conclusion. For his observation, Hrvibm turned and zapped him. He crumpled across the couch.

"What have you—"

Hrvibm cut off Jessie's cry with, "He is only stunned. He will come around in a few minutes. Where are Viator and Qilana?"

Jessie stared at the bulldog-faced woman. "Tim was right. *You* helped Dr. Cenamola. You are the traitor."

"Where are they?" Hrvibm repeated. "They know too much. I cannot allow them to return to the ship."

This was Cenamola's accomplice. And she meant to harm Marcus and Veronese. "They aren't here." Jessie backed up toward the kitchen. *Please, Marcus, don't come downstairs.*

"You are lying." Waving the blaster wildly, Hrvibm followed her.

"Veronese went back to the ship already." Jessie was making this up as she went along, hoping Hrvibm didn't see through her deception. "Didn't you see her?"

Hrvibm blinked in confusion.

"And Marcus...Marcus went into town. He went to meet his twin."

"His twin?"

Jessie backed into the door. "I know you know. Everybody on the ship knows that Marcus is Terran. That he was a victim of Cenamola's experiment. Like me and Veronese Qilana. You were in the Medical Center when Marcus announced he's Terran."

Hrvibm nodded.

"I found his twin. So, I called him up, and he and Marcus made plans to meet in town. I guess he—"

"Do not talk so much, Wyndom." Hrvibm sounded confused. "Before the Captain made his announcement, I did not know he is Terran. Cenamola did not confide that piece of information."

If Jessie opened the door and ran out into the backyard, would Hrvibm follow? Or would she think that Jessie was deliberately trying to get her out of the house? Like she was.

"So, Cenamola got you to do the dirty work and left you out in the cold."

The Security Chief motioned with her weapon toward the back door. "We will join the happy reunion."

Okay, this is what she wanted. Jessie prayed Marcus wouldn't come downstairs. If she got Hrvibm away from the house, Marcus could come up with a plan. After grabbing her keys off the hook near the door, she stopped for her boots on the back porch. She didn't bother to lace them up. She just stuffed her feet in them and then clumped her way to her truck. She hoped Hrvibm wouldn't question the muddy shoes Marcus had left on the porch or the other vehicle, Scott's, in front of the house. Maybe she'd think it was Tim's.

If what Hrvibm said was right about only stunning Tim—oh, God, she hoped he'd be all right—by the time Marcus and Scott came down, Tim would wake up and could tell them what happened.

"W-Would you put that weapon away? It makes me nervous." She fumbled with the key in the ignition.

"Good. It will prevent you from doing something foolish."

"Y-You must buckle up." Jessie pulled her own seatbelt across her protruding belly. At Hrvibm's questioning look, Jessie pointed. "'Click it or ticket.' It's the law."

Hrvibm stared in incomprehension. "Enough with these odd expressions. Start this vehicle."

Jessie didn't know why she even bothered trying to get Hrvibm to buckle her seatbelt. She deliberately ground the starter. Marcus and Scott were in the upstairs back bedroom and, even though they couldn't hear what happened in the living room, they'd hear the noise of the truck. If she delayed just long enough, they would see where she went. "P-Please put the gun away. I promise not to fight you."

"Of course, you will not fight. You are no match for my superior strength and intellect. Start this vehicle. I must find Viator before he returns to the ship."

Jessie started the engine.

***

In amazement, Marcus pondered Scott and Veronese's plan. Scott wanted to switch places with him.

"I'm going downstairs to tell Tim you're considering it," Veronese said with delight.

"I have not agreed," Marcus said to empty air. She'd already left. He turned to Scott. "You do realize there may be consequences of my disobedience to a direct order, do you not?" He gave Scott a hard stare. "You should not have to pay for my actions."

"Always the hero, right? You can't let someone else—"

"Captain, Scott, come quickly!"

At Veronese's frantic call, they rushed downstairs to the living room. Tim was sitting on the floor, rubbing his head. "I feel like I was hit by a truck."

"Did you fall?" Scott knelt beside Tim.

"What happened?" Marcus looked around. "Where's Jessica?"

"Some creepy woman beamed into the living room and zapped me. She wore a uniform like yours, Marcus, only dark green. Jessie seemed to know her. Called her Herbie-something."

"Hrvibm," Marcus and Veronese exclaimed.

"But, why—" Veronese began.

Marcus cut off her with "I always wondered if Cenamola had an accomplice."

"Hrvibm?" Veronese asked in disbelief.

"Who better than the Security Chief?"

He raced out to the porch just as Jessica's truck slowly negotiated the turn from the drive to the road. Through the back window, he could see a squat figure in the passenger's seat.

"Come on," Scott yelled as he bounded down the steps to his car. "Let's go get them."

Marcus stopped him at the driver's door. "This is my responsibility. Give me the keys. You need to go now."

Scott handed over the keys without protest. Momentarily, he looked confused. "Go now?" Then understanding dawned. "Yeah, now." His face split into a wide grin. "Yes." He punched the air.

"You will help him?" Marcus asked Veronese.

"Of course, Captain."

"You must call *him* 'Captain' now." Marcus nodded to Scott. "This could be dangerous."

"Don't go having second thoughts. This'll be a kick." Scott grinned.

Marcus gave Scott his password to the ship's computer and the code for his apartment. "You will not have time to wait for the depilatory pills to work. The crew knows I am Terran. You can tell them you have decided not to hide your true identity." He slid into the driver's seat. "And another thing—"

"Go," Scott ordered. "Don't let Jess get too far ahead of you."

Observing Earth—its inhabitants and customs—prior to the war, Marcus knew enough to be able to pilot the primitive vehicle. Still, Scott gave him a few basic instructions then Marcus floored the accelerator. He had to rescue Jessica.

Veronese stood on the porch with Scott, watching Marcus race down the drive. A feeling of dread swept through her. She had had that feeling before, when the drug dealer was stalking her. 'A kick', he had called it? Switching places with the Captain was a kick? Scott thought this was going to be a game? He had better take this seriously.

"We have to hurry," she said. "We must return to the ship."

Scott continued to stand on the porch. He looked like he was in a state of shock. She called again. What was the matter with him? When he still did not answer, she tugged on his sleeve then promptly dropped her hand. Serenians kept a proper distance and rarely, if ever, touched each other. She would have to remind him of that.

But, not now.

"Scott," she spoke firmly. "If you are switching places with Marcus, we must go now." This was not a good idea. Definitely not a good idea.

He shook his head once, as if to clear it. "Yes." He followed her into the house. Then he stood in the middle of the living room and stared.

This was not going to work, she thought. She knew he would not be able to convince anyone he was Captain Marcus Viator. She should never have gone along with Tim's hare-brained idea. And she should never have agreed to help. She was in enough trouble as it was with her own hare-brained idea of switching places with *her* twin.

The Captain was gone. They had to return to the ship and return to Serenia before this detour was detected. There was no one else to take charge. It was up to her.

"Change into the Captain's uniform," she ordered.

Scott blinked.

Would the man snap out of it? "Scott, now," she said firmly.

He drew himself up and squared his shoulders. "I am Captain Marcus Viator of the starship *Freedom*. You will address me as Captain, Lieutenant Qilana."

TWENTY-THREE

"Why are you not going faster?"

Jessie glanced in the rearview mirror. No car had come out of her driveway. Was anyone coming to her rescue? "Can't you see how rutted the road is? It rained last night and washed away the loose dirt. If I go any faster, I'll wreck the suspension of my truck."

"Primitive vehicles," Hrvibm derided.

Then Jessie saw Scott's car race onto the road. Only one person was in the car. The driver, Scott. It was too much to hope for Marcus to follow her. He had to get back to his ship, she thought in disgust. She knew where his priorities lay. Not with her.

She'd thought Marcus was different. She'd thought she could count on him. He was more like her father than she'd thought. What was wrong with her that the men in her life, the men who mattered to her, didn't find her worthy of their time or attention?

Her children would never know that feeling, she vowed.

Okay, Tim and Scott found her worthy, and they would be good father figures. But, why didn't Marcus understand how much she needed him? Why didn't he put her first?

When she got to the stop sign at the main road, she thanked God there was traffic. Maybe Scott could catch up with them. At least someone was coming to her rescue.

"What are you waiting for? Go." Hrvibm pointed the weapon at her.

"Shoot me, and you'll never find Marcus."

"I would go back to your farm and wait for him."

Jessie floored it, cutting a little close in front of an oncoming car. The driver blew his horn and gave her the one-finger salute. She returned it.

"What was that?" Hrvibm demanded. "A secret sign?"

Obviously, Hrvibm was not a researcher. "It's a universal good-luck gesture."

A car passed them.

"Why did you not salute that car?"

"I, uh, I didn't know her."

"You knew the first driver because he made a noise?"

The horn blast. "Right. Say, Chief, you catch on real quick. I've got to hand it to you. You really are smart."

Hrvibm preened. Just like Cenamola. "Of course."

Jessie worked hard to keep sarcasm out of her voice. "Yeah, that intellect of yours is really superior."

Now, Hrvibm was fairly beaming with pleasure. *Okay, feed her ego.* "You and Cenamola really confused those people on the *Freedom*. They never did figure out how he managed his tricks."

"Dr. Cenamola came aboard the ship many times in disguise. No one ever notices an Engineering technician working in a conduit. He had rudimentary mechanical knowledge. Enough to cause a few problems."

From Hrvibm's disparaging remark, Jessie had a flash of insight. "But, you were the brains of this operation."

The Security Chief beamed. "*I* reprogrammed the ship's computer. Cenamola thought he was so smart. His Great Master Plan to overthrow the Alliance. Bah. Serenians are such an egotistical race. They use others to accomplish their ends and then discard them."

"*You* locked the Captain and me in his quarters and disabled the analyzer, didn't you?"

"You were very clever to discover the problem with the analyzer and to find a way out of the Captain's quarters," Hrvibm groused.

Maybe bringing that up wasn't a good idea. Jessie glanced in her mirror. Scott got caught at the stop sign. Three cars separated them, but he was still following.

"I'll bet *you* fixed the computer to throw suspicion on

Klegznef."

Hrvibm's bulldog face split into a grin. "Do not forget Melora. It was easy to cast suspicions on her."

"Only it didn't work because you didn't know Marcus wasn't related to her."

Hrvibm shot her a nasty look. "Cenamola did not see fit to give me all the information he possessed."

"Now it makes sense why you never came up with a proper suspect. Talk about the fox guarding the henhouse."

Hrvibm turned. Jessie glanced over to see confusion written on her face. "The traitor looking for a traitor," she explained. "Cenamola made you do all the dirty work. He used you, and then he skipped out on you and left you holding the bag. What a chump."

Hrvibm waved the weapon. "You will die for your insolence, just like Viator."

Jessie closed her mouth. She'd pushed too far. Scott was still behind her, but traffic was too heavy for her to stop. "I don't get it. You knew Cenamola was dead. You were in the clear. He never said a word about an accomplice. So, why come down here? Why come after Marcus?"

"The *good* doctor," she sneered, "took the communication device." She clasped the oval red stone pendant hanging around her neck. "I could not contact the others without this."

"Others? You mean the rebels? I thought the Praetorium surrendered."

Hrvibm laughed harshly. "Not all. Cenamola left orders for the rebels to gather in this sector."

"How? I thought he was a prisoner on the *Freedom*?" Jessie thought for a minute. "Wait a minute. He relayed messages through you, didn't he?"

"Yes. Now, they will need a leader. Finally, I will have the command the Alliance denied me because of my race."

"This is about discrimination? I thought the Alliance accepted all races. Look at Glaxpher and Klegznef. The Alliance—"

"Tegrors and Zorfans are the puppets of the Alliance." She looked around as they drove through the city streets.

"Where did you say Viator was meeting his twin? I must find him."

So much for trying to talk her way out of this situation. "Why go after Marcus?"

"He has something I need."

"What?"

"Quit asking so many questions." Hrvibm rubbed her forehead. "I cannot think with so many questions. I cannot think. Have to find Viator. Have to get the code."

"What code?"

"I must get the code," Hrvibm rambled. "I must get the code and then destroy him. No one must know." She almost sounded as if she'd lost her marbles.

Jessie had no idea what she was talking about, but Hrvibm was bent on destroying Marcus. Well, she could just think again.

Jessie turned toward the University of Michigan, still keeping Scott in sight behind her. She couldn't lose him in the late afternoon traffic.

They stopped at a light. Hrvibm turned in her seat to look out the back window. "There is a green vehicle behind us? I have seen it before." She sounded perfectly lucid now.

Jessie's palms began to sweat. "Really? It's a popular car. There must be a lot of them around here. I think it was named Most Popular Car of the Year or something."

"No, Wyndom. I saw that vehicle near your domicile."

Jessie made a show out of looking in the rearview mirror as she pulled away from the light. "You know, it does look a lot like my brother's car. Of course, that couldn't be my brother, since you shot him. That was a nasty thing for you to do. He hasn't walked for six months thanks to getting shot by another bad guy. You didn't have to—"

"Quiet. I cannot think with your chattering." Hrvibm waved the blaster in Jessie's face. "I want to get out of this vehicle."

"Wait," she cried. Scott was two cars behind them. "We're almost there. They were going to meet at the bell tower. There." She pointed to a stone structure ahead.

"I knew you could be cooperative." Once again, Hrvibm sounded coherent. "You just needed motivation."

"Oh, I'm motivated, all right." Again, she tried to keep the sarcasm out of her voice. No need to give away too much. All she needed was a few more minutes to give Scott a chance to catch up, and then she would find some place to park.

"The code. I have to get the code," Hrvibm mumbled. "Stop this vehicle. The cars, the people. Too much congestion."

Jessie noticed nothing different about the area. There were always a lot of cars, and the street was narrow. University students often crossed the street in groups without looking for oncoming traffic. Nothing out of the ordinary but, apparently, too much for Hrvibm.

"We will get out here." She pointed to a no parking zone in front of the tower.

"I can't park here. The cops will come." *Hurry up, Scott.* "They would see your weapon and—"

"Stop now." Hrvibm's menacing tone convinced her.

As soon as Jessie pulled the key out of the ignition, the Security Chief grabbed her arm. With hard fingers digging into Jessie's upper arm, Hrvibm dragged her across the seat and out of the passenger door. She must have paid some attention to Jessie's comment about the police because Hrvibm kept the blaster close to her side, hiding it between them. She hurried Jessie across the wide expanse of grass in front of the old bell tower. Nobody even glanced at them, as if it wasn't out of the ordinary to see a person in a dark green jumpsuit who looked like the Tasmanian Devil.

Hrvibm tried to open the building's door. The bell tower was locked, as Jessie knew it would be. She glanced over her shoulder. Scott had stopped his car in front of hers and jumped out. Someone honked at his opening the door without looking. He ignored it as he rounded the front of his car.

At the noise, Hrvibm stopped yanking on the door and looked back. "Viator."

"No, it's his brother. Scott, go back," Jessie yelled.

The man in ripped jeans and red flannel shirt kept coming. Red flannel shirt? Jessie looked back again. That's what

Marcus had been wearing when they walked out to the fields. Scott had changed into his old clothes?

"His brother?" Hrvibm sounded confused.

Oh, God. That wasn't Scott. It was Marcus. He *had* come for her. Her heart gave a spurt of joy before she realized Hrvibm would kill him after she got some code. Hell, that loony woman was going to kill them both.

The Security Chief aimed her ziff blaster at the lock. A flash of light later, she jerked the door open. Still gripping Jessie's arm, she dragged her into the building.

Jessie had never been in the tower. For safety reasons, it was always kept locked. Despite the dimness inside, they could see that a barricade blocked the stairs. Hrvibm urged Jessie over the gate. Despite the bulk of her pregnancy, Jessie managed. She was surprised that Hrvibm, with her short, squat stature, was able to easily leap over. From her agility and the grip she had on Jessie's arm, Hrvibm could easily overpower her. Jessie would have to come up with a better idea.

The stairs were shrouded in darkness. What little lighting there was was provided by two narrow window slits high above. Dust motes floated in the dim light as Hrvibm pulled Jessie up the wooden stairs.

Built against the rough interior walls, the stairs rose in roughly a spiral fashion with a hole in the middle through which hung the rope from the bells. Not trusting the rickety handrail on the outside, Jessie held onto the stone wall for support. There were no risers between the steps. You could look through and see the floor below. Oh, God, with his fear of heights, Marcus would never be able to climb these stairs.

Hrvibm had told her too much. She wasn't going to let Jessie live. She was the bait to draw Marcus there. He may have come this far for Jessie, but he wouldn't be able to go any farther. One look at those stairs and Marcus would stop.

It was up to her to rescue herself.

***

Marcus's heart thudded in his chest. His Security Chief had dragged Jessica into a narrow building roughly twenty meters high. As he raced across the grassy space, he looked up. It appeared to be a campanile. Through the open archways at the top of the tower, Marcus could see large bells clustered in the middle.

Hrvibm had taken Jessica into that building. He had to follow.

All during the drive into the city, he'd prayed to the Intrepid Ones not to let him lose sight of her vehicle. He had quickly mastered the operation of Scott's car, unused as he was to actually driving on land. When cars wedged between them, he thought surely she would disappear and he would never find her again. He would have given anything for his speeder to rise above the land-bound vehicles.

Marcus threw open the door through which Hrvibm and Jessica had disappeared.

"Scott, go back." Jessica's voice came from up the blocked stairway. "She doesn't want you. She wants Marcus. Something about a secret code."

So, Hrvibm wanted the code. Cenamola had alluded to the strategic defense system locked into the *Freedom's* computer. The *Freedom* had once been General Porcazier's ship. The code had been embedded deep within the computer's memory banks as a backup system in the event of the invasion of Serenia. With the defense code in the rebels' hands, the Alliance would be powerless. Obtaining the ship had been Cenamola's goal—and now Hrvibm's—in order to capture the Intergalactic Alliance's headquarters.

Even the Security Chief had no way to access the code, though she must have tried. For a brief moment, Marcus wondered why Cenamola and Hrvibm hadn't held him hostage on board ship to get the code. Why wait until now?

They must have known there was nothing they could do to Marcus—or threaten him with—that would make him give up the code. But, Hrvibm had quickly identified Jessica as his weakness. He would do anything to keep her alive. Yet, as soon as he gave Hrvibm the code, she would have no reason to keep Jessica alive. Or him, for that matter. By surrendering the code, he would sign their death warrant.

"Go back, Scott," Jessica called down from about halfway

up.

Marcus hesitated at the bottom of the stairs. He had climbed vertical ladders in Engineering to reach Jessica. Together, they had climbed down conduits and the conveyance shaft to reach freedom after being locked in his quarters. But, none of them held the terror of this type of stairway. The stretch of wooden steps with open spaces between them, loomed in front of him. In order to reach Jessica, he had to climb the stairs.

"That is Viator. Why do you call him Scott?" Hrvibm demanded.

"You have the wrong brother. I'm telling you that isn't Marcus. It's his twin, Scott."

"His twin?" Hrvibm sounded confused.

Marcus leaped over the railing and bounded up the stairs. They thought he was Scott. That should keep Hrvibm off balance until he could reach them. The Security Chief had hurt too many people helping Cenamola. She was not going to get the chance to hurt Jessica.

Yet, if Jessica thought he was Scott, that meant she thought he—Marcus—had abandoned her once again. She had no faith in him that he would come to her rescue. A sharp pain sliced through his chest as he raced up flight after flight of stairs that curved around the walls of the narrow building. The pain had nothing to do with his fear of heights but, rather, his fear that he had lost his soul mate.

He kept as close to the wall as possible. He dared not look past the railing, dared not look where he put his feet, or else he would see his worse nightmare. A heavy door slammed above.

He looked up. A rope cascaded down through a hole in the ceiling approximately two meters in diameter. The rope was attached to the bells hanging in the center of the tower. Jessica was out there, on the platform that circled the inside of the tower. The bell chamber.

With nerves strung tight, Marcus reached the top of the stairs. Cautiously, he opened the door. Hrvibm had taken Jessica around to the opposite side. They stood on the circular platform mid-way between the open arches and the hole in the center. Either way—to the ground outside or the stone floor below—a drop of twenty meters would probably kill him and Jessica. If Hrvibm didn't vaporize them first.

His heart jerked as dread shot through him. He could not stand here in the doorway paralyzed. He stepped onto the platform and let the door close behind him with a thud.

"Hrvibm, it is me you want. Let her go."

"Ha! It is you, Viator."

"No, it isn't," Jessie cried. "It's his twin. Marcus is afraid of heights. He would never be able to climb those stairs."

Hrvibm looked momentarily confused. "The Captain is afraid of heights?"

Thanks, Jessica. Give the enemy more ammunition.

"Let Jessica go, and I will give you the code." Keeping his back against the stone wall, Marcus side-stepped to the first arch, closer to where Hrvibm and Jessica stood.

"I cannot let her live, Viator. She knows too much about Cenamola. And me."

He would have to walk past the open arch to get closer to them. "Who could she tell? I will not give you the code if you harm her," Marcus vowed. "Let her go."

"If I let her go, you will not give me the code." Hrvibm edged Jessica closer to the bells, closer to the opening in the center of the platform.

Willing his legs to hold him up, Marcus walked past an open archway. His knees were trembling by the time he felt the stone wall behind his back again. "We are at an impasse, Hrvibm." He stopped across from them. Two meters separated him from the woman he loved.

"Give me the code, or watch your woman go over the edge." Inexorably, Hrvibm pulled Jessica toward the edge of the opening.

"No!" Marcus cried out.

Jessica dragged her feet, trying to slow Hrvibm down, all the while struggling to get free. Her boots were not fastened properly. The laces trailed on the platform. One false move, and she would trip.

"Come here and stop me," Hrvibm taunted. "You are afraid of heights, Viator. You will not come any closer."

Marcus felt his gut twisting with each step she took closer to the edge. "Chief, you have had a long and successful career. Why throw it away?" His palms slicked with sweat. Jessica was just beyond his reach. If he came closer, Hrvibm would fulfill her threat. If he didn't reach Jessica in time, she would die. "I can forget this incident. No one will ever know what happened here. We can work this out, Chief."

"No. It is too late." Anger turned Hrvibm's face red. "You will never forget I helped Cenamola. You will never forgive me for destroying your woman."

At a trilling sound, the Chief became confused. The sound came from the pendant she wore around her neck. It must be a communicator. Hrvibm had a problem. She could not hold her weapon and Jessica and activate the device at the same time. She released Jessica's arm and pointed the weapon at Marcus. "Stay." Hrvibm told Jessica as she tried to edge away. "Or I will kill your lover."

Jessica stopped, but Marcus was afraid she was about to do something that could endanger them both.

Hrvibm touched the pendant.

"Are you ready for transport?" The voice came from the pendant.

"One moment. On my signal," Hrvibm said, her eyes gleaming madly. "Viator, this is what comes from denying me what I wanted. You wouldn't give me the code, now watch your woman die. And your child."

"Not on your life, lady." Jessica lashed out with her foot.

Her muddy workboot caught Hrvibm's knee. Surprised at the attack, the Security Chief seized Jessica's leg. They both tottered on the edge of the platform.

"No-o-o," Marcus cried, leaping the last steps. He caught Jessica's wrist. For several heart-stopping moments, Jessica was stretched between the two. He circled her waist with his other arm, trying to prevent her from following Hrvibm over the edge.

Hrvibm's hands slipped down Jessica's leg then latched

onto the workboot while she dangled in space. Then, the boot which Jessica had not laced up, had not tied, slipped off. Both it and the Security Chief plummeted.

Nausea swirled up his throat as he saw Hrvibm fall. He clutched Jessica as fright roared up inside him. He shut his eyes at the thought of Jessica's body hurtling downward.

"She's gone. Marcus? Marcus, don't look down. Look at me," Jessica demanded. "Hrvibm disappeared. There was a transport light, and she just disappeared. Let's go. We gotta get out of here."

He could not move. They were too close to the edge. The opening was drawing him. He had to step back, but his feet would not move. He looked straight ahead, past the bells. The arches began to swirl, whirling past him. His balance. He couldn't maintain his balance. Had he gotten Jessica away from Hrvibm only to cause their deaths by his irrational fear?

"Marcus, we have to go before somebody comes." She was clinging to him, expecting him to lead her. "Marcus!"

Her frantic voice shook him out of his trance-like state. He had to get them down from this tower. He looked across the platform and focused on the door, not on the opening in the center of the floor mere centimeters away from their feet. Not on the open arches which, thank the Intrepid Ones, had stopped whirling. He put one foot in front of the other. The door. They had to reach the door.

"You came for me." She was breathing heavily—from fear or exhaustion, he did not know. "You didn't go back to your ship."

He could not concentrate on the awe in her voice. Nor on her limping. He had to focus on getting them both to safety. He opened the door. The stairs loomed before him.

The nausea returned. The circular stairs began to recede, as though he were looking through the wrong end of a telescope. He blinked. They began to move in and out, swirling in a spiral motion until he had to release Jessica and grip the doorframe with both hands.

She got as far as the top step and sat down. "I can't do it. I can't go down those stairs."

His worry for her superceded his fear. He hastened down three steps and knelt to face her. "What is wrong? Were you injured when Hrvibm went—" his voice cracked. "—when she went over."

Jessica buried her head in her hands. "No. I'm not hurt. It's just— Marcus, my knees are shaking. I don't think I can stand up."

He clasped her hands. "You must. We cannot stay here. As you said, the authorities will come to investigate."

He put his hand under her elbow. She tried to stand. "I can't." Tears formed in her eyes as she huddled against the wall. "I can't go down those stairs. My legs feel like cooked spaghetti noodles. Is this how it is for you, Marcus? I just know I'm going to fall through, between those steps."

Yes, that is how it is for me. That mind-numbing, gut-clenching fear that he would fall. His brave Jessica was terrified. Jessica, who wise-cracked her way through being 'kidnapped by aliens', who refused to be intimidated by Klegznef, whose initiative had rescued them from captivity. His courageous Jessica had been reduced to the terrified woman cowering at the top of the stairs.

In the past, he'd had to reach deep inside himself for the courage to face the terror. Each time, he had found a way to escape without conquering the fear. Inner peace in high places eluded him. Never had he faced such a challenge as this. Getting himself down would be no mean feat. But being responsible for Jessica and their child? What if he couldn't do it? What if he failed them?

"Marcus?" She brought her small hand up to cradle his jaw. "I love you. I need you to get me down the steps."

He could not do this for himself. But, the woman he loved, the woman who carried his child, needed him. Her love would hold the terror at bay.

"I will carry you down. Put your arms around my neck."

"You can't carry me, Marcus. I'm too heavy."

He looped her arms around his neck. "Impugning my strength?" He lifted her into his arms. "Casting aspersions on my manhood?"

"How can you joke at a time like this?" She buried her head into the crook of his neck.

"Is that not how you deal with difficult situations?" As he turned around, his back grazed the railing which separated him from the opening down the middle of the tower.

"Don't lean on the railing, Marcus! It's not safe."

Her voice shook. Almost as much as his knees. If the railing broke, they would both plummet several stories to the concrete floor below. Fear swamped him again, making him dizzy. He stopped, shutting his eyes.

"Why aren't we going down?" Jessica's voice was strained. "Please don't close your eyes, Marcus. Please don't stop."

He called on the Intrepid Ones. He called on her God for help. He cursed his weakness.

"I need you, my love," she said softly. "Your babies need you. You must get us down the stairs. I can't do it by myself."

Jessica needed him. His child needed him. He opened his eyes and looked straight into her blue ones, shimmering with fear. Then, they changed to hope.

"That's better. You can do this." She smiled up at him, making him feel as if he could do anything—even walk down stairs. "I love you, Marcus. Our babies love you."

Her eyes filled with love. She held his gaze while slowly he started down the stairs. He slid one tentative foot forward until he felt the edge, then he stepped down. To keep as far away from the flimsy railing as possible, he hugged the wall with his shoulder. One step at a time. One step at a time.

His arms quivered from his burden. His precious burden. She depended on him. She needed him. His self-sufficient woman needed him. His heart swelled at that thought. How had he ever thought he could leave her, even for a short while?

After two flights, he stopped. He tried to catch his breath, swallowing his fear, keeping Jessica and the child's needs planted firmly in front of his eyes.

"You can do this, Marcus. You *have* to do this. You have to get me down before I wet my pants." She laughed nervously.

He shook his head to clear it. "Jessica, only you could reduce my—my weakness to a joke."

She clutched the back of his neck. "I'm not joking."

Another flight. And another. He dared not look to see how much farther.

"Only one more flight, Marcus. I knew you could do this." Her voice still sounded shaky, but she infused her words with hope. She waved her bootless foot. "Just like old times, huh, Marcus? The first time I met you, I was wearing only one shoe. Can you just see Hrvibm arriving on that rebel ship with a muddy boot in her hand?" She started to laugh. "Oh, God. Marcus, I really am going to wet my pants."

Finally, they reached the bottom. He set her down before climbing over the barricade. Then, he lifted her over. They clung to each other. Trembling, Marcus's knees gave out. He slid to the floor with Jessica still in his arms. He cradled her on his lap and buried his head in her neck.

"Thank you, Marcus. Oh, God, thank you." She wept. "I was so scared when Hrvibm took me up there. I didn't think you would come. And, then when I realized it was you and not Scott, I thought you'd take one look at those stairs and say forget it. But you came after me. You saved me. You saved all of us."

"How could I not? You are my soulmate, my love." Tears stung behind his eyes. Tears clogged his throat.

Tears? He never cried. Not since he was a child and suffered punishment from his Serenian father for not controlling his emotions. Now, he cried in gratitude for the life of the woman he loved. And their baby.

Hold it. Twice, she'd said *babies.*

He lifted his head. "Babies? More than one?"

She smiled through her tears. "Surprise!"

TWENTY-FOUR

"Damn, this is better than watching soaps." Tim slapped his knee after Marcus and Jessica returned to the farmhouse and explained what happened. "Kidnapped by aliens again, Jess?"

Marcus glared at the younger man sprawled on the couch. Tim looked chastened. "Glad you're okay, Jessie."

Marcus guided her to the rocker. He still worried even though she claimed she was all right after the trauma of the past few hours.

"So that weird woman just disappeared?" Tim asked incredulously.

"You remember that necklace that fell out of Cenamola's pouch when we thought he was Dr. Rindor?" Jessica said. "Apparently, it was a communication device. Cenamola said something about waiting here for transport—after he did away with us, of course."

Marcus nodded. "She must have been transported to that ship as she went over the edge." He still couldn't think about what might have happened to Jessica without fear racing through his body.

"The old bell tower's been closed up for years. You guys are lucky Campus Security was too busy to catch you in there."

"Surprised the heck out of me, too," Jessica said.

"I heard on the news that one of the biology labs had a fire." At Jessica's gasp, Tim added, "Not Dad's. I checked. The news also said someone broke into the bell tower but Campus Security was too busy with the fire to check it out until later."

"Well, that's a relief. Guess we won't get arrested for

trespassing." Jessica grinned at Marcus. "I still can't believe you came after me."

"I'll always be here for you, Jessie."

"Sure. After you return from Serenia." She leaned her head back against the top of the rocker. "When are you leaving?"

"I'm not." He knelt on one knee beside her and clasped her icy fingers. Her blue eyes searched his in disbelief, as if it was too much to hope for.

"What?"

"This just keeps getting better," Tim said with glee.

"Quit it," Jessie chided. "You sound like that little troll, Drakus."

"Huh?"

"Never mind. Wait a minute. You called me Jessie." She looked at Marcus who smiled. "Turning over a new leaf?"

"Do you not—I mean, don't you—have a saying about 'when in Rome, do as the Romans do'? If I'm going to live here, I'll have to start talking like a native."

"You're staying? You're really staying?" She threw her arms around his neck. "Thank you, Marcus. You don't know how happy that makes me." She looked around. "Where's Scott? Veronese?"

Marcus stood and exchanged glances with Tim.

"What's going on?" she asked.

"The *new* Captain Viator has returned to his ship, with his trusted companion, Lieutenant Qilana," Tim chortled.

"What are you talking about?" she demanded.

"Scott switched places with Marcus." Tim stood, stretched, and walked slowly over to his computer. "There were some *real* technical difficulties with the communications system, Marcus. They finally left about an hour ago."

"What?" Jessie cried, jumping to her feet.

"C'mon, Jess, you know Scott," Tim said. "The guy's been dying to go into space. My God, it killed him to be released from NASA because of budget cuts. He's wanted to be an astronaut since he was six years old."

"Scott is gone?" She clutched Marcus's arm.

"Yep," Tim said.

"He can't pull it off. Nobody'll believe he's Marcus. He's hairy, for God's sake."

Marcus placed his fingertips on her lips. "They know I—he is Terran. He will tell the crew he has decided not to deny his heritage."

She stepped back, breaking their contact. "You knew about this?"

He nodded, but Tim cut him off before he could explain. "Neesie will help him. Remember all those drawings Scott did of the *Freedom*, Jess? He took lots of notes when you described every last detail of the ship and the crew. I'll bet he knows the ship almost as well as Marcus does."

Tears welled up in her eyes. "I'll never see him again?"

Marcus felt a moment of uncertainty. Perhaps her feelings for Scott were stronger than he thought. Then, Marcus remembered her fervent proclamation of love for him as they came down the stairs. She loved him, not his twin. Marcus put his arms around her. "Do not worry. They will be safe."

"They promised to keep in touch," Tim said. "Neesie made a couple of modifications to my computer, so I could get transmissions from them. They called down a little bit ago. They're fine. They saw what happened in the bell tower, so they know that Herbie woman escaped."

"Contact them now," Jessie demanded. "At least I can say good-by to Scott and Veronese."

Tim gave her a look of chagrin. "In the middle of their transmission, everything went blank. Before it did, Scott said he thought Hrvibm deliberately screwed up some of the instruments—mainly, transport and communications."

Jessie looked up at Marcus. "She said the rebels are gathering here in this sector. Could they be jamming transmissions again?"

"It's possible," he said thoughtfully. "Hrvibm would have made certain no word about her defection could get back to Space Fleet Command...Jessie, do not worry. Your sister will help Scott." He dared not tell her of his fear that Scott would make a serious mistake and give himself away. Second thoughts assailed him at what he had done, at the peril he had allowed Scott and Veronese to go into.

No, Marcus thought. He had done what needed to be done. He'd needed to rescue Jessica. He had no regrets.

"They promised to come back when the baby is born," Tim said.

"Plural," Marcus interjected.

"What?"

"*Babies.*"

"Twins?" Tim exclaimed. "How come you never told me you were having twins?"

Jessie shrugged. She sat down in her rocker. "I hope Scott and Veronese are going to be okay."

"They will be," Tim said. "Marcus, Scott left instructions for you on the kitchen table. His wallet—driver's license, credit cards, everything he could think of. He also said that you were to take Jessie to meet your mother."

His mother. Marcus had given no thought to his biological mother. He had not thought any further than making certain Jessie was safe. Now, the implications of what he'd done rained down on him. How was he going to fit in on this alien planet?

"Scott said," Tim continued, "that the two of you were to decide if your mother is strong enough to tell her about what's happened. He said she'd understand why he wanted to go. Oh, and he said one more thing. Watch out for the Wicked Witch of the West a.k.a. your sister Irene."

"You knew all about this, Marcus?" asked Jessie.

"Not about the sister." He wondered what Scott meant by calling her a witch. "I knew about the rest. I thought I had to get back to the ship but I could not leave you. Scott, Tim, and Veronese came up with this plan while we were out walking. When Hrvibm abducted you, I agreed to let Scott take my place."

"I don't believe this." She shook her head. "I guess you're really staying, huh?"

"You betcha." He grinned.

"You're staying here with me." Tears formed in her eyes.

"If she's going to start bawling, you'd better take her outside," Tim groused. "She's been blubbering ever since she found out she was pregnant. God, I can't stand cry-babies."

She swiped at her tears as Marcus pulled her up into his arms. She would not have reason to cry again. He would make sure of it. He pressed her head against his chest.

"You guys aren't going to make out, are you?" Tim gave them a pained look.

She lifted her head and sniffed. "Oh, stick a sock in it, Tim." She took Marcus's hand. "Let's go outside where there's peace and quiet."

He was bemused by the sparring between them, but the affection in her voice made him smile. Then, the enormity of what he had done settled in the pit of his stomach. Leaving his ship, his crew, everything he had known. He swallowed hard. He had done the right thing. He was sure of it.

He followed her out to the porch. He had nearly lost her. Chills still ran down his spine as he thought of Jessie nearly going over the edge and the long walk down the stairs.

"You stayed for me," she said in amazement.

"I could not leave."

"But what about your uncle's farm? After wanting it, asking for it, for so long, how could you give it up?"

That may have been the deciding factor in his reason to stay on Earth. "Cam wanted the farm to remain in the family, as it has always been. I wanted to pass that heritage along to my offspring." He held her face between his palms. "But, my children are here. Their heritage is here. Most important of all, you are here."

"What about your crew? Your ship? Your duty?"

"They mean nothing without you." As he said the words, he knew they were true. Nothing mattered without her. He pulled her into his arms.

"You put me first," she said in amazement. She laid her hand against his cheek. "You put me first."

He turned to press a kiss into her palm. "Always."

"I love you, Marcus." Her love shone out of her eyes, shimmering with tears, glittering in the light streaming from the open door.

Marcus bent to capture her mouth. He infused his kiss

with tenderness, reverence, admiration for her strength. And, all of his love.

"Would you two make out where I can't see?" Tim called from inside the house. "I can't stand that mushy stuff."

Jessie broke away from Marcus. "Timothy John," she hollered back, "you sound like a kid." She sat down on the porch swing then patted the space next to her. "Ignore my brother, Marcus. He always was a pest."

"I heard that," Tim yelled.

Marcus put his arm around her shoulders and drew her close. She snuggled against him.

The sky was bright with stars. And one large moon. He looked for the others before catching himself. This was Earth. One moon. Earth. His home. How different that...felt. How right. Like now with Jessie in his arms.

She looked up at him, her eyes wide. "Why is it whenever I'm around you things happen so fast?"

He raised his eyebrow.

She punched him lightly on the chin. "You know, I actually missed that supercilious eyebrow of yours."

He grinned.

"I mean, you've only been here—what?" She checked her watch. "You've been on Earth all of five hours and look what's happened. Cenamola has come and gone—literally. Tim can walk again. Hrvibm tried to make smashed pumpkins out of us." She shivered. "And Scott has switched places with you—I still don't know about that part, though. And look at what happened at the beginning. In the span of two weeks, I was kidnapped by aliens, flew through space, visited an alien planet, fell in love, got preg—"

"I get the picture." Marcus tapped her nose. Then he became serious. "Do you regret being kidnapped by aliens?"

"Not this alien." She leaned toward him and whispered, "Want me to show you how Terrans make out?"

Author's note

There is a bell tower on the University of Michigan's campus—the Burton (no relation) Memorial Tower. However, it does not resemble the one in this story which came from the writer's imagination with help from the Alfred Hitchcock movie *Vertigo*.

ABOUT THE AUTHOR

Diane Burton believes in fairy tales, the Easter Bunny, and happy-ever-after, which is why she loves reading and writing romance. She met her own hero on a blind date 29 years ago and has followed his job from the Detroit-area to Missouri, sw Michigan, and Chicago-land. Diane and her husband currently reside in mid-Michigan with a wimpy Lab-cocker mix whose favorite place to sleep is under her desk. They have two grown children. Diane's love of romantic comedy and "Star Trek" led to the writing of her first futuristic, *Switched*.

Diane loves to hear from her readers.
email: DBurton72@aol.com
or
P.O. Box 504
St Johns MI 48879

website: www.dianeburton.com

ONCE UPON A TIME
ON A PLANTATION

Other books by the author:

THE GRAND STRAND: An Uncommon
    Guide to Myrtle Beach and
    Its Surroundings

CAROLINA SEASHELLS

TALES OF THE SOUTH CAROLINA
    LOW COUNTRY

MORE TALES OF THE SOUTH CAROLINA
    LOW COUNTRY

COASTAL GHOSTS

Once Upon a Time on a Plantation

By Nancy Rhyne
Illustrated by Joan Holub

PELICAN PUBLISHING COMPANY
GRETNA 1988

Library of Congress Cataloging-in-Publication Data

Rhyne, Nancy, 1926-
  Once upon a time on a plantation / by Nancy Rhyne ; illus-
trated by Joan Holub.
      p. cm.
  Summary: A collection of short stories following the lives
of two young boys living on a plantation in antebellum South
Carolina.
  ISBN 0-88289-702-0
  1. Children's stories, American. [1. Plantation life—South
Carolina—Fiction.   2. South   Carolina—Fiction.   3. Short
stories.] I. Holub, Joan, ill. II. Title.
PZ7.R34790n 1988
[Fic]—dc19   88-9896
                                                       CIP
                                                        AC

Manufactured in the United States of America

Published by Pelican Publishing Company, Inc.
1101 Monroe Street, Gretna, Louisiana 70053

CONTENTS

Some of the stories in this book were inspired by tales told to the author by Will Alston of Hampton Plantation. Mr. Alston's late parents, Sue and Prince Alston, are mentioned frequently in the books of the late Dr. Archibald Rutledge, a Poet Laureate of South Carolina whose family owned the plantation for seven generations.

ONCE UPON A TIME
ON A PLANTATION

THE
ALLIGATOR

WHY DO PEOPLE call your papa 'King Robert'?"
dark-skinned Will asked his friend, Cartrette
Middleton.

Twelve-year-old Cartrette jabbed a thumb toward
the mansion in a clearing in the trees. "See that big
house with the white columns?"

"And the big rooms?" Will added.

"Well, Papa owns that house, and this plantation,
and lots of other things. And he has lots of land,
some on the river and some on the Atlantic Ocean.
People call him 'King Robert' because he owns such
a big plantation. He's not a real king."

"But you don't call him 'King Robert.' " Will
said.

"No. He's Papa," Cart answered. " 'King Robert'
is a nickname. Papa's real name is Robert
Middleton."

"Well, your father has all of that stuff," Will answered, "but my father doesn't have much of

anything. How come you're my best friend?"

"Because I like you best of all the people here on Midcliffe plantation," Cart explained. "And besides that, we were born the same year. We're the same age." Cart looked toward the forest and creek, trying to decide on something that would be exciting to do.

"My mammy says you're white and I'm black and you might not like me forever and ever."

Cart turned back to Will. "I'll always like you best of all. In my whole life I'll always like you best. Don't ever forget that."

"I won't," Will answered.

"Know what happened this morning?" Cart asked.

"What?"

"Well, that big black alligator in the creek, the animal we call Brute, ate up one of my mother's roosters. Boy, she's mad at Brute! She wants Papa to kill him, but I begged her not to have Brute killed."

Will thought about that. "We couldn't have all that fun if they killed Brute. Do you think they'll really kill him?"

"I don't know. He ate a pig one night, and now my mother's rooster. He's not behaving as he should. That alligator's in trouble!"

"Let's go see if we can spot him," Will said.

"I'll beat you to the creek," Cart answered, taking off in a run. Bijou, his dog, caught up with him and ran beside him. "Come on, Bijou. Let's beat Will."

Will ran as fast as he could and finally caught up with Cart and Bijou. They raced neck-and-neck and arrived at the bluff overlooking Chapel Creek. Cart ruffled the hair on Bijou's head, and the dog's eyes, within pinkish rims, danced. He wagged his tail.

Will was breathing heavily from running so fast. "Do you see Brute?"

Cart eyed the black cypress water. Tree limbs were hanging over the water, and some cypress trees grew in the creek. It looked dark, although above the trees the sun was shining. "I'm looking. Sometimes Brute is hard to see."

Just at that moment, Will saw the shiny, slick black spots that seemed to be floating on the water. "There he is! Just under the surface. See his back?"

"That's him," Cart answered. "He's sly. Just floating along, waiting. He doesn't know we can see him."

"He looks like a log," Will said. "He must be trying to trick us into thinking his *is* a log." Will picked up a stick and threw it into the water. "Brute! Get away from here!"

"Don't do that!" Cart scolded. "My father said not ever to annoy an alligator or a wild hog. They'll sometimes come at you. They could eat you up!"

"Uh-oh," Will said. "That stick didn't come close to Brute, and I'm glad."

"It's getting late," Cart said. "Almost suppertime. I'm going home. Come on, Bijou."

"I've got to go home, too," Will answered. "Will I see you tomorrow?"

"Sure. You see me every day. Come after breakfast, and I may have some good news."

"Like what?"

"Papa said next year, when I'm thirteen, he's going to get me a gun. My mother is angry about that. She says I'm too young, but Papa says I have to learn the ways of the plantation and how to take care of myself."

"Oh, boy! I hope you get a gun. We'll put the boat in the creek, and if anything starts to get us we'll shoot," Will exclaimed.

"I don't know if Papa will get me a gun or not. I'm trying to talk him into it, although it's against my mother's wishes."

Will ran toward the caretaker's house, where he lived with his parents and baby sister. "See you tomorrow," he called back. He looked forward to every day as there were so many wonderful things to do and places to explore on the plantation.

"Sleep tight," Cart called. Bijou barked.

Cart and Bijou ran up to the white-columned porch where Mr. and Mrs. Middleton were sitting. They enjoyed sitting on the porch in May, when the cool air came in from the ocean and pushed the heat away. "Cartrette, I know you must be ready for your supper," Mrs. Middleton said. "And you too, Bijou." The dog ran over to her, and she patted his head. "Let's go inside."

As Cart and his father took their seats at the dining room table, Mrs. Middleton took a small plate and filled it with meat and vegetables. "Come on, Bijou," she said, leaving the room. Bijou ran at her heels, for he knew that she had his supper on the plate. And he knew his usual place to have his meals was in the pantry. Mrs. Middleton put the plate on the floor of the pantry, and Bijou began lapping the food.

Each night at supper, the Middletons ate leftovers from lunch, and their beverage was buttermilk. The grownups had coffee for breakfast and lunch, but everybody drank buttermilk at supper.

Cart turned up his glass of buttermilk and drank deeply, for he was thirsty and tired. When he put the glass back on the table, there was a white mustache on his upper lip. His mother motioned for him to remove it with a napkin. She passed to him a platter of sliced ham, a bowl of rice (they ate rice every day for rice was produced on the plantation), and tomatoes and cabbage.

Cart ate all that he desired, but before he was ready for dessert, Bijou had finished his meal and was standing by Cart's chair. The dog wagged his tail as he licked his lips.

"Sit!" Cart commanded.

The dog curled up near Cart's feet.

After a dessert of orange marmalade spread on thick slices of bread, Cart and Bijou went to the drawing room. Before long, Cart's eyes were heavy and he could hardly keep them open. Bijou was already asleep, on a rug near the hearth.

"It's time for bed, you two," Mrs. Middleton said. Cart pulled himself up and yawned. "Come on, Bijou," he said, sleepily. Mrs. Middleton walked with Cart and Bijou up the winding stairway, and when they reached the bedroom at the top of the stairs, Cart put on his pajamas and climbed into the tall tester bed. It was a high bed and had a canopy of lace, draping over the high posts. Bijou settled down on a rug on the floor. As always, Mrs. Middleton folded back a corner of the rug, and Bijou wiggled himself into the fold. Before Mrs. Middleton left the room, Cart and Bijou were sound asleep.

Back downstairs, she talked with her husband about some of the dangers of the plantation.

"Cart's just a little boy, Robert. I think you should caution him not to go so close to Chapel Creek and the alligator. In fact, I think it's time to do away with Brute. We don't know which farm animal he'll eat next."

"You know," Mr. Middleton answered, "all plantations have a certain amount of danger. There are canebrake rattlesnakes, and some of the alligators walk up the bank of the creek and come rather close to the house. Evidence of that is that Brute came close enough to eat a rooster and pig. But I grew up here and learned early how to take care of myself. I think my son should do the same."

"Well I don't want to hear any more talk of a gun," Mrs. Middleton snapped. "Cart's too young and it's dangerous. Don't promise him a gun for his next birthday."

"I had my own gun before I was his age. I want to teach Cart to draw a bead with his gun, and by the time he's sixteen, he'll bring down a deer with a set of antlers that will decorate the walls of our library."

"All of this worries me," Mrs. Middleton said. "Danger lurks everywhere on a remote plantation like this."

The plantation consisted of a large tract of land that extended from the Waccamaw River in South

Carolina to the Atlantic Ocean. Much of the property was in marshland, where crabs, shrimp, oysters, and nearly every conceivable kind of shorebird lived. Then there were the forbidding woods. Huge oak trees, draped in Spanish moss, darkened the land on the brightest days. And there were the pine woods, where pine needles crackled under your feet when you walked. The cedar grove was eerie and dense. Wild hogs, turkeys, and herds of deer made their home in the forests.

Besides the forests, there were rivers and lagoons that were the haunts of dozens of huge alligators, and many species of snakes. One had to be constantly on the alert to keep away from ugly hazards. Yet, this land was the perfect place for boys to have a good time. There was never a shortage of places to explore, although Cart and Will had been cautioned to keep a safe distance from Brute and sometimes from the Old Wagon Road, if Mr. Middleton knew wild hogs were running there. Cart had also been told to stay away from that out-of-the-way chapel where a ghost rang the bell in the tower. But Cart and Will never saw the peril in playing in the woods or near the creek. They believed that Mrs. Middleton just got her dander up for no reason at all.

The next morning Will and Cart went back to Chapel Creek to see if they could spot Brute. They again had some free time to go off in search of adventure, although on certain days Cart studied with a tutor, a young man from Scotland who lived with his wife on the plantation. Will didn't study with them, but he listened as Cart tried to explain the lessons to him later. Will and the other blacks on the plantation regularly attended the Sunday religious service, where Cart's tutor would teach the catechism. The Middletons were members of an Episcopal church near Pawleys Island, but they sometimes came to these services too.

Today Cart and Will could play at the creek. When they reached it, they saw that just as yesterday Brute was floating under the surface, and the shiny parts of his hide that were above water appeared to be black coins, floating on the surface. At midday the boys went to their homes for lunch, but Cart couldn't get Bijou to come with him.

"I called Bijou, but he wouldn't come home," Cart said to his parents. "He wouldn't budge, so I left him at the creek."

After lunch, Mr. and Mrs. Middleton and Cart were standing on the porch when they heard Bijou barking, in the distance. Just then, Bijou let out a loud yelp, and then all was quiet.

"I think I'd better go see what happened," Mr. Middleton said.

"I want to go too," Cart said.

"All right. Come along."

When they reached Chapel Creek, at the very place where Cart had left Bijou, the dog was not in sight.

"Son, I'm afraid I have bad news," Cart's father said.

"What are you talking about?" Cart questioned.

"See that little bit of dog hair on the bank?"

"Yes."

"I think Brute has killed Bijou."

"No!" Cart cried. "Surely Brute didn't eat Bijou."

"I think Bijou is the latest casualty," Cart's father said. "And that means that the 'gator has got to go."

"What do you intend to do?" Cart asked.

His father thought about that. Then he said, "Well, I'm going to rig up a hook inside a ham. I'll tie a rope around the ham and throw it into the creek where Brute will be sure to find it. When he swallows the hook, I'll shoot him."

"I didn't want you to shoot Brute, but I didn't want him to eat Bijou. Shoot that mean alligator!" Cart cried.

"Now you're talking. You know that Brute ate a rooster and pig, and now your dog. We don't want to take any chances of this 'gator coming for a child." Mr. Middleton and Cart turned back toward the mansion. They walked to the kitchen, which was a building separate from the house.

Fire was one of the worst enemies of plantations, and kitchens were not a part of the main house. Cooks attended the kitchen, where there was a fireplace big enough in which to cook an ox.

"Sue," Mr. Middleton called to a cook, "go to the smokehouse and bring me a ham."

"Are we having company?" Sue asked.

"No. I'm going to hook the big alligator and shoot him. He has killed Cart's puppy, Bijou."

"Bijou come to his end in the jaws of that 'gator?" Sue questioned.

"That's right."

Just then Mrs. Middleton stuck her head in the door. "What's going on?"

"The alligator killed Bijou, and I'm going to shoot that reptile."

"I'm so relieved," Cart's mother answered. "Cart and Will have become too interested in that animal and they could get careless. One of them could be next."

"If I can't find a big hook in the carpenter shop, I'll have to go to Georgetown and buy one," Mr. Middleton explained. He walked across the yard to the carpenter shop and asked a worker for a large hook. The man looked on all of the shelves but couldn't find a hook as large as Mr. Middleton desired. "Then it's settled," Cart's father said. "I'll go to Georgetown and buy what I need."

Late in the afternoon, Mr. Middleton returned from Georgetown. He had a hook that looked to be big enough to hook a cow.

"Are you going to kill the alligator now?" Cart asked.

"No. It's getting late. I'll do that in the morning, after breakfast."

Cart was crying when he went to bed that night. He couldn't remember going to bed when Bijou wasn't on the rug beside the high-poster bed. The door cracked, and Cart's mother peeked around it. "Are you asleep?"

"No. I'm sad about Bijou."

"I'm said too," she said, coming in and taking a seat on the bed. "I thought I would read you a story. Or would *you* rather read it?"

Cart turned over and stretched. He was sleepier than he realized. "You read it."

"Once upon a time," she began, "there was a little boy who lived in England."

Cart sighed and moved slightly. Mrs. Middleton stopped reading and watched him until he was sound asleep. She doubted that he had heard even the first word she had read. It had been a sad day for him.

When Cart went downstairs the next morning, his mother told him that his father was in the little kitchen building, preparing the hook which would kill the alligator. Cart flew out the door. Just as he ran into the small building, Mr. Middleton cut open a side of the ham and pushed the big hook inside.

"Wait," Cart screamed. "I want to get Will. I don't want him to miss this."

Mr. Middleton waited until Cart ran to the care-taker's house and got Will. The boys were quiet as they watched Mr. Middleton. After he had placed the hook inside the ham, he took a needle that had thread in it and sewed up the ham. It looked just like a regular ham, except an end of the hook pro-truded from an end of the ham. Mr. Middleton tied a rope to that end of the hook. "Come on, boys. Let's go get rid of the 'gator."

"We're with you," Cart said.

"This is a broken-hearted day," Will said.

"Why do you say that?" Cart asked.

"Because that 'gator ate Bijou, and now we are going to kill the 'gator."

"It's the only thing to do," Mr. Middleton

explained. "If we don't kill the 'gator, there is no telling what he will kill next."

The boys watched intently all that Mr. Middleton did next. He tied the end of the rope that was not attached to the ham to a tree on the creek bank. Then he laid the ham aside for a moment and went into the bushes to get a small boat that he kept concealed by foliage. After that, Mr. Middleton cut down a small tree, and whittled it until it was no more than a heavy stick that had forked limbs on one end. After he had placed the forked limbs and the ham in the boat, Mr. Middleton pushed off and jumped inside the boat. He took a paddle from the boat bottom and maneuvered his way to the middle of the creek.

"Papa," Cart called. "Where is Brute? Don't let him get you."

"Don't worry. He's not here right now." When Mr. Middleton got to the middle of the stream, he pushed the limb into the floor of the creek, leaving the forked branches above water. Then he threw the ham into the water and placed the rope in the forks of the limb. The forks kept the ham in the right place for Brute to find it and prevented it from moving with the flow of the water.

Mr. Middleton rowed back to shore and insisted that the boys go home with him. "I'm going to load the gun and have it ready. And, boys, I trust you not to go near the creek until we have disposed of that alligator. He's a vicious animal and would think nothing of killing all of us. Don't get near him until this is over."

Cart and Will stared at the rope that was tied to a

tree and stretched across the water to the forked limbs and then went down into the water. The ham on the end of the rope was underwater, and not in sight. All the rest of the day, Cart and Will played around the mansion. But nothing was fun that day.

The next morning Cart asked Will if he was brave enough to go to the bank of Chapel Creek and see if the rope was still in place.

"But your father told us not to go there."

"But it's no fun here," Cart said with a pout on his face. "We won't get hurt. I want to see if Brute has swallowed the hook."

"Let's go," Will answered.

As the boys ran toward Chapel Creek, Cart missed Bijou. Perhaps his father would get him another puppy today, he thought.

"The rope is still in place," Cart said, as soon as he reached the bluff overlooking Chapel Creek. "Brute hasn't found it."

"Do you think the ham with the hook in it is still hanging on the end of the rope?" Will questioned. "The water is dark, and we can't see under it."

"I don't know," Cart answered, a thought crossing his mind. "Will, what do you say we pull that boat down and row out there and check on the hook?"

"Let's go," Will answered.

Back at home Mr. Middleton was getting his gun ready to shoot the alligator as soon as it swallowed the hook. Mr. Middleton loved guns, and he loved hunting in his woods. As there were no supermarkets in that day, that is where he got much of the meat that came to the plantation table. Wild turkeys were always available, as well as many other kinds of wildlife. He fingered the smooth grain of the hand-rubbed gun handle. Then he "broke" the gun and peered down the barrel. He loaded the firearm and placed it back on the rack.

Cart and Will were pulling the boat down the bank of the creek when they heard the faint sound of a church bell.

"What was that?" Will asked.

"That was the chapel bell," Cart explained. "There's a chapel by this creek, and that's why it is named Chapel Creek."

"Where is the chapel?"

"Beyond the bend of the creek, in a deep thicket," Cart explained. "Papa told me never to go there."

"Why do you think he doesn't want you to go to the chapel?" Will asked.

"Because some of the people who work on the plantation believe that a ghost lives there. The chapel is haunted."

"Why do they think a ghost is there?" Will wanted to know.

"Because, when it is least expected, the chapel bell rings. Like it did just then," Cart explained.

"Do you want to see the chapel?" Will asked.

"I want to see the chapel, but I don't want to see a ghost," Cart answered.

"Would you go there? Ever?"

Cart thought about that, and finally said, "I might. Would you?"

"I might," Will answered.

Cart got in the boat, and Will pushed it out onto the surface of the water, jumping in at the last minute.

Cart and Will took paddles from the floor of the boat and began to guide the vessel toward the forked stick that was holding the rope in place.

"WATCH OUT!" Will called. "You almost made the boat bump into the stick. What would your father do if he came here and found out that you had knocked down the stick?"

"He'd be angry. He'd be angry with me if he knew that I came here, even if I didn't knock down the stick," Cart added.

Just then the boys maneuvered the boat close to the rope.

"Will," Cart said. "Steady the boat. I'm going to lean over and pull the rope and see if the ham is still there."

"All right." Will sat in the middle of the boat in order to keep it from tipping over.

Cart leaned over the side and caught hold of the rope. He pulled, but it was heavy. "I think the ham is still there. This rope's heavy. So heavy I can't pull it from the water."

"LOOK!" Will screamed. "Oh, Cart, LOOK!"

Cart pulled himself back in the boat and glanced at the bank, toward the place where Will was pointing. A monster of an alligator was sliding across the mud and into the water.

"Oh, it's Brute!" Cart yelled. "Let's get out of here." He grabbed a paddle and started rowing.

"He's coming toward us," Will yelled, also paddling for his life.

"If we don't get out of this creek, Brute will eat us," Cart yelled.

Cart and Will were so scared that they splashed

water as they paddled, and some of the water was coming inside the boat. "The boat is getting heavy with water," Will said.

"Pray!" Cart called out. "Pray to God that He will save us."

"Okay," Will answered. "I'll pray just like I do in church."

They were paddling so furiously that a wave came over a side of the boat and overturned the vessel, pitching Cart and Will into the water.

"Don't look back," Cart said, treading water. "Swim to shore."

Water splashed into Will's nostrils, and he began to cough.

"Keep going, Will," Cart called out. "Don't let Brute get you."

Will didn't answer. He was now coughing very hard. His eyes were full of water, and he couldn't see where he was going. Low-hanging limbs came down so low they almost touched his head.

"Will," Cart called. "Turn! Go another way."

"I'm going as fast as I can," Will called, not looking back.

"But there's something on a tree limb, near you."

"What is it?"

"A snake."

Will gazed up and saw a snake slithering around the limb that was just over his head. "Mercy. I don't think I can make it."

"Sure you can! You can make it. You're almost there. Turn and go another way."

Will took a deep breath and turned. It seemed he

was going backward instead of forward. He wasn't
making any headway at all.

"Keep going," Cart called. "Don't look back and
don't look up. That snake could make a move."

"How did we get into this?" Will screamed.

"I don't know," Cart answered. "I sure wish we
hadn't gotten in the boat."

Just then Cart was so near the bank that he believed he could walk out of the water. He stopped
swimming and his feet touched the bottom of the
creek. Mud oozed up between his toes. Suddenly his
feet began to slide and he fell down in the water.
Pulling himself back up, he tried to walk, but the
mud was slick and his bare feet were sliding on it.
He fell face down in the creek and swallowed some
water. When he came up, water was coming out of
his eyes and nose and ears, and he was coughing.

Will's eyes went to a tree limb that wasn't too far
away, and it had no snake on it. He swam under the
limb and caught hold of it. Swinging his feet up and
clasping them around the limb, he pulled himself
up and over. Now he could look down at Cart, and he
saw that Cart was in trouble. Then Will's eyes went
to Brute. The alligator was nuzzling on the ham
and was unaware that the boys were so close.
"Hurry up, Cart," Will called. "If Brute swallows
the ham and hook, he might stir up this creek. Get
out now."

"I'm trying to get out," Cart said angrily. "But it's
too shallow to swim and my feet are sliding in the
mud. What can I do?"

"I'll help you." Will climbed to the trunk of the

tree and shinnied down. He ran toward Cart and held out his hands. It felt so good to have his feet on solid ground and be away from Brute. But Cart couldn't reach Will's hands, and his feet were miring in the mud. He was stuck!

"Should I go and get King Robert?" Will asked.

"No! Help me get out of the mud," Cart yelled.

"I'll go find a stick, and maybe you can hold onto one end and I'll pull you out," Will said. He ran up the bluff and looked around frantically. Finally, he found a stick. Back at the creek, he held the stick out as far as he could. Cart took hold of the stick and pulled with all his might. His feet didn't move even the slightest bit, and instead of Will pulling him out, he pulled Will in.

"Help me," Will cried. "Now *I'm* stuck in the mud."

"HELP! HELP!" Will cried. Brute could come at any minute, Will was thinking. There wasn't a second to spare.

"I wish I had Bijou," Cart said. "If I had Bijou, he'd bark, and my mother would come to see about us."

Will leaned over, and his hands went down in the mud as well as his feet. "The mud is swallowing me up," he cried. "We're just as good as dead. Why did we do this anyway? We knew we shouldn't go out in the boat."

"I'm sorry that I disobeyed my father, but that's not helping me get out of this mud," Cart answered. "I wish somebody would come. HELP!"

At that very moment a great bellow exploded in the air, and it was like the biggest cannon in the whole world being fired. Cart and Will looked around, a quizzical expression on their faces.

"What was that?" Will asked.

"I think Brute just swallowed the hook," Cart answered.

Creek water began to churn and splash and the sounds coming from Brute were unlike anything that Will and Cart had ever heard.

"Oh, mercy," Will screamed. "I've heard the old folks say that they have heard alligators talk like a man. Brute's talking like a man."

"He's not talking like a man, Will, he's talking like an alligator with a hook in his mouth. Get moving!"

The alligator threw his head back and rammed it down into the water, making a great splash. His bellow was so loud that it reverberated in the forest.

"Cart, he *is* talking like a man."

"No, he's not! He's in pain, and he's bellowing like you've never heard in your life."

The head and tail of the animal were rising up and dipping down, and the creek churned like milk in the kitchen. But instead of butter coming to the top of the churn, mud was coming up in the water. It was brown and black and dark red.

"What are we going to do, Cart?" Will blubbered, tears running down his cheeks. "Tell me what to do!"

"Hold on, boys!" Mr. Middleton was running through the forest. He had on rubber boots and was carrying his gun. He stopped under the big oak tree and looked at the alligator. There was no time to lose.

"What are you boys doing in the creek?" Mr. Middleton asked, not waiting for an answer. He flew down the hill and into the water. Although his boots began to sink into the slimy goo, he pulled them up, and grabbed a boy under each arm. Taking big, high steps, he carried them to the bank. "I thought I told you boys to stay away from the creek until I killed the alligator."

"You did, Papa, and I'm sorry," Cart said.

"I'm sorry too, King Robert," Will said. "We didn't mean to do nothing wrong. We were just checking to see if the ham was still on the rope."

"Hush," Cart said to Will. "He's going to punish us anyway."

"No, I'm not going to punish you," Mr. Middleton said. "I'd give you a good spanking right now if I wasn't so glad that I got here in time to save you." He picked up his gun and as he tried to sight the alligator, he asked, "Do you boys realize how much danger you were in?"

"We sure do," Cart answered.

"But you saved us," Will answered.

Mr. Middleton kept moving his gun, but the alligator was going under the water, and stirring up mud, and the gun couldn't be focused on him.

"Drat!" Mr. Middleton said. "I can't get a bead on him."

"Kill him, King Robert," Will called out. "He almost ate us up."

Mr. Middleton kept on moving his gun, but every time he thought he had the gun pointing in the right direction, the alligator showed up in another part of the creek.

"I can't get a focus on that 'gator," Mr. Middleton

said. He paused and tried to decide what to do. "Will, go home and get your father and tell him to bring two helpers with him. Tell them to come quickly. I need some help."

"I'll go, too," Cart answered, catching up with Will, who was already running toward his house.

Will's father was working in his vegetable garden. "Come quick. To the creek," Will screamed. "King Robert needs you. He's hooked Brute, the alligator."

"And bring two helpers with you," Cart added. "Papa needs several men to help him. Oh, hurry!"

Will's father put his hands by his mouth and called to some men who were on the Wagon Road, riding in a cart pulled by two oxen. "Come here. King Robert needs you!"

Will and Cart ran back to the creek. Mr. Middleton still was unable to shoot the alligator, for it had gone under the water and couldn't be seen.

"Are the others coming?" Mr. Middleton asked.

"Yep," Will answered.

When the helpers arrived, Mr. Middleton told them to pull the alligator out of the water by yanking on the rope. "When his head comes up," Mr. Middleton explained, "I'll shoot right between the eyes."

The men untied the end of the rope that had been tied to a tree on the bank. They summoned all of their strength as they pulled, but Brute wouldn't budge. "That 'gator's heavy, Boss," a helper said.

"I believe he *is* too heavy for us," Will's father answered.

"Will. Cart. Go and get some more men," Mr. Middleton said.

The boys ran back to the mansion, and Will asked

his mother whom he should get to help his father. She thought about it a moment, then said, "Well, I believe Prince and Abraham are working in the carpenter shop today. Go and find them." She left the house and started running toward the creek.

Abraham and Prince arrived on the scene with three other men, as well. Mr. Middleton had the children stand back as all of the men pulled on the rope. Brute was dead weight, but he finally began to move, and the men backed up as they pulled his head out of the water. His jaws were open, and the people on the bank could see many sharp teeth.

"That's the biggest 'gator I've ever seen," Abraham said.

Minutes later, when the animal had been pulled up on the bank, Mr. Middleton said, "He's fifteen feet long if he's an inch. Now everybody get out of the way. I'm going to shoot."

"Kill him, Papa," Cart yelled.

Mr. Middleton squeezed the trigger, and suddenly there was a great thrashing and whipping of the huge tail, which looked like black armor. Then, all was quiet.

"Boss," Abraham said, "if you don't use that 'gator, I take the tail home to my wife. She make stew out of 'gator tail."

"If you meddle with them thing," Prince added, "I want some of such as that."

" 'Gator go good with corn," another said.

"Oh, I eat 'gator till I bust," someone called out.

"All right, folks," Mr. Middleton said. "We'll cut him up and divide him."

The alligator was stretched out on the ground, and Mr. Middleton took a knife from a boot where he carried it and cut off the tail. That part of the alligator was divided into as many pieces as possible, because everybody wanted a piece of the tail.

"Does anybody want the hide?" Mr. Middleton asked.

Nobody answered, as they had no use for the alligator hide. After the reptile had been equally divided among those who had helped kill him, the men went home to give their wives the meat.

Cart looked at Will as though they had just endured a horrible storm, and he wanted to run to release the tension. "Let's run, Will." As Cart took off, with Will behind him, he looked back and said, "I sure miss Bijou."

THE
WILD HOG

Happy birthday, Cartrette," Mrs. Middleton said, as she came into Cart's room.

He opened his eyes. It *was* his birthday. He remembered that he had gone to bed last night thinking about it. He sat up quickly. "Did Papa get me a gun for my birthday?"

"Oh, Cartrette," Mrs. Middleton said as she gave her son a hug. "Wait until you see the present your father and I have for you."

"What is it?"

"I'll allow your father the privilege of telling you, or better still, giving it to you."

"Happy birthday, son," Mr. Middleton said, as he walked up to the door. The tall man with luxuriant brown hair wore leather boots. "Do you feel older now that you are in your teens?" Mr. Middleton walked to the bed and hugged his son.

"No. I don't feel any older. But did you get me a gun for my birthday?"

"I talked this over with your mother, and we decided to hold off for probably another year. But we do have something for you. A gift I believe you will like."

"Oh, Papa. You didn't get me a gun? Will wanted me to get it as much as I did."

"Guns are dangerous. Your mother and I have decided that I will give you some careful instruction on the use of firearms before we gift you with a rifle. You and I will go into the woods and have target practice, maybe today, if you want. But come along. I want to give you your gift."

Cart was disappointed over not receiving a gun for his birthday, but he could understand his father's reasoning to a point. However, Cart felt that he and Will were growing up now, and they could be trusted with a gun. He'd insist that his father take him for target practice unless something more exciting came up.

Cart was still in pajamas as he walked down the winding stairway, in front of his mother and father.

"We're going outside, to the kitchen," Mr. Middleton said. "That's where your present is."

"In the kitchen! Is it something to eat?" Cart asked, disappointment showing on his face.

"No, no. It's nothing to eat."

They left the big house and walked across the yard, and just before they reached the kitchen a tan and white puppy ran out.

"That's your present," Cart's father said. "A puppy."

Cart ran to the dog and stooped down and nuzzled the fuzzy face next to his neck. "What's his name, Papa?"

"He doesn't have one. You can select a name."

Cart moved back and looked at the puppy. "He has orange-brown spots, like, uh, like marmalade. That's what I'll name him, Marmalade."

Mrs. Middleton stooped down and held the puppy's face between her hands. "You have a new name, and it's perfect. Welcome to the plantation, Marmalade."

"Drat!" Cart said. "I have to go back upstairs and put my clothes on before I play with Will." He broke into a run toward the mansion, calling, "Come on, Marmalade. I want Will to see you."

Up in his room, Cart pulled on blue trousers, and buttoned a shirt and tucked it inside his britches. All of his clothes were made by seamstresses who worked in a room in the attic of the mansion. They made clothes for every member of the family and their own families as well. Mrs. Middleton bought cloth by the bolt, and what she didn't use, she gave to the other people on the plantation.

Cart held Marmalade under an arm and flew downstairs to the porch. "Hey, Will. Come over. See my present."

Will loved Cart's birthdays even more than his own. As he and Cart had been born in the same year, the Middletons always celebrated Will's birthday on the same day as Cart's.

"Will, this is Marmalade."

"Let's take him in and show him the house," Will suggested.

Inside the house, Marmalade looked disoriented, and for a moment he stood still. "Let's go to the hall," Cart said.

In the hall Cart carried Marmalade to the far

side, and then Cart went to the other side of the room. "Come," he begged. "Marmalade, come to me."

Marmalade hesitated for a second or two, then ran on the pine floors that had been rubbed with beeswax. Before the puppy reached Cart, he stopped abruptly, and just then his stiff little legs started sliding and he skidded right into Cart's arms. Cart hugged him. "He came to me," Cart said to Will. "And he liked sliding on the floor."

"Cart," his father called from the porch, "you and Will come here. I want to caution you about something."

Cart picked Marmalade up and Will followed them to the porch. "What is it, Papa?" Cart asked.

"Don't go anywhere near the Wagon Road. I've been noticing lately that a wild hog has been going there."

"How can you tell?" Cart asked.

"I've seen his tracks. Now, be warned. He's every bit as dangerous as Brute was. I'm going to try to kill him, but right now I don't know exactly how to do it."

"I've never seen a wild hog," Cart said.

"Well, let me tell you, they're devils. You wouldn't want to come in contact with a wild hog. The correct term is wild boar, as *boar* is the name for a male domestic hog."

Cart hugged Marmalade. He was so happy to have another dog. He didn't want to concern himself with the hog problem.

"Cart, please give me your attention," his father lectured. "This may be one of the most important conversations you and I ever have."

"Why, Papa?"

"Because if you ever encounter a wild hog you must recognize the danger." Mr. Middleton turned to Will. "You listen too. Both of you need to keep this in mind."

"I'm not going close to such as that," Will said.

"The wild hog is not as large as our domestic pigs. Wild ones are grayish-black and have short hair and coarse bristles. The lower jaw has two powerful tusks which are used for fighting."

"Tusks?" Cart asked.

"Those tusks can kill a man and tear him to pieces. I believe the wild boar that has been coming into the Wagon Road is at least two feet high and could weigh about two hundred pounds. Do you understand me? *Don't go near the Wagon Road!*"

"We won't," Cart answered. Then he looked at Will. "Let's take Marmalade for a tour of Midcliffe, and we'll show him some of the things we do to have a good time."

"Let's show him how we make rabbit boxes and catch rabbits," Will answered.

"That's what we'll do," Cart said. "And we'll catch a rabbit and let Marmalade chase it."

Mrs. Middleton poked her head around the door. "Will, you are invited to lunch in the mansion today. We're celebrating your birthday, too. There'll be cake."

"Will the cake have white icing and red berries on it?" Will asked.

"Oh, that's a secret," Mrs. Middleton answered.

Cart grabbed Marmalade and said, "Come on,

Will. Let's go to the carpenter shop."

Prince and Abraham were repairing a carriage. The Middleton carriages were elaborate vehicles, and each one bore the Middleton family's coat of arms.

"Prince," Cart said. "Look at my dog. His name is Marmalade. He's a present. Today's my birthday."

Prince looked at the dog and nodded. "Pretty fine dog," he said. "Wish I had a present for you."

"You don't have to give me a present," Cart answered.

"I can't give you anything less I make it." Prince spread out his large, dark hands. They were gnarled and scarred from hard work in the carpenter shop. "You want anything made for you?"

"Will and I want you to make us a rabbit box," Cart said. "We are going to catch a rabbit and let Marmalade chase it."

"Oh I can make good such as that," Prince answered. "Make rabbit boxes all the time. Catch all rabbits what the old woman cooks in the pot."

Just then the wheels in Cart's brain started turning. The most marvelous thought had come to him. If Prince could make a huge rabbit box, perhaps he and Will could catch the wild hog that his father hated. After all, Papa had said that he didn't know how to capture the animal. "Will," Cart said, "come outside."

The boys stepped out of the carpenter shop and whispered. Cart said something, and then Will spoke, and they got excited and almost talked aloud. Finally, they came back inside.

"Prince," Cart said, "for my birthday I want a

rabbit box most of all. But I want a very big rabbit box."

"What for you want one so big?"

"You know I might catch a rabbit that's about two feet high and weighs about two hundred pounds." Cart looked at Will, and they giggled. Cart hoped that Prince didn't catch on to the reason he wanted such a large box.

"You want rabbit box so big?" Prince questioned. "No rabbit on plantation be two feet high and weigh two hundred pounds." Laughter bubbled up in Prince and he motioned for Abraham to come across the room. Abraham put down a barrel that he was making, dusted his hands on his britches, and walked over. "What be going on over here?"

"These boys ask for rabbit box that be big enough to catch a rabbit what be two feet high and weigh two hundred pounds!" Both Prince and Abraham laughed so hard that tears came to their eyes. Cart was annoyed at the laughter.

"Can you make it, Prince?" Cart asked.

"What you plan to do with such as that?" Prince questioned.

"We're, uh, going to take it to the Wagon Road and set the trap door. And if it catches an animal that's not a rabbit, that'll be all right. Maybe a mean animal that worries Papa will get in that box, and we'll be helping Papa." Cart looked at Will, and they giggled.

"When you catch them rabbit and fetch him in, I want to see him," Prince said. "You gonna eat him?"

"No. We're going to let Marmalade chase him."

"You not aiming to catch no sickly rabbit," Prince said, laughing so hard that tears again came to his eyes. "That must be a mighty big rabbit!"

"If a rabbit that big come after me," Abraham said, joining the merriment of Prince, "I run and I ain't stop!"

"Rabbit what be two feet high and weigh two hundred pounds," Prince said, laughing. "That devilment must be the terriblest looking sight you ever saw!" He stopped laughing and wiped his face. "All right. I never rassel with rabbit box what be that big, but come back in an hour and your box'll be ready."

"Will you make it big?" Cart queried.

"Big enough to catch rabbit what's two feet high and weighs two hundred pounds," Prince said.

As Cart and Will left the building, Cart heard Prince say, "Some kinder rabbit!"

Will asked Cart if he thought it was a good idea to set a rabbit box on the Wagon Road and try to snare a wild hog.

"Of course," Cart snapped. "You heard Papa say that he didn't know how to catch the hog. We can do that for him."

Lunchtime came, and the boys came back to the house. Cart put Marmalade down in the hall, and the puppy ran to the other side of the room. A little past the midway point, Marmalade stiffened his legs and skidded the rest of the way. Mrs. Middleton called that lunch was ready.

Marmalade's food was put on a plate and carried back to the pantry. In the dining room, Cart and Will and Mr. and Mrs. Middleton dined on chicken cooked in batter, rice, guinea squash, peas, and oysters. A pitcher of sweet milk and a bowl of yellow butter were on the table. Cart was pleased that his father was having lunch with the family, as he didn't come home in the middle of the day very frequently. The huge rice fields near the Waccamaw River needed his attention. But as Cart thought about it, his father had always come home for lunch on his birthday.

After the main course was finished, Mrs. Middleton said, "Now for dessert." She got up and went to the pantry. When she came back she carried a high, four-layer cake that was covered in soft, white icing. Red berries decorated the top.

"Looka!" Will yelled. "Man!"

"Oh boy!" Cart said. "Cut that cake."

Mrs. Middleton took a knife from the rack on the sideboard and cut two pieces of cake, adding a little extra icing and berries. She served Cart and Will. After that, she sliced two smaller pieces for her husband and herself. Will's and Cart's eyes met over mouthfuls of cake.

After lunch, Cart and Will went back to the carpenter shop. The big box had been completed and was sitting in a corner of the building.

"Oh boy!" Cart exclaimed. "It's ready."

Prince lifted one side of the box and let sawdust that had collected on the top slide off. "How you gonna move this thing?" he asked.

"I don't know," Cart said, thinking that he hadn't thought about that. Just how *was* he going to move such a heavy box to the Wagon Road? The box was a secret, and he didn't want his father to know about it. If he found someone who could help him, it would have to be a person that would not come into contact with Mr. Middleton.

Just then Cart heard a wagon scraping and clanging. He ran outside and saw Gabe, holding the reins on two oxen. Gabe would be the person to move the box, Cart thought. Mr. Middleton rarely saw Gabe.

"Gabe," Cart called, "today's my birthday. Will you give me a present?"

"Don't know nothing 'bout what you say," Gabe answered.

"Today's my birthday, and I need you to haul a big rabbit box to the Wagon Road. Will you do it?"

"I going to Wagon Road to find one or two plum on the tree," Gabe explained.

"Then you can take the rabbit box," Cart said. He turned to Prince. "Put the box on Gabe's cart." As Prince lifted the heavy box, Cart said, "Thank you, Prince. This is a perfect birthday present."

Cart grabbed Marmalade and he and Will climbed onto the wagon. Prince hoisted the box up, and said, "I spec you to catch a rabbit what's two feet high and weighs two hundred pounds."

"We'll catch something that big, and you can count on it," Cart, sitting on a board with Will and Gabe, answered.

The oxen moved so slowly that Cart was worried that his father might see him on the wagon with the big box. The last thing in the world he wanted his father to know was that he and Will had slipped to the Wagon Road and rigged up a trap-box to catch the wild hog. When the hog was safely in the box, then he would show it to his father.

Finally, the oxen pulled the wagon around a curve

and Cart relaxed a little. They now were out of sight of the mansion.

"Stop!" Cart yelled. He handed Marmalade to Will and hopped down. "I see some tracks. Gabe, can you pull the box off the wagon?"

"I fix it," Gabe answered. He climbed down and went to the back and slid the box off the vehicle. "This be the place?" Gabe asked.

"Pull it over here," Cart said, motioning to some tracks obviously made by an animal.

Will put Marmalade down and he walked around the trap-box. Cart observed it too. It had been perfectly made. There were probably no finer craftsmen in the South Carolina Low Country than Prince and Abraham. The box was oblong, and on one end there was a trap door that was pulled up and attached to a trigger near the back of the box. Cart stooped down and looked in the door, which was facing the road in order to lure the hog. "Come here, Will."

"What are you going to do?"

"I'm pushing my hand in the box. Now watch. The door is being held up by the string that is attached to the trigger. See what happens when I tap the trigger." Cart rammed the trigger with his hand, and the trigger, which was a long piece of wood about the length of two pencils and as big around as four, flew up. The trigger loosened the right string that had held it in place, the slack string no longer held up the door, and the door slid down.

"See!" Cart exclaimed. "It's working." He reset the trap. Will tried out the box. As his brown hand moved through the open door and touched the trigger, it flew up and the door banged down.

"Will, we need to bait this box," Cart said. "The

hog won't be tempted to go inside unless he smells or sees food."

"What do hogs like?" Will asked.

"I don't know, but I bet they like corn. Papa feeds his other hogs corn."

"I've got to go home for supper in a minute, and I can go by the corn crib and get an ear of corn," Will said.

"Let me get the corn," Cart said. "I'm afraid someone will see you in the corn crib and get suspicious."

Cart and Will went to their homes for supper, and Mrs. Middleton fixed Marmalade's supper and took him to the pantry. Marmalade was getting used to eating in the pantry now.

During the meal, Cart had an opportunity to talk with his father. "How big is that wild hog?" he asked, although he knew the answer to the question.

"He's plenty big, son. As I told you and Will, he could be two feet high and weigh two hundred pounds."

"Do people eat wild hogs?" Cart asked.

"Yes. In England, hunting wild boar is a favorite sport. It's a sport of kings and nobles," Mr. Middleton answered.

"What do they do after they kill one?" Cart questioned.

"Sometimes the head is cooked, and it is brought into the dining room with great ceremony."

"The hog's head?"

"Oh, yes. Usually an apple is in the hog's mouth. It's an important ritual in England, a feast."

"If you, uh, if you kill that wild boar do you think we could have such a feast?" Cart asked.

"I don't see why not. We've never done anything like that at this plantation, but perhaps we could start something, the beginning of a yearly banquet featuring a wild boar's head."

"Yippee," Cart squealed. "Papa, I want you to get that boar."

"That is precisely my intention," Mr. Middleton answered.

"I'm fairly stuffed," Cart said. "And it's early. May I go outside and play with Marmalade?"

"Of course," Mrs. Middleton said. Just then Marmalade ran into the dining room. Cart grabbed him, and they left the house. Cart slipped to the back of the mansion, and made his way to the corn crib, where he took an ear of corn from a bin. When Cart and Marmalade reached the rabbit box at the Wagon Road, Will was waiting for them.

Cart put Marmalade down. "Don't run away," the boy said. Then Cart put the ear of corn at the very back of the box and set the trap door.

Suddenly there was a great snort. Cart jerked his head around at the same moment the wild hog burst from the woods. The animal's head was down, and he was grunting with the most ferocious sound. White tusks came from the menacing face. There was no question that the creature was savage. Besides that, he seemed so angered his blood must have been boiling.

"Run, Will. There's the hog!"

"Climb a tree, Cart," Will shrieked.

"Where's Marmalade?"

"I don't know, but get up a tree before you get killed!"

The hog eyed Cart, and picked up speed. The grunts were now more menacing.

"HELP! The hog's after me!" Cart yelled.

"Climb a tree," Will screamed. The closest tree to Cart was a holly, and the leaves had stickers on them, stickers that were as sharp as needles. *I can't climb that tree,* Cart was thinking, his eyes searching for another tree to get into. He didn't have a second to lose. The hog was getting closer—the snorts were louder and nearer.

Cart looked around for his friend and couldn't see him. "Where are you, Will?"

Will yelled from a loblolly pine tree, on the opposite side of the road. "I'm here, Cart, but hurry. The hog's right behind you."

Suddenly, Cart saw an oak tree, with low-hanging limbs. He fairly jumped toward it. Only a few more steps and he would be there.

Unexpectedly, the hog appeared between Cart and the oak tree. "Oh, no!" Cart cried. "HELP! Somebody help me."

"Cart," Will called, "there's another tree, over there." He pointed to a nearby oak tree.

Cart turned his direction and hoped from the depths of his heart that he could make it to the tree. He was spreading his legs out as far as he could to make big steps. Then he leaped to the tree. His arms and legs worked frantically to get him up high enough that the wild hog would not be a threat. Finally, he reached a limb that stretched out, and he worked his belly on that limb. "I'm so tired. And I'm so afraid."

"Hang on," Will called. "We'll have to stay here until the hog leaves."

"But it's late," Cart answered. "It's almost dark. What'll Papa do to me when he finds out?"

"You'd better watch that hog," Will cautioned.

"I've got to go home," Cart said. "My parents are probably looking for me."

"If the hog goes inside the box, we can leave," Will said.

"I'm hoping he'll go in the box. I'm really wishing that with all my heart," Cart said.

Cart didn't take his eyes off the hog. Its snout was rooting in the sand near the box. The hog seemed to be hungry. Cart was glad the hog hadn't caught up with him, as Mr. Middleton had said many times that wild animals are brutal.

Something moved in the woods. Cart, his arms around the limb, wiggled around to get a glimpse of it. What could it be? Then he saw it. There in the woods, Marmalade was walking on dead leaves and pine needles. He didn't appear to be aware of any danger.

"Marmalade," Cart called. "Go back. Go into the woods." But Cart knew that Marmalade didn't hear him. Marmalade was coming out of the woods right where the hog was rooting in the sand with his snout. Just at that moment, the hog started toward the dog.

"Run, Marmalade," Cart called. "Run for your life. That hog's going to eat you!" Cart started down the limb toward the trunk of the tree.

"What are you going to do?" Will called.

"I don't want the hog to kill Marmalade."

"But if you climb down the tree, the hog will kill

you!" Will screeched. "Get out of the way, Marmalade," Will yelled.

The dog still had no sense of danger. He walked over to the big box and nosed the front. The hog was just inches away.

"Oh, Will," Cart cried, "the hog is going to eat Marmalade."

"Marmalade," Will screamed, "get away."

Just then Cart had an idea. "Go in the box, Marmalade," Cart called. Then Cart yelled to Will. "If Marmalade goes inside the box, and the trap door slams down, Marmalade will be caught in the box and the hog can't get him."

"Get in the box, Marmalade," Will called. "Go in! Go in!"

Marmalade sniffed the box, but he was not fond of corn. Cart waited, his breath coming in short gasps. "I wish Marmalade would just amble in."

"He might do that," Will answered.

"Will, I'm going down the tree and push Marmalade into the box," Cart said. "I can beat the hog back to the tree. He won't get me."

"Don't do it! The hog'll attack you," Will cautioned.

"I don't want him to attack me, but I don't want him to eat Marmalade either."

Just then the hog rushed up beside the puppy. Marmalade jumped back and yelped. The hog snorted. "Marmalade, RUN!" Cart yelled.

"Get away, hog! Get away, hog!" Will screamed.

Marmalade edged up beside the open door without realizing it.

"Cart, look," Will said. "I believe Marmalade is

going inside without knowing it. He's about to *back* in the door!"

"But he still has to go back as far as the trigger in order to drop the door," Cart explained. "Oh, Will, wouldn't it be awful if the hog and Marmalade both went into the box? Oh, mercy, I wish we'd never had Prince build this box."

"If Marmalade goes inside the hog can come after him, and then the trigger could lower the door and trap them both," Will said, as if he just now realized that the worst was yet to come.

"Will," Cart yelled, "I'm coming down. I'm not going to let that hog eat Marmalade."

"Don't, Cart! Think of King Robert and your mammy. They love you."

"I'm a big boy," Cart reasoned. "I can go down and get the hog's attention, and make him start after me. Then I can shinny back up the tree in a hurry."

"What good will that do?" Will asked.

Cart thought about that. "Will, I need you to help me. After I get the hog's attention, and he starts coming after me, you throw Marmalade in the box and trigger the door."

"Do you think we can do that?" Will asked.

"I'm willing to try," Cart answered. "Are you?"

Will felt that he wasn't as ready to try it as Cart, but they were best friends. Friends had to help one another, and Marmalade needed help. "I will if you will," Will promised.

"Wait," Cart called. "Look at the hog. He's going to go after Marmalade. We're not going to have time to get the hog's attention."

The hog gave a huge snort and lunged toward

Marmalade. But the puppy jumped out of the way in the nick of time. The hog snorted at the corn and now was filled with a new interest. He rumbled inside the box.

"Look, Will, the hog has smelled the corn. He's going to the back of the box after it."

"Yes. Get back, Marmalade."

A side of the hog's head hit the trigger and it flew to the top of the box and the door slammed down.

Will fairly jumped to the ground, and Cart slid down the oak tree. Cart ran to Marmalade and picked him up. The puppy looked startled. "Marmalade, are you wondering what's going on?" Cart asked.

"Call King Robert," Will said. "Tell him to bring his gun."

Just then the hog began to bellow and snort and he pushed himself against the sides of the box. He went from one end of the box to another, charging the door.

"Oh," Will said. "He's going to get out. Let's go."

"Come on."

The boys flew toward the mansion. Cart, carrying Marmalade, was in the lead.

When they had darted through the woods and came out in the clearing, Cart saw his mother, in the yard. "Cartrette," she called as she spied him. "Where in the world have you been?" Not waiting for him to answer, she added, "I've been looking everywhere for you."

"Where's Papa?" Cart called breathlessly. "Get Papa and tell him to bring his gun."

"Forever in the world why?"

"We caught the wild hog," Cart called.

"He's in a rabbit box," Will added.

Mrs. Middleton opened her arms and caught Cart and Marmalade as they flew to her. "Oh I'm so glad to see you," she said. "But what is this about the wild hog?"

"We caught him in a rabbit box. Prince made me a rabbit box for my birthday, and Will and I wanted to surprise Papa."

"Are you saying that you and Will trapped the wild hog?" she asked, pushing Cart back so she could look at him.

"Marmalade helped too," Cart said.

"Is all of this true, Will?" Mrs. Middleton asked.

"Yes, ma'am. It be true," Will answered.

Mr. Middleton heard the commotion, and he came around a side of the house.

"Papa," Cart called. "We've trapped the wild hog."

"Bring your gun, King Robert," Will yelled.

After talking with Cart and Will, Mr. Middleton went back to the mansion and got his gun. Cart and Will begged to go back to the Wagon Road and watch the shooting, but Mr. Middleton wouldn't allow it.

"You two come inside with me," Mrs. Middleton said. Cart, still carrying Marmalade, followed his mother into the house. Will came too. As they went into the hall, Cart put Marmalade down, and he ran across the waxed pine floor, then stiffened his legs and slid the rest of the way.

"How would you like to have another piece of cake?" Mrs. Middleton asked Cart and Will. They looked at each other and licked their lips. She knew what that meant.

"And you?" Mrs. Middleton asked Marmalade. She went to the pantry and cut three pieces of cake. Marmalade was at her heels, and he began nibbling the cake as soon as she placed it before him.

Just then there was the sound of a gunshot in the distance. Will and Cart looked at each other. Without saying a word, they communicated the message that the wild hog had been killed. They ate the cake in silence. After awhile, Mr. Middleton walked to the doorway. He was so tall he almost filled up the entrance. "Cart and Will, I thought I told you boys not to go to the Wagon Road. You disobeyed me."

Cart thought his heart came to his throat. Will looked lonely and afraid.

"Well," Mr. Middleton continued, "I'm glad you figured out how to catch that hog. I couldn't have worked it out better myself." He laughed heartily.

"You're not angry with us, Papa?" Cart asked.

"I'm disappointed in you," Mr. Middleton explained. "I asked you not to do something and you did it anyway."

"Papa," Cart said, "we've already suffered enough. You'll never know how I felt when I was in the tree and that hog started after Marmalade. Just before the hog went into the box, I was starting to come down that tree and rescue my puppy."

"You were coming down from the tree?" Mr. Middleton asked.

"Yes. And I was going to get the hog's attention, and Will was going to throw Marmalade in the box and trigger the door and shut it."

Mr. Middleton began to laugh. "You boys certainly had everything figured out." He laughed some more, and he thought about the possibility of finding Will and Cart in trees and Marmalade in the rabbit box, and the wild hog snorting about. Mr. Middleton turned to Will. "How would you like to have supper with us tomorrow night?"

"Oh, Papa," Cart said. "Please invite Will to eat with us tomorrow night."

"I'd be happy 'bout that," Will answered.

"That is," Mr. Middleton said sternly, "if the two of you don't get into any mischief tomorrow."

"Oh we won't, Papa," Cart promised.

The next night, Mr. and Mrs. Middleton and Cart and Will sat at the table in the dining room. Marmalade was eating his meal in the pantry.

Cart looked at the food on the table. There were beans and tomatoes and hot rolls. All of that smelled so good, and he was starving.

Just then Mr. Middleton got up and excused himself. After a moment, he stood in the doorway, a massive silver tray in his hands. On the tray was the boar's head. The eyes were open and an apple was clinched in the sharp teeth. Native greenery decorated the tray, around the boar's head.

"This is the first of our annual boar's head feasts," Mr. Middleton said. "But next year, *I* want to have the pleasure of capturing the animal."

"That sure be the truth," Will said.

"If ever I heard it," Cart answered.

THE HAUNTED
CHAPEL

DID YOU HEAR that, Will?"

"Yes. That be the bell in the chapel."

"Who do you think rang that bell?" Cart asked.

"I don't know. Do you?"

"They say it's a ghost. There's a ghost that rings the bell in the chapel," Cart said. He thought about the ghost a minute, then asked, "Would you be afraid to go to the chapel?"

"I don't believe there is no ghost in the chapel," Will said, a little weakly. He wasn't absolutely sure that he didn't believe in ghosts.

"There must be an explanation for the bell ringing," Cart said. "If we went to the chapel, we could probably solve the mystery. Are you brave enough to go there?"

"I might go," Will said. He was thinking that he was afraid to go to the haunted chapel, but if Cart was brave enough to go, he didn't want to be a coward. In his mind he was thinking about the chapel

55

and wondering what it looked like. "What about that old chapel? Did it once be a church?"

"Papa said many years ago, before he built the chapel that Dr. Glennie preaches in when he comes to Midcliffe, the old-timey people built a little church by Chapel Creek. Nobody uses it today. Except the ghost that rings the bell."

"What does that chapel look like?" Will asked.

"I've never seen it," Cart answered. "But I'm willing to go over there and take a look. If we are afraid of the ghost we can run away fast!"

In his mind, Will pictured himself running away from the old church and telling his family that he had seen a ghost. They would think he was special if he had seen the ghost that rang the chapel bell. "Let's go," he said.

Cart flew off in the direction of the forest, and Will followed. Marmalade was running behind. "What is the church made of?" Will called out.

"Tabby," Cart called back.

"What is tabby?" Will asked. All he would think of was a striped cat.

"It's a construction material of sand, burned oyster shells, and water. Tabby is hard and concrete," Cart explained.

"Have I ever seen tabby?" Will asked.

"That old round water cistern near the stableyard is made of tabby," Cart explained. "A long time ago rain water was stored in the cistern. But now Papa has a good well. It's called an artesian well."

"Why is it called that?"

"Because the water that comes from deep in the ground is called artesian water. It's clear and good."

"Why is it better than other water?" Will didn't think he had ever heard of artesian water.

"Because the well is deep-bored and Papa says artesian water rises under pressure."

"I'm glad we get our water from your artesian well," Will said.

"Papa says everybody needs a well, and there are a lot of old wells on the plantation."

"Where are they?" Will asked.

Cart stopped running, and Will caught up with him. "I don't know where they are. I suppose they are where people once lived."

"Would there have been a well at the chapel?" Will asked.

"Yes. The old-timey people had to have water when they went to church. I'm sure a well was there."

"What do they look like?"

"Papa says they are holes in the ground, and he told me to be careful and never fall into one. But he said some of the old wells have filled up with leaves and rubbish. Just the same, I'm supposed to watch out for them."

"Let's go," Will said, taking off into a run. Before long, they had come to the forest, and vines and bushes covered the ground. Cart called Marmalade and picked him up. "You can't walk here," he said. "We'd lose you in the bushes."

"I can't walk so fast," Will said. "Some of these bushes be nearly as high as I be."

Just then from across the ravine the sound of a church bell rang out. Cart gasped, and Will stopped walking. "What was that?" Will asked.

"It was the chapel bell," Cart said. "You know

that was the chapel bell. You've heard it before."

"I know. But I'm scared. Do you think the ghost rang it?"

"Are you a fraidy-cat?" Cart asked.

"No," Will answered shakily. "But what if we see that ghost?" He knew that he *was* a fraidy-cat but he didn't want to admit it.

"We'll run home faster than we ever ran in our lives if we see that ghost," Cart said reassuringly.

"What does a ghost look like?" Will questioned.

"I don't know. I've never seen one. But if we see the bell, and it starts to ring, we'll know that the ghost is there. C'mon, Will."

Finally, the boys came out of the woods into a clearing. "Let's run," Cart said, dashing off, still carrying the puppy.

Will caught up with him. "When we get to the chapel, if the bell rings, I'm going to run home as fast as I can," Will admitted. "I'm not going to wait for you and Marmalade."

"We'll be in front of you," Cart laughed.

"How much farther?" Will called out.

"Not much," Cart answered. "Keep running."

When Cart and Will reached another forest, they picked their way through briars and a jungle of tropical growth. Sharp-pointed Spanish sword jutted out of the leaves and vines. Palmettoes grew among the oaks, pines, laurels, and magnolia trees.

"Watch out, Will," Cart called back. "Here's a ditch." Cart carefully climbed down one incline, and as he climbed up another, Will came down the hill behind him. Flies, gnats, and other insects were swarming around their heads, and they constantly swatted at bugs.

"What's that over there?" Will asked as he rubbed his eyes.

"It's an old bridge, but it has fallen down," Cart said.

"I'm not going to try to walk on that," Will said, "as it looks splintery."

"Not only that," Cart added, "but we've just seen our first snake of the day." A black snake was slithering over an ancient log that had once been a part of the bridge.

The woods were darker now, as the trees met overhead and the sun couldn't shine through fully. Only shafts of sunlight penetrated the cover of foliage, and the boys slowed their progress. They were on the lookout for snakes and were giving attention to their every step. Suddenly Cart and Will caught their breath. From somewhere ahead came the sound of a cry. "What was that?" Cart asked.

"I don't know. It sounded weird. Oh my, it be scary."

"Don't be so chickenhearted," Cart growled. "It's just an animal."

"Do you think it be a bear?" Will asked.

"No. It's not a bear, but I don't know what it is."

"Is the animal in trouble?" Will asked.

"It could be."

"Looka!" Will screamed. "A cemetery."

"Drat!" Cart looked at the scene before him as though his eyes could scarcely take it in. Cypress trees with no leaves protruded from a swampy place that was covered with ancient gravestones. Spanish moss hung from the grotesque cypress limbs, making the burial ground eerie and ghostly. In the cover of gray cypress and Spanish moss, a blue haze seemed to be hanging over the symbols of death. Gnarled and deformed cypress limbs extended forward and outward like phantoms.

"It be spooky," Will said. "I'm going back."

"I know about this place," Cart said, slowly and with awe. "It's an old graveyard where the old-timey people who worked on this plantation buried their dead. I've heard Papa talk about this place. He said some of the old markers are of wood."

"Are you going to look at them?" Will asked.

"Of course. I'm not afraid." But as he heard his words, Cart knew that he *was* afraid. Gazing at the hideous and grisly spectacle, he realized that the earlier mood of adventure had now been overtaken by a sense of discovery. Some of the ancient markers were of wood, and they were cracked and half-covered with mold. None of them sat straight; they leaned this way and that. Cart walked toward one of the markers, wondering if it had been inscribed with a name.

"Can you read anything on those gravestones?" Will shouted.

"I'm trying," Cart said, easing Marmalade to the ground. He wiped off some green mold.

"What does it say?"

"One word," Cart called. "Pompeii."

"Who was that?" Will asked.

"Just somebody who was buried here!"

Nearby was a stone that had been engraved with a man lying under a fallen tree. "It's clear that this man lost his life when a tree fell on him," Cart explained.

Will was braver now, and he ventured into the old

cemetery. A quiet, mopy feeling came to him as he stepped among the old stones that marked the resting places of the people who had died maybe even a hundred years before. He was thinking that he had been to a few cemeteries and had never taken the time to look at the markers. But Cart seemed to be loving every minute of looking at them. He was reading one now.

"Look, Will, this one says 'Le Baron of France.' " Cart stood back and stared at the marker. It had been carved in the shape of a nobleman, in knee britches and buckled shoes. The hair looked to be a wig. As he took it in, he remembered hearing his father talk about it. Cart's eyes went as big as saucers as he yelled, "Hey, I know about this one. Look at it."

"What do you know?"

"Papa said many years ago a ship docked on the Waccamaw River. The mates carried off a man who had yellow fever. They asked the owner of this plantation to help the man and restore his health. They promised to come back and get him when he was well."

"Did they come back?" Will asked.

"No. The ship was never seen again. But before they left, one of the mates left enough funds to pay for a burial should the man die. And the mate said the man had been a baron in France."

"What was the man's name?"

"Nobody knew. That's why they inscribed the stone 'Le Baron of France.' "

"Are you going to tell King Robert you saw the marker?" Will asked.

"I think so," Cart answered, wondering if he should let his father know that he and Will had come so deep into the forest.

"Looka here, Cart," Will called, pointing to a small grave with a tiny marker. "What does it say?"

Cart fell down on his knees and took a stick and scraped mold from the marker. "I believe this is the grave of a baby," he said. "It's too small to be a man or woman." After he had wiped the marker, he read, "Mariah, Life stole away without warning."

"She musta died in a hurry," Will said.

"Must have."

"Say, Cart," Will said, "don't ghosts come from cemeteries?"

"That's what they say." Cart got up quickly. "A ghost is supposed to be the spirit of a dead person."

Just then the sound of the animal resounded in the woods.

"That be some kinda animal," Will said. "Or could it be a ghost?"

"Don't get scared! It probably is an animal that's been hurt."

"I'm for getting away from this cemetery," Will said. "That ghost what rings the chapel bell might come out of one of these graves."

"You could be right," Cart concluded. "Let's look at the chapel. It is not far away from here."

As the boys hurried from the bluish grotto, gnats flew at their eyes and mouths, and they were constantly fighting insects. "How much farther?" Will asked.

Just at that moment the chapel bell rang out

loudly. "We're almost there," Cart said. "That bell is beyond the next stand of trees."

Excited now, the boys flew ahead, going toward the sound of the bell that had just sounded. Suddenly, Cart stopped. "Will," he whispered, holding a finger to his mouth to indicate quietness, "come here."

"What is it?"

"The chapel!"

"Where?" Will asked.

"Over there, in the thicket."

Remains of a tabby structure were all but covered in vines. A fallen tree had knocked down half of the roof, and the door was completely covered in thick, lush growth. Cart wondered where the bell was. The roof was mostly fallen and there was no steeple. He was speechless and Will seemed unable to utter a sound. Just then, the bell clanged in their ears. Cart rubbed his ears. "That shrill sound almost deafened me," Cart said, shaking his head and again rubbing his ears.

"It be squally, all right," Will said. Just then he broke into a run. "I'm leaving. A ghost from the cemetery just rang that bell!"

"Come back here!" Cart howled.

Will stopped running. "I don't wanta go near the chapel," he whined. Looking apprehensive, he inched back toward Cart. "Do you see the ghost?"

"I believe something is up there in that old wood tower," Cart murmured.

"Where?"

Cart thrust a finger toward the treetops. "Up there in the tower."

Will's heart was beating furiously. He thought he had never been so afraid in his life, and he wanted Cart to agree to go home. They didn't really need to see a ghost. "Let's go!"

"Wait a minute," Cart mumbled. "I'm going to walk around the bell tower and look it over."

Will and the dog looked on as Cart picked his way through undergrowth and vines, stopping now and then and gazing up to the bell. Finally, he had made his way around the bell tower. Again he looked upward, his eyes taking in every detail of the bell. Slowly, he froze with fear. *Something in the tower moved.* With Cart's eyes plastered on the bell, again the cry of an animal split the quietness of the woods.

"I'm not staying," Will screamed.

Cart's attention had been snatched from the tower to a place beyond the church. He walked past the old tabby building with oyster shells protruding from the walls. He stopped. For a moment he was deathly quiet. Finally he called, "Will, come over here."

"I'm not coming over there!"

"Yes you are. An animal has been hurt!"

"What kind of animal?"

"I don't know, but there's a six-foot-wide hole in the ground, and an animal has fallen in."

Will eased himself through some prickly vines and peered at the hole.

"I can't see down inside," Cart said, as he pulled some briars from his shirt. "I'm going around to the other side."

"How deep is the hole?" Will asked.

"So deep that I can't see the animal inside." Cart

stopped and thought about the hole. "I believe this is an old abandoned well."

"Would it be the one the old-timey people who worshipped at this chapel used?" Will asked.

"Yes." Cart surveyed the church ruins and the well. "This is the perfect place for their well to be located. I'm sure of it. This is an old well."

Will cleared the way as he gingerly walked to the far side of the well. Cart was looking inside. Luckily for them, the sun slanted through the trees and a shaft of light extended into the well.

Deep inside, a furry brown animal with white spots moved. "It's a deer!" Cart yelled. "We've got to get him out."

"How you gonna do that?" Will asked, still eyeing the small animal.

Cart's eyes went one way and then another. He spotted a fallen tree. "Help me move that tree."

"What you gonna do?" Will asked as he lifted one end of the tree. He wasn't so scared now that he was becoming interested in rescuing the tiny deer.

"I'm going to put the tree in the well," Cart explained, "and then I'll go down and try to lift the deer and pull him up."

"How do you know it be a 'him'?" Will questioned.

"I don't know that. It might be a doe, and that's a her."

"What you donna do with that deer?"

"Take it home and have a new pet."

"Oh, boy!" Will shouted. "Let's get the deer out of the hole. What you gonna name him?"

"I don't know that yet, Will. Right now I've got to get him out of the hole." Cart moved his end of the tree to the hole and yelled, "PUSH!" Will pushed his end and Cart guided the tree into the old well. The very instant the tree was in place, Cart shinnied down. "Oh, Will, he's so lovable."

"You sound like your head be in a drum," Will called down.

"And so do you! Will, hold the tree and steady it. I'm bringing up the deer."

Will put both arms around the tree and hugged it. As Cart started up, the tree moved slightly, and Will held it tighter to his chest. He could feel Cart coming up, and he pictured him holding the deer. Just then the bell in the tower rang out. Will turned loose of the tree and ran. The tree moved away from the side of the hole, and Cart, holding the deer, fell back into the hole.

"Will!" Cart screamed. "Don't leave me now. I can't get out if you don't help me."

Will was so frightened that he didn't think of Cart and the deer. He did think of Marmalade, who had been standing beside the well. "Come here, Marmalade." Will grabbed the puppy and flew toward home.

"Will, please come back," Cart called. "The tree isn't steady, and I'm sliding back down every time I try to climb up. Please come back."

Will, carrying Marmalade, was fleeing, trying his best to remember the way home. When he came to the cemetery, he knew that he was on the right track. But he was suddenly afraid that the ghost who rang the chapel bell was the spirit of someone who had been buried in the cemetery. He sprinted well away from the burial ground. After a few minutes, he wondered if he had made a wrong turn. Nothing looked familiar. He couldn't see the abandoned bridge, and he didn't know where the ditch was. It came to him that he was losing his bearings and was getting lost in the forest. He stopped and took everything into account. He *had* left Cart in a bad place, at the bottom of the well. He'd go back to get Cart.

Will turned around and around, and he discovered that he didn't know in which direction he should walk. Trees were all around him, and they all looked the same. Oh, what will I do, he was thinking. Cart needs me and I can't find him. Why did I ever leave him? I won't leave him again. Will was about to cry, when the chapel bell rang, giving him the true direction to the chapel. Will was so glad that the ghost had rung the bell and showed him the way back to Cart and the deer. In his heart of hearts he would rather see a ghost than be lost in the forest and probably never be found. Besides that, he couldn't leave a friend in such a dangerous place. When Will and Marmalade got back to the old well, Cart was still calling him.

"I'm here, Cart. I came back." Will peered down in the hole.

"Hold that tree and get me out of here," Cart said, annoyed at Will for the first time in his life. Cart was hot and sweaty and bugs were about to eat him up, he thought.

Will put Marmalade down and again hugged the tree to his chest. Cart started up, carrying the deer. Will could see the top of Cart's head. Finally, Cart was near the top. He handed the deer to Will, and

Will pulled him to safety. Cart scrambled the last few steps. "Whew!" he said. "I thought I wasn't going to make it. Why did you run away?"

"I be so afraid I didn't know what to do. I wanted to go home. I'm sorry."

"Oh, forget it," Cart snapped, now looking at the little animal. The deer was trying its best to stand up on four legs, but they buckled, and the fluffy brown and white deer fell to the ground.

"He's hurt," Will said.

"Sure he's hurt. You'd be hurt too if you had fallen into an abandoned well," Cart said. Then he realized he had spoken unkindly to his best friend, and was sorry. "I'll forget you left me if you'll help me carry the deer home," Cart promised.

"Let's go," Will said.

"I think I can carry him, but you'll have to help," Cart said. "But I'm tired. Why don't we sit under a tree for a little while?"

Cart's forehead and cheeks were red. He was hot and so exhausted. He took deep breaths as he stroked the deer's head. "I feel almost like taking a nap," he said.

"Put your head on the moss," Will urged, pointing to a clump of soft green moss at the foot of the tree.

Cart stretched out and closed his eyes. He couldn't remember when he had been more tired. He almost fell asleep when all of a sudden the chapel bell rang so loudly it jarred him to his feet. He looked up at the bell in the tower. Then he held his breath. *Something was moving up there.*

"I see something in that tower," Will whispered. "Is it the ghost?"

"If it's a ghost," Cart said, "it has eyes."

"A ghost has eyes?" Will asked.

"No. But that thing in the tower has eyes. I can see them."

Will looked as hard as he could, and he saw the eyes. "They be the blackest eyes I ever saw," he said.

"Will," Cart said, as everything was being revealed to him, "there's no ghost that rings the bell. Those are raccoons, and they have a nest up there."

As the boys' eyes searched the bell tower, a furry raccoon climbed out of the nest, which was just under the bell. As he went from the nest to a limb of a hickory tree, he bumped into the clapper, suspended inside the bell cup. A chime sounded and reverberated throughout the forest.

"That's probably the mother, and she's going after food," Cart said.

"What do raccoons eat?" Will asked.

"More than likely they eat hickory nuts, from the hickory tree. But Papa says they can ruin a corn crop."

"Do they eat crawfish and frogs?" Will asked.

"I wouldn't be surprised," Cart said. "The creek is just over there." He pointed toward Chapel Creek.

"My pa has a coonskin cap," Will said, just as a tiny raccoon came out on the limb. "Oh, look! He be so little! He didn't ring the bell."

"His black eyes have white fur around them," Cart said. "And his tail is striped. He's looking at us!"

"You want to try to take him home?" Will asked.

"Papa says raccoons are friendly if kept as pets,"

Cart said, "but we don't need a raccoon. We've got a deer!" Cart stooped down, placed the deer across the back of his neck, and pulled its legs to his chest. "Will, can you watch out for Marmalade?"

"Come on, Marmalade," Will called. "We're going home."

"When we get home I'll tell Papa that no ghost rings the chapel bell," Cart said. "He'll be glad to know why that bell rings."

Cart walked as fast as he could, carrying the deer on his shoulders. Will, carrying Marmalade, followed. Cart slowed down when he reached the cemetery. Instead of stopping, he walked around the edge and hurried on.

"What'll you feed the deer?" Will asked.

"Probably oats. But he might eat things from the table like Marmalade does."

"Will your mother let you keep him in the house?"

Cart thought about Will's question. He pictured the huge house with the fine rugs and mahogany furniture and damask curtains. He didn't know what his mother would think about keeping a deer in the house. "I hope so," he said.

Just then the boys came to the ditch. Cart slowed down and looked at the ravine. He wondered how he would get the deer across.

Will put Marmalade down. "We'll carry the deer by the legs," he suggested.

"Good idea." Cart stooped down and let the deer slide from his shoulders. He took two of the legs and Will lifted the other two, and they carried the deer down one incline and up the other. When they had completed that task, they sat down and rested. Just then Marmalade barked. He was on the other side of the ravine.

"Oh my mercy!" Will cried. He ran down into the ditch and up on the other side where Marmalade stood, looking like he had been forsaken. Will grabbed him and carried him to the other side.

"I believe the deer is scared," Cart said. "He doesn't know how lucky he is that we rescued him. He'd have died if we hadn't found him."

"What are you going to name him?" Will asked.

Cart laughed. "You always want to know what I'm going to name my pets." He thought about it, and his mind went into a kind of reverie. He never in his life had known anyone who had a deer for a pet. What did people name deer? he wondered.

"What do you think be a good name?" Will prodded.

"Well," Cart said, "I have an aunt in Charleston who calls everybody 'dearie.' Why don't we name him 'Deerie'?"

"That be a fine name," Will said. "I like Deerie."

Cart jumped up. "Come on, Deerie, we're going home."

Cart and Will were weary as they approached the mansion. Cart was dragging his feet, with the burden of Deerie on his shoulders. Will carried Marmalade.

Mrs. Middleton was on the porch, and she saw the boys coming in the distance. She called her husband. Mr. and Mrs. Middleton ran to meet Cart and Will.

"Cartrette!" Mrs. Middleton said. "I've been looking everywhere for you. Where in the world have you been?"

"Your mother and I have been worried, son," Mr. Middleton said.

"Look at Deerie," Cart said, stooping down and allowing the animal to slide from his shoulders. "He's been hurt. He fell into an abandoned well."

"Where did you find him?" Mr. Middleton asked.

"We went to the chapel," Cart explained.

"Oh, no!" Mrs. Middleton shouted.

"It's all right," Cart explained quickly. "There isn't a ghost there. Some raccoons have a nest in the bell tower, and they bump against the clapper when they go in and out of the nest."

"Oh, what will you get into next?" Mrs. Middleton questioned.

"Papa, can I keep the deer for a pet? We've named him Deerie."

Mr. Middleton looked at his wife. "What do you think?"

"Does a deer *make* a pet?" she questioned. "I've never known anyone to have a deer for a pet."

"I've always heard that a small deer, if found when injured and nursed back to health, makes an excellent pet," Mr. Middleton said.

"Can I keep him?" Cart petitioned his mother. "Please let me keep Deerie."

She thought about it. Cart wondered what was going on in her mind. He couldn't tell by her face whether she would agree to keep the deer or not. "Please let me keep him," Cart begged.

"I hope Cart be able to keep that deer," Will

added. "We sure like to have a deer for a pet."

Finally, Mrs. Middleton smiled. "All right. We'll keep him in the back room and nurse him back to health. We can decide then whether to keep him or turn him back to the wild."

"Oh that's splendid," Cart said. He turned to Marmalade. "You've got a brother. His name is Deerie."

Mr. Middleton laughed. "You say there's no ghost at the chapel?"

"No," Cart said. "Raccoons ring the bell."

"Well," Mr. Middleton said as he winked to his wife, "I'm glad we don't have to worry about a ghost."

"We don't have a ghost to worry about," she answered, "but we have Deerie to nurse back to good health. Let's take him inside and introduce him to his new home."

"I know he be happy here," Will said. "It be better than an abandoned well."

Just then Mr. Middleton asked Will and Cart to come to the morning room in the mansion, a room that he used for his business matters. The boys followed him to the house and to the morning room.

Mr. Middleton sat at a tall secretary-desk. He looked straight at Cart. "Cartrette, I've asked you and Will to stay out of trouble. Moreover, I have asked you not to go near any abandoned well. You have no idea how dangerous such a well can be."

"I know, Papa, but I was helping you."

"How do you rationalize that?" Mr. Middleton asked.

"You always talked about the people saying a

ghost rang the bell at the chapel, and I wanted to find out if there was a ghost there. Now you know that no ghost rings that bell."

"That is true, but you still disobeyed me," Cart's father said, a stern look on his face.

"And Papa, we found Deerie. If we hadn't gone to the chapel, Deerie would have died."

"There is no doubt about that," Mr. Middleton said. "But the fact remains that you disobeyed me."

"But Papa, don't you want me to get to know the ways of the plantation? You said so yourself!"

Mr. Middleton got up and went to a window. He pulled back a curtain and looked out across the vast acreage toward the river. "Yes. I want you to learn the ways of the plantation, just as I did when I was your age. But you and Will have to start obeying me." He let go of the curtain and turned and faced Will and Cart.

"I'm sorry, Papa, but I thought I was helping you by identifying what rings the chapel bell."

"Well, be that as it may, it's almost time for the rice harvest. The field hands could use some help. I want you two to help carry the sheaves from the fields up to the stableyard."

"That be a heavy load," Will said.

"I think the two of you can manage it," Mr. Middleton said. "Cartrette, you are to report to me in the morning, and I will give you your task. I'm going to come down on you until you learn to obey me."

"Yes, Papa," Cart answered. "I'll help with the sheaves. Whatever task you give, I'll be glad to perform."

"You and Will are dismissed," Mr. Middleton said.

"Come on, Will, let's go see about Deerie."

THE HURRICANE

"DEERIE, IT'S ME," Cart said as he flew into the room where Deerie had spent the night. The small deer stirred and pulled himself up, but his legs wobbled and he fell down on his front knees and then lay down on the floor. Doleful, moist eyes looked at Cart with a hint of gratitude. Cart patted Deerie's head.

"Come on, Marmalade," Cart said. "Will's waiting on the porch."

Will was sitting on the top step and looking at the sky, which was perfectly clear.

"Will," Cart said, "I'm sorry Papa is punishing us and making us help carry rice sheaves up to stable-yard from the fields."

Just then Mr. Middleton came to the porch. He wore a three-piece suit, and of course, his boots. "Boys, now behave yourselves today and help carry sheaves to the stableyard. That's your task for dis-obeying me."

"Papa, are you not going to be here?" Cart asked.

"No. I've had a communication from my sister in Charleston, and she needs my help as soon as I can get there."

"Is that the aunt what calls everybody 'dearie'?" Will asked. "That's the one," Cart answered. Then he looked at his father. "But Papa, you're always here during rice harvest. Something important must be going on in Charleston."

"I don't know if you can understand it or not," Mr. Middleton replied, "but I have to go to the bank with her and sign a promissory note. If I don't sign the note, she will lose her Charleston mansion."

"How will signing the note help?" Cart asked.

"You know her husband died recently," Mr. Middleton explained as he motioned for a servant to fetch his carriage. "She is in debt. She cannot pay the mortgage on her property. But I have assets, and if I sign the note, then the bank will allow her to retain her property."

"That *is* important," Cart answered. "But don't worry. We'll see that the rice sheaves are all carried to the stableyard."

Mr. Middleton took his watch from a pocket and checked the time. "You boys have been getting into mischief lately. It's time you put a brake on some of that stuff and helped around the plantation."

"We'll help you, Papa. We'll try to do everything you would want us to do while you are gone."

"This is a tedious time," Cart's father said. "The rice has been cut by the women who work in the rice fields, and the plants are lying on the stubble in order to dry. They are dry now and the whole crop has to be on the racks in the stableyard by tonight."

Mr. Middleton eyed his son. "Cart, you know that it would be devastating if we should lose the rice crop. That would mean a whole year's work would go up in smoke. We *have* to get the rice in today so it can be flailed tomorrow."

"What do you mean by *flailing?*" Will asked.

"After the women use the circular hooks and cut the rice plants, the plants have to lie on the stubble for about twenty-four hours. That dries them out. Then the women go back into the fields and gather up the dried rice plants and tie them in bunches, and they carry them to the stableyard. The next day the rice is taken to the winnowing house and the product is flailed, or beaten until the grains are separated from the straw. The grain is packed in barrels and the straw is put on wagons and taken away to be used for food for some of the farm animals."

"There sure be a lot of things to be done to rice," Will said, shaking his head.

"It *is* a long process," Mr. Middleton agreed. "After the rice has been flailed, and we have the grain in barrels, we still have to remove the husks from the grain before the product is considered 'clean' enough to bring a high price."

Just then a groomsman pulled the carriage up to the foot of the steps. The driver, a man called "Daddy Thomas," was sitting on the box, holding the reins to four matching bay horses. A servant came from the mansion and tied Mr. Middleton's trunk to the top of the carriage. Mr. Middleton climbed into the carriage, and as it moved away, he waved through a back window.

"C'mon, Will," Cart said. "Let's go to the rice fields and get started with our work."

The boys ran to the Wagon Road, then through a forest, and they came out on a bluff that overlooked the Waccamaw River. For as far as they could see, women were working in the fields, grabbing armfuls of rice plants and tying them in bunches. Other women, coming from behind, picked up as many bunches as they could, and began the long walk to the stableyard. With the rice sheaves on their heads, only the legs and feet of the women could be seen. Golden rice plants hung over their heads, arms, and below their waists.

"Will," Cart asked earnestly, "did you see any animals standing in the Wagon Road?"

"I saw some deer," Will answered.

"There *were* deer, but I thought I saw some cows coming from the woods."

"So? What if you did?"

"It's a bad sign. The cows that have been turned into the forests only come out into the roadways if a hurricane is coming."

"But no storm be brewing today," Will said, pointing to the clear, blue sky.

Cart consulted the sky. "It *is* a sparkling day, and it doesn't look like a hurricane could be threatening. Still, the wildlife is acting funny."

"Do you want to go back and see?" Will asked.

"Yes."

"But King Robert said for us to carry rice sheaves today. He be angry if we don't do that."

"We're going to carry rice sheaves," Cart said. "But first I want to check on those animals. If a hurricane strikes while the rice is in the stableyard, the whole year's work will be ruined."

"What'll the storm do to the rice?"

"You know what a hurricane can do!" Cart fairly screamed. "It's awful. Papa said if one ever came while the rice was in the stableyard, the rice would be soaked with water, and the rice fields would be damaged if not washed out. All the work would be sacrificed."

"We better check on the animals," Will agreed.

The boys flew back to the Wagon Road and spotted a group of cows standing in the sandy lane. They seemed muddled and confused. Nearby three deer, also looking mixed up, stared toward the sky. Just then a rabbit hopped from the underbrush and sat near Cart's feet. "Will, I believe a terrible storm is coming and I must do something to help Papa. He said I'm the man of the plantation today."

"What are you going to do?"

"First of all I'm going to find Abraham and ask him if he will take me to see his mother. She's over a hundred years old, and she knows everything about storms and things."

"Can she tell you about such as that?" Will asked.

"Yes. She'll tell us what to do."

"Are you going to tell your mother about the animals coming out into the open spaces?"

Cart thought about that. Finally he answered, "No. My mother stays in the house much of the time, and she doesn't know the ways of the plantation like Papa. She wouldn't know what to do. I'm the man of the plantation today and I've got to prove that I'm worthy of the task."

Cart and Will ran back toward the mansion, and

as they darted along they spotted Abraham going from the carpenter shop toward his house. "There's Abraham," Cart said. "Let's take a shortcut and meet him near his house."

The boys were breathless when they met Abraham, and both of them talked, trying to tell him that they wanted to see his mother. Abraham motioned them on.

When they reached a row of identical cabins, Abraham went to one near the middle of the street. An ancient woman was in a rocking chair on the porch. Her hair hung down to her waist, and she had a pipe in her mouth. She smiled at Cart and Will. Abraham's mother had no teeth, and her gums were blue.

"Please answer a question," Cart begged of the old woman.

She looked at her son quizzically as she didn't understand what Cart had said. She spoke Gullah, a language native to the black people on South Carolina plantations. Abraham translated the message.

The old woman smiled broadly and shook her head to indicate yes. Cart explained that the animals were coming out of the woods into the roadways, and he believed a hurricane was approaching. It was crucial that he know immediately, because he would have to gather all the people on the plantation to help with the rice. Instead of carrying it to the stableyard, it would have to be stacked in the barn before the storm hit.

Abraham's mother looked at the sky. Then she said something to Abraham. He told the boys that his mother said she had seen a ring around the moon the night before. "Ring around the moon, rain come soon," Abraham stated.

She said something else. If the seagulls were flying inward, or high into the clouds and above them, it was a sign of a storm. She also indicated that she could not turn her wrists away from her body, and that always indicated a sudden weather change.

"Thank you," Cart called, flying toward the stableyard. Will was behind him. A groom reined a horse and helped Cart and Will climb on. They flew off in a cloud of sand.

Cart reined the horse to a stop at a salt marsh near the sea. As the ocean was two miles from the mansion, he felt he didn't have time to go all the way to the beach. From the salt marsh he could survey the sky over the sea. Clouds were moving in an unusual, circular motion. When he looked overhead, swarms of seagulls were flying inland.

"Look! Look at the seagulls. They're going inland, and that means a storm is coming."

"Looka!" Will shouted. "The clouds."

"The clouds are moving mysteriously," Cart said. "An east wind is blowing."

"How can you tell?"

"Papa showed me how to detect an east wind. And he said an east wind blows no man any good. It indicates a storm is coming from the south or southwest." In an instant Cart turned the horse and was flying back toward Midcliffe. Just then the wind began to moan. "That's the strangest sound," Cart observed. "I've never heard the wind sound like that before."

"Me neither," Will agreed.

Cart directed the horse past the mansion to the carpenter shop. "Prince! Abraham! Go quickly to the stableyard and get every wagon and cart available. Then go to the rice fields and help the women bring rice to the barn. Don't put the sheaves on the racks, but put them in the loft and the feed room, and anywhere else where there is room. But get the rice inside! A hurricane is coming!"

Prince and Abraham put down their work and left the carpenter shop at once. Cart and Will flew to the street of houses where the workers lived. They saw a man on an ox cart, pulling a load of wood that would be burned in his simple kitchen as he cooked his meals. "Turn around!" Cart screamed. "Get every man on the plantation and go to the rice fields. Remove the wood and pile rice sheaves on your cart and take it to the barn. Don't put the sheaves on the racks in the stableyard. PUT IT IN THE BARN. A HURRICANE IS COMING!"

Then Cart and Will ran to each house in the street and slapped the doors and yelled for the men to join their women in the rice fields and transport the rice to the barn. "A HURRICANE IS COMING!"

Back at the barn, Cart yelled to the grooms to go to the rice fields and help transport the rice to the barn. "GO!"

It seemed that all the men and women on the plantation, except for those who worked in the mansion, were working in the rice field by now. There was a continuous line of people carrying sheaves from the rice field to the barn. Others were piling sheaves on wagons and carts which were then driven to the barn. Someone had already removed the sheaves that had earlier been placed on the racks and had put them inside for protection. It seemed to Cart that everyone was working perfectly in the emergency, but little did he know.

A man named Gainey, a white man, marched up to Cart. "I'm the overseer here. Your pa named me overseer. What do you mean getting the people all stirred up? Them rice sheaves supposed to be hung on racks in the stableyard, not put in the barn."

"But Papa's not here today, and a hurricane's coming, Mr. Gainey," Cart replied.

"And just what makes you think a hurricane's coming?"

"I just know it's coming. The animals have come out in the roads. You can go to the Wagon Road and see them. The seagulls are flying inland. And an east wind is blowing."

Gainey frowned. "Let me tell you something. If you have all these people move the rice sheaves into the barn and no storm comes, me and your pa is gonna have a little talk."

"Yes sir. I expect we'll do that anyway, Mr. Gainey. Now get going and help us get the rice in the barn."

Cart took the horse to a bluff overlooking the rice field. "Will, the Waccamaw River is rising. If the tide doesn't turn soon, the field will be flooded. If any rice remains in any of the fields it will be ruined as all the fields will be under water. HURRY!" Cart called to those working in the nearest field. "THE TIDE'S RISING AND IT WILL COME OVER THE BANK. PLEASE HURRY!"

Just then there was earthquake-like thunder that rumbled overhead and shook the very earth.

"Hurry!" Cart shouted as he turned the horse around. He and Will took the horse back to the barn and they ran as fast as their legs would carry them toward the rice fields. As they came to a boggy place, they spotted Abraham and his mother, on a cart piled high with rice sheaves. Abraham's oxen had stopped at the boggy place and refused to budge. Abraham was shouting at them, but they wouldn't move. The sky was now black with clouds, and wind was bending trees over toward the ground. Just then Abraham's mother got off the cart and went to the oxen and spoke softly in their ears, urging them. An ox took a step forward, and then the other ox moved. Finally the wagon rolled forward.

Cart and Will flew into the rice field, grabbed a load of rice, and carried it to the barn. They couldn't move very fast as the rice was heavy and the wind was fierce. Cart, under the heavy load, listened to what the other people were saying. A man on his way back from the barn said, "I take thought in this storm." A woman answered, "I been have this dream about this storm. I see it in my dream. The beach dunes be washed away and the river tide rise and wash out all them rice field."

"Oh Will," Cart called from under the rice sheaf. "Did you hear that? That woman dreamed the rice fields washed away."

"Let them wash," Will called back. "King Robert be able to fix them back. But he can't fix the rice if we don't save it."

Finally they reached the barn, and Cart estimated that most of the rice had been stacked inside. It looked to be one of the largest crops he had ever seen. Just then his mother stuck her head in the barn. "Cartrette, come home. I believe a terrible hurricane is crashing on the plantation."

"I can't go home now," Cart called out. "I'm trying to save the rice crop and if I don't get it in the barn, it'll be destroyed."

"But I don't want *you* to be destroyed," his mother cried. "It's dark and getting darker all the time."

"Don't worry about me," Cart said. "When I think we have done all we can, I'll come home. But I believe we're almost finished."

Mrs. Middleton pulled a coat over her head and started walking toward the mansion. It was raining so hard she could hardly see. A woman came from the street of cabins and said that the street was flooded and water was gushing inside the small houses. Cart and Will ran in the wind back toward the rice fields. They met Prince on a wagon that was loaded skyhigh with rice sheaves. "This be the end," Prince said. "All rice be gone from the field." Cart and Will ran on to the field and saw that the Waccamaw River had risen over the bank and was now flooding the fields.

"All the rice been taken to the barn," Will said.

Cart sighed heavily. "It has been saved," he answered. "Let's go."

As they ran toward the mansion, Cart and Will noticed that the animals had moved to a side of the road, in order to allow the wagons to move by. But the livestock and wildlife had not gone back into the woods. The storm was still ahead.

"That Spanish moss swinging from the oak trees moan same like human," Will commented.

"It's moaning, all right," Cart agreed.

"That wind sure enough be spanking that moss," Will added.

Just then a man came running and said for all the field workers to go to the little plantation church. The people who lived and worked on the plantation were going to pray for their lives. The storm was so bad it could mean the end of the world, the man believed.

"Will," Cart said, "do you want to go to the mansion?"

"I be to my own house," Will answered.

"It's not really the end of the world, of course, but some of the big oaks are falling and the rice fields are being washed away. You can go to the mansion if you want to and wait for the hurricane to pass over."

Will didn't answer. He broke into a run for his own house. When Cart ran in the front door of the mansion, his mother hugged him so tightly he thought she was going to squeeze the breath out of his chest. "I don't know how you sensed the approach of such a terrible storm," Mrs. Middleton cried.

"When do you think Papa will return?" Cart asked.

"I don't know. Damage must be terrible all the way from here to Charleston. I doubt that the carriage can move very fast with many trees down."

After the storm, Cart and his mother assessed the damage to the plantation. Most fences were down, and many trees. Some of the small dwellings on the plantation had been damaged, and a part of the rice

fields had been washed away. On the side of the
plusses, no lives had been lost. All of the damage to
buildings could be repaired, and rice fields could be
restored. But best of all, the rice crop had been
saved. A year's work hadn't gone during the
hurricane.

Six days later Mr. Middleton returned from
Charleston. His clothes were soaked and he was exhausted. His horse seemed near death. Its head was
hanging down to its knees and foam dropped from
its mouth. A groom at once took the horse to the
barn to be treated.

After Mr. Middleton checked his family to see that
they were safe, Cart escorted him to the barn. As he
surveyed the enormous number of rice sheaves that
were stacked there, Mr. Middleton shook his head.
"Son, I couldn't have done any better myself. And
I'm totally surprised that all of the crop was saved. I
expected to come home and find a total loss of the
crop. You have learned the ways of the plantation,
not as I did, but much better."

CHRISTMAS EVE

CART AND WILL were playing near the stableyard when Mr. Middleton rode up and pranced his stallion to a stop. "Boys, I'm going into the forest for greenery to decorate the house for Christmas. Want to go?" As usual, Mr. Middleton had on his boots and a three-piece suit. A gold watch chain draped over his vest.

"Whoopee!" Cart said. "Are we going to get a Christmas tree?"

"Not today. We'll get that in a day or so. But your mother wants the house servants to start making ropes of greenery to drape on the staircase banisters."

"Let's go," Cart said, as he looked at Will, whose eyes were dancing in anticipation.

Mr. Middleton maneuvered his horse over to the boys, reached down and pulled Cart up. After he slid in front of his father, Mr. Middleton reached and grabbed Will's arm. Will pulled himself up and sat in front of Cart. The wind blew in their faces as they flew off toward the forest.

If there was one thing that Mr. Middleton knew how to do, it was ride his stallion. He was pushing the horse to its peak of endurance, and it was reaching its top speed as it fled across the field. Cart's face felt as though it was pulled back in a rigid mask, slanted eyes and all. Will's body pressed back against Cart.

As they approached the forest, Mr. Middleton slowed the horse. "We're looking for holly and cedar and mistletoe," he said. "I have a sack to carry it in."

"There be a pretty holly tree," Will called out.

"And it's a good one," Mr. Middleton answered. "It's full of red berries." He stopped the horse and slid off, then he helped Cart and Will slide down the side of the animal.

Mr. Middleton took a knife from a boot and cut several branches of holly that were full of red berries. "Now let's see if we can find a cedar tree." He climbed on his horse and pulled the boys up.

Deeper into the woods, some cedar trees grew close together, in a sort of thicket made by tall trees. Cart and Will pulled down branches which Mr. Middleton cut. He added them to the holly branches in the sack. "Have you boys spotted any mistletoe?" he asked as he threw a leg over the back of the horse.

Cart and Will were looking everywhere. Mistletoe grows as a parasite on the branches of various trees. It especially likes sycamore and poplar, among others, but it doesn't grow on every tree, and sometimes it is difficult to find. "There's some mistletoe, Papa," Cart said, "but it's too high to reach."

Mr. Middleton stopped the horse, and as they sat on its back, they surveyed the thickly clustered leaves with white shiny berries.

"You're right," his father said. "It's too high but it's a perfect specimen. Your mother would like that bunch of mistletoe. She'll probably tie it to the chandelier in the dining room."

"How are you going to reach it, Papa?"

"I'm not going to try. Tomorrow I'll have Gabe come over in the ox cart and he can cut the tree down. We can always use firewood, and he can bring wood and the mistletoe also."

"When are we going to get our Christmas tree?" Cart asked, as his father turned the horse toward home.

"If you see one that you like, let me know," Mr. Middleton said. "We want a cedar, and it has to be as high as the ceiling in the ballroom." The ballroom was a room that extended the width of the mansion. It was used only on special occasions. People still talked about George Washington visiting the plantation when he was on his tour of South Carolina in 1791, and he dined in the ballroom.

"That sure enough be a big tree," Will said. "A tree that reach the ceiling of the ballroom be a big tree, all right."

"I see one," Cart yelled. Mr. Middleton slowed the horse.

"That one looks good. It's perfect." He guided the horse around to another side. "It's filled out all around. I'll tell Gabe about it and he can cut it when he comes to get the mistletoe."

"Can we come with Gabe?" Cart asked.

"I think he'd probably like to have your help in locating the mistletoe and Christmas tree," Mr. Middleton said. He pressed his knees into the sides of the horse and moved the reins, and the animal turned toward the mansion. Within seconds, he had again reached his peak of speed.

The next night, the mansion smelled of the strongly scented cedar, pine, and holly. "It smells like Christmas," Will said. Cart had invited Will to help decorate the tree. Mr. Middleton stood on a ladder next to the tree, which had been placed near the fireplace. Cart and Will handed him decorations made from beads, colored paper, and popped corn. Other ornaments had been made of wood, in the carpenter shop.

All the talk was of Christmas Eve, two days away. The cooks were already preparing hams from the smokehouse, wild turkeys from the forest, and oysters from the marshes. Duck was a specialty at Christmas, and Mr. Middleton had shot several, which would be baked, sliced, and served on a silver platter. A Christmas cake would be baked, but it was much like birthday cake, with white icing and berries on the top. Everyone in the room was tingling with expectation. Marmalade nosed around the room, and Deerie, on his blanket, blinked big moist eyes.

"I just can't wait until Christmas Day," Cart said, bubbling over with excitement. "How about you, Will?"

"Me, too. We get presents," Will said, clapping his

hands. "Everybody on plantation come to the mansion and say 'Christmas gif' and they all get presents."

Mr. Middleton looked down from the tree where he was hanging decorations. "When we hear our workers calling out 'Christmas gif' we'll be ready with presents. The gifts are ready."

Just then Cart whispered, "Will, come out into the hall with me."

Will couldn't understand what Cart wanted to tell him. It must be important to take him away from decorating the Christmas tree. When he was in the hallway, he said, "It sure smell like Christmas around here."

"Will, do you know that old superstition about Christmas Eve?" Cart asked as his eyes went to the ropes of greenery draped on the stairs and bunches of mistletoe hanging in the doorways.

"What you mean?"

"Have you ever heard that at midnight on Christmas Eve the brightest star in the heavens shines to show where the baby Jesus lay?"

"I hear tell something about that," Will answered.

"Listen. On Christmas Eve, about thirty minutes before midnight, let's slip down to the bluff that overlooks the river and see if we can spot that star." Cart's face reflected his excitement.

"You think that be all right?" Will asked.

"Nobody'll know but the two of us. We won't tell anybody."

"Can you slip out without Marmalade hearing you?" Will asked.

"I'll tiptoe. Nobody'll hear me."

"All right," Will said. "I'll go if you will."

Christmas Eve came, and after a sumptuous supper, one that was considerably more than leftovers, Cart was sleepy. His mother went upstairs with him, and she folded the rug over for Marmalade. She blew out the lamp and left the room, believing that Cart was already asleep. But Cart was careful not to go to sleep. He listened until he heard his mother and father blow out the lamps downstairs and come upstairs to bed, and he was as quiet as the sea mist as he waited for the perfect time to slip away from the house.

Finally the mansion was deathly quiet. Mr. and Mrs. Middleton were asleep, and Marmalade was sleeping soundly. Surely Deerie was in slumber.

Cart eased out from under the quilts, put on his shoes, britches, shirt, and coat, and ever so quietly made his way downstairs. It was so dark that he had to feel his way. He looked out a window before opening the big door. Luckily for him, a full moon was shining. As he stood there, looking out across the field, he wondered if this was the kind of night on which the baby Jesus had been born.

Cart unlocked the heavy front door, pushed it open just a crack, pulled in his stomach, and eased through the opening. From the doorway, he heard the grandfather clock strike 11:30. He had thirty minutes in which to get to the Waccamaw River where he hoped Will would be waiting.

Running across the field in the moonlight, he missed Marmalade. Up to now, his parents hadn't let him take Deerie out of the house, but before long they would surely allow it. Deerie had almost recovered from falling into the old well.

Now Cart could see the open space that was the river. He ran down the Wagon Road, and the woods were black but shafts of moonbeams spread across the sandy lane. He looked up. The stars seemed almost to touch the trees. They were bigger than Cart had ever seen them, he thought. As he came out into the opening, Cart saw the outline of Will, standing on the bluff overlooking the river.

"Will, is that you?"

"It be me, all right. But all the stars are so big. Which one be the one showing where the baby Jesus lay?"

"I don't know. But we may not see it until midnight," Cart explained.

"When will that be?"

"It's almost midnight. In about five minutes we'll know the truth," Cart said.

"It not be long before tomorrow morning," Will said, "and then I can go to the mansion and say 'Christmas gif,' and I'll get a present."

"Hush!" Cart scolded. Then he whispered, "I think it's almost midnight."

Just at that very moment a star that was even bigger than the moon appeared somewhere on the far side of the Waccamaw River. It was so bright that Cart and Will rubbed their eyes. Far away, under the huge star, the land was as bright as day.

"Looka that star!" Will exclaimed.

"It's just like the one that appeared on the night that the baby Jesus was born," Cart whispered. "When I came here tonight I believed we would see the star of Bethlehem, but now that I'm seeing it, I can hardly believe it's true."

"It hurts my eyes," Will said.

Just then a guinea hen flew down from a tree where it had been roosting, and then a wild turkey showed up and fluffed its feathers. The turkey opened its tail out and looked in the direction of the star.

"Looka, Cart," Will called out. "It be the old peacock."

A big peacock spread its handsome feathers into the most gorgeous fan, and it was the showiest of any of the plantation animals. The feathers in the peacock's tail were five times as long as the peacock's body. Then the bird dropped down the colorful feathers and paraded slowly and majestically as it eyed the star.

"I hate to leave that star," Cart said, "but we'd better go home and go to bed."

"I be for that," Will answered. "It not be long before I say 'Christmas gif.'"

The boys ran down the Wagon Road, but before they had gone very far, Cart said, "Stop!"

"Looka!" Will exclaimed.

Suddenly, a beam of light from the star lighted the lane just ahead of where Cart and Will had stopped.

"I don't know the meaning of this," Cart said.

"Me neither."

Just at that very moment eight reindeer pranced from the forest and played and danced as they led the way back to the mansion. Before Cart said goodnight to Will, he cautioned, "You and I will always know what happened tonight, but don't ever tell another person."

"I won't say a word," Will promised.

"Even if you described it all," Cart said, "no one in the whole world would believe what happens on this plantation at Christmas."

KIAWAH ISLAND SUMMER

C ART," Mrs. Middleton said, "malaria fever is spreading across the Low Country, and I'm worried."

"Don't worry, I'm not going to have malaria fever. I'm strong and healthy."

Mrs. Middleton got up and went to her son and gave him a squeeze. There was a special closeness between Mrs. Middleton and Cart. "Sure, you're healthy, but one has no control over malaria fever."

"What causes that ailment?" Cart wanted to know.

"We don't know just now, but some people in science are trying to find out. Although we have believed for generations that the illness came from the warm, moist air, there has been some indication that a certain type of mosquito that breeds in the low-lying rice fields may carry it."

"Drat! I have lots of mosquito bites." Cart rubbed his arms.

"We all do. And if it is true that mosquitoes carry the infectious disease, then we have no control over it. The only prevention is to leave this semitropical region until cooler weather arrives."

"What does *malaria* mean, anyway?" Cart asked.

"The word *malaria* comes from two Italian words that mean 'bad air.' And that is why we associate the disease with the musty, bad-smelling air of the swamps and rice fields."

Cart rubbed his eyes. He was getting sleepy because he had played all day with Will. "If I get malaria, what will it feel like?" he yawned.

Mrs. Middleton got up. "It's time for bed." She called to Marmalade, "Come on, puppy. Let's go upstairs." As she led the way up the steps, she explained to Cart, "If you should have malaria fever, you would probably suffer chills and fever and weakness, but I'm going to do all that I can to see that you don't come down with such a terrible illness."

"What are you going to do?" Cart stopped on the steps and faced his mother.

"I'm going to see about sending you to Kiawah Island for the rest of this summer. Rice is not raised on Kiawah, and there are cool breezes from the ocean. The people who live there are not affected by the rice fields."

Cart was suddenly worried. "But I don't want to go to Kiawah."

Mrs. Middleton ran her fingers through his hair and patted his cheek. "You would have a swell time there. Everybody wants to spend a summer at Kiawah, but only the VanderHorsts are afforded that opportunity. They own the whole island."

Cart started up the stairs. "They won't let me visit them. I don't even know them."

"They know who you are. I mentioned to Mrs. VanderHorst when I saw her in Charleston that I was worried about the fever. She insisted that we bring you to the island and leave you there until after the first frost. We won't be bothered with mosquitoes after the low temperature that comes with the first icy frost."

Cart sat on the rug for a moment, and he gave Marmalade a hug. Then he put Marmalade on the fluffy rug, and Cart climbed up into his bed. It was a huge bed, high off the floor, and it was necessary for him to step on a footstool in order to reach the mattress. He spread out his arms and flopped down on the soft featherbed, but he didn't get the happy, cozy feeling that he usually got when his mother tucked him in. On this night he had a nagging worry about going to Kiawah Island for the summer. Just at that moment, he thought about Will. Sitting up in bed, he said, "I won't go if Will doesn't go with me. I cannot leave Will." Marmalade heard him mention Will, and the dog crawled from under his fold in the corner of the rug and wagged his tail.

"Marmalade, who told you that you could get into this conversation?" Mrs. Middleton asked. She tucked him under the fold of the rug. "Go to sleep and dream your puppy dreams." Her eyes went to her son. "Don't worry, Cartrette. If you go to Kiawah Island, you will never forget the experience. There are many groves of trees, and large herds of deer, and all kinds of wildlife. Besides that, the VanderHorst house is huge, and there will be many rooms to explore." Cart yawned and closed his eyes, and his mother believed he was asleep as she left the room.

Cart tried to stay awake and think about Kiawah Island but his eyelids were so heavy they would not remain open. Within a few minutes, there was no worry about the summer visit to the island seventeen miles south of Charleston.

The next morning, when Cart's mother came into the bedroom, she told him that she had talked with his father and they had decided to ask Mrs. VanderHorst if Will could also go to Kiawah. Although black people were not susceptible to malaria fever, she realized that Cart would miss Will, and Will would be lonely with Cart gone. "I'll send a communication today, and if the VanderHorst family will agree to it, then Will can go too."

"Oh, thank you, thank you," Cart exclaimed, as he stepped on the footstool and down onto the rug with Marmalade. "Can Marmalade go too?"

"Don't you think you are pressing your good fortune?" Mrs. Middleton asked. "After all, Mrs. VanderHorst only invited you and now you've added Will to the list and are asking about Marmalade." She tried to look aggravated, but a smile crept across her face, and she said, "I suppose the VanderHorsts have dogs and one more won't make that much difference. Will you help take care of Marmalade?"

"Of course I will. I'll see that he gets food every day and I'll fold over the rug beside my bed every night." Cart had begun to think that going to Kiawah Island for the rest of the summer was a good idea. There was an old man who told stories, and he wanted to see a cotton gin. Sea Island cotton was raised on the island as the land was not suited to rice production. Four days later the Middletons, with Will and Marmalade, left for Kiawah Island.

After the carriage had crossed the river on the ferry, Cart's eyes were wide as he tried to take in the island. Marmalade, in his lap, was also looking around, and Will was looking too. They were not talking, as they wanted to get a good view of the place where they would spend the next three months.

"King Robert," Will said to Cart's father, "do you think there be any alligators on this island?"

"I expect there are plenty of them," Mr. Middleton said. "There are many lakes and lagoons that make a perfect place for alligators to live."

Mrs. Middleton looked around at the dense bushes and trees. "There is so much foliage here that it's spooky. Robert, do you think the boys will be all right?"

"Yes, my dear," he answered. "I believe that Kiawah will be a pleasant change for them, and of course, Cartrette will be away from the malaria threat."

Her husband's words seemed to reassure her. "Yes, I know we are doing the right thing, but I had forgotten how luxuriant the plant life is on an island. It is so close and dense you cannot see very far away."

"Kiawah has been known for that feature," Mr. Middleton explained. "That is why the pirate, Captain Kidd, hid his treasure on Kiawah."

"A pirate buried his treasure here?" Cart asked.

"That's what they say," his father answered. "But none of it has ever been found."

"Do you think it's true, Papa?" Cart asked.

"I don't know. It very well *could* be. For about two hundred years people have told tales about Kidd's supposed buried treasure and bloody deeds."

"Where would he have buried the treasure?" Cart asked.

"Somewhere just back of the sand dunes," his father answered. "According to old records, Captain Kidd seized much treasure, things like gold and silver and Indian goods, and the accumulation was buried in many different places."

"Where Cap'n Kidd get that stuff?" Will asked.

"He attacked rich ships sailing under French commissions," Mr. Middleton explained. "This was considered lawful as Kidd was English, and England was at war with France."

Cart was suddenly so happy that he wanted to jump up and down but he had to remain in his seat. As the carriage rumbled on, he said to Will, "We have three whole months to search for Captain Kidd's treasure."

"That sure be the truth," Will answered.

When the driver, sitting on the box at the front of the carriage where he could hold onto the reins and watch the bay horses, turned the next corner, the VanderHorst mansion came into view. The house was four stories high, the upper three stories of wood. On the inland side, a piazza (porch) extended from the main wing.

A servant notified Mrs. VanderHorst that the

guests had arrived, and she came from the mansion to greet them. She hugged Mrs. Middleton and spoke to the others. "I'm so glad you will be spending the summer with us on Kiawah," she said, looking at Cart. "And I'm delighted that you brought along your friend Will and your dog."

Will eyed Cart. "Miz VanderHorst sure be a nice lady."

"Yes," Cart answered. "And I'm glad we came to Kiawah. There are lots of things to do on an island."

"That sure be the truth," Will said.

After a servant removed the trunk from the top of the carriage and took it to a bedroom off of a hallway on the second floor, Mr. and Mrs. Middleton kissed Cart goodbye. They explained that they would be back in three months. Before the carriage was out of sight, Cart and Will had run into the woods between the mansion and the ocean. They were about to start a search for Captain Kidd's treasure when they heard the sound of a horn and returned to the big house. The horn signaled that dinner was on the table.

Food at the VanderHorst house was special. For dinner Cart and Will were served fowl with white sauce, and oysters that had been taken from the marsh. For dessert, plates of a sweet, lemony cake were brought to the table. Mrs. VanderHorst called it "Prince Albert's pudding." She said she was planning to serve Huguenot torte the following day. When she asked Cart and Will if they liked cooter soup, the boys eyed each other. "We'll try it," Cart answered.

Mrs. VanderHorst had put Marmalade's food on a plate, but as the pantry in this island house was far away from the dining room, the dog was allowed to eat in the room with the people. Cart wondered if Marmalade would refuse to eat in the pantry when they returned to Midcliffe. Thinking about that, he wondered where his mother and father were. It would take a long time for them to return home. Cart was just about to get homesick when Will interrupted his thoughts. "Wanna go back and looka 'bout that buried treasure?"

"Let's go," Cart said. He asked to be excused, and Mrs. VanderHorst allowed the boys to leave the table, but she cautioned them to be careful.

Cart and Will walked around the mansion before they went on their treasure hunt. They peered through the fence around the cooter pen, and watched the turtles. "We be eatin' one of those," Will said.

Just then Mr. VanderHorst came over and said, "Boys, tomorrow my servant Squash and I are going to search the island for deer and other wildlife. I want to make sure there is plenty of game and lots of animals here when the weather cools and I invite my friends to the island for a hunt. Do you think you can amuse yourselves tomorrow when I'm gone?"

"Yes, sir," Cart answered. "We're going to search for Captain Kidd's treasure."

"Well, I'm going to make a rule for you youngsters: you must never take a dip in the ocean unless I am with you. There are large sea turtles out there, as well as a shark that we've sighted."

"We won't, Mr. VanderHorst," Cart answered.

"And you may call me 'Major,' if you choose. My friends call me 'the Major.' "

"All right, Major," Cart said.

Just before the Major turned to go, he said, "If you should desire some diversion, there is a white-bearded man who lives at the end of the lane leading from the avenue of oaks. He can regale you with his tales and narratives of this island. You may go to his house anytime you like. He likes nothing better than having visitors."

"I've heard of him," Cart explained. "We'll go to his house for a visit, but not today. Will and I are going to search for Captain Kidd's treasure."

As the Major turned to go, he called over a shoulder, "I doubt you'll find it. We've been looking for years. But give it a try, if you like."

As soon as the Major was out of sight Cart and Will flew to the dunes. They searched for the treasure, but found nothing. They also hunted for it the following day, but their exploration didn't turn up any buried treasure. Two days later, the Major had returned home.

"Boys, the Major brought you something from the store," Mrs. VanderHorst said.

"What is it?" Cart asked as he patted Marmalade's head. It was a warm day, and Marmalade's tongue hung from his mouth as he breathed heavily.

Just then the Major came in and handed each of the boys a straw hat. "I'm going to the cotton gin tomorrow, and every man I know wears a straw hat to the cotton gin. I thought the two of you would like to have your own straw hats."

"Thank you, Major," Cart exclaimed.

"Looka," Will said as he plopped the straw hat on his head. "We see the cotton gin?"

"Yes," the Major answered. "It will be a new experience for the two of you. We'll leave the house with the wagonload of cotton early in the morning. The gin is on the other side of the island."

"What's a cotton gin, Major?" Cart asked.

Major VanderHorst pulled up a chair and sat down, stretching his long legs in front of him. He wore boots. "The cotton gin is a machine invented in 1793 by Eli Whitney for separating cotton fiber from the seed. Tomorrow, when we get to the gin, a man will be holding a suction pipe that pulls the cotton from the wagon into the gin. Inside the building, the seed is removed from the cotton. The cotton is then packaged in bales, which are stored at the gin until they are sold at the highest price. We bring the seed back for next year's planting."

Early the next morning, Cart, Will, and Marmalade were allowed to ride in the cotton instead of sitting with the Major on the seat at the front of the wagon. Cart and Will laughed joyously as they jumped and dived into the huge mound of soft cotton. Marmalade was also jumping, and he was sinking so deep into the cotton that Cart had to keep pulling him up. They were having a swell time playing in the cotton, but after two hours of the frolicsome romps, they arrived at the gin.

The cotton gin was a two-story building, with a place for the wagon to be unloaded. A river flowed at the back of the building, and after the cotton had been cleaned and baled, it would be loaded on boats that would take it to Charleston where it would be sold.

The driver was now maneuvering the horses carefully in order to position the wagon in the perfect place for the cotton to be sucked up into the building. Cart and Will, in their new straw hats, stood aside. Cart was holding Marmalade.

"Now, boys," the Major called, "stand back so that you won't be in the way. The man here at the gin is going to drop the metal pipe into the cotton, and when he turns on the machine, the cotton will be sucked up to the second story of the building."

Just at that moment a machine started grinding and clanging and cotton flew into the pipe. The machine frightened Marmalade and he barked. "I've got to hold you tight, Marmalade," Cart said, "or that machine'll suck you up along with the cotton."

Marmalade went into a rage and barked furiously at the machine. He jumped from Cart's arms and ran toward the pipe that was sucking up the cotton. Cart dived for his dog but didn't catch him. Suddenly, his new straw hat was sucked into the pipe, and Cart reached into the swirling cotton that was being pulled into the tube. The suction air was so strong that it pulled Cart's head, shoulders, and arms into the pipe, along with the cotton.

"Cap'n! Cap'n!" Will was screaming and jumping up and down. "Cart's going up in the pipe!"

The noise was so loud it was like thunder, and the Major didn't hear Will. His eyes were on the window at the second story of the building.

Marmalade, seeing that Cart was being dragged

into the pipe, barked furiously. Trying to alert someone to help his master the dog went into a maddened rampage, but just then a ball of cotton flew to Marmalade's nose. The dog shook his head to free it of the tickling sensation, but he only stirred up more cotton balls. They were now floating around his nostrils, and Marmalade appeared to believe he would choke on the lint. He coughed and sneezed.

"Major!" Will yelled. "Come quick!" But Major VanderHorst heard nothing.

Cart was shouting and shrieking, but with all the noise being made by the machine he couldn't even hear his own yells. He wondered what his fate would be.

Will ran to Cart and pulled on his legs, trying his best to drag him from the suction pipe. Marmalade, thinking that Will was doing something dreadful to Cart, sank his teeth into Will's britches and pulled with all his might. But Cart didn't budge, and Will was unable to free him of the pipe. The suction was very strong.

Just then the Major saw what was happening, and he flew to Cart. "Stop the machine!" the Major yelled. He pushed Will and Marmalade out of the way and grabbed Cart's legs and pulled with such force that when the machine suddenly shut down the Major and Cart both fell back into the wagon. Cart was pale and trembling. "My straw hat is gone," he wailed.

"Don't worry about the hat," the Major said as he pulled himself up. "We can always get you another hat."

The men who had been working inside the building ran outside to see what was happening. Will and Marmalade were wide-eyed as they gazed at the Major and Cart, both of whom appeared to be sick. Finally, the Major pulled himself together. After picking some of the lint and cotton from his shirt and britches and checking to see that Cart was all right, he said, "Let's go into the building." He jumped off the wagon and caught Cart and Will as they jumped off. The Major lifted Marmalade out of the vehicle, and the dog wagged his tail furiously.

The boys followed the Major inside the cotton gin. There on the floor was a huge pile of cotton and on the very top of the pile was Cart's hat. It didn't look any the worse for wear and tear, but Cart and the Major looked as though they had survived a hurricane.

Coming home in the empty wagon save for the cotton seed, Major VanderHorst told Cart and Will that he was going to show them something impressive. The boys climbed up on the front seat with the Major and beamed their eyes straight ahead.

"What is it?" Cart questioned.

"It's the Mosquito Fleet," the owner of the island said.

"Cap'n, why you call it Mosquito Fleet?" Will asked.

"Just you wait. You'll see."

The Major stopped the wagon on a knoll that overlooked the Atlantic Ocean. "We'll wait here. If you boys keep your eyes on the horizon, just before the sun sets you'll see what appears to be mosquitoes coming toward you."

A few minutes later, just as the Major had said, there appeared to be three mosquitoes on the horizon. "Are they boats?" Cart asked.

"Yes," the Major explained. "We refer to them as the Mosquito Fleet. When the boats come closer, you can see the sails, and when they get even closer, you can see men on board the ships. The men will be cleaning fish, the catch of this day."

"What do they do with the fish heads and tails?" Cart asked.

"The waste parts are thrown into the ocean. That's why you'll see seagulls flying around the boat. Although the fishermen on the vessels furnish their tables and ours with fish, they sell most of their catch in Charleston before returning to the island."

Cart held Marmalade up so that he could see. "There they are, Marmalade. That's the Mosquito Fleet."

Tired now, Cart and Will sat quietly and watched the boats sail toward a dock. What had at first appeared to be a misty cloud now materialized into a flock of seagulls. They soared and dived into the water, picking up every scrap of fish that was thrown into the ocean.

"What be the names of the boats?" Will asked.

"Those vessels have quaint names," the Major explained. "Watch them closely and see if you can make out the names."

Cart and Will squinted their eyes, trying to read the words. They decided that one was named *The Cootie.* "What does that mean?" Cart asked.

"The people on those boats call cooters, or turtles, *cooties,*" the Major explained.

Another of the vessels was named *My True Love,* and the last boat to arrive at the dock was titled *Kiawah Island Lady.*

When the Major turned the wagon around and headed for home, Cart and Will were so exhausted they almost fell into slumber. Marmalade went to sleep in Cart's lap. The Major talked constantly, trying his best to keep the boys awake until they had eaten supper.

For the next several weeks, Cart and Will searched frantically for Captain Kidd's buried treasure. When they found none, they decided to pay a visit to the white-bearded man at the end of the lane.

"C'mon, Will. Let's go see the old man with the white beard. Perhaps he'll tell us some stories."

"Where's Marmalade?"

"He's running ahead of us." Marmalade had become so accustomed to the thick foliage of the island that he was no longer afraid to explore on his own.

Going down the sandy lane was almost like walking the length of the aisle in a huge cathedral. The tree limbs met and intermingled overhead, bringing dusk to a sunny day. Spanish moss swung from overhead limbs and blotted out any light that managed to filter through. As Cart and Will proceeded, the road became darker and eerie. But they were not afraid. If they could reach the old man's house, they believed, it would be a place of light, and much good conversation. Finally, they saw the house at the end of the road, but it was more of a shack than a house.

"Looka!" Will said.

"How about you knocking on the door, Will?"

"No. You knock on it."

The boys walked slowly to the front door, which was closed even though it was a warm day. Cart knocked, but there was no answer.

"Knock again, Cart."

Cart knocked a second time, and a booming voice yelled, "Come in. The door's not locked."

The door squeaked as Cart opened it with one hand. He was holding Marmalade under the other arm. Will stood back, his eyes nearly as big as moons. "C'mon, Will. Don't be afraid."

"Leave Marmalade outside," Will suggested.

Cart eased the dog down, not taking his eyes off the room he was now seeing. "Everything looks all right. C'mon in."

Unexpectedly, an ancient man loomed before them. Cart was thinking that he looked like Old Saint Nick, with such a luxurious beard.

"Is that Moses?" Will asked.

"No! It's not Moses." Cart wished that Will had been braver. Will seemed to be holding back.

"You boys visiting the VanderHorsts?" the man's booming voice asked.

"Yes, sir," Cart answered, a little nervously. "My parents believe it's safer here than on our rice plantation."

The old man pulled his beard as he thought about that. "A rice plantation you say? Well, it's time you become acquainted with Sea Island cotton. You ever see any before you came here?"

Cart and Will shook their heads to indicate they had not.

"It's the finest cotton in the world," the old man

said. "Some say it's silkier than any silkworm's co-coon in China. And it brings a big price." He looked at Cart squarely, and Cart thought that the man had the bluest eyes he had ever seen. "The Sea Island cotton makes rich men out of the planters," the man explained. Without awaiting an answer, he went on. "VanderHorst is so wealthy I doubt he knows how much he has in assets."

Cart glanced around at the room. Although the house was plain and simple, there were many books lying around. The overhead shelves were crammed with them.

"You're looking at my books and wondering why I have them," the old man said, obviously reading Cart's mind. That is precisely what he was thinking.

"It may surprise you, but I am a physician. Stud-ied in Charleston."

"Do you practice medicine?" Cart asked.

The answer began with a laugh that shook the man's shoulders. "You wouldn't believe it to look at me now, but many years ago I was considered the most prominent physician in Charleston. But now? I just take care of the island people. And at no charge to them, I might add."

"What be your name, Cap'n?" Will asked in a faint voice, obviously still a little afraid of the old man.

"Dr. Pennywhistle! You may call me Dr. Penny, if you like."

"That's a funny name, sir," Cart said.

"And I'm a funny man!" The old man pulled his chair up close to the sofa on which Cart and Will were sitting. "Do you boys want to hear something melodramatic?"

Neither Cart nor Will knew what the word melodramatic meant. But they nodded their heads to indicate that they wanted to hear what Dr. Penny was referring to.

"Now listen carefully," Dr. Penny said, looking first at Cart and then at Will. He spoke very distinctly. "I have something in this house that everyone has but few people are willing to reveal to others."

Cart jabbed an elbow into Will's side. "What's he got?" Cart mouthed silently.

"It be something that scare us," Will said aloud.

Dr. Penny pulled his beard. "Oh, it might frighten you just a tinge, but don't you boys believe that it is good to be frightened once in a while?" Not waiting for Cart or Will to comment, he added, "Sure it is. It makes your minds go to work. You are required to figure something out when you are frightened. So don't worry about 'the thing' I have in my hall closet. It won't startle you too much."

"I don't want to see it," Cart said firmly.

Will shook his head in desperation. "It sure be something that scare me."

"Have you given any thought to the clue I gave you?"

Cart looked at Will. "I didn't hear any clue. Did you?"

"No."

"Listen carefully. Use your minds!" Dr. Penny scolded. "I'll repeat the clue. It is: I have something in this house that everyone has but few people are willing to reveal to others. That is the clue. Think about it for a moment." The old man got up and went to a back door and let a huge tabby cat in. When he came back to the sitting room, he asked, "Have you figured it out yet? What is it that I have that everyone else has but few are willing to reveal?"

Cart shook his head, saying, "I don't have the faintest idea."

"That thing sure be something that I don't know," Will agreed.

"Then come with me," Dr. Penny said. He led the way into the hall. As Dr. Penny walked toward the closet door, he repeated, "Inside this closet is something that every family has but few are willing to reveal."

Cart stopped walking and Will stood as close to Cart as he could.

"Don't be afraid," Dr. Penny said. "Come close to the door, for I am just about to open it."

Cart inched his way over to the door and Will joined him. The boys were standing immediately in front of the closed door.

Just at that moment Dr. Penny yanked open the closet door, and Cart and Will screamed loud enough to wake up the dead. There in the closet stood a stack of rattly old bones, the framework of a person. No eyes were in the deep sockets of the face, and the large, protruding teeth were grinning. Arms, hands, fingers, and toes, all were of many bones. Cart recoiled and Will also jumped back from the closet door. "What is it?" Cart mumbled.

Dr. Penny stood back and pulled on his beard as he laughed heartily. "Why it is just as I told you in my clue. That is something that every family has but few are willing to reveal. It is a skeleton in the closet."

"That not be clear to me," Will said. His mouth was agape and he shifted his eyes back and forth afraid to give his full attention to the skeleton.

"I'll explain it to you," Dr. Penny said, as his big cat brushed against his ankles. "There are few people who do not have some sort of family scandal that is concealed to avoid public disgrace. Most people keep some shameful secret hidden, so to speak, 'in a closet.' In other words, they cover up the dishonor, the shame, so that others will not know about it. Consequently, their unpleasantness is hidden from the public." Just then Dr. Penny smiled widely and threw out his arms in a wide gesture. "But as you can see, I am perfectly happy to share my skeleton in the closet with anyone who cares to see it. There is no camouflage regarding my skeleton, which I used in Charleston when I was a student at the Medical College of the State of South Carolina."

Will backed away from Dr. Penny, as he had never before seen anything so appalling as the skeleton in the closet. Cart was scared too, and he made up an excuse to leave the house. "I left my dog, Marmalade, outside, and I'd better go see about him."

"Well, I trust you have enjoyed your visit with me," Dr. Penny said. "How long will you be on the island?"

Cart thought about the question. He didn't really know how much longer he and Will would be at Kiawah Island but he believed that their visit would end soon. Almost every day a chill came to the air, and fall couldn't be far away. His parents would

come for him after the first frost. "We'll be here until the first frost," he answered Dr. Penny.

"Then you should take in all of the island experiences," the old physician said. "Have you been to a
shout?"

"What be a shout?" Will asked.

"It's a musical and religious event," Dr. Penny explained. "And the people who have lived their lives
on this island can sing in a way that you will never
know unless you hear them. I suggest that you attend a shout to round out your summer on this
island."

"Where are the shouts held?" Cart asked.

"They are in different cabins." Dr. Penny pulled on
his beard as he thought about it. Finally he said, "I
believe the shout this week will be held at Squash's
house, tomorrow night. Do you boys know Squash?"

"Squash be my good friend," Will said. Squash,
the dark-skinned servant of the Major, had been especially friendly to Will.

"Then you should go to his house tomorrow night
and listen to the singing. You won't ever forget it,"
Dr. Penny promised.

"I'll tell Squash I want to go," Will said. "C'mon,
Cart, let's be getting home."

When the boys reached the mansion, Squash and
the Major were sitting on the porch, discussing a
hunt that the Major was going to organize. Squash
agreed to travel to several plantations on other is-
lands and on the mainland and deliver invitations.
He also agreed to lead the procession of men on
horseback as they raced through the woodlands of
the island in search of wild turkeys, deer, ducks,

and any other wildlife to their liking. "Squash,"
Will interrupted, "you be having a shout at your
house tomorrow night?"

Squash looked surprised. "How you know 'bout
that?"

"Dr. Penny say you have a shout."

"Dr. Penny," Cart added, "said we shouldn't go
home without attending a shout, and we know we
won't be on the island too much longer."

The Major got up from his chair. "Dr. Penny is an
intelligent man, and very perceptive. I don't know
why I didn't think of it, but I'm glad he did. Yes, you
should attend a shout while you are here."

The next day Mrs. VanderHorst insisted that
Squash eat supper at the mansion and accompany
the boys to his cabin for the shout. She also made
Squash promise that he would bring the boys home
after the meeting. Supper was served on the brick-
floored porch, and Marmalade's food was put on a
plate and served to him there. The cooks had prepared turtle or cooter soup that was cooked with cit-
ron. After the soup bowls had been removed from
the table, a platter of turkey hash and sweet pota-
toes was brought to the table. Palmetto cabbage and
bread pudding were served before dessert, which
consisted of ginger cake and pickled damsons. Cart,
Will, and Marmalade were fairly stuffed when they
left the mansion with Squash.

Squash whistled merrily as he led the way
through the woods. They had traveled about a mile
when they could hear music. Will and Cart, carrying Marmalade, ran the rest of the way. Squash
went into the small cabin where the crowd had

gathered, and Will and Cart and Marmalade sat on the floor of the porch. They looked through the open door at the people.

A woman was singing in a minor key, and her voice was of high range. She took a haunting melody through runs, trills, and other florid decorations in vocal music. Cart leaned over to Will. "That woman has a beautiful voice."

"It be about the best I ever heard," Will answered.

After a moment, another woman got up and joined in the song. Then others stood up and they also joined in. Their bodies swayed right to left and back. The voices heightened and became a clearly defined pattern, producing a hammering beat that was almost jolting in its primitive intensity.

"That singing be shocking," Will said.

Marmalade barked at the singers, but they didn't notice. "Shh," Cart hushed the dog. "That's good music. You won't ever hear singing that's any better than this," Cart said to Marmalade.

Suddenly, all went quiet. The woman who had sung the song that was still lingering in Cart's head walked to the center of the room. All was as quiet as death. She raised her arms heavenward and began to pray:

> Lord, You can make the danger road smooth
> And You can make the crooked path straight.
> You be able to slow the mighty wind and
> Hold back the big wave . . .

"She's praying," Cart whispered.

When she had finished praying, the woman stood for a moment of utter quietness, her eyes closed. A tear escaped her eyelids. Then she began to sway, and her friends joined her in a song that reached a wild, intense pitch.

"That song sure be frisky," Will observed.

"And her prayer was simple but imaginative," Cart answered.

Just at that moment a man shuffled his feet in a kind of dance, and the people around him continued to sway back and forth and hum a rhythmic tune. After a while, the man danced away from the group, and he went into a dance technique that bordered on excited violence. The people in the room with him clapped their hands and called out to him. His name was Felix. When the unrestrained, turbulent dance ended, all of the people joined in singing "Honey In The Rock," a favorite hymn of the island.

"Will," Cart said, "I believe that tonight we have seen the true island ways of these people."

Will didn't answer. It was clear that he had been singularly moved by the beauty of the island music. His face appeared to be floating in tempo with some of the haunting and grievous tunes.

"You be ready to go?" Squash asked as he came to the porch.

Cart grabbed Marmalade and jumped up. "Yes."

Will didn't say anything. In his heart, he knew that he would never forget the music and the people involved in the Kiawah Island shout. The next day he told Mrs. VanderHorst that he would never be able to have enough of the music.

"The shouts are the island people's social activity," she explained. "They sing and pray about the things they are familiar with," she went on to say.

"Like the perilous ocean. Sometimes they sing and shout until you wonder if their lungs ache."

"It be frisky," Will answered.

The next day dawned clear and crisp. Knowing that their days on the island were numbered, Cart and Will again searched for Captain Kidd's treasure. They poked under bushes, and scratched in sand dunes that were covered in beach vegetation, but they were unable to find anything that had been buried. The closest they came was when they found something solid in the sand, but it turned out to be a large piece of driftwood, and it was too heavy to pull from the earth. Two weeks later the boys awoke one morning to look out the window and see a covering of lacy ice crystals on everything. The first frost had appeared, and that meant that Mr. and Mrs. Middleton would come to the island and take the boys back to the plantation on the Waccamaw River.

"I'm going to miss Kiawah Island," Cart said.

"Do you think the Cap'n allow us to come back someday?" Will asked.

Cart's eyes still gazed across the land to the marsh in the distance. "I don't know. If someone invents a cure for malaria fever, we won't come back."

"This be a summer I won't forget," Will surmised.

"What was the best part, do you think?" Cart asked.

"The shout."

Cart thought for a moment, then answered, "Well, for me, I believe the best part was not getting killed in the cotton machine."

THE BEACHED WHALE

WHEN CART AND Will arrived at Midcliffe, Cart ran into the house to see Deerie. How his pet deer had grown since he'd been gone! As Cart hugged the deer's neck, he said, "Deerie, you may not remember me now, but pretty soon you'll know that I am your best friend."

"That sure be the truth," Will said.

"Hey, Will," Cart said suddenly. "Let's go to the carpenter shop and see Prince. We can tell him all the things we did at Kiawah Island."

"That be a good idea," Will answered.

Prince was working on a bed when the boys arrived with Marmalade. The bed on which Prince was working had large posts at each corner, and Prince explained how he intended to carve rice plants on the bed posts. He referred to the project as making a rice bed. Cart and Will were impressed with the intricate work that Prince was doing. "You're an expert carpenter, Prince," Cart said.

While they were examining the rice bed, Abraham rushed in and announced that a whale had washed ashore, on the beach portion of the plantation.

"How big it be?" Will asked.

"Big enough to have swallowed Jonah!" Abraham declared.

"Let's go see the whale," Cart said. Will jumped up, and by the time Cart had grabbed Marmalade he was on his way to the beach.

Cart, carrying Marmalade, caught up with Will, and they flew across the field. Soon they had reached the marsh, and within minutes they were standing on a sand dune where they had a clear view of the beach. There on the sand was a black whale that appeared to be as big as a house.

"He sure enough be big," Will exclaimed.

Cart took a deep breath. "I didn't know whales were so big. Let's go tell Papa."

The boys flew back to the mansion and told Mr. Middleton that a whale had washed ashore, and the animal was as big as a house. Mr. Middleton went with the boys to the barn, where he got a hoe. He asked his groom to bring his stallion, and when he had climbed on the horse, he pulled Cart and Will up so that they could ride with him to the beach. Cart, holding Marmalade, sat between his father and Will. All of them held onto the handle of the hoe. When they arrived at the beach, Mr. Middleton was astounded at the size of the whale. He was a tall man, and when he stood close to the whale and held the hoe as high as he could, it only reached about halfway up the side of the black mammal.

"You were right," Mr. Middleton said. "I believe this whale is truly as high as a house."

Just then some plantation workers arrived, and they all exclaimed about the size of the creature. None of them had believed that whales could grow to be so big.

"Papa, can we play on the whale?" Cart asked.

"No, son. This mammal belongs to someone."

"Who does it belong to?"

"Come with me." Mr. Middleton walked around the huge black mound of rubbery substance and pointed to the top. "See those spears?"

"Yes," Cart and Will said in unison.

"They are harpoons. Some whalers on a ship offshore harpooned this whale, but before they could capture it, it got away and then died and washed ashore. I feel sure that the harpooners are looking for their bounty and will find it."

"When will they come?" Cart asked.

"I don't know, but you can be sure they'll arrive here within the next few days."

Word of the beached whale spread, and the following day people from many Low Country plantations arrived on the scene to take a look at the monster. Mr. Middleton remained at the beach for several days and he always held up his hoe so that the visitors could get a clear idea of just how large the animal was. Four days later, the harpooners arrived in a canoe.

"Mate," one of them called to Mr. Middleton, "we been looking for our whale."

"It beached several days ago," Mr. Middleton explained, "and it has caused quite a sensation. None of us believed that whales were so large. How did the animal get away from you?"

"We harpooned him, mate," a whaleman said, "then the monster began to swim and he pulled our boat along with him. We had to do something to save our boat and our lives, so we cut the ropes loose. The whale swam away with the harpoons in his hide."

"What do you intend to do now?" Cart asked.

"We intend to cut off the blubber, lad."

"What will you do with it?" Cart wanted to know.

"We'll cook the blubber, lad. When it cooks, grease just pours out, and we'll put the grease in barrels."

"Is whale oil valuable?" Cart asked.

"That it is, lad. It's used as machine oil."

"We wanted to play around the whale, but Papa wouldn't let us," Cart complained.

The harpooner scratched his head, as though he were thinking about that. Finally, he said, "Lad, we'll be glad to leave the skeleton for you, if you like."

Cart looked at Will, and they laughed. This wasn't a skeleton in a closet, and they were not afraid of it. Cart told the whaleman that he would appreciate it if he would leave the skeleton so that they could romp in it.

Just then another canoe with men in it arrived, and they each carried a knife on the end of a long pole.

The men looked at the huge whale and shook their heads. They said that they didn't know how to remove the blubber on the top.

"How do you remove blubber when the whale is in the ocean?" Mr. Middleton asked.

"We tow the whale alongside the boat, mate," the whaler answered. "Wood to black skin; that is, the boat almost touches the whale. Then we peel the blubber off in one long spiral strip as the whale is rolled over in the water." He glanced back to the beached animal. "But we cannot use that method here. We need a ladder."

"Well I can furnish you with a ladder," Mr. Middleton said as he turned around. Then he glanced back at the monster and added, "A ladder that's two stories high."

"C'mon, Will," Cart said as he picked up Marmalade. "Papa's going to see Prince. Let's go, too."

Prince was working on the bedpost and he didn't take his eyes off the wood that he was sanding. After he was told to make a long ladder, he answered nonchalantly, "Ladder be ready tomorrow."

The next day, Prince and Abraham loaded the ladder on Abraham's ox cart and transported it to the beach. Cart and Will went too.

"That sure be a huge whale," Prince observed.

"It be that all right," Abraham answered.

After Prince and Abraham had situated the ladder against the whale, the whaler commanded his men, "Peel the beast."

Using the knives on long poles, the men peeled off the blubber. The whalers called the lengths of meat "blanket strips." The blanket strips were loaded in the canoe and boated back to the three-masted schooner that rode at anchor, beyond the breakers. It took many trips in the canoe to transport the blubber back to the ship. Abraham and Prince decided to return to the plantation, but the boys stayed behind to watch. When all the blubber had been transported, the whaler said to Cart, "Lad, the skeleton's of no use to us. It's yours."

"Will you prop the ladder up on the skeleton?" Cart asked.

"I'll oblige, lad, but be careful. That would be a long way to fall."

"We'll be careful."

The ladder was situated on the monstrous framework of whale bones, and Cart shrieked, "Perfect!"

Cart was first up the ladder, and Will was close behind. Marmalade watched from the sand beach. When Cart reached the top, he grabbed a rib bone and pulled himself up on top of the whale frame. "C'mon up, Will."

"I be afraid," Will answered.

"What's there to be afraid of?"

"Look down," Will said.

Cart looked down and saw that they were as high as a house. "Sure we're high, but come on up."

Will didn't answer, and Cart reached down to him. "Here, catch my hand. I'll pull you up."

Will caught Cart's hand and squeezed it for dear life. With his other hand, Will took hold of a rib, and as he pulled and Cart yanked, Will's feet flew out and pushed the ladder away from the whale. Suddenly there was a thud, and when Will was safely on top of the whale and he and Cart looked, they saw that the ladder had been knocked to the ground.

"Drat!" Cart said. "The ladder's down."

"What we do now?" Will asked.

"I don't know," Cart answered. He looked around. No one was in sight. "We can't call loudly enough to attract attention," he said. "And Papa won't come back until after he has completed the evening chores, and then it will be dark."

"We'll be dead then," Will said.

"No, we won't be dead!" Cart scolded. "We may be scared half to death, but we won't be dead."

As the day waned, Cart and Will sat very still on a whale rib, and they held tightly onto another rib for safety.

"How long it be before King Robert come see about us?" Will asked.

"I don't know, but I hope it is soon," Cart answered. "I'm cold and tired."

"I be hungry," Will said.

"Me, too. Say, wouldn't it be nice if Marmalade would go and get help?"

Cart called to Marmalade but, as he expected, the dog only looked at him. "Go get Papa," Cart ordered, but Marmalade just sat on the sand. "We're doomed to wait on Papa," Cart said to Will.

Sometime later, Will said, "Cart, that be Abraham on his ox cart?"

Cart looked and saw Abraham on his cart, probably going for oysters at the inlet. Cart and Will screamed at the very same time, as loudly as they could yell. But Abraham kept on going.

"He be singing," Will said. "Abraham sing when he travel in ox cart."

"Well, let's scream so loud that he'll hear us," Cart said.

The boys yelled until it seemed that their lungs would burst, and Abraham slowed down and looked around. But he didn't see them.

"You know, Will," Cart said, "it's a good thing we are this high. If we were not on the very top of the skeleton we couldn't see over the dunes, and we couldn't see Abraham."

"Call again," Will said.

The boys cried out for help, and Abraham spotted them and waved an arm. He turned the cart back and started in the opposite direction. "He be leaving," Will said, forlornly.

"No. He's going for help. He can tell by looking at us that we're in trouble. He'll come back, and Papa will be with him, and probably some other men as well."

Cart and Will were very quiet as they awaited help. After awhile, Mr. Middleton and some helpers, including Abraham and Prince, arrived.

"What are you two doing up there?" Mr. Middleton questioned.

"Papa, we were playing on the skeleton," Cart explained.

"Well you should have waited until you could talk with me about that. I would never have let you climb so high. Of course you can play in the skeleton, but I forbid you to crawl around on the top. If you fall, you could break your back!"

"If you'll put the ladder back in place, Papa, I promise that I'll never come back this high," Cart assured his father.

"I not be coming back here," Will asserted.

Mr. Middleton and Prince stationed the ladder so that the boys could climb down. When they were safely on the ground, Mr. Middleton said, "Prince, destroy that ladder. I don't want it lying around for the boys to be tempted by."

The next day Cart and Will went back to the whale skeleton to play, but they didn't use a ladder.

INDIAN FEVER

"WILL, IF A pirate ever buried any treasure on the plantation where do you think he would have put it?"

Will thought about Cart's question. "Under the big oak on the bluff that overlooks the Waccamaw River?"

"Drat! Why didn't I think of that? That is the perfect place to bury something. Let's go dig there and see if a pirate buried something there."

"That be a good place to bury treasure," Will agreed.

Cart picked up Marmalade and flew toward the barn. Will ran beside him. At the barn they found two shovels, and they carried them back to the big tree near the river.

"I'm glad the ground is mostly sand," Cart said as he dug into the earth.

"It not be too hard," Will said.

"We'll have to dig deep, because if a pirate buried

treasure here it would have been a long time ago," Cart said. For the next hour both of the boys dug into the ground, stopping now and then to rest. When they were just about ready to give up, Cart's shovel struck something solid.

"Will! What is this?"

Will got down on his hands and knees. With his hands he moved some earth away, and something colorful and shiny caught his eye.

"Looka!" Will shouted. "Buried treasure."

"It *is*," Cart said. "It really is buried treasure. Those are beads like my mother wears to a ball."

Will scooped up a handful of the beads and quickly stuffed them into a pocket. "Can we keep all the treasure?"

"I don't know," Cart answered. "Perhaps we should tell Papa."

"Do you think that be right?" Will asked.

"Well, if it is or not, we'll never know, because I see him coming toward us now and he is going to find out about the buried treasure."

Mr. Middleton rode up on his stallion. "What are you digging for?"

"Papa, we're digging for buried treasure, and we found some."

Mr. Middleton slid from his horse. He got down on his knees and pushed away some dirt. "Move away, boys. This is not buried treasure. These are Indian trading beads."

"How did they get here, Papa?" Cart asked.

Mr. Middleton pulled himself up and brushed himself off. "Many years ago a tribe of Indians had a trading post on this bluff."

"Who were the Indians?" Cart asked.

"They were the Waccamaws."

"Why did you tell us to move away?" Cart asked. "Can't we keep the beads?"

"I don't know. Sometimes this type of bead was used in burials, and if there are any skeletons here, that means some Indians were buried here. If they had an infectious disease, some of the bacteria may be lying dormant in the beads, and if you handle the beads you could be infected. It's not worth the chance."

"When will we know for sure, Papa?"

"I'll go get Prince to come and do a little digging. If no skeletons are found, then you and Will can have the beads." Mr. Middleton rode away on his stallion.

"Cart," Will said, "I be glad you didn't tell King Robert I put beads in my pocket."

"You have already handled the beads," Cart answered, "and if you are infected with the bacteria, then it's too late. There is no need to upset Papa, but I hope nothing happens."

About an hour later Prince and Mr. Middleton returned to the bluff overlooking the river. Cart and Will were sitting on the ground talking. Marmalade was taking a nap.

"Prince," Mr. Middleton said, "clear away some dirt and see what's here. If there is nothing but the Indian trading beads, then the boys may have them. However, if you find any bones, let me know. That's another matter entirely." Mr. Middleton headed back to the mansion.

Cart and Will watched as Prince moved the dirt.

He worked carefully, mostly with his fingers, in order not to disturb any bones that he might discover. Just then Prince smoothed away some earth and the face of a skull glared up. Prince jumped up and stood back. "Looka that carcass," he said. "I not be fooling with that carcass."

Prince and Cart and Will left the bluff and walked back to the mansion. Cart told his father that a skull had been found.

"Tomorrow I'll go over there and conduct a dig," Mr. Middleton said. "I'll find out what was buried under the tree. However, you boys must not go back to the scene. As I told you, it is likely that some bacteria are lying dormant, and if you handle anything that was buried in that hole you could become infected with a contagious disease."

"What could it be, Papa?"

"Any number of diseases, and all of them quite deadly," the man answered.

"Let's go outside, Will," Cart said.

Outside the mansion, Will asked, "You think I be getting sick?"

"No. I think Papa is being overly cautious. That's his way. Don't fret about it."

The following morning after breakfast, Mr. Middleton told Cart that he was going to the tree on the bluff to do some digging. "When I have finished, we'll have some idea what was buried there and whether or not it is safe for you and Will to handle the beads."

"I'm going to get Will, and we'll watch you dig, Papa."

"That's fine with me."

Cart flew to Will's cabin, but he didn't see Will. "Will!" Cart called, but there was no answer.

Just then Will's mother eased open the door and poked her head around it. "Will be sick."

"Sick! Will's sick?"

"Yes. He be sick."

"What's wrong with him?" Cart asked.

Will's mother shook her head to indicate that she didn't know.

Cart turned around and started walking toward the bluff. He was very worried. Will had taken the Indian trading beads home with him, and now he was sick. He could have any number of deadly diseases. Papa had said it was likely if they played with the beads. Oh, how Cart wished that he hadn't allowed Will to take the beads home with him.

"Papa, Will's sick," Cart said when he reached the bluff.

"Well I trust it's nothing serious," Mr. Middleton answered.

Cart and Marmalade sat on the ground and watched Mr. Middleton dig in the earth. Cart became more distressed with every passing moment. Mr. Middleton was digging up one skeleton after another. When he had finished, he had unearthed eleven bony skeletons. All of the bones were there, and the skulls were frightening. The teeth were large and yellow, and they were grinning, just like the face of Dr. Penny's skeleton. "Papa, do you think Will and I can have the beads?"

Mr. Middleton had raked the beads into a pile. Indian trading beads had been buried with each body. "No. Indeed not. It is now clear that these people died of a serious disease, for they were all buried at the same time. Eleven people probably would not have died at once had it not been for a disease on the rampage. You and Will must not touch a single bead."

Cart felt as though he was sinking into the ground. He didn't know what to do about Will. As he thought about it, he realized that he *must* tell his father about Will taking the beads. That was the only way he could get help for Will. "Papa," Cart said weakly, "yesterday Will took some beads and put them in his pocket. Today he is sick."

Mr. Middleton faced his son. "Will is sick?"

"Yes."

"What do you think the trouble is?"

"I suppose the beads caused it."

"You think Will has Indian fever?"

"Yes."

"Then let's go to Will's house and see if we can find out what the trouble is."

Cart picked up Marmalade. Marmalade was growing now, and becoming larger, but Cart still carried him when they went somewhere in a hurry.

As they walked along, Cart thought he had never before been so worried. Digging for buried treasure had been his idea, and Will had grabbed for the beads as any boy would do. None of this was Will's fault, and now it was likely that he would die. What would Cart do without his friend, he wondered. Cart was so sad he thought he would die, but he didn't want his father to see him crying.

Just then Cart heard Will call him. "Is that Will?" he asked.

"It's none other," Mr. Middleton answered.

"Oh, Will, I am so glad to see you!" Cart exclaimed when Will ran up to him.

"I thought you were ill," Mr. Middleton said.

"I be sick, all right," Will answered, "but after I drink a pot of warm water I be well again."

"A whole pot of warm water?" Cart asked.

"That be right. I have dyspepsia a lot and that be what it takes to make me well."

"Papa, what is dyspepsia?" Cart asked.

"It's a digestive ailment," Mr. Middleton explained. "And there is no medicine better than a pitcher of warm water. It flushes out the system."

"Then Will didn't get sick from carrying the Indian beads?"

"I doubt it," Mr. Middleton answered. "He would have to handle the beads for some length of time in order to contract an illness from them. But I still don't want either of you to play with those beads. Although you are not ill now, that doesn't mean that it couldn't happen."

"I won't touch those beads," Cart answered, so relieved that Will didn't have Indian fever.

Will took a cloth from his pocket. "Here, King Robert, you keep these beads. I don't want them in my house."

Mr. Middleton unfolded the cloth and looked at the red, yellow, and blue beads. "I'll put these with our other Midcliffe relics."

Cart and Will and Marmalade ran off to play.

THE BEETLE BRACELET

"CART, WHAT BE that thing what the sun be shining on?" Will asked as he pointed to an object in a cabinet in the Midcliffe drawing room.

Cart glanced at the jewelry that was glimmering in the morning sun. "The one you're pointing at is a bracelet that my grandfather gave to my grandmother, many years ago."

"Who be your grandfather?" Will asked, his big eyes accenting his dark skin.

"My grandfather was the owner of this plantation, and my father was a little boy when my grandmother was given that bracelet."

"Did King Robert play with a black boy when he was little?"

"I hope so, because I sure like being with you."

"Can we see that bracelet?" Will asked. His eyes were almost popping out of his head.

"Well," Cart said as he thought about it, "I'm not supposed to unlock that glass-front chest and take anything out. But I suppose it would be all right for us to look at that piece of jewelry." He took a key from a small drawer near the bottom of the cabinet and unlocked the glass doors. Carefully he lifted out the bracelet. "C'mon, let's go to the piazza." Will followed Cart as they ran to the white-columned porch, where they could get a better look at the bracelet.

Cart held the bracelet in both hands, and Will lowered his head for a good look. "That sure enough be shiny."

"Have you noticed that the links are in the likeness of beetles?"

"They be bugs?" Will's face shot around to face Cart and his eyes became even larger.

"Look carefully," Cart said, not taking his eyes off the bracelet. "There are wings, eyes, and tiny claws."

Will leaned his head toward the circlet for the wrist. "And the claws be sharp!"

"My mother says this jewelry is made of diamonds and rubies and gold," Cart explained. "And all of the gems are valuable."

"My mammy never saw anything what be like that," Will said, dejectedly. "How about we take it to my house so she can see it?"

Cart gazed in the direction of the caretaker's cottage where Will lived. He wondered if he could get by with taking the bracelet to the cabin for Will's mother to see. It was true that the hardworking woman had never in her life seen anything so beautiful. It would be unthinkable not to allow her to feast her eyes on the valuable jewelry, if only for a moment or two. "Let's go," Cart said without hesitation. He dropped the bracelet into a pocket. "Do you think your mother would ever tell my mother that she had seen it?"

"No. She not tell about things like that," Will assured Cart. "She surely think this jewelry be the most bee-oo-tiful thing she ever laid her eyes on."

As the boys ran down the steps, Marmalade joined them. His tail was wagging. He was larger now, and Cart didn't carry the dog when they went flying across a field or through the woods.

Will's mother was sweeping her porch when the boys arrived. "Cart have a bracelet in his pocket what sure enough be something you want to see," Will screamed, before he reached the cabin.

The woman stopped sweeping and leaned on her broom. "What be that in your hand?" she called to Cart.

"It's a bracelet that my grandfather gave to my grandmother many years ago. I'm not supposed to take it from the glass-front cabinet, but Will wanted you to see it."

Will's mother propped her broom against a wall, went to the edge of the porch, and reached for the jewelry. Cart held the bracelet up and quickly slipped it over her hand and onto her arm. "See? That's the way you wear it."

Just then Will's mother whirled around, holding her arm in the sun. The diamonds, rubies, and gold caught the sunlight and dazzled like nothing the woman had ever seen before. She seemed to be speechless and unable to express her feelings. Finally, she asked, "This glow in the dark?"

"No," Cart answered. "But the links are beetles. If you look closely, you will see wings of diamonds, eyes of rubies, and claws of gold."

"That sure enough be a bee-oo-tiful thing," Will said, grinning from one cheek to another. He was so pleased to see the glittering jewels on his mother's bony arm. She loved the bracelet so. Her eyes were flashing with brilliance as she observed the beetles.

Suddenly, the woman went into a dance, and she grabbed the broom and swung herself around the broom, dancing from one end of the porch to another. It came to Cart that she had probably stood in the trees and observed people dancing at parties in the mansion, and she was imitating them. In her daydream, Will's mother looked as though she had taken leave of time and place and was lost in her pretense. Engaging in the merriment and frolic of the moment, she was footloose and fancy-free. Then she began to sing a lively tune.

Will called Cart aside. "My mammy want to wear that bracelet for the night. I bring it back to you tomorrow."

"You want to keep the bracelet overnight?" Cart asked, his eyes wide and questioning.

"This be the best time of her life. She never go anywhere other than on this plantation."

Cart's eyes dropped. What could he do? He could tell that the woman didn't want to part with the jewelry. Surely he could allow her to indulge in her fantasy for one night. As Will had said, she had never ventured anywhere beyond the borders of the plantation property, and all she knew was what she had seen and learned on the land. Cart's mind raced on as he visualized the frail woman, probably from time to time hiding in the trees, gazing into the mansion windows and observing ladies dressed in full feather. Some of them wore dresses and jewelry from Paris. Will's mother didn't know where Paris was. She had probably dreamed of wearing such a dress or piece of jewelry, at least one time in her entire life. This was that time. What kind of person would Cart be if he denied Will's mother her one night of reverie? As she continued her pretense, showy and grandiose, Will's mother lost some of her primitive and rustic ways. She had become someone else, someone living a dream. "Let her keep the bracelet for the night," Cart finally said, "but never under any circumstances tell my mother that I allowed her to do so."

"I won't tell her," Will promised.

Cart called Marmalade, who was sniffing underneath a bush, and they ran toward the mansion, leaving Will with his mother.

The next day dawned rainy and dreary, and Cart looked forward to Will's arrival at the manor house. When Will came, the first thing they would do would be to put the bracelet back in the glass-front cabinet, and then they would likely go to the attic and rummage through some old trunks. That was always entertaining on rainy days. On this day they would even take Deerie with them, as they hadn't spent much time with the pet deer lately.

Will arrived, dripping wet. "Hey, Will," Cart said. "Let's take Deerie to the attic and go through some of the old things in the trunks."

"And see some of the old clothes?"

"We might even put on some of the old clothes,"

Cart answered. "Where's the bracelet? I have to put it back in the cabinet."

Will spread out his hands and a look of innocence spread across his face. "My mammy, she not be serious like she used to be," he explained. "She wear that bracelet and not take it off, even when she sleep."

"You mean she is still wearing it?" Cart asked.

"That sure enough be the truth."

Cart glanced outside. Rain was coming in torrents. "You should have taken the bracelet from her," he said. "It's raining too hard to go after it now. We'll play in the attic today, but you have to bring the bracelet back tomorrow. You know what'll happen to me if my mother finds out I took the jewelry from the cabinet."

"I sure enough bring it back tomorrow," Will promised. "Let's go to the attic."

In the garret room under the roof, the boys opened a big wooden trunk. They carefully removed a hat with a feather on it, and velvet britches, and a wig that had powder on it.

"Looka," Will exclaimed. "That be a book?"

"It's a scrapbook that was made by my grandmother."

"The woman who had the bracelet?" Will asked.

"Yes. Let's look at the scrapbook." Cart gently lifted it from the trunk and he and Will sat on the floor as they stared at the cover. There was a colorful picture of a woman. She wore a floppy hat covered in roses of the most delicate hue. The woman's cheeks and lips were of the same pinkish red as the roses on her hat.

"That woman be bee-oo-tiful," Will said.

Cart lifted the cover, and they peered inside. The first page was labeled:

THE FAMILY TREE
Ancestral History

On the following page was a picture of a bride and groom coming through a large door. In front of them were dancing children. The girls wore fluffy pink dresses, covered with roses, and there were garlands of flowers in their hair. On their feet were pink satin slippers.

Cart read words that had been recorded in a spidery script:

> Few minds are endowed with the capacity to recall in retrospect the dates and details of all the important incidents of an eventful life. Memories of even the most significant experiences are distorted or lost forever during the passing of ten or twenty years. I shall now record some of the dates and details of the Middleton family, but as is my custom, I shall begin with scripture . . .

On the page that followed, the first letter of the first word in each paragraph was huge and it was surrounded by flowers painted in red and purple and leaves of green. The background of these letters was painted gold.

"Looka!" Will shouted. "That writing's bee-oo-tiful!"

"Yes," Cart answered, "the old folks wrote like that." He continued to read:

> And it came to pass, that, as he was praying in a certain place, when he ceased, one of his disciples said unto him, Lord, teach us to pray, as John also taught his disciples.

After the last word was a wreath of green leaves intermingled with red berries.

Cart flipped over several pages and just then both his and Will's eyes, at the very same instant, saw a drawing of the bracelet that was at that very moment on Will's mother's arm.

"Looka!" Will shouted. "That's the bracelet from the glass-front cabinet."

"It sure is," Cart answered. "And there's a story about it."

"Read the story to me," Will begged.

"Well it might take me a long time to make out this fancy writing," Cart said. "But I'll try my best to read the story about that bracelet. Sit down and be quiet, and don't rush me."

"I won't rush you," Will promised.

"Oh, Will," Cart said, as though something had just occurred to him. "I want to get Deerie. We haven't played with the deer in several days."

"Don't get him now," Will snapped. "Read what the words say about the bracelet."

"Drat!" Cart snapped. "I wanted to play with Deerie today. But if you insist, I'll read about the bracelet first."

"Then we can play with Deerie," Will agreed.

Cart began to read:

> From the hour that my husband gave me the Beetle Bracelet, I was afraid to wear it. I have always believed that bracelet means death.

"Death?" Will asked.

"That's what the book says," Cart answered. "Let me read on."

My husband was not superstitious, and he believed only in the beauty and value of the jewelry. But I believe there is something deep and mysterious about the bracelet because it took the life of the Withers girl. After her death, I beseeched my husband not to accept the bracelet from the Withers family, but he insisted that there was no danger connected with it. However, that bracelet never slipped over my hand onto my arm. To this day I would never wear it under any circumstances. It all happened on August 4, 1800, and this is my account of it.

The Withers girl met a striking young ship's officer in Georgetown. She fell as deeply in love with him as he with her, and their wedding was planned upon the return of his vessel to the Georgetown Port of Entry. He was to leave on the morrow, and would return in about three months. After his vessel sailed beyond the horizon, plans got underway for the wedding. Although the bridesmaids' dresses were made on the Withers plantation, the bride's dress was fashioned by the most noted dressmaker of that day, in Charleston. When the ship's officer returned to Georgetown he brought his intended bride a gift from Egypt. It was a bracelet of diamonds, rubies, and gold, and had belonged to an Egyptian princess. It was said that she wore the jewelry as she reclined by her lotus pool at her father's palace. Of course the Withers girl was pleased with the gift and the very next day when she was dressed in her wedding finery, the bracelet was on her arm. She held onto her father and they paused at the top of the circular stairway in the drawing room. Her young man was resplendent in his white uniform with braid of gold. But just at that very moment, the girl fell down the stairs and her wedding dress crumpled all about her. Her father and intended groom ran to her, and they shouted for a physician. As it happened, Dr. Taylor was a wedding guest, and he ran to the bride. After examining her he declared that he could find nothing wrong, but just at that moment her father noticed blood on her wrist. When Dr. Taylor held out her wrist, all whose eyes were on that spectacle saw that each tiny beetle had moved from its usual place in the bracelet, and had squeezed the white flesh of the bride's wrist, and had dug their sharp claws into her arm. But there still seemed to be some doubt as to what had caused the death which now was confirmed by Dr. Taylor.

"Oh, Cart . . . my mammy. . . " Will stammered.

"There is no cause for panic yet," Cart assured Will. "Let me read on a little."

"Read on."

The Withers girl was indeed dead, and her funeral was conducted the following day at Prince George Winyah Church in Georgetown. After the burial in that cemetery, when the remains had been interred in the Withers mausoleum, the father of the deceased mailed the bracelet to a chemist in London. In three months, Mr. Withers received the bracelet, and the conclusion of the chemist was that each beetle claw had expelled a bit of potent poison, of a kind only known to be in existence in Egypt. The mystery has not been solved until this day, and although Mr. Withers gave my husband the bracelet, I will not wear it. However, let me state unequivocally that I have all faith in my husband, and it is my belief that he always thought the death of the bride to be from other causes.

"Cart, let's go," Will shouted.

"Let's get that beetle bracelet off your mother's arm and back into the cabinet."

As they raced across the field, huge tears splashed down Will's cheeks. Oh, how he hoped he could reach his mother in time.

Cart fretted over why he had allowed Will's mother to keep the bracelet so long. What if they found her dead? What would they do if the beetles had moved out and expelled some deadly poison from their claws—poison that was known only in Egypt? It was too awful to think about.

Will's mother was nowhere in sight when they reached the cabin. "Cart, what I do if my mammy be dead?" Will cried.

"Don't be so afraid," Cart said with more courage than he was feeling at that moment.

Will ran to the doorway. "Mammy! Mammy!" But there was no answer.

"Where would she be this time of the morning?" Cart asked.

Will wrung his hands. "I hope she not be dead."

"She has to be somewhere," Cart surmised. "Let's look for her."

"Maybe that bracelet be inside," Will reasoned. He ran inside the cabin, and Cart came behind him. Their eyes flew over everything in the small house, but they did not see the bracelet.

"Cart," Will cried, "my mammy not be dead from that bracelet! She not be dead!"

"No, Will. Your mother is very much alive. All we have to do is find her."

As Cart and Will headed toward the rice fields, they saw a figure weaving toward them in the distance. "That be my mammy!" Will shouted.

Cart squinted his eyes. "I believe it is." He broke

into a run, and Will caught up with him. "Oh, Cart, it be my mammy. She be alive!"

"I told you she was alive. All we had to do was to find her."

Just then, Will's mother recognized him and she lifted an arm. Something on that arm flashed in the sun.

"Cart, she has the bracelet! It be on her arm. The beetles not kill her." Will ran so fast that he had a pain in his chest and was gasping for breath. "Mammy! Mammy!"

Cart stumbled on a twig and picked it up.

"Mammy! Give me that bracelet."

"No," his mother shouted. She held up her arm and looked at the bracelet.

"Will," Cart said, out of her hearing, "we'll have to take the bracelet away from her."

"I hold her arm tight and you pull it off."

Cart thought about that. He didn't want to touch the mysterious gift from Egypt. Just then the twig in his hand caught his attention. "Will, you hold her arm and I'll pull off the bracelet on this limb. I can carry it home without touching it."

As Will pulled his mother's arm away from her body, in one swift move Cart looped the bracelet on a hook in the twig. He jerked it from the woman's arm before she realized what was happening. Without waiting to see what Will's mother's reaction was, Cart jounced into a run that took him to the mansion in minutes. As he was walking gingerly across the carpet toward the glass-door cabinet, the bracelet still on the hook in the twig, Mrs. Middleton called, "Cart, what are you doing?" He went weak in the knees.

Without turning to face his mother, he mumbled, "I'm just returning something."

"What is it?"

He turned his head around, but still balanced the bracelet on the twig, in front of him. "It's, uh, the beetle bracelet."

"It's WHAT?"

"It's the beetle bracelet."

Mrs. Middleton flew to her son and took the bracelet from the twig.

"Mother! Don't touch it. The beetles have poison from Egypt in their claws. They could kill you."

Mrs. Middleton turned around. "How did you know about that old legend?"

"I read it in grandmother's scrapbook, in the attic."

Mrs. Middleton went to the glass-door cabinet and placed the bracelet inside. She locked the cabinet and put the key in a small drawer near the bottom. Then she turned around and faced her son. She noticed that Will had come into the room. "Cart, have I not warned you about removing any of the valuable jewelry in the case?"

"Yes."

"Then why did you disobey me?"

"I didn't intend to disobey you, Mother. But Will wanted to see the bracelet, and then we decided to let his mother look at it. She loved it so much we almost couldn't get it away from her."

"You took this bracelet to Will's house?"

"It be the most bee-oo-tiful thing," Will said. "And my mammy, she love it so."

Something in Will's voice moved Mrs. Middleton as she had rarely been moved. "Come here." Both

Cart and Will went to her. "I don't know whether or not that old legend is true. I rather doubt it. However, it is for reasons that you sometimes don't know that some things are off-limits, and I expect you to abide by my requests."

"We won't do it again, Mother," Cart said.

"Someday, when I think you boys are old enough to appreciate it, I plan to take the jewelry out of the case and show it to you. There is a story that goes with almost every object in the case."

"Frightening stories, Mother?" Cart wanted to know.

Mrs. Middleton nodded. "Some of the tales are quite frightening."

"When you be going to tell us the tales?" Will asked.

"Not for some time yet," Mrs. Middleton explained. "But the time will come when you will appreciate the old things, and you will want to preserve them, like my husband and I do. When I think you have reached that stage of maturity, I'll tell you all of the stories, and you will appreciate each object that is attached to some bygone era."

"I hope that time be soon," Will commented.

"Perhaps it will be," Cart answered.

"Perhaps," Mrs. Middleton said. "But in the meantime, you need to straighten up the trunk in the attic, and Deerie is longing for some companionship. Run along now," she added, as she left the room.

"Cart, I sure be glad she not punish us for taking the bracelet."

"I don't think she had to punish us. She could tell

we had already been punished. I thought I'd die when I read that story in the scrapbook. It sure made me sorry I had disobeyed my mother."

"I be scared all right," Will answered. "We not do that again."

"C'mon, Will, let's go up to the attic and straighten up the trunk, and then we can play with Deerie."

Will and Cart raced each other up the three flights of stairs to the attic.

DATE DUE			

90-37

Bound to Stay Bound Books, Inc.